MUSIC HALL

THE SAGA GOES ON

Stephen P. E. Lees. LL. B.

This book published 22 December 2014 by SPEL Publications
prodev@globalnet.co.uk

ISBN No. 978-0-9571629-8-3

A CIP catalogue record of this book is available
from the British Library.

Book and Cover design by SPEL
Typeset in Garamond

Printed and bound in the United States

SPEL Publication acknowledges kind permission from Bloomsbury
Publishers to reproduce some images from '*Visions of Architecture*' also by
Stephen Lees ISBN 978-1-4081-2881-7.

SPEL Publication further acknowledges kind permission from
The Calderdale Museums to reproduce the painting
entitled '*Briggate*' by John Atkinson Grimshaw on this book cover.

Contents

Introduction

MUSIC HALL – THE SAGA GOES ON is the sequel from **ROYAL AQ. – QUEEN OF MUSIC HALLS** and continues to chronicle the hilarious exploits of two Vaudeville artistes out of New York City, who accompany an impresario back to England to perform in various London Music Halls. They do so in the erroneous belief that Music Hall in England is the same as Vaudeville in America.

What they do not understand is that Vaudeville in America is not the same as Music Hall in England. And what in England might be considered Burlesque would, in America, be termed Vaudeville!

However, what our Vaudeville artistes crucially fail to grasp is the fact that Music Hall originated from the saloon bars in *Public Houses*. These emerging *Quality Wets* replaced the *Pleasure Gardens* such as those at Vauxhall, Ranelagh, Marylebone or Cremorne, where debauchery and licentiousness were rife and on a grand scale. And, vestiges of that *Unbecoming Behavior* could occasionally manifest themselves at awkward moments on the stage, even in the well appointed red plush Music Halls!

This was very much the case during our American Vaudeville artists' début at the Imperial Theater. There they totally misjudged a staid and respectable, if unrelenting audience, who thought them a pair of imbeciles!

MUSIC HALL, with an extensive index, continues the saga of Music Halls and their intrepid performing artistes, with more drama – on and off stage – making this book informative, humorous and enjoyable.

Dedicated

to the real hero of the book

'Judd'

the

Ventriloquist's Dummy

for his useful suggestions

&

practical help

Chapter 1

The Unrelenting

My stage partner, of thirty one years, Jack Mitchell and I had performed at the Imperial Theater, in the Royal Aquarium & Winter Garden in Victoria. The general consensus held that our début was an unmitigated disaster on a grand scale equal to the recent sinking of the *Titanic* ocean liner. However, our agent, the impresario Michael W. Lodge did not in appear particularly trammeled, or in anyway full of deep misgivings at our spectacular failure on the stage. Rather, he has invited Jack and me to luncheon at his town house in the Bergen Avenue, ostensibly to discuss a new revolutionary stage *act,* an innovation so daring that it will take unsuspecting London audiences by storm, and sweep all before it.

"Well Theodore Houston, my long suffering friend and stage partner, last night, we managed it! We achieved it with the ease of Eurydice entering the underworld, and plummeted to new depths of mediocrity during our inaugural performance at the Imperial Theater in Victoria. What should have been our début evening, instead developed into organized concentrated idiocy worthy of a pantomime of the lowest order."

Jack, tetchy at the best of times, was not in an amiable mood or in a forgiving frame of mind, uttered these words. He did so whilst we were taking break-fast in the ornate Grand Dining Room at the even more extravagantly opulent St. Pancras Hotel, in which we are staying.

"We were not to know what kind of audience was going to frequent the Imperial Theater on that particular evening. Nor did it help us that Judd, our ventriloquist's dummy and his head falling off his shoulders and rolling about the stage, when he ought to have been playing the pianoforte with you Jack," I said.

"I know there were several reasons," replied Jack, "why we agreed to come to London with Lodge. Chief amongst which was because, whilst we are accomplished performers, we recognized that our act may need rejuvenating. We therefore considered that coming to London may provide that initial spark or opportunity as a means of gaining inspiration. We neither of us could have known that Music Hall in England is not the same as Vaudeville is in America."

"We did know Jack, albeit too late..," I said.

"What," interrupted Jack, "when the Imperial Theater manager George Leybourne told us about three minutes before we were due up on stage. What did he warn of when he turned up to wish us all the best; something along the lines of? 'Firstly,' he had said, 'music Hall in England is not the same as Vaudeville is in America. Secondly, what you term as Vaudeville in America is not the same as Variety Theater in England. And thirdly, what in England might be considered Burlesque would be termed Vaudeville in America.'"

"I know Jack," I said, "but even that Bella Elmore, Lodge's new soprano..,"

"What, the one who has replaced, or indeed, supplanted Marie Lloyd, as the soprano singing the lead rôle in that Choral Anthem Symphony?" asked Jack, again interrupting.

"The very same person Jack," I replied, "in that what she had to say, I felt was instructive. She alluded to the fact that breaking into Music Hall in London or in the provinces in England is difficult enough, even for indigenous artistes. And that we ought not to delude ourselves. One has to gauge the audience sitting in the crimson plush seats in the stalls, in the balconies or in the private boxes, watching closely the artistes performing on the stage. There were, she continued, different rôles extant which catered for various audiences.

"In her estimation she thought that we simply failed to differentiate amongst Vaudeville, Music Hall or the Burlesque. And, that was the probable reason why were heckled way back at the Majestic Theater in Chicago. That fact was apparent to her, whilst she was sitting there in the audience at the time, during her visit to the Chicago World's Columbian Exposition on Manhattan Day!"

"I do not remember seeing her round blank face sitting there in the audience," said Jack.

World's Columbian Exposition Ticket – Manhattan Day

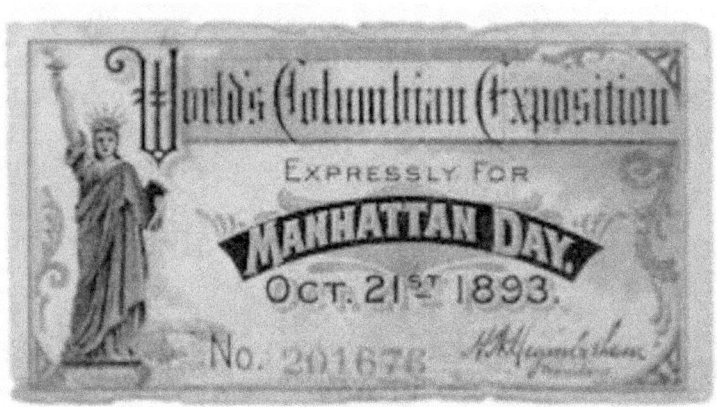

"Never the less Jack, I think what Bella had to say kind of makes sense to me. I remember she remarked at the time that we failed to pick up certain facts, obvious to even the rawest of Music Hall artistes starting out treading the boards. They were, at least recognizing the fact that Music Hall, however plushed up with crimson furnishings and brass ornamentation, originated from the new style of saloon bars of *Public Houses*.

"They themselves replaced the *Pleasure Gardens*, such as those in Vauxhall, Marylebone, Cremorne or Ranelagh. And, more importantly, the historical relevance of such places, and their impact on what is performed in today's Music Halls.

"In those former *Pleasure Gardens* aforementioned, Bella went on to state that, debauchery and licentiousness were extant and vestiges of that *Unbecoming Behavior* could occasionally manifest themselves at awkward moments on the stage, even in red plush Music Halls! Or, the exact opposite, in advocating respectability, as we both experienced earlier that evening on the stage at the Imperial Theater, embedded as it is, in the depths of the Royal Aquarium & Winter Garden, at Victoria.

"We failed to read an unrelenting audience; and our well rehearsed rôle resulted in what reputation we have being irretrievably dented! This is the price that we may now have to pay. So it is a well that we hear what Lodge and Bella have to say about their new innovative sensation that he intends to let loose on an unsuspecting London audience," I said.

"What would Bella know?" was Jack's only comment.

"Possibly more than we do Jack," I responded

"Right, so now we know," said Jack, "and we sure as hell can now figure out the differences amongst the various types of establishments and audiences; be they in Music Hall, Variety Theater, Burlesque or Vaudeville."

We finished taking our break-fast and spent the rest of the morning reclining on the various buttoned down red leather Chesterfields or, alternatively, green moiré silk covered chaises longue. In the silence of our well-appointed salon a clock chimed out the hour of eleven o'clock, which had the effect of bringing us out of our break-fast induced reverie.

At length, we decided to make a move and head off to Lodge's town house in the Bergen Avenue, where ever that is. We made our way in to the hotel's foyer complete with its extravagant purple flocked wallpaper and red plush décor. However, even on experiencing this extravagance on several occasions whilst staying in the hotel, it can never fail to move me nor prepare one for the sheer feeling of beauty emanating from its lavish decoration and extensive opulence.

In particular, the pleasure one experiences whilst looking at the murals decorating the walls of the main foyer in the Entrance Hall, illuminated by several bright and incandescent glittering acetylene gas-fuelled chandeliers. This extravagant luxurious décor continued in to other areas of the foyer, especially on the walls. Some of which were covered in a purple flock wallpaper, complete with raised velvet floral designs, and bearing large pictures in gilt frames, augmented the sumptuous feeling of opulence affecting the place.

The impressive cantilevered Grand Staircase progressing dramatically up into the vaulted ceiling of the fifth floor from the foyer was a sight always to behold. The walls of the staircase were covered with maroon coloured wallpaper punctuated with golden fleurs de lys integral raised designs added a further beauty to the vision of the place.

We approached the ornately carved mahogany Reception Desk and in particular the Concièrge. He simply stood there behind his counter, wearing his black morning coat and silk top hat with a blue rosette affixed to the side, complete with all the dumb aloofness of a Greek god. It was Jack who initially dealt with this arrogance with a curt remark.

"Our keys my good man," said Jack, whilst dropping the keys onto a silver salver.

Jack motioned me to follow him out to the Porte Cochère. I did so. Accordingly, we both stepped down through the honey colored Ancaster stone-framed doorway, flanked by columns of polished green and pink limestone and into the protection from adverse weather, afforded by the ornately carved stone vestibule of the western Porte Cochère.

Waiting on the cobble stone yard of the vestibule was a Phäeton carriage into which we climbed, giving the address of our destination to the liveried coachman. He flicked his chestnut mares and we rattled out into the still pervasive and acrid fog in which London had been enveloped since our arrival here several days ago.

We made ourselves comfortable on the buttoned down green leather upholstery of our Phäeton carriage, as it progressed past the formidable façade of the St. Pancras Hotel. The magnificence of this red brick High Victorian decorated neo-Gothic edifice to extravagant lavish monumentalism, never fails to impress me. The building, of course, was designed to do precisely that; and, it is easy to witness that intention, as confirmed in the majestic spectacle and majesty of the phäntasmagoric façade of the huge St. Pancras Hotel, which affords the observer.

It was also evident that the magnificent and impressive façade to the St. Pancras Hotel, represented a fusion of functionality, exuberance and beauty. All expressed as a

St. Pancras Hotel

mass of decorated stone and red brick, assembled to create an ostentatious High Victorian Gothic edifice to Romanticism. Complete with pinnacles, turrets and towers, one of which, the tallest, houses an illuminated clock that even the all-pervasive fog laden aether was powerless to shroud or obscure.

"Do you know Jack," I offered, "we have been to Lodge's town house before, but apart from the address being 536 Bergen Avenue, we possess no clue as to just where it is located. This was because of the presence of the fog which prevented our seeing just where in fact, we were headed on that previous visit to his house!"

Chapter 2

The Lost Journey

Over break-fast, Jack and I were discussing our less than perfect performance at the Imperial Theater the previous evening. We had now both of us come to realize that our act failed to recognise the essential differences amongst Music Hall, Variety Theater, Burlesque or Vaudeville, and accordingly, the type of audience attending those places. However, we are now to take luncheon with Lodge, the impresario responsible for our being in London, to consider a new innovative sensation he wishes to let loose on the Music Halls ranged across the Metropolis.

Having driven past the imposing façade of the St. Pancras Hotel, and traversed the sweeping drive down to the Euston Road, we paused before entering it and joining the vicissitudes of traffic coursing along this thoroughfare. As we waited we could see, coming out of the fog towards us a series of green tender lamps suspended in the aëther, almost as ghostly apparitions. Vehicles of every description; pantechnicons, military wagons, carriages, dray wagons or indeed omnibuses, went lumbering by. And as they did so, heralded their departure with a red tender lamp bringing up the rear. All of a sudden our carriage driver whipped up his horses and we plunged into the carriageway turning right and heading west.

Portland Road Metropolitan Station

We had not gotten very far when we came across on our left the decorative Portland Road Metropolitan Station,[1] I think. But do remember Lodge saying to us that it was one of the first urban rail road stations in the world serving the first rail road ever constructed, here beneath the very road that we are now traversing along.

The urban rail road station looked impressive complete with classical details impressed into its white façade. On either side of the elongated main hall entrance, addressed by low steps leading up into it, were adjacent circular rotundas which were crowned with dominating domes finished in blue slate. The building was low in height and displayed aspects of elegance in its architecture, which reflected an eclectic mixture of Renaissance and Italianate styles impressed into the overall design of the building. The window reveals were generous and allowed light to flow into the interior space of the edifice. Surmounting the walls of the structure addressing the flat roof level was a parapet wall of balustrades, upon which affixed cupolas were placed at regular intervals, further adding a Baroque elegance to structure.

I also knew that just beyond this station was a bronze bust of a dead president on a granite plinth, shaded by an apple tree, which still bore late fruit. Gradually as our Phäeton carriage, progressed down the road, we saw the Park Crescent Pavilion. It was Jack who commented on this structure.

"I cannot believe that subterranean bar we visited a few days ago. It is too difficult even to imagine that such an extraordinary establishment could even exist, and beneath a main road such as this," said Jack.

"It was built into the arches," I added, "supporting the carriageway. But what surprised me was the sumptuous appointment of the place, complete a series of rusting cast iron walls supporting cast iron vaults, forming arches upon which clearly part of the Marylebone Road above was constructed. Adorning the rusting cast-iron walls of the establishment, which gave off a reddish hue, were large pictures in gilt frames of ethereal and classical scenes. Most were reminiscent of Thomas Cole's *Course of Empire* or Claude Lorrain's *Landscape with Psyche and the Palace of Amor*, being particularly impressive."

"Other paintings ranged around the establishment, we recognized, were of known dignitaries and modern interpretations of concepts. Various polished brass objects were placed around the large vaults, reflecting the light radiating from several chandeliers suspended from the curved cast-iron roofs. Upon the floor was laid a luxuriously thick deep-piled red silk carpet punctuated with gold *fleurs de lys* in the pattern, which certainly added to the opulent ambience of the place," commented Jack

"Indeed the iron vaults were teeming with respectable professional gentlemen in frock-coats, pin-striped trousers and top hats. Some were reading newspapers, others chatting amiably amongst themselves, and a few drinking at an extremely well appointed zinc covered bar. The whole atmosphere was one that exuded understated gentility and courtesy, in which the members of this unexpected assemblage were generally behaving as though they were in their own drawing rooms at their place of residence. They acted in a totally unabashed and relaxed manner; quite the epitome of a Gentleman's Club, albeit in an Iron Vault!" I enthused.

"I liked the well-appointed zinc-topped bar," said Jack, wistfully, "and wish that Lodge were here right now. We could then get in an and avail ourselves of that well-appointed bar."

"Remember Rosine Bernard, or rather Sarah Bernhardt as she likes now to be known, chatting nonchalantly to a group of well-dressed professional gentlemen as though they were at a garden fête? It is a possibility that even as we are driving over the place, there will be famous persons drinking quietly amongst themselves. We should talk to Lodge about our becoming members!" I offered.

And so it was that we chatted about our experience of the Iron Vault. That is until we came across that strange looking house at the top of Harley Street we had encountered previously.

"Remember when we were here before, with Lodge, Theo?" asked Jack.

"I do indeed, and especially Lodge asking had we noticed the protuberance between the ground floor rooms and the first floor," I replied.

Looking at the edifice now, as our Phäeton carriage

Park Crescent Pavilion

rattled by, the building was clearly of indeterminate architectural design, but did reflect a combination of pseudo classical Greek and Roman motifs and renaissance styles. It was designed clearly to impress and impart the success of a wealthy patron, who had caused the structure to be created, and in so doing, resembled, very much, a prosperous merchant's house.

On considering the building's façades through the still pervasive swirling yellow fog, I gradually realized what precisely what had caught my attention previously. Immediately above the ground floor window frame arches, where the keystones were fitted, was a protuberance of stone resembling a balcony three feet in height and jutting out by about twenty or so inches. This regular undecorated masonry projection girdled the building, creating an overhanging plinth upon which, so it appeared, the rest of the upper section of the building had been constructed.

"Lodge also mentioned something about this house not being the first building in London to hold within its walls, a dark hidden history, which was only revealed recently. It became the sensation of the time and all society talked incessantly about it," I informed Jack.

"Well it may not have made news in New York Times Theo," said Jack, "but I was here at the time on my previous trip to London when the news broke out. There was much more to it than Lodge had at first, led us to believe. It involved a remarkable individual called Adam Worth, otherwise rather fancifully known as the '*Napoleon of Crime*' [2] and this was not his stage name! He was an *éminence grise* - a mastermind and an accomplished criminal whose actions in the annals of criminality surpass even those of Conan Doyle's fictional Professor Moriarty!

"You may remember Theo, some time back, about a daring bank robbery in Boston, Massachusetts, where the robbers got into the bank's vault by tunneling into it from a neighboring shop. Worth actually organized that robbery, in which the thieves made off with several trunks loads of gold bullion. Worth, having organized that robbery, left New York, aboard the RMS *Olympic*, the same boat we later used to steam across the Atlantic to come here to England. Worth then arrived at Liverpool, where he assumed the alias of a financier, called Henry Judson Raymond.

"Worth then moved to London, where he took rooms in Mayfair and, with associates from New York, formed his own criminal fraternity. At that stage, it was probably Worth had an encounter with another existing London based arch-criminal. Almost certainly, a power struggle ensued, with Worth coming out the victor. He then employed the vanquished arch criminal, as a 'tool of convenience' as it were, to administer their combined criminal empire. Accordingly, Worth, through him, organized major robberies and burglaries using a series of subordinates, none of whom ever knew Worth personally, or indeed even his name. His skill here was to detach himself from any potentially incriminating evidence, accept in one singular case.

"As part of an elaborate deception to steal art work destined for the World's Columbian Exposition in Chicago a minor villain and artist called Lyons was employed by Worth to make a copy of an original painting and return the fake to the real owner and give the original to Worth. However, Lyons decided to cheat Worth of his art work by making, not one copy, but two, keeping the original for himself, and giving the real owner and Worth the fakes! This would be, at the time, a very dangerous game to play, especially with a venal person such as Adam Worth.

"When Worth found out about the double crossing, his vengeance was swift, as it was effective. He wrote a letter to Lyons about some none descript remark, along the lines of *'Can I trust you with valuable information?'* You have to imagine Lyons sitting on this *moiré* silk covered Biedermeier chair in his bedchamber, on the *piano-nobile* in this house in Harley Street. Holding that paper with his fingers, and also thinking he was secure in the belief that he was safe from Worth, whilst in the depths of his apartment.

"What Lyons had failed to realize, as he tried to make sense of the message, by reading it and re-reading it, was that paper he was holding, with his fingers, had been soaked with strychnine poison and later dried. The effect of this strychnine poison, as he held the infected paper with his fingers, was actually killing him, as the vegetable alkaloid poison seeped through the skin of his fingers and into his body.

"When they eventually found his corpse, *Risus sardonicus,* had, of course, set in, with a vengeance, producing a fixed grin on the face. Not unlike that fixed grin on the face of our own ventriloquist's dummy, Judd!

"That protuberance between the ground floor rooms and the first floor was in fact a secret mezzanine floor, into which that particularly venal villain Lyons, had constructed a secret space in order to hide his caché of stolen artwork. It was only discovered when he was found dead on the premises. Even his house keeper and other tenants living in the building were totally unaware of those rooms on that secret mezzanine floor.[3] In fact, if one examines the front façade of that House in Harley Street one can make out that bulging protuberance supporting the first floor," completed Jack.

"My God Jack," I responded, "this house is very similar to our mysterious Castle Hotel in Chicago, with its chamber of horrors built into the very structure of the building, and in which the hotel proprietor, perpetrated all types of murder when we were resident there!"

We clattered through the fog-bound Metropolis heading toward Baker Street. Whether it was my nervous state resulting from our consideration of horrors perpetrated in that house in Harley Street. Or the presentiment of abject fear, for some reason of that secret floor embedded in that ill-omened house in Harley Street where murder had occurred, I could not say. But all of a sudden, my recollection of the horrors associated with the Castle Hotel in which we stayed whilst in Chicago recently, did much to subdue my spirits further.

The fog, as with snow, has the effect of muffling

The House in Harley Street

sound, and can be made the more sinister by the blindness that its shrouds produce. The fog, on this occasion was not welcomed as an occasional mysterious or romantic experience. Rather its claustrophobic presence created in me a feeling of anxiety and repressed panic. And so it was under such conditions in the swirling yellow cloud that we came across what looked like an ancient Egyptian Pyramid looming out of the fog and into our vision.

Of course we had seen this structure before during a

similar journey to Lodge's town house. But even the expectation of seeing the building in no way could diminish the sinister impact the building's presence presented to us. The impact of this image of the pyramid rising up as it did into the fog-laden aëther, from a London street, still haunt me, as we continued to make our way through Marylebone. My re-action was made all the great, simply by the fact of my feeling nervous.

This presentiment of this pyramid caused uneasiness in me, even though I knew of the existence of the structure and expected the vision to manifest itself again in the fog as we drove past it. But that fact did not in anyway make its acceptance any easier. And the vision of the structure, especially located, as it was, in a London street, made it presence all the more incongruous and difficult for me to accept.

Jack seemed pre-occupied with more important matters; for with his ornately patterned paisley handkerchief, was too busy attempting to wipe off his face, the oily sensation, caused by the acrid fog through which we were travelling in our open Phäeton carriage.

My resistance to this expected vision was further weakened by our temporary mental vulnerability to our immediate vicinity. What had caused this concern was the vision of a building located at Devonshire Street and the junction of Devonshire Close. Or at least so a road plate informed me. The structure was constructed of brick and three stories in height. Both Jack and I now sat there in our Phäeton carriage transfixed by the vision of this pyramidal structure.

Rising up from the third floor, and forming the attic, was a tiled clad structure in the distinct shape of a pyramid with the fog swirling around it. It seemed out of place and menacing and yet strangely hypnotic, almost

Devonshire Street Pyramid

as if one were being drawn to its magnificence, making it difficult to ignore or disregard. Two ornate cast iron Victorian lamp posts, rising up from the street next to it, illuminated the pyramid and the fog in a pale yellow incandescent gas light. In so doing they gave added credence to this *Sur-real* form that dominated the building, and, conferred, as it were, acceptance of the pyramid's presence in a Victorian London street.

Having recovered from this unsettling experience, I

engaged Jack in conversation about more enlightened, if humorous times back in New York, to add a bit of light relief during our journey to Lodge's town house in the Bergen Avenue.

"What of this Bella Elmore; is she as bright as one could suppose?" I asked Jack.

"To be honest Theo," Jack responded, "I do not know. Certainly she has an innate understanding of Music Hall in London. Her acute observations, I have to concede, make kind of sense. But then I am learning pretty quickly that Music Hall in London is so very different to what you and I have experienced in Vaudeville in America."

"I agree. That other woman we met, the one I call the Woman in Red, we experienced on stage the other evening, was a revelation. Not least in her control of Lodge at the Crush Bar at the New Bedford Music Hall in Camden Town. Not only that, I noticed, but also her magical, if not hypnotic hold, over an intelligent audience of which the auditorium on that particular night was comprised.

"It is my intention Jack, irrespective of Lodge's discomfort with that Woman in Red, to try and make her acquaintance. For I do believe Jack, we could benefit by her instruction. She not only is clearly an accomplished Music Hall artiste; but also remains a devastating *Femme Fatale,* and in so being, could dispense with ease to oblivion those Sirens on the island of Anthemœssa.

"Even more important was her electrifying presence on the stage. Be honest Jack, we neither of us has witnessed any person such as her performing quite like that on the stage, in our thirty one years of treading the boards, have we? Even the accomplished Marie Lloyd when in New York, did not achieve quite what the Woman in Red could do with the ease of the mercurial Proteus changing shape for advantage!" I said

"You are right Theo, and I remain much impressed with her action both on the stage, but more so in the Crush Bar!" replied Jack.

"Yes, but Jack it is much more than that. Listen to her ad lib and unrehearsed language. What did she have to say about the *Titanic* ship, a boat that could only do but one thing; sink on its maiden voyage? Hardly what one might describe as a fertile source from which material for Music Hall songs or anecdotes could be drawn? And yet she was able to transcend the mundane with these powerful words;

"'How many of us here have lost dear ones, friends or sweethearts when the ill-fated *Titanic* went down? And in so doing, the *Titanic* took with it, their souls and dreams as it plummeted to the depths of the Atlantic Ocean, consigning their memories to a permanent Iron Mausoleum which the *Titanic* has now become.'

"And she then went on to say even something more profound.

"'My friends, I want to remember all those who perished during that terrible night, by sharing with you the sentiments in a new work called the Choral Anthem Symphony. Contained in this work is a particular anthem appropriate for this sad occasion, which I should wish to sing for you. It is the one that addresses *Hope*! It deals with those *deep feelings of sadness which have pierced our hearts, causing our love to leak away though the wound.'*

"'…deep feelings of sadness which have pierced our hearts, causing our love to leak away though the wound.'"

"Jack these words speak volumes; not least for the person saying them. That is how she captivated her audience; because she spoke directly to their hearts," I said.

"I am beginning to understand what it is you are

driving at Theo," remarked Jack, "in that I do distinctly remember her performance of that Choral Anthem Symphony. Especially her rendition of the sentiments and the rôle expressed in addressing *Hope,* which opened with a low sustained D minor chord to give life to the words enshrined in the anthem."

"I also recall then at the time," I responded, "that an aura of ethereal grace and nobility seemed to intensify about her person. And, that she did look to be almost angelic!"

"That could have been the beam of limelight shining upon her Theo!" advised Jack.

"Yes but what happened was incredible," I continued, "as if by a hidden signal and literally in total unanimity, the whole audience instinctively rose from their seats; be they in the stalls, Dress Circle, private boxes or on the raked stairs. They stood there Jack; some swaying in synchrony with the music, other motionless but with moist eyes from which, unashamedly, tears ran down their cheeks, as the Woman in Red, reached the apotheosis of the anthem. And then, as she approached the tumultuous crescendo, it was attended by the thunderous applause, from a very appreciative audience, which followed on.

"And also Jack, consider what then happened when the Woman in Red had finally finished singing. The applause was tremendous as it was sustained for several minutes after the finalé had been reached. That woman, that Woman in Red had a profound power over a very intelligent and discerning audience. As you remarked at the time; that the New Bedford Music Hall in Camden was no two bit obscure Vaudeville theater. Instead the audience comprised wealthy, witty or clever patrons located in a prosperous district of the largest Metropolis on earth. And yet this Woman in Red could reach out to this audience and make it re-act and respond unanimously to her ability to exploit emotions positively," I said.

Jack was thoughtful, but then replied.

"It has just occurred to me. Is it not the intention of Michael Lodge to supplant Marie Lloyd with his new favorite soprano, Bella Elmore to sing the sentiments expressed in that rôle addressing *Hope?*"

"It is indeed," I replied.

"Interesting, because is not that rôle addressing *Hope* also expressed by the Woman in Red. And might not that Woman in Red have something to say on the matter of Bella Elmore subsuming her rôle in addressing *Hope?*"

At that precise moment our thoughts, if not observation, were directed towards a building looming up out of the fog on our right.

"Have we not seen that building before?" inquired Jack, pointing with his cane to it.

"We have indeed seen it before," I said, "it is called the Exhibition Building of 1862 and was considered as a possible home for the Royal Aquarium & Winter Garden, including its notorious Imperial Theater. Well so I remember Lodge telling us on that occasion on our way to Victoria."

"Victoria," asked Jack, with a questioning look upon his face, "are you absolutely certain?"

"Just where is this Bergen Avenue coachman?" Jack eventually asked, in tones that implied a rising impatience at our situation.

"Not far now gentlemen," muttered the carriage driver, "not far now."

And so it was that we continued our journey in the fog. I looked at my steel-case watch to ascertain the time and motioned to Jack that we were going to be late when

Exhibition Building of 1862

arriving at Lodge's for luncheon. He merely shrugged his shoulders.

Our respective thoughts drifted off into the fog laden aëther, with eventually mine to thinking about that remarkable Woman in Red.

Our reveries were interrupted abruptly, for in that instant we all of us in our Phäeton carriage felt a shudder and a jarring immediately followed by a crunching sound, as we move in a sideways motion. I then realized that we had just collided with a Barouche carriage. In that other carriage, sitting upright, totally unperturbed was a gentleman of aristocratic bearing wearing pin-striped trousers, a black frock coat and top hat and smoking a Trichinopoly cigar. He looked at us; such was his manner, as though we had been personally responsible for the accident. The two carriage drivers had, in the meantime, begun a heated argument, in their manner of trying to apportion judicial blame.

"You two, yes, you two in that carriage!" came a command from the gentleman sitting in the Barouche, "try and make yourself useful and see if you can disengage your carriage from mine. Taking care not to scratch the varnish on the coachwork of my Barouche!" he instructed.

I did not hear quite what Jack's reply was to this gentleman, due to the increasing shouting of the carriage drivers next to me. However, we both remained seated and instead got out our Trichinopoly cigars and enjoyed a smoke whilst the impromptu street pantomime continued to its inevitable conclusion. Whilst smoking I chanced to glance up and was rather surprised to see a building the significance of which momentarily escaped me.

It was Jack who recognized the building.

"Theo, this is the famous Wigmore Street building, I think!" he said whilst smiling.

The building loomed up into the fog, but from its façade, appeared to be of a design, which was prevalent in New York and Chicago or indeed other big cities. It certainly looked very modern and impressive. And, reminded me of that Vigo House in the Regent's Street, the one of ill-repute that we drove past the other day, and especially the antics that went on in the dome on the roof. This building too, also had a gaunt almost minatory look about it, suggesting hidden factors affecting its interior. However, the design of the building, did in no way, detract from its overall beauty or overwhelming presence in the street.

At length our liveried coachman, having disengaged his front axel of his Phäeton carriage from that of the Barouche's wheel, regained his bench on our carriage and we commenced our journey to Lodge's town house, where we were expected some time ago for luncheon. It was whilst Jack and I were discussing those bizarre

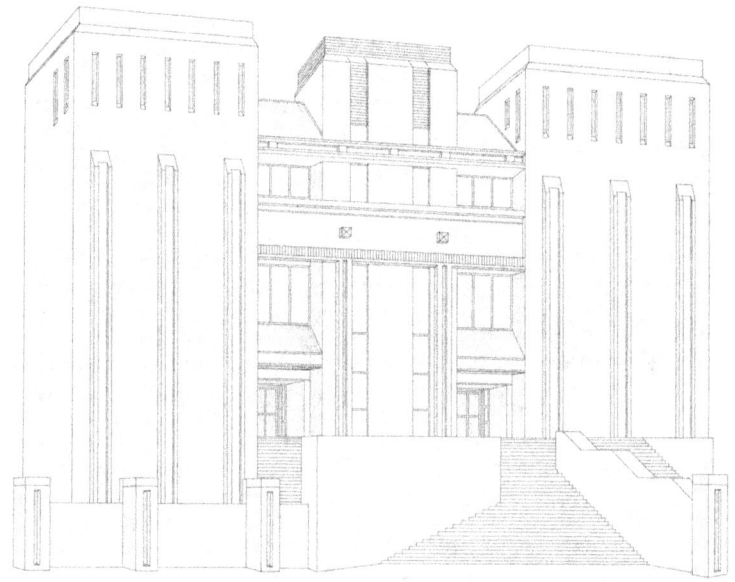

Wigmore Street Building

practices which took place in the roof top dome on Vigo House, that we encountered a most singular experience.

We were progressing up a wide road, the name of which was obscured by the fog, when gradually a building in the distance began to become visible to us as we approached it. It looked impressive with classical details to its façade which were becoming more defined as we drew near to the structure. The building, I could now discern, had a dome.

In fact the building, from what I could now see before me in the fog, had two domes, each one of which were positioned on top of circular rotundas, adjacent to an elongated hall with steps leading up into it.

The building was low in height and displayed aspects of elegance in its architectural style which reflected an eclectic mixture of Baroque and classical designs impressed into its white painted façade. The large window reveals allowed light to flow into the building. Surrounding the flat roof of the building, on the parapet wall were decorative items of masonry in the form of cupolas placed at regular intervals and which added a certain refined elegance to the structure.

Even Jack agreed with me in confirming the building's overall elegance and understated charm worthy of a temple or place of retreat for contemplation. The building, especially enveloped in the fog, might have been taken as an original classical structure, were it not for a very pertinent and obvious sign affixed the front façade. Even in this fog it was not difficult to read the sign which proclaimed its message in very clear lettering: 'Portland Road Metropolitan Station.'

"My God, what have you been doing," shouted Jack at our liveried coach driver, "we have been going around in circles? We passed this Portland Road Metropolitan Station building over an hour ago!"

I could scarcely believe my eyes. We had driven past this Portland Road, or whatever it, is urban rail road station, as Jack said, over an hour ago. We had been on a grand tour driving around in a circle in the fog.

"Not far now sirs, not for now," was the only chant this liveried coachman knew.

The phrase, 'not far now,' turned out to be an under-statement of monumental proportions in every sense. We did not arrive at Lodge's town house in a reasonable time. Instead we travelled almost blindly around parts of London the locations of which were but a mystery to us.

Occasionally Jack thought that he recognised a partic-ular building. But this recognition, so I got the impres-sion from Jack, confirmed to my mind, even more that fact that our carriage driver was still no where near our

Olympia

destination. At one stage Jack made a comment whilst pointing to a building with his cane.

"That is Olympia; for I remember distinctly being inside that building," he muttered, which means that we are some place else other than the Bergen Avenue.

Whether Jack was referring to Olympia as being the abode of the ancient classical Greek gods, I could not venture to say. Save that when he had uttered these words, they were done so with a tinge of dismay in his voice. He pointed, with his gold capped cane, vaguely to a monumental building, inside of which he had been, that did not in any manner resemble Olympia or even a Mount Olympian temple structure.

1. Now called Great Portland Street Metropolitan Station
2. More about this character in the book, **The Iron Soul - A case of Sherlock Holmes and the Napoleon of Crime. ISBN No. 978-0-9571629-2-1**
3. For a fuller account of this remarkable story see **The Iron Mausoleum – A case of Sherlock Holmes and the Titanic. ISBN No. 978-0-9571629-0-7**

Chapter 3

The House of the Impresario

Whilst journeying in the fog to Lodge's town house, for luncheon. Jack and I had discussed the remarkable Woman in Red, whom we had seen at the New Bedford Music Hall in Camden Town. And, in particular the extraordinary effect she had on her audience and how indeed we might avail ourselves of instruction from her. She had obviously been alienated by Lodge some time in the past and a certain acrimony still existed between them. However, Jack and I are of the same opinion that a meeting with her is of the utmost import and not a moment should be lost in our endeavoring to arrange one.

Eventually, our Phäeton carriage pulled up outside 536 Bergen Avenue. We had arrived at Lodge's town house at long last, late and not, in good temper. This was as a result of frolicking around the Metropolis due to our liveried Phäeton coach driver's inability to navigate the fog-bound streets of London, let alone find a direct route to the Bergen Avenue. I was in the mood for a drink and hoped against hope that Lodge had a decent supply of whisky.

Though partially obscured by the fog, one could just make out some interesting architectural details in the design of the houses of which the thoroughfare was comprised. In so doing, they reflected the prosperous and affluent quarter in which they were constructed. We alighted from our carriage and stood in front of Lodge's impressive town house.

Jack and I were, of course, not strangers to this four storey house at 536 Bergen Avenue, which formed part of a terrace of town houses. The façades of these town houses were clad in reddish brown terra-cotta slabs, and resembled nothing more than an eclectic representation of design details under the general style of Italianate Renaissance.

The house we were about to enter comprised three bay windows punctuating the façade. Each containing three window reveals, on each floor of the building, from the basement below the street level, up to the piano-nobile. The three-sided bay window structure was crowned, at this piano-nobile level, with a substantial over-hanging decorated architrave, formed of ornate recessed alternate deep consoles.

These were used for corbelling, supporting a lesser detailed stepped cornice, typical of the Renaissance style. These designs details were repeated, in the arrangement addressing the roofline above the flat fronted top floor attic, defined by an unadorned deeper cornice fronting a parapet wall capped with coping slabs.

The building, I was looking at, was remarkable. Not least for its front door, located at the top of the steep flight of steps, we had just ascended, in between ornate metal handrails rising from the footpath to the first floor. The main door to the front of the town house, was adjacent to the first floor bay window, framed in terra-cotta block work. The reveals and sills of which were immediately above a series of half balusters impressed into the masonry transom wall and forming a false balustrade for decorative effect only.

The House in Bergen Avenue

Jack pulled vigorously at a rusting iron bell rod, several times.

We were waiting for our summons to be answered. In the meantime; my attention was taken up with the decoration adorning these front double doors. Or rather, I thought, the over ostentatious and extravagant integral decorative excess, adorning the doors, which conferred, as it were, an air of overt sophistication. The two over-ornate double doors were set into an arched timber door-frame which formed the door reveal surrounded by masonry.

The doors themselves were of timber and painted gun metal blue. Each door had an opaque glazed panel, at the base of which was an acroterion, set in front of a metal grill reflecting ornate tracery in the form of curved and flamboyant floral designs. This design was more reminiscent of the Parisian style, currently in vogue, than that of formal Renaissance in design.

These front doors were odd for a number of reasons, including the obvious absence of the lock plate, which contained no integral barrel-lock. Surprisingly, there were no other items of brass decoration or paraphernalia, such as door furniture, in the form of door handles, knocker or nameplate one would expect to see on a front door of a town house. Their not being present made for a strange sensation when viewing the doors.

What was even stranger, I noticed, than any lack of ornamentation in the form of door furniture, was the absence of a letterbox! But what I found more alarming and disturbing was the absence of brass kick-plate to the base of each door; it was as if one were about to enter the abode of the destitute.

At length the front door began to open slowly to the accompanying sound of creaking.

I noticed that the person who had eventually opened the door was Lodge's man-servant. And he was still wearing his flamboyant, if ostentatious powder blue tail-coat complete with gold-braid emblazoned on to the front and gold tasselled epaulettes to match. Not only did he seem decidedly uncomfortable, he appeared vaguely ridiculous wearing this rather over ornate and extravagantly designed tunic, the uniform of which, was of indeterminate rank. He looked as though he had just stepped out of an historical pageant at some European palace or some other such place.

"What do you want?" he asked, with characteristic bluntness.

I now recalled, this was an all too obvious and pertinent trait of his personality. An unwelcome aspect that was very much apparent when he waited upon us at luncheon during our last visit here, not so long back.

"Well, what do you want?" repeated the voice in the door way of Lodge's town house.

"I beg your pardon," replied Jack, some what put out by his rather truculent attitude.

"Can I be of assistance then?" asked the voice.

"Yes you can. You may inform your lord and master that Theodore Houston and Jack Mitchell have arrived to take luncheon with him."

The voice in the door way I recognised, of course, as being that of Aloysius, Lodge's irascible and over confi-dent man-servant. Indeed it would have been difficult not to have recognized Aloysius, irrespective of his sartorial preferences in wearing his distinctive uniform.

"Lord and what did you…" responded Aloysius.

I think Lodge hove into view in the background, and this fact was noticed by Aloysius, who promptly changed his treatment of Jack.

"Certainly sir, if you would just wait a moment," he mumbled, and then promptly closed the door in our faces!

At length the door was opened again by the truculent man-servant.

It was only when a commotion erupted on the landing behind Aloysius, that he relented and at last deign to let us into the dimly lit hall way. Upon doing so we were immediately intercepted by Lodge looking very dapper in his electric blue bellowing dressing gown and smoking a cigarette from an inordinately long black cigarette holder.

"Jack and Theo my good friends, how good to see you again after all this time," he said, looking at his gold Hunter, "please, please do come this way. And Aloysius; bring drink for my esteemed guests; the larger glasses and the best of my wines!"

We followed Lodge from the hallway and up the creaking bare timber staircase to the *piano-nobile*. On this occasion, we were not subject to the ritual of our host or his man-servant testing which doors opened into rooms before allowing us to enter. No, this time Lodge opened one door leading into a room, and then another door which led into other areas on the *piano-nobile*, with an inordinate confidence and knowing smile upon his face.

This was in direct contrast to when Jack and I were here previously. Then, Lodge seemed equally lost in his own town house or trying doors that were locked, and had evidently been so for some time.

At the time I remembered visions of the good Doctor Holmes of murderous intent and his peculiarly designed Castle Hotel in Chicago, all of which came flooding back to me like a deluge of biblical proportion. Not so on this occasion; and we all three of us made rapid progress to where ever it was that we were headed to.

On reaching the third door on the second floor he opened it with a flourish and ushered us into what I suppose one would call a parlor. Lodge then promptly left us.

"We have been in this room before Theo," said Jack, pointing to a remarkable work of art set in an over ornate gilt frame placed above the chimney piece.

I walked up to it. And, upon closer inspection of the exquisite drawing, could read from a small brass plate fixed into the lower section of the gilded frame, that indeed the work was entitled *Visions of Architecture*.

I stood back to look at the large ornately decorated gilt frame that contained one of the most exquisite drawings I have ever witnessed. Without doubt this fascinating drawing radiated a remarkable beauty which emanated from its creator's patience and detailed execution of a difficult perspective vision. The drawing combined an

Visions of Architecture

ethereal elegance with serenity interpreted as a perspective of an idealized vision of several classical buildings from antiquity. Alas, it was unsigned lending even more of an air of mystery to its skillful creator.

With the exception of this drawing in its gilt frame, the walls remained devoid of any other paintings or decorative objects. The walls of the parlor were finished in yellow paint complimented by a white oiled based finish applied to all the timber surfaces, including skirting, window and door frames.

Presently Lodge did return and asked that we follow him to meet with an important friend. With expectation, we duly obliged and entered the Dining Room in order to take luncheon, and meet with his friend.

"Jack, Theo my good friends, let me please re-introduce you to actress and soprano extraordinaire, Bella Elmore. With whom I remain exceptionally confident, that now has an even brighter future on the Music Hall stage, under my exclusive patronage, as her agent, whilst still impresario! Bella's *tessitura* [1] is remarkably wide, in fact from C below middle C to high A, which that supplanted and vulgar Lloyd does not, alas, possess!"

Lodge said these words whilst looking at Bella intensely, as if to reënforced just what he was stating to Jack and me, whilst gathered in the Dining Room.

Whatever, Bella's re-action was predictable, and it was quick in coming; as she accordingly, responded by lapsing into a fit of high pitched giggling.

"As I have without any exaggeration said a thousand times before, that I like to get out and about and be seen in the right places. That is how I make my contacts you know, as a result of my numerous *perambulations.*"

Lodge said this last word slowly, as though not entirely convinced it was the correct word to use. Not for the first time have I noticed Lodge confusing his words before, and did so on an all too regular basis. I think the word he was looking for on this occasion was *peregrinations*. Unless of course he was referring to something quite different; which, knowing Lodge, probably might well have been the case. That, or I concluded, he not only suffers from a chronic monomania; that of periodically looking over his shoulders, for no apparent reason. But that he was equally afflicted with chronic metathesis [2] too, and in more than equal measure.

I stood up and offered my hand to Bella, which she took nonchalantly. Jack's, she did not bother to acknowledge.

She wore a dress of luxuriant red velvet, interspersed with opulent layers of mauve and pink silk. Her hair was dark and tied up with ribbons of electric blue silk, matching Loge's extravagantly ostentatious and voluminous dressing gown. Upon her head she wore an outsized hat in the shape of what looked like a bowl, with fruit in it. Sticking out, and at an awkward angle, was a feather, a long blue feather, of an indeterminate species of bird.

These were the exact same clothes she wore last night when we were first introduced to her by Lodge, in the dressing rooms after our débâcle on the stage at the Imperial Theater. Only now she looked a bit dishevelled. And those big round blue eyes, with which she stared out into nothing, looked tired and were rimmed with redness. Her pretty, but blank face was not quite so appealing at this precise moment. But nonetheless, despite these shortcomings, it still exuded all the qualities of profound ignorance and overwhelming anonymity as she out-stared oblivion.

Her refusal to shake Jack's hand may have been an oversight or that she simply failed to notice it. Though

The Acropolis

how that can be when two persons walk into a room was beyond my comprehension. Jack in the meantime was occupying himself with admiring another of Lodge's acquired drawings that we had encountered before. I turned around to look at it whilst Lodge was talking some interminable nonsense to Bella.

I walked up to it. And upon closer examination, also remembered this particularly exquisite fine drawing too.

It was very much in the same style as the drawing we had just encountered in the parlor, suggesting it was created by the same artist, who had refrained, out of modesty, from lending his signature to the work. As with the other drawing, I could read from a small brass plate embedded into the lower gilded section of the frame, that here this work was called *Acropolis*.

This large ornate gilt frame was hanging, in pride of place, from the wall immediately above the white painted chimneypiece. The scene depicted in this drawing was of several ethereal classical buildings, almost certainly by the same creator as *Visions of Architecture*, since both styles were all too similar, though as I realized, unsigned. Both Jack and I instantly recognized this drawing as representation in ink, of that group of temples, of which the Acropolis, in Athens, Greece, is comprised.

"Ah Aloysius, drinks at last!" said Lodge, in re-action to Aloysius as he walked into the Dining Room, and did so, complete with his St. Vitus' Dance affliction attending him.

Aloysius came shuffling towards us. In his arms he carried an elm tray containing four of the smallest wine glasses which I have ever seen in my long and varied life. All contained a greenish blue liquid, that I determined instinctively there and then, I should not wish to pour down my throat. This was despite the fact that I was actually by now, quite thirsty and in desperate need of some refreshment. I merely held it in my hand until I could dispose of it someplace else. The fire-clay green glazed urn contain a ubiquitous palm tree looked to be a suitable candidate for the dubious blue liquor.

"You may serve luncheon now Aloysius since we are nearly done with our pre-prandial," instructed Lodge to his man-servant

My reluctance to drink what ever it was Aloysius offered me in no way stopped Bella from downing in one go the contents from her glass. After which she breathed out noisily. She then looked about her.

"Thank you Michael, needed that drink," she informed us.

"No, no, no Bella, please, please let us not be too formal here," insisted Lodge, "I prefer that my new close acquaintances, including Jack and Theo here, call me '*Loge*.' Apparently all my acquaintances do so in honor of the only noble character in the opera *Das Rheingold*, which I believe emanates from Wagner's *Ring Cycle of the Nebulous*? [3] A rather amusing little tale the libretto from which is based on one of those interminable Völsunga saga-fuelled legends by Hildebrand.

"A saga of Teutonic gods, mortals, , including our erstwhile female warrior friends, the Valküre,[4] together with an assortment of heroes plotting, in the depths of the Nebulous, on how to get their grubby little hands on an ill-fated golden band. In addition to a demented woman, another Valkürian, no less, who will insist on throwing herself onto a flaming funeral pyre, for the sake of self-immolation, in order to be re-united for all eternity, with her burning dead hero lover!" advised Loge.

"Was not *Loge,* in Wagner's opera, a really horrible man?" asked Bella, from the blankness of her round face.

1. Comfortable vocal range
2. Transposition of letters or sounds
3. Der Ring des Nibelungen
4. Daughters of the Teutonic god Wotan

Chapter 4

The Undeviating Stratagem

Irrespective of Bella's faux pas, if indeed it was one, because I am inclined to agree with her blunt description of Wagner's operatic character *Loge*. More importantly, what close acquaintances of Lodge's felt the need to confer this name upon him? However, we are here to discuss our respective rôles in Lodge's *innovative sensation* that will take the London Music Hall audiences by storm and, according to Loge, sweep all before it.

"My friends welcome to my humble abode," said Lodge, whilst sweeping his arm back in an arch to clearly indicate possession.

In the absence of kick-plates to his front door, I was inclined to agree with him on the description of his abode.

"Please, please take your seats at the table," said Lodge.

We duly obliged.

"When last we met," continued Lodge, "yesterday evening I believe, at the Imperial Theater, it was after a disastrous a performance as any on the stage. Now that is all behind us and I shall not mention any names."

To this magnanimous gesture, Jack just looked up, to the bare ceiling of Loge's Dining Room.

"But, as with all things," Lodge continued, "which may be considered to be an adversity; now is the time to convert them into advantage and increase Box Office receipts!

"Last night showed an inability to read the audience in the auditorium at the Imperial Theater, and as a result of that oversight, a fiasco of monumental proportions, erupted on the stage…"

"I thought we were not going to mention any names Loge?" interrupted Jack.

"Well Jack one can hardly avoid it. For whom else in this room was on stage at the Imperial Theater yesterday evening?" responded Lodge.

"Theo was," informed Bella.

"Yesterday evening," Lodge pronounced clearly, in order to gain attention, "destiny walked with us. After the débâcle on stage, the Fates intervened, and by fortuitous grace presented to us with a solution to hand.

"The distinction amongst Music Hall, Variety, Vaude-ville or Burlesque, by their very nature, must be considered arbitrary. Rather than performing for a certain audience in a certain theater on a certain night and hoping against hope that our *act* fulfils the crowd's expectation, we should make them respond to us!

"Bella, gentlemen, attend me. It can be done. Our new innovative style of entertaining the audience with a range of emotions will go down in the annals of Music Hall legend," said Lodge.

"Loge, there is nothing new in what you are proposing," I said, "we saw such innovation in action the other night at the New Bedford Music Hall, in Camden Town, did we not? The woman, you know the Woman in Red, with whom you were discussing old times in the Crush Bar? Well as you may have noticed, she appeared on stage unannounced by the Compière or indeed was scheduled to do so, in the published list of *turns* occurring that night.

"Within minutes she had the audience in her hand. In fact she did not sing, dance or do anything for a full seven minutes, during which she was applauded continuously," I said.

"Oh her, *that* woman, she sang but one song, that is all," replied Lodge, looking uncomfortable at even the mention of the Woman in Red, especially in his Dining Room.

"Lodge, she held her audience captive and attracted a standing ovation at the end of that so called song, which lasted twelve minutes…!" I responded.

"No, No Theo," Lodge interrupted, "you are wrong! You see only half of what I propose. We spoke yesterday about Freud's concept of *subjectivity* and *objectivity* and the interplay between them.

"Bella, gentlemen attend me. We discussed this innovative approach last night. Have you forgotten already? In your dressing room of the Imperial Theater, we concluded that we thought it was quite possible to create totally new *acts* which would take the London stage by storm with their breath-taking scientific and highly innovative approach in applying Freud's ideas about *subjectivity* and *objectivity*?

"And, that we could address *objectivity* by Bella's controlled pathos in her singing, with all the dignity at her disposal, the rôle of *Courage,* or whatever in that Choral Anthem Symphony? This will, of course, lend verisimilitude to the proceeding, as it were. And then, the reverse, in having Theo and Jack do their routine in reflecting the humorous element of *subjectivity,* including their headless ventriloquist's dummy playing a seven octave pianoforte encased in walnut paneling, whilst his head rolls around the stage floor!

"Our audiences will not know what has become of

them, as we subject their emotions to the extremes of our innovative stage show! We will drain them emotionally, and they shall leave us in a total state of mental exhaustion; which, of course, is precisely what they have paid for. Now I know just where to launch our new kind of Music Hall *act*, before we take it on tour around the Music Halls of London, for the whole of humanity to witness. The Music Hall that I have in mind, is in a place with gravitas, and is located in the depths of Soho," informed Lodge, to anybody interested in such details.

Whilst still waiting for luncheon, Lodge intimated at other ideas in his stratagem which he had in mind. And elaborated further on his detailed, if defective plans, during which he also spent some time explaining why this would involve Bella singing all manner of songs, including some of an outré nature.

What I found unnerving. And to an extent, even more disquieting was the certain probability that Lodge was living proof that a little knowledge was still too dangerous. Somehow, he managed, to inveigle us all into a discussion about the essential altruistic rôle of the Music Hall in society. In particular, Loge argued, there were educative aspects of the Music Hall and its ability to lend dignity and imbue the soul with nobility of purpose.

For example, he proposed, emanating from those eminent establishments, were such noble ideals as *hope*, *aspiration* or *courage* and even fortitude in the face of adversity.

"And indeed," continued Lodge, unabated, "such magnanimous intent should be conveyed in the idiom of music and song for the whole of humanity, in its diverse forms, to endure, and not just for clever people like us."

Jack looked at me; and I at Bella.

"Might not the Music Hall," Loge suggested, "be used

to convey such ideals as perfection in harmony, and indeed, thought? This of course my learned friends, is the quintessential rationale of my Choral Anthem Symphony, which I concocted with an old friend of mine in Gustav Mahler.

"We did so more out of recognising instantly each others talents in the sphere of counterpoint! And to deliberately address those noble ideals of *hope*, *aspiration* or *courage* now enshrined in the Choral Anthem Symphony for eternity, at least in the metaphysical sense!"

Lodge pronounced the word metaphysical slowly as though not convinced it was the correct word to use. I think the word he was looking for was metempsychosis. Unless of course he was referring to something entirely different which again, knowing Lodge, would almost certainly have been the case. That, or Lodge was afflicted with chronic catachresis as well. [1]

"Bella, Theo and Jack we have but work to do in carrying out our undeviating stratagem. We shall begin to perfect our act immediately; within the confines of the proscenium arch, we will forge our *Innovative Sensation!*

"Yes I have hired out the Royalty Theater at seventy three Dean Street, Soho. I have some sway there, and can perfect our stage début in presenting our *Innovation Sensation*. Thereafter I shall, by using my contacts, you understand, arrange to have our instructive Music Hall sensation rehearsal, before we have a go on the London Music Hall circuit, for the enlightenment of all.

"Our stratagem involves Theo and Jack doing their normal stage *acts* in between sections of the performance of the symphony. At any time the audience will be invited, no compelled, to consider such noble ideals as *hope, aspiration* or *courage* and then when they are reeling from the effects of such deep consideration, subject them with the antithesis in the form Jack and Theo brash style of *turn* on stage," completed Lodge.

The defective thinking in this strategy stratagem, or whatever, was assuming alarming proportions in my mind. Bella appeared totally oblivious to her crucial rôle in this, this innovative venture.

"It is a risky business, but of course, one has to take chances. It is called innovation, and if scientific, then all the better," said Lodge.

Jack was about to say something, but checked himself and desisted, which was ominous, because at that very moment Aloysius returned with a trolley, upon which were more drink and the same dented and tarnished soup tureen.

1. Incorrect use of words

Chapter 5

The Man-servant

Loge, as he likes to be known by his close acquaintances, was trying to explain to us his undeviating stratagem, as he calls it. His defective strategy appears to change shape almost as frequently as did Proteus for advantage in classical mythology. I could not help but think that this idea by Lodge, ought to be consigned to realms of classical mythology as well. However, as far as Jack and I are able to determine, Lodge's idea deploys the subtle but innovatively clever device involving the mass delusion of a Music Hall audience without their realizing it!

Aloysius having returned with a trolley upon which was a soup tureen, looked at the assembled diners seated at the dining table. Jack and I had been served soup from this container before. We were therefore fully aware and familiar with the rigmarole which attends Aloysius' attempts to serve soup. However, it was the wine Aloysius poured first, or attempted to.

The man-servant made his way around the table, and with his shaking hand, attempted to fill each of our small wine glasses. It was with trepidation that I allowed him to come to my side to pour wine into my glass. The inevitable happened and not only did my glass receive a splash of wine but so did my linen jacket sleeve. Almost immediately, the spilled wine on my jacket sleeve gave off an indescribable musty odor that was most unpleasant inducing immediately a faint feeling of nausea in me.

I decided there and then to desist from drinking that wine from my glass. This was evidently cheap wine, which had obviously corked and gone off, quite possibly, some years ago. As usual Lodge was oblivious to the antics of his erstwhile employé in the person of Aloysius. The man-servant, had managed somehow to eventually fill our wine glasses, despite spilling most of the wine on my sleeve and the threadbare tablecloth. Whether his clumsiness was by design or accident, I remain unde-cided. Continuing his magnanimous gesture, Loge got up from his seat and offered a toast.

"To my very good friends and colleagues; working with whom, in order to take the London Music Hall audiences by storm, using our new innovative stratagem will be a distinct pleasure for all of us, and in achieving acceptable Box Office receipts! I am pleased to welcome you all in to my humble home!"

"Well Loge, we too are pleased to be in your house again," responded Jack, returning the compliment. I knew that Jack was being facetious and would simply prefer to call Loge, Mr. Lodge, and dispense with the Wagnerian connotation altogether.

"Jack, Theo and now Bella," Loge said, devoid of any such reserve, "to the future," and drank deeply from his cut glass goblet with a chipped gold rim.

I put my glass to my mouth but did not dare drink the wine for fear of becoming violently sick. A real fear confirmed by the most appalling smell now coming off my wine drenched linen jacket sleeve.

"Would you care for some more of this excellent vintage wine sir?"

I turned my head to respond only to find myself inches

away from Aloysius' unshaven face and inhaling the heavy smell of alcohol coming off his breath.

"No." I responded decisively, whilst instinctively covering the wine glass with my fingers.

It was only then that I discovered that Aloysius, despite the fact I had declined his offer of more wine, was pouring the wine over my fingers and through into my wine glass.

"A bit of vintage wine is good for you sir, takes the tension out of your neck, I find it helps one to relax," advised Aloysius, as he made his way round the table to Lodge.

"The usual refill in your wine glass there Michael?" inquired Aloysius.

I confess to being quite shocked at hearing Aloysius, yet again, address his lord and master in such tones of familiarity.

"Aloysius, I have told you before," said Loge, looking over his shoulders and clearly put out by Aloysius' confident behavior, "do not address me in term of such over familiarity. And, do desist from being over confident in front of my guests. You are man-servant to me, and shall know your place," instructed Loge.

The man-servant shuffled over to me again and stood to my side, his chronic St. Vitus' Dance affliction, I noticed, much to my apprehension and dismay, considerably increased.

"Good day sir; will you be taking luncheon per chance?" asked Aloysius.

Astounded at his audacity, I replied to him.

"That question is rather a ridiculous one it would seem to me; since I am quite clearly sitting at the dining table. Do tell me? For what other possible reason would I be seated at this table?" I asked Aloysius, with deliberate and pronounced aspersion in my voice.

"Why Sir, any number of excuses, how could I know? It is possible you might want to play cards or even poker or indeed any other immoral past-time," he replied.

Insolence noted, I thought, as Aloysius without my consent nonetheless served up what he described as being the *London Particular.* [1]

This same question, Aloysius asked of Jack, and even more remarkably, his master, in the person of Lodge.

I was rather amazed that such unbridled arrogance could be overtly displayed by an employé towards his master. I found this situation to be incongruous, to say the least.

"Bella, gentlemen, attend me!" announced Lodge, "we have discussed this thorny subject before, but it is as well to do so again; for it can qualify the foundation of our very existence and rationale. You perhaps do know gentlemen, but in England, especially in London, there are but three perennial enemies, *Three Apocalypses of Doom*, as it were, of the Music Hall and, by implication, of drink.

"One concerns the on-going activities of the interfering and infamous Metropolitan Board of Works, [2] which was established in 1855. This organization, with a seemingly innocuous name, has begun the remorseless process of trying to impose strict licenses on our Music Halls. It remains but their intention, their avowed and unequivocal intention, and that of any organization that might succeed them, to put Music Halls out of business and quite simply, to legally bankrupt us."

"You mean that laudable organization dedicated to protecting the public from the excesses emanating out of those Music Halls which, if not checked will have us all deteriorating back into the immorality of the Pleasure Gardens of previous ill-repute," said Lodge's man-servant.

"It has assumed legislative powers," continued Lodge, "under which it is able to impose draconian conditions in governing our Music Halls and our social responsibilities to the public. Previously, these powers were exercised under the old Theatrical Regulations Act 1843 [3] by more considerate and understanding magistrates..."

"Do you not mean by a corrupt and easily influenced bevy of Justices of the Peace," interrupted Aloysius, whilst serving the *London Particular* to Bella. "Most of whom were either drunk, and therefore perforce, lenient. Or, easily persuaded with fat purses or complimentary tickets to the best seats in the very Music Halls they were supposed to be regulating?"

"I do not think that was the case at all Aloysius," replied Lodge, albeit meekly.

"Well I know it to be the case," replied Aloysius, whilst progressing with his tureen to where Jack was seated.

"This meant," continued Lodge, "that every Music Hall premise had to acquire a license to allow music or dancing to be performed. And this license could be revoked at any time for even the most minor infraction of the conditions under which it was issued...,"

"Quite, quite right!" butted in Aloysius, "allowing persons to frolic around in public in an abandoned way remains not only objectionable, but could be considered immoral too. If we, and by that I mean the laudable and upstanding Metropolitan Board of Works, did not check this social malaise, we almost certainly would find ourselves in the depths of social anarchy and a return to the days when antics in Pleasure Gardens were rife. Complete with their reckless behavior, to say nothing of the licentiousness and debauchery taking place there, on an unimaginable vast scale.

"Do not delude yourself Mr. Lodge," continued the

man-servant, "you could not surely have condoned such acts, which by their very nature, involved promiscuous or permissive behavior that were rampant before? Especially in those aforementioned infamous Pleasure Gardens I have already alluded to and will you be taking the soup Sir?"

"The Metropolitan Board of Works is notoriously sympathetic to any number of misguided moral or social reformers, notably the deranged and malevolent Mrs. Ormiston Chant. That woman and her cohort of malcontents constantly wage an unceasing campaign against what they see as the immoral style and operation of Music Halls..." said Lodge.

"But Mr. Lodge, Sir," interrupted Aloysius again, "that fine upstanding lady represents a vast silent majority. The same people who prefer to live a decent fulfilling life untainted by the goings on in those Music Halls, where morals are easily corrupted, by a continuous onslaught of innuendo, euphemism or in verse coming from those, those degenerate artistes. Who themselves are certainly not above exhorting their audience to even higher levels of disrespect for decency, religion or authority. She is a fine woman, a fine woman indeed!"

"In particular she saves her venom for the Empire Theater in the Leicester Square," emphasized Lodge, more so for Aloysius' benefit, "that woman and other meddling crusaders have convinced the puritans who run the Metropolitan Board of Works, of the efficacy of banning drink in all new Music Halls constructed after 1909. That and the preposterous imposition of safety regulations, have made being a Music Hall operator or impresario, extremely hard and fraught with ever-increasing difficulties. Challenges that would, by comparison, make Hercules' task of cleaning out the Twelve Stables, appear easy."

"The second threat to our Music Halls, "stated Lodge, "emanates from that accursed Valkürian woman, Lily Langtry, who never tires of promoting the strictures of her loathsome society.[4] An organization, which is committed to the ridiculous notion of banning alcohol in drink..!"

"It is a well-known fact Sir," interrupted Aloysius, "that when the lower orders, including the undeserving poor, drink excessively, they become emboldened in their opinion of others, who are not as they are, or indeed, different to them. This is very much the case when encourage to do so through song or verse by those, those Music Hall artistes frolicking around on the stage in the limelight which exposes them to the full sight of God. In particular those same lower orders reserve their contempt for all decent persons not wishing to go to the Music Hall and thereby become tainted with the immorality extant in such places.

"In addition to the fact that alcohol, without doubt makes the audience, which comprises nothing more than the inherently disrespectful and their brethren, the undeserving poor, obstreperous and contemptuous of authority, temporal or spiritual. Free from any moral constraints the audience are given to behaving in an inordinately confident manner. Especially, when they are sitting in their comfortable red plush velvet covered seats with brass division rails, oblivious to the decent things in life."

Having served up our specialité food in a haphazard manner and interrupted Loge, Aloysius withdrew to the far end of the dining room. There he produced a carton of cigarettes from the front pocket of his blue and white striped cotton apron. I watched him more out of curiosity, as Lodge, was at the time engaged in trying to inveigle Bella to take more wine. Presently the man-servant put a cigarette to his lips. I confess to being quite astounded at this confident act by Aloysius, an employé no less. He then produced a match from a box of Bryant & May improved phosphorous matches. To my utter amazement Aloysius struck one on the sole of his boot and offered the flame to his cigarette.

I looked at my host, Lodge who was still busy conversing with Bella about her taking more wine, to notice his man-servant's behavior. Presently he became aware as the smell of burning tobacco assailed his nostrils. Upon doing so Lodge, this time, had good reason to look over his shoulders. He then returned to his food and the rest of us sitting around the table.

The luncheon, set before us simply defied description and was indifferent or lukewarm where, I would have thought, it should have been hot. Unless of course one is supposed to consume stone cold soup or the *London Particular* or whatever. Needless to say we all of us kept our counsel to ourselves, rather than risk a full retaliation from the man-servant, who presumably was responsible for preparing our so-called specialité food.

Lodge had let go that previous insolence, of smoking in the Dining Room during our luncheon, because clearly he was more concerned now, about describing the second of the three apocalypses, which was re-incarnated as Lily Langtry.

"As I was saying, the second of the *Three Apocalypses of Doom* is that Valkürian woman Lily Langtry. She and that venal brigade of hers are dedicated to abolishing alcohol in drink and in so doing constantly attack our social organizations which of course, Music Halls are. For reasons that are not apparent to me, the woman considers, without any shred of evidence, that our

Royal Aquarium & Winter Garden

Music Halls to be harbingers of reckless drunken behavior. Where unbridled drinking to excess with all the concomitant implications arising from such licentious behavior is not only a normality, but, is encouraged enthusiastically by the management of such august establishments.

"That Valkürian warrior in Lily Langtry has for example, acquired a monetary stake in our beloved Royal Aquarium & Winter Garden and precious Imperial Theater. I fear that she intends change irretrievably the operation of the Royal Aq by lobbying the management there to return the establishment to its original purpose and style of entertainment. She will endeavor to return the Royal Aq to a place, more resembling a temperance chapel, than a place where one's emotional sensibilities may be elevated to the ethereal heights of existence!" said Lodge.

"Would that be the famous lady who single-handedly and valiantly attempts to save the souls of the damned who enter the Music Halls, as though lambs to the slaughter, as it were?" inquired Aloysius.

"No Aloysius, that woman is neither the heroine you think her to be nor valiant, and indeed remains an interfering eccentric who has rejected the social convention of being convivial. Without doubt the woman is a deranged failed thespian and courtesan, who is motivated by her jealousy of others more fortunate than she is.

"Indeed, her re-action to a society, which shuns her social behavior, is to lead a revengeful puritanical crusade against all that is impeccable or dignified in our Music Halls. And, those high minded ideals, of course which we all endorse, and emanate from such places, with noble intention, as our esteemed Music Halls. And, which, by popular consensus, exist for all to enjoy," said Lodge, with a passion, Jack nor I, had in fact quite witnessed before.

"Preposterous," said Aloysius, uninvited, "such misplaced sentiments only go to reiterate precisely what that shining beacon of light, in what would be everlasting night, that Lily Langtry is, in her quest to rid society of mindless entertainment, fit only for the unthinking and undeserving poor.

"And if I may be so bold as to say so Mr. Lodge, Sir, yours is a futile argument, in trying to justify the uplifting rôle of Music Hall in this respect. And, I am not only referring to the Royal Aquarium & Winter Garden and its embedded den of inequity known also, I believe, as the Imperial Theater.

"And, I might add, especially in the light of your attempt to imbue the place with an aura of intellectual sophistication for the enlightenment of all, is fatally flawed. For the simple reason, any visit to that or other Music Halls will invariably show this to be very much the case. And this fact will be made abundantly clear, and demonstrated unequivocally to those who dare to attend such places. Those precious high minded ideals, seemed somewhat to have alluded the promoters of Music Halls and instead, have dissipated into the fog-bound aëther, all too extant here in London," said Aloysius.

"What is this other third *Apocalypse of Doom?*"

The person who asked this question was none other than Bella Elmore.

"Ah yes," replied Loge, "by far the worst of the *Three Apocalypses of Doom*, "is that all pervasive and interfering Salvation Army. By comparison, the two other *Apocalypses of Doom*," pale into insignificance by the actions of that venal organization, which constantly endeavors to drive our patrons away from exercising their inalienable rights to attend Music Halls.

"They on occasion invade our Music Halls. And there, attempt to inveigle our patrons into what they erroneously believe to be more righteous and salvationary pursuits. Leading inevitably into mental decay and amaranthine oblivion and adherence to religious ideals! Think about it, what is religion," asked, Lodge, "but a game of semantics used to protect an outmoded belief?"

Aloysius looked hard at Lodge.

"However, my friends," Lodge continued, "that vile organization is in deadly earnest and has actually managed to close down one or two Music Halls, including the famous and legendary Eagle in the City Road. As I have stated before, our Music Halls have not evolve over the decades unchallenged. I need only allude to the sad case regarding that inestimable loss of The Eagle *Public House*, in the City Road, which was re-built by its then landlord 'Bravo' Rouse, as he was known, and renamed it the *Grecian Saloon*.

"It achieved a sort of notoriety, due mainly to an author fellow, I believe called Charles Dickens, who frequented the place and wrote of his experiences there in his *Sketches by Boz*. Despite this apparent fame The Eagle *Grecian Saloon* was acquired by that scourge of humanity, the Salvation Army in 1899. Accordingly, they purchased the premises and then promptly closed the establishment down on the premises of moral turpitude; causing widespread anguish throughout London and indeed the Empire, on that terrible day; a terrible day that will live on in infamy.

"Before The Eagle was closed by the Salvation Army, it did a roaring trade as one of the first Music Halls. The Eagle *Grecian Saloon* still had other claims to fame, for it was there, that fourteen year old Lloyd made her stage début in 1884. But of course now she is considered passé, and in chronic decline, by many who attend the Music Halls." [5]

Lodge said these words whilst looking intently at Bella.

"Though the closure of The Eagle *Public House* and *Grecian Saloon* was an irreplaceable great loss to humanity, it was as a direct result of the Salvation Army concentrating all its resources for an all-out campaign to discredit The Eagle. The Salvation Army was motivated to undertake this extreme draconian action, on account of the fact that they considered one particular song, sung there frequently, to be lascivious and lewd. And, they thought, altogether symptomatic of the immorality which emanated out of that fine establishment. You may know the lyrics:

'Up and down the City Road
In and out The Eagle
That is the way the money goes
Pop goes the weasel.'

"One might possibly consider it a little *Burlesque,* common perhaps, or even risqué, but certainly not lascivious nor lewd," said Lodge.

"I would consider it absolutely offensive to any decent person's moral sensibilities," responded the man-servant, "you surely cannot fail to see the immoral implications raised within those lewd, yes Mr. Lodge, Sir, lewd verses. It is nothing short of an invitation by the singer of such a verse to invite the audience into a frenzied behavior of the utmost disgrace and would you like some more gravy Sir?"

Neither Jack nor I could not even remotely consider the verses of this song as anything other what it sounded as, since their meaning entirely eluded us. And, I suspect Bella too, though with that constant blank expression upon her face, it was difficult to be absolutely certain.

"The great loss of this famous Music Hall, in the continuing campaign the Salvation Army is waging against us, clearly indicates, if nothing else the depth of their resolve to eradicate our necessary social establishments," said Lodge, visibly moved by this blow to humanity, and Box Office receipts. At length he recovered his suave composure,

"The evolution of our Music Hall, my friends, is not complete," Lodge continued, "as a result of the activities of the Metropolitan Board of Works and that, that Lily Langtry, there is now what they call the emerging *Variety Theater.* Complete with the application of red plush and brass division rails, on a pervasive and almost monumental scale. This is so in order to give the impression of the utmost respectability and lend, as it were, verisimilitude to those new establishments."

"Quite right," interjected Aloysius, "quite right! It is about time those out-dated and lascivious Music Halls finally gave way to the more resplendent establishments designed by your man there Ebenezer Saunders with plays acted out properly and sensible drama, albeit of the *melo* variety. Respectability and decorum are, thankfully the mainstays of the…" said Aloysius.

"This type of *Variety Theater*," interrupted Lodge emphatically, "was promoted and accepted when they decided to rebuild the old London Pavilion at the Regent's Circus end of the Shaftesbury Avenue during 1885. And, I might add, to the deliberately extravagant and opulent designs of James Ebenezer Saunders, an employé, no less, of the Metropolitan Board of Works.

"In this case a concerted attempt was made to sever, in one fell swoop, all connections with the Pavilion's, so-called, gaudy if tawdry origins, in the roofed over stable yard of the Black Horse Inn, which previously occupied the site. Typically, in this Music Hall, exotic and other such strange acts and demonstrations were performed. From now on, the new Variety Theater, their promoters declared, would conform to abstemious decency, for that is what they are. And shall be places of opulence and respectability in every aspect of their design and appointment," advised Loge.

"You may sneer at such establishments Mr. Loge, Sir, but I have had the pleasure of attending a show, and very good it was too at that London Pavilion, a place you appear eager to denigrate without in my humble opinion, justifiable reason. What made it particularly enjoyable was the absence of alcohol and the riff-raff who infest the Music Halls," stated the man-servant, bluntly.

Indeed one was somewhat compelled to think. Was Aloysius, in fact Lodge's actual man-servant; for he seemed to display an extraordinary and deep contempt for someone who was supposed to be his master? We all of us sitting around the table could see Lodge's mounting exasperation with the unchecked confidence, if not mounting disrespect, with which the powder blue tunic wearing Aloysius felt, at his convenience and liberty, to extend to his master in a forthright manner.

And did not Aloysius call his master *'Loge'* albeit prefixed by Mr? Indeed the relationship was peculiar, but then anything which attends Lodge, his house or his loquacious man-servant, abandoned the ordinary for the bizarre quite some time ago. Could it be that this man-servant retains a hold over Loge? I would dread to think of the ramifications resulting there from.

Who was this Aloysius? I wondered. Where did he come from and how came he to be working as a flunky, albeit an arrogant flunky, for Loge? That he was intelligent could never be in doubt. That he possessed inherent humility and politeness certainly could. I remembered when we came here previously his manner, personality and characteristics were less than one would expect from a servant of the household, in which we found ourselves as personal guests of his master. Why even earlier his blunt response to Jack on arriving at the front door of this town house were in some respects not remarkable and in retrospect, entirely to be expected.

'What do you want?' he had asked Jack, and later followed, 'Well, what do you want?'

This encounter at the front door lasted all but eight seconds! Finally the man-servant, on seeing Lodge approach the commotion at the front door, abruptly changed his attitude. Aloysius then immediately, for the benefit of Lodge, qualified his previous refrain with the words, 'Certainly sir, if you would just wait a moment.' He then promptly closed the door in our faces.

Again, who was this man-servant, I asked myself whilst studying him. He was tall and had a shuffling gait exaggerated by his being afflicted by St. Vitus' Dance, which was in perfect synchrony with a defective eye that twitched almost constantly. His hair, though thick was dark and unkempt. His face was pocked-marked and blotched, as were his hands, as though he had at some stage in his life, handle vast quantities of acid.

His eyes, when not twitching, were of a dark brown and set deeply beneath a bulbous forehead. He often looked into the middle distance with eyes which expressed a sadness at times, as if they had witnessed great sorrow.

His ability to return wit, instantly and succinctly with unerring and devastating accuracy was remarkable to say the least. And, could in my experience of over thirty years treading the floorboards on stage, earn him an enviable reputation in Vaudeville or indeed in any English Music Hall as a Monologist or in some such similar rôle.

He, on numerous occasions, had elicited a surprised re-action from both Jack and I, and now also Bella, as a result of his open disregard for his master in Michael Lodge. I have been entertained in houses across the States. And in such places, any flunky of the household, be they a humble housemaid, or senior butler, paid unceasing deference to their masters in demonstrating respect and obedience.

Clearly in the case of this man-servant Aloysius, unerring deference was but a concept to him. This situation in itself would not normally have engaged my attention, or that of Jack's, I would suspect. But my knowing Jack as I do, he would be thinking similar thoughts to the ones that I too was now doing.

What makes this situation vaguely implausible and therefore incongruous, but in keeping with things appertaining to Lodge, is the rather fanciful, if ridiculous uniform Aloysius has elected to wear. And does so apparently with confidence and a certain degree of overt pride in his choice of a powder blue tunic with gold braid!

His rather over ornate and extravagant outfit looked as if he had just taken part in a pageant at the Versailles Palace. It consisted of a flamboyant if ostentatious powder blue tail-coat complete with gold-braid emblazoned on the front and gold tasselled epaulettes to match. He may take great comfort and be proud of his extravagant uniform of indeterminate rank, but to me and possible others, including Jack and Bella he must, per force, appear vaguely ridiculous. His trousers were baggy and black and the boots he wore were not black, but brown and scuffed.

Notwithstanding Aloysius sartorial preferences, Lodge attempted to establish his precedence over this mercurial man-servant.

"From the luxurious and elegant foyers found in such Variety Theaters," Lodge continued, "all the way to their lavishly appointed auditorium and promenades, illuminated brilliantly by glass chandeliers fuelled by acetylene gas creating a myriad incandescent light radiating down on to deep red carpets and brass fixtures and fittings. In such places, no expense shall be spared in reaching the empyreal heights of opulence. Certainly banned now are the *Specialité Acts* that pulled in the crowds," informed Lodge.

"So what are you arguing about and would Sir care for more cabbage?" inquired the man-servant.

Lodge laid down his cutlery.

"That is precisely the whole point. One does not go to the theater to gawp at the fixtures and fittings, however well appointed, or not, as they may be. No, one goes to the theater for entertainment and to have one's spirits raised to empyreal heights. Not to be subject to instructive lessons in boredom of amaranthine proportion of a type advocated by that woman Langtry and her misguided blue ribbon wearing malcontents bent on their puritanical desire to rid the realm of pleasure. And no, I do not care for more cabbage," answered Lodge, clearly working himself into an abandoned feverish pitch.

"The Variety Theater is the successor to a place," said Lodge, "originally where tables were ranged around a hall with a stage at one end, and in which drink was served. That has now changed forever, and these Variety Theaters have become the smug respectable auditorium where drink is not permitted under any circumstances. So why bother attending such places, one is tempted to ask. That is why you probably like it Aloysius. The Variety Theater achieved its recognition and, I suppose, apotheosis recently, when the first Royal Variety Performance commanded by King George V[th.] took place during the 1912 season.[6] And accordingly, the Variety Theater was acknowledged as a respectable form of entertainment, now far removed from its rather exotic origins.

"During the recent first Royal Command Performance, it was instructive to note that the unsurpassable Marie Lloyd, sorry, I mean Lloyd, even though it must be said she may have been at the height of her career on the stage, that is before her very evident decline, was considered to represent the old Music Hall style. Especially, with her lasciviousness and avalanche of innuendos, euphemisms and catch phrases, to the extent that she herself was thought to be too *gregarious* to perform in front of a reigning monarch. But then you see that is precisely what Variety Theater is; smug and tame," said Loge.

"Well what would you rather have?" replied the man-servant, "a hall full of drunks. All attempting to out sing each other. Out drink each other or exceed each other in what can only be described as, profound disrespect to all and sundry male and female alike, and doing it regardless of shame, in front of God and in clear sight of a reigning monarch too. And, being whipped into a frenzied trance and becoming delirious by the very stage artistes themselves cavorting on stage.

"Most of whom indulge in trying to inveigling the audiences in to committing all manner of outré acts and responses in what must merit some form of legal attention because of the implicit encouragement embedded in their lewd songs and verses. And I am not restricting myself to that heathen woman, that danseuse, [7] that Flora Millar, and her wretched brass plated Aëolian pianola making a mockery of the sacred hymnal the *Lost Chord*, a childhood favourite of mine."

"I beg your pardon; what did I hear you call Flora Millar?" asked Lodge of Aloysius.

The man-servant mumbled some inaudible reply and fiddled around with the pots and pans on his trolley, before plunging his ladle back into the tureen containing the remains of the *London Particular*.

"I did not quite hear what it was you said," insisted Lodge.

"Heathen I said, the woman Millar is a heathen, and her blackened soul is destined for eternal damnation!" replied Aloysius.

Loge looked at his erstwhile man-servant and replacing his tarnished silver plated knife and fork on the table cloth for the second time during this luncheon.

"What did I hear you say?" demanded Lodge, "how dare you, how dare you utter such words in the presence of my guests and…"

"I dare utter these words, Mr. Lodge, Sir, because as the Christ is my witness, they are true," responded Aloysius.

"Ha ha, you cannot know about Flora Millar since you by your own admission, do not attend the Music Hall," said Lodge.

"I do not have to. One need only read the *Investors' Chronicle* or *The Daily Telegraph* to be appraised of such unbecoming behavior by her on stage, or indeed off it," replied Aloysius.

"Your attempt to denigrate her is based on rumor, whispers and ill-informed, goss..," offered Lodge.

"She lures her audience in," interrupted Aloysius, "by presenting herself in a contrived and deliberate manner to suggest that nothing but sweetness and light emanates from her person. Indeed she has had caused to be painted, an image of her, dressed in a long white cotton gown with ribbons, with her curly locks, flowing over her back, sitting at some monstrously oversized Aëolian pianola, and playing along with it contently. She is depicted, looking into the middle distance with her soft brown eyes, almost as though in a state of grace complete with angels fluttering above her to suggest the divine angelic in her.

"Of course nothing could be farther from the reality of it all and her shameful attempt to complete the allusion and delude an easily gullible public as to what she really is; a fraudster and charlatan, to say nothing of the fact she is also an immoral cavorting danseuse with a lack of integral morality."

"She is nothing of..," Lodge tried to interject.

"Indeed, a recent dispatch in the very same *Investors' Chronicle* relates a detailed account of her appearance in some salubrious place, I think the Imperial Music Hall, where the lights are permanently dimmed. On that occasion, the report described her as being rather diminutive and embonpoint[8] looking woman who appeared on the stage. Followed by two stage-hands who wheeled on to the stage, that monstrously oversized brass-plated Aëolian pianola on to which ornate intricate raised designs had been etched in to its metallic surface. The report then went on to describe the fact that Flora Millar looked about her in a furtive manner, and then produced from her bellowing deep red colored silk gown, a not inconsiderably sized brass handle which she inserted into the side of the Aëolian pianola. The danseuse then proceeded to wind up this ornate pianola in a very lewd and overtly suggestive manner, which even surprised some members of the audience, notably those seated not in the Upper Dress Circle, but rather in the cheap seats of which the stalls were comprised.

"Then having wound up the Aëolian pianola apparatus to its limit, Millar turned and faced the audience, and with a flourish and a bow, immediately launched off into bouts of singing. She sang in the most appalling voice, and did so whilst waving her head from side to side, which apparently, for some reason got her audience to re-act in sympathetic response. The verses she sang were of a blatant nature. Typically, the newspaper report went on to describe, about her being in the garden shed looking out amongst the cabbages and leeks. During the course of her unbridled candid performance on stage, Millar

Imperial Music Hall, Victoria

constantly looked over both her shoulders, as though a premonition, or presentiment, was imminent, no doubt, fuelled by guilt.

"She continued singing to the accompaniment of the sublime tinkling of arpeggios emanating from her brass plated Aëolian pianola that struggled to keep up with her frenzied attack on musical harmony, yes and verse. Such depravity appeared acceptable to those seated in the Balcony which made up the more expensive of seats. It is reported that some in the audience felt physically revolted and ill at Millar's repulsive behavior on stage.

Involving as it did, an Aëolian pianola, with which she cavorted around and without any vestige of shame. In addition, it was also reported that Millar stroked tenderly the Aëolian pianola, during her recital of verses. Some of which were so licentious to a degree, that the Lord Chamberlain may well now have to intervene in order to curtail such wanton acts of depravity being performed on the London stage, and in public too.

"It followed that her singing these verses caused acute embarrassment, to say the least, to the audience in the stalls, No such feelings of sensitivity or embarrassment attended the occupiers of the seats that made up the Upper Dress Circle who chanted out their equally vulgar responses with inordinate and overt enthusiasm, some even clamouring out for more and encore increased in as she approached her crescendo to one particular obscene series of linked verses.

"What Millar had to sing about the *Lost Chord,* so upset, and profoundly, many in the audience, to the extent that some felt moved to abandoning the auditorium there and then. Indeed it was later reported that such was the degree distress suffered by some members of the audience, that several felt a need to make vigorous and sustained representation to the theater management. In particular, various persons in the audience, later complained to the Music Hall manager that they had bought tickets in the reasonable expectation of seeing a woman dressed a white flowing gown wearing ribbons. That, and looking the very picture of an angel, whilst she tossed her golden locks back as she sang *the Lost Chord* accompanying the keyboard, releasing a cascade of exquisite arpeggios emanating from her Aëolian pianola as depicted in the various advertisements displayed clearly on the front of the theater.

"This was not to be so; the audience were instead shamelessly subject to a blatant travesty of the *Lost Chord* complete with all manner of gesticulation and profane innuendo. When she finally concluded her lewd interpretation of the *Lost Chord* and parody on the virtuous, it had the unsettling effect. It caused many in the audience to reëvaluate their deep understanding of lyrical sensibilities and emotional response to profound music, especially when subject to abusive interpretation in Music Halls.

"Now Mr Lodge, Sir, those observations are not based on rumor, whispers or ill-informed, gossip, as you previously intimated. But rather on hard irrefutable facts, as reported by an unbiased national newspaper, and would you care for more gravy Bella?" inquired Aloysius.

We had all been listening, with attention, to Aloysius' description of the antics on stage of a certain Flora Millar, danseuse. And particularly, her remarkable brass plated, with integral raised designs etched into its metal surface, of her Aëolian pianola, with which she performed enthusiastically to the delectation of the audience.

It was not so much the antics of Millar that I think occupied Lodge's thoughts; rather it was the antics of his so-called man-servant and his all too ready back-chat to his master, which did. This fact became indicative as the expression on Lodge's face crystallized from one of surprise into one of contempt and intolerance. Especially, with someone who, irrespective of being an employé of his, has failed to recognise that Lodge, or Loge to his close acquaintances is, and always shall be, impresario with portfolio to Music Halls. Therefore, I concluded, an attack upon Flora Millar, must inevitably mean an attack upon Lodge.

"So your only knowledge of the reputation of Flora,"

Lodge said, "is based on what you have garnished from the newspaper…?"

"It is indeed and…." replied the man-servant, butting into Lodge's inquiry.

"I would not have thought," said Lodge, interrupting Aloysius' attempted interjection, "that both the *Investors' Chronicle* and *The Daily Telegraph* would have much interest in the proceedings extant in Music Halls. Their interests reside in the reporting of tame shows put on at the smug Theaters of Varieties, such as the new London Pavilion."

"As I have stated before quite categorically, the woman is heathen, without morals. And, that she derives great pleasure in cavorting around on a public stage in an overt licentious and lascivious manner and all for the delectation and gratification of an undiscerning intoxicated audience, which in the main, comprises the undeserving poor. She and her like kind, are destined to reap the reward for such a blatant and lewd performances, whether in public or not. In particular, that woman, especially her singing and acting in such an outrageous manner and enthusiastic corruption of the revered *Lost Chord*, a fovorite anthem of mine, and other good persons, and since childhood, in my case."

"Have you quite, quite finished?" demanded Lodge.

Even Bella laid down her fork she held in one hand and also the wine glass she held in the other, such was her interest in Lodge.

"The woman is sinful, sinful I tell you, and an abomination in the sight of the Christ. And do you want more gravy Bella or not?" asked Aloysius impatiently and for the second time.

"Really," replied Lodge, "Flora Miller teaches religious instruction at the sanctimonious Marylebone National School!"

The man-servant put down the gravy jug on the table and ignored Bella who was holding her plate up for more gravy.

Capitalizing on his coup de grâce, Lodge continued his advantage.

"As I have stated quite clearly before, you are man-servant to me and shall know your place!"

And with that injunction, Lodge, with a dismissive waive of his arm, instructed, with a renewed confidence, his man-servant to repair to the basement and to remain there until summoned.

"The devil take the man," I heard Aloysius say of his master, as he left the Dining Room.

Jack, Bella and I were truly impressed. That was an effective a coup de grâce, that I have ever witness from Lodge. Though I could not help but think that while Lodge may have vanquished his man-servant to oblivion on this occasion, Aloysius did not strike me as a person who would forgive, or indeed forget. And it would invariable be only a matter of time before such an inevitability would manifest itself, probably at a most inconvenient time, certainly for Loge.

1. Pea soup
2. Replaced by LCC in 1889
3. Sometimes known as the Theaters Act 1843
4. Blue Ribbon Brigade
5. Lodge and Lloyd have ceased being friends
6. Held at the Palace Theater at Cambridge Circus
7. Performing dancer to song
8. A person of plump proportion.

Chapter 6

The Royalty Music Hall

In keeping with anything or anyone appertaining to Loge, and this might involve one being exposed to an unmitigated series of bizarre episodes which, if properly scripted into a libretto or scenario, could form the basis of a successful comic opera or even pantomime. It would be hard to invent what occurred as a natural consequence of singular events erupting in the Lodge house in the Bergen Avenue, culminating in the resounding defeat of his man-servant Aloysius whilst he waited upon us at the luncheon table. However, renewed with his new found confidence, Lodge was leading the conversation as we headed into Soho. In particular to the Royalty Theater in Dean Street to rehearse our new innovative type of show, which, Lodge assures us will be an *innovative sensation* that will take the London Music Hall audiences by storm. And, according to Loge, sweep all before it, involving as it does mass delusion on a grand scale of an entire audience without their realizing it.

All four of us were sitting in our Brougham carriage talking about our impending rehearsal of our innovative show. And, more importantly, the all important eventual Box Office receipt the show will generate for us concerned including us. With this delightful possibility in mind we were in a cheerful mood as we made our way down Regent's Street, still in the grip of the perennial fog. However, as we approached Piccadilly we rattled by Vigo House, looming up out of the fog. Lodge pointed with his gold capped ebony stick at the building in question.

"Yes it was astounding what they got up to on the roof of that building," said Lodge.

"Got up to what?" asked Bella, with her big searching vacant eyes focused on nothing in particular.

Lodge looked at our carriage driver, and satisfied that he was not listening, lowered his voice and head and then looked at Bella furtively.

Of course Jack and I remembered. Lodge had explained to us only a few days ago the true significance of this building, and our having good cause to remember it. Who could not have done so? The whole of polite society, not only in London, but America too, was shocked at the revelation of the bizarre and peculiar practices, which took place in the circular domed structure on the roof of the infamous Vigo House! And there was even talk about introducing, as a matter of urgency, legislation to curb such outrageous or outré behaviour!

Even now some years later, just looking at the building mannerism, it retains a peculiar aspect in its presentation to the street, albeit a fog-bound street. The designs in the façade to this building incorporated strong references to repressive monumentalism, expressed in the building's style and especially in the entablature, progressing upward from the roof line architrave to that, that infamous dome.

Indeed, there were features of a face in the façade of this edifice, extenuated by the horizontal deep recessed openings cut into the building's upper section.

Lodge commenced his description of the building for Bella's benefit.

Vigo House, Regent Street

"The designs in the façade to that building, Vigo House Bella, represent features of a masked human face with the dome being the top of a head! It was this pertinent fact Bella, that of the building resembling more a human face, which attracted several individuals to it at night.

They would meet, on an all too regular basis, in the dome, located on the roof. And then, commit the most bizarre of rituals or diversions of an outré nature, which are better left un-chronicled. What they certainly did not do Bella, was to admire or appreciate the innate intricacies of the building's façade or integral architecture!" said Lodge, whilst tapping his nose with his index finger and smirking.

"I simply cannot imagine for the life of me, what they could have possibly ever got up to in that dome at night," responded Bella, whilst looking over her shoulder at the building, now gradually fading out of vision, as the fog re-claimed it once again.

Lodge raised his eyes up to the fog-laden aëther, then looked at Bella.

"Yes gentlemen believe in me, I kid you not, our *innovative sensation* will make us considerably richer. But first things we must commence rehearsal at the small intimate theater called the Royalty Theater in Dean Street and is managed by Arthur Bourchier, an old acquaintance of mine, albeit through Violet Vanbrugh, his wife.

"I thought we were going to launch this new type of show of ours at that establishment you called the Alexandra Palace or some such place, not some small theater embedded in the depths of Soho? " asked Jack.

"We have to start some where Jack, "replied Lodge, "or would you rather I hired out at considerable costs the huge hall at the Alexandra Palace just for rehearsals? Aside of which, I do not want to expose our *innovative sensation* to anyone who happens to be watching our rehearsals, before we have introduced it ourselves and claimed the copyright. I am having no one getting rich at my, sorry, our expense. In addition to which, it is possible we may scale the Choral Anthem Symphony down to a more manageable size to allow it to be performed in West End Music Halls. I am thinking the Criterion Theater."

Presently our liveried coachman drove his chestnuts horses into Piccadilly Circus, passed the resplendent Criterion Bar and Theater, looking very inviting and turned into the Shaftesbury Avenue. We made our way along this *Avenue of the Theaters* until we reached Dean Street into which we turned left and headed up to the Royalty Theater. In so doing I noticed that we passed a street called Bourchier Street.

"Is there a connection with the name of that street, and the manager of the Music Hall where we are headed?" I asked Loge.

"Absolutely," replied Lodge, "the street was named for him."

A few moments later we pulled up outside the establishment. Even in the pervasive fog, one could easily make out the features embedded in the façade of this Music Hall. The front of the theater was about as featureless as one could ever hope to see anywhere. It was essentially a four story flat-fronted building that clearly comprised two small Georgian town houses, clearly fronting the theater. The façade had little or no external decoration or ornamentation as one would expect to see adorning any Music Hall in a big city, such as here in London. The only ornamentation was in the form of pedimented window reveals addressing the *piano-nobile*.

Looking at the front of the Royalty Music Hall it was quite probable that it had indeed started out as two private houses that had been converted into a Music Hall. I seem to remember Lodge talking about the establishment being converted to the designs of an architect, name

Royalty Music Hall, 73 Dean Street

of Beazley, Samuel Beazley. In addition, the Music Hall had an ill-fated opening and for the first decade of its existence was not fully used and in fact changed its name twice. Perhaps that factor may be instrumental in Lodge being able to hire it out for our rehearsals.

However, on entering the place we made our way quickly through a modestly decorated foyer and straight into the auditorium

I confess at being rather surprised at the amount of activity both on the stage and off I, especially in the front stalls. There were several people ranged about the stalls all seemingly with some purpose in organising the rehearsal. Lodge does seem to be able quietly and efficiently to organise these events, almost as though with the ease of Theseus strolling through the Labyrinthine tunnels. I was looking around this scene of organized chaos when we all of us were brought to attention by a person who had ascended the podium in front of the stage below the proscenium arch. He was gesticulating frantically; it was Loge.

"Ladies and gentlemen, may I have your attention please? We have but a few hours to day to rehearse before our opening night the day after tomorrow, so let us be about our business. Maestro I leave it to you," announced Lodge, waiving to a diminutive looking person to join him on the podium. Presumably he was the maestro and it was into his small hands we were to commit our destiny and therefore fortune, via the all-important Box Office receipts.

They commenced their rehearsals of the Choral Anthem Symphony, and Jack and I went through our routine directed by Lodge as to our timing.

It became apparent to not only me, but others too, that Bella, what ever else she can do, and it is quite feasible that she may be a good cook, but alas she cannot sing; well at least not for her supper. This fact was made abundantly and unequivocally clears to all but the deaf during the first part of our rehearsal.

One can only assume the conductor of the orchestra was being paid in advance, irrespective of the fact that this *turn,* in essence, was a Vaudeville act and not really a symphonic experience. Even though the dignity inherent in the words and lyrics of the verses could at times express a profound significance to those who might appreciate them. And indeed they were to be applauded, especially with such sentiments as;

'Look down upon us from your majesty,
That we may, with your light, see your greatness;
And though we know we are but mortal,
Live in hope to be with you for all eternity.'

'With the eternal light from thy saving grace,
Radiate down upon our parched souls;
And with it give us strength to gaze upon thy face,
With renewed faith our hopes with you embrace.'

However, the undoubted majesty of the verses served only to emphasize the absurd juxtaposition of our *act*, which involves our ventriloquist's dummy Judd, and his decapitated head rolling the stage floor. Even more so when set against that stupidity of Judd's headless performance at the seven octave pianoforte with mahogany paneling playing works by the Abbé Liszt, but more surprisingly more modern music by Schönberg or Mahler. This proposed major *act* incorporating the headless Judd and the symphony still appear to me to be just too incongruous as to be literally incredible!

None the less, we are here and presumably have little option but to possess our souls and hope to God it works on the opening night. After repeated performances, which nearly induced ennui, in all but the brave, we at last decided that a finely honed polished had been achieved and our creation was ready for the limelight, in a more substantial Music Hall.

Accordingly, we at length left the Royalty Music Hall, clearly harboring more doubts than we had when we arrived seven hours earlier.

Having stepped out of the Royalty Theater we started walking down Dean Street. Suddenly Lodge stopped and pointed with his gold capped ebony cane at a green painted doorway on the other side of the road, opposite Bourchier Street.

"That is where it all started and, I have spent many a pleasant hour in that green and pleasant place, within the precincts of that establishment. It was in there that I met Thomas E. Clay, of the *Cremorne Belles* and Wilton's Music Hall fame. And, it was in that club too where I introduce Gustav Mahler to the members of that august establishment and I recall, he took to it instantly as a refuge for Bohemianism. It was also the place in which I commissioned Gus, sorry I mean Gustav Mahler to compose the Choral Anthem Symphony, after I had undergone an inspiration of particular profundity whilst within the precincts of the establishment!" [1]

"Well, Loge, what are the goods on that place, just what is it?" asked Jack.

"Why Jack, that is the famous Colony Room Club!" replied Lodge.

We all stood there for a few moments, as though in awe of the place. Presently a London four wheeler carriage came clattering out of the fog towards us. Lodge hailed the liveried carriage driver.

"Criterion on Piccadilly Circus," he instructed the coachman.

"Where is that place?" asked the coachman.

"You mean to tell me that you, being a coachman, a liveried coachman, does not know where Piccadilly Circus is my good man?" asked Lodge with tone of incredulity in his voice.

"I have been driving my carriage abroad this Metropolis for five and thirty years and I do not know where Piccadilly Circus is, where ever that is," replied the coachman.

"Well, "said Lodge, "it is down this street, Dean Street,

Colony Room Club, Soho

make a right when we get to Shaftesbury Avenue and along the avenue. Do you know where Shaftesbury Avenue is?"

"Of course I do, but alright then guv,' get in," said the coachman, in as surly a manner, as I have ever experienced in London.

We progressed down the *Avenue of the Theaters* until we came to a circus with a large aluminum statue in the middle. At length we pulled up outside the Criterion Building containing the famous Bar and adjacent theater. Lodge jumped down to the footpath and looked up at the coachman.

"Where are we my good man?" inquired Lodge, with a smile on his face.

"We are at the Regent's Circus; where else could we be at this moment?" retorted the carriage driver.

"Do not be preposterous; this is Piccadilly Circus, replied Lodge, with a sweep of his ebony cane, as though encompassing the area.

The coachman viewed Lodge with a seasoned eye whilst checking the fare offered by Bella.

"When the Regent's Street was built by John Nash in 1826, its junction with the Oxford Road, as Oxford Street was then known by, was called the Regent's Circus. Farther down the Regent's Street is another circus that intersects Piccadilly and Coventry Street over there," said the liveried coachman, pointing with his whip to a thoroughfare vaguely shrouded in the fog. "It too, was known as the Regent's Circus. Gradually both circuses were known as the Regent's Circus 'North' and the Regent's Circus 'South.'

"This peculiarity prevailed, until the advent of the rail road, when two competing rail road companies built underground rail road stations at each circus, respectively.

The Central London Rail Road Company decided to call their station in the Oxford Street, 'Oxford Circus.' And, the Great Northern – Piccadilly & Brompton Rail Road Company's station at the beginning of Piccadilly was, naturally enough called, 'Piccadilly Circus. In other words, the term *Piccadilly Circus* is rail road slang not carriageway nomenclature, and you will never hear a paid-up carriage-man call it by any other name!"

"The devil take you!" I distinctly heard Lodge mumble under his breath.

By now, Lodge, was obviously somewhat put out by the loquacious coachman's arrogant, if supercilious behaviour, and resolved to put the carriage driver in his place. Rather as he done previously with Aloysius.

"Really, and I suppose you will be telling us next, that the monument over there, in the fountain, is not the statue Eros?" said Loge, with a flourish and a grin on his face as he delivered his coup de grâce.

"It is not Eros; it is the Angel of Christian Charity, showing the Greek god Anteros [2] and not Eros!"

And with that Parthian shot, the coachman flicked his horses and disappeared into the folds of fog, and oblivion, probably hoped Lodge.

Whilst Loge was engaged in that fascinating discourse with the coachman Jack and I had been watching a commotion on the other side of the roadway. A few bystanders had gathered outside a somber-looking store and were pointing in an excited manner to a window display of some sort. Curious Jack and I accompanied by Bella made our way to investigate the cause of the excitement. Having gained upon what was effectively a notions store, we were able to see clearly the cause of the excitement. Behind the store's plate glass window was a display almost like a stage set.

"What in tarnation is that?" asked Jack, pointing with his Trichinopoly cigar to the window display.

"Oh that," replied Bella, "that is the funereal emporium."

"It is the what?" I inquired.

"It is an emporium, a funereal emporium" replied Bella, with a cheerful expression upon her normally blank face, "in which clothing for funerals and the like, may be bought, complete with black ostrich feather plumes, and black *crêpe* material. Decking out this window display has become an attraction, indeed quite a feature around here!"

"A funeral parlor - quite a feature?" asked Jack, incredulously.

"Rather! People flock to the window from all over the Metropolis to view the shop's display of the latest in funereal garb and accessories. Only a month or so ago, they were showing the latest in *catafalques,*[3] wreathed in black silk. You might recall, that black *crêpe* material, is only a recent innovation, in the perceived correct sartorial arrangement during such a profound and moving occasion, as a funeral, to say nothing of the perceived strict requirements of the Requiem.

"Indeed, I am informed reliably that such accessories are all the rage and one is considered improperly dressed if not disporting such garments or accessories," informed Bella, with an enthusiasm for death-laden concern that seemed a variance with her capricious character and blank face.

1. Alcohol induced
2. Often mistaken for Eros
3. A structure for displaying or conveying a coffin.

Chapter 7

The Criterion Theater

Our rehearsal had been marginally successful but did show weaknesses, quite a few weaknesses, which will need attention. It is to be hoped the importance of the occasion will in itself make all the persons involved, performed to their utmost. Naturally, I include both Jack and myself in this expectation. Despite our being exposed to the latest in funereal garments and inclined catafalques, whilst at Piccadilly Circus, we were also open to another more worrying concern, represented in numerous persons forming a *concentration* of Nihilists. Over the last few minutes we all of us had become aware of a growing concentration of Nihilists, complete with their distinctive black beards and coats, looming out of the white acrid fog and gathering outside the Criterion Bar. They were a furtive-looking lot, who viewed us with their dark venal eyes as they chanted their contempt in our direction. Memories of the Majestic Theater in Chicago came flooding back like a deluge of almost biblical proportions. Had they caught up with us, I thought. Had they reconvened at the Piccadilly Circus, or whatever this place is called?

"Jack, are we going to have a repeat performance of their disruptive tactics we were forced to endure at the Majestic Theater in Chicago?" I asked with mounting trepidation in my voice indicating deep rooted agonies of despair.

Jack too had a look of repressed anxiety in his knitted eyebrows.

"I do not know Theo, I simply do not know," was all he could muster in his reply to me.

Evens as we spoke more Nihilists seem to appear from out of the shrouds of fog, particularly around Alfred Gilbert's newly erected sculpture of the Angel of Christian Charity,[1] or whatever it is. This aluminum-sculptured statue had attracted their contempt, because they regarded it as an arrogant and provocative symbol of the abandoned and reckless affluence of the profligate upper classes, and by implication, Music Hall artistes – us. On this occasion however, their *concentration* was considerable and they were clearly agitating in a confident manner, for an all-out final reckoning with someone or something.

A reckoning with whom or what, it seemed, was neither apparent to them, or indeed to us. However, that uncertainty did not in any way deter them from shouting their dreadful chants or blood-curdling slogans, such as; *'Be it now or never,'* or the more dread-filled, *'Dispatch forthwith the upper classes to their oblivion,'* or, even more alarmingly, *'Our failure to act now; shall be to our utter detriment!'*

They chanted whilst clenching their fists at all and sundry, including ordinary members of the public passing by, and on one occasion, a horse, pulling a Phäeton carriage.

I pretended not to be alarmed by their verbal threats. Instead, I feigned visible interest in an adjacent poster advising the reader of the benefits, now, of a revolutionary treatment for rupture.

"Do not be unduly concerned my friends," soothed Loge, "we are not the focus of their unbridled fury. It is almost certain that they will vent their wrath on the innocent members of the Criterion Bar, inside there. The Nihilists periodically assemble outside and chant the indescribable, in order to unnerve the drinkers inside the Criterion Bar.

"It is all part of their avowed intention of waging unceasing terror by repeatedly shouting such dreaded chants as, *'Destroy their places of leisure,'* or the fear-laden injunction, *'Inconveniencing the rich is our prerogative; our failing to do so shall be at our utmost peril,'* to the assembled patrons at the Criterion establishment. The Nihilists, encouraged by their numbers forming a *concentration,* were clearly in the mood for a show down – with anybody, or at least so it would seem.

"It is all a sport and the members inside the Criterion Bar consider it entertainment of the highest order. Some members have even been known to take glasses of champagne out to the more vocal of the Nihilists, in order to relieve their sore throats, brought on by their shouting!" informed Lodge.

Both Jack and I remained unconvinced and even Bella viewed them with an expression of hostility clearly recognizable even upon her normally blank facial features. We turned to enter the Criterion Building.

The Criterion Building looked to be a sumptuous place to be in. I could well understand the Nihilists' resentment at such profligate persons enjoying themselves, absolutely. The façade to this five storey building clad in grey Portland stone, was designed by Thomas Verity in the French Renaissance style with suggestions of Second Empire addressing the attic level. Complete with an ornate Mansard roof structure, that was punctuated with ornate lucarne window reveals and crowns of metal fencing. Traces of Art Nouveau were evident, especially in the decorative detailing to the building's façade.

The Criterion was completed in 1870 and interior decoration carried out by Simpson & Sons to a very opulent and extravagantly ornate finish. Jack and I had, of course, been here before, whilst waiting on Lodge a few days' ago, before heading off on our aborted visit to the Oxford Music Hall, due to a fire breaking out there.

Jack, who knew the Criterion establishment from his previous visit to London, informed me that the place was a veritable *Emporium of Tastes*.

"An interesting fact," Jack informed me, "is that most of the entire theater and auditorium is below ground in the basement and even Dress Circle can only be attained by walking down stairs to it! The rest of the building, of course, is above ground, and rises through five floors, and comprises the Ballroom on the fifth floor, a Marble Hall housing a salon, an a la carte restaurant, the Long Bar. It was to this well-appointed Bar that we now headed with indecent haste and commendable determination.

Notwithstanding this potential inconvenience to our persons, we threw open the main double doors of the place and stepped into a brilliance of incandescent light emanating from large lanterns of glass and chandeliers suspended from the ceiling which illuminated the plush red silk carpet below. The whole effect was to create a crescendo of light, a euphoric sensation of ecstasy and warmth, all of which we needed so desperately having travelled through the acrid all-enveloping fog to reach here.

The light filled our senses as though experiencing the final closing chords of a symphony by Mahler, music so close to our hearts! Presently we found ourselves inside

The Criterion Building

what I took to be the salon in the Marble Hall. Lodge lead us through various large salons into what we knew to be the focus of our quest; the Long Bar, which was large, noisy and decorated extravagantly and exuberantly throughout. It combined Queen Anne and Baroque styles, with a suggestion of the Byzantine theatrics, and built of highly polished mahogany woodwork with brass fittings, handrails, marble surfaces and ostentatious acetylene gas-fuelled globe lanterns.

Complementing this style was incorporated the generous neo-Byzantine opulence of mirrors and mosaics on various walls and surfaces. There were rich, red velvet drapes framing engraved windows and decorative glazed panel openings in the internal timber partition walls. The ceilings were of painted and gilded moulded plaster looking down on elaborately patterned carpets with fleur de lys, upon which were positioned several indoor palm trees. The back bar, set in front of a mirrored wall, displayed decorated bronze stands on which were fixed curved glass globes containing various liquors.

In between them, and dominating the whole, was an enormous brass till of such intricate and ornate raised filigree design as to be almost a work of art, rather than a cash depository. The decorative effects and appointment of the bar were those which augmented the feeling of an opulently sumptuous, if meretricious establishment clearly patronized by a wealthier clientèle.

We pushed past a variety of patrons and at length we managed to gain the pale green *Emperador Chiaro* marble covered bar, whereupon surprising it was Lodge who ordered the drinks by intercepting a passing bar-tender.

"One large gin and tonic and three large whiskies, two neat, the other with the Coca~Cola, if you serve it," instructed Loge.

"We certainly do not serve it Sir; this is a respectable establishment and not a drug store," said a jovial red-faced bar tender, wearing a white apron and sporting a large handlebar moustache. "all of our customers prefer Schweppes' range of aërated waters and will have nothing else in their drink. They certainly would not dream of drenching their drinks with that dark cocaine-laced abomination. Why only yesterday a group of top hat wearing gentlemen advised the manager, Henry J Byron that if they ever saw the stuff being offered at this Bar, they would forthwith abandon the Criterion for a place which did not offer such a concoction, such as Kettner's or the Café Royal!"

We did eventually get our drinks and made ourselves comfortable on red damask covered sofas surrounded by the usual plethora of indoor palm trees ranged around the place.

"Quite a building, do you not think so Bella, gentlemen?" asked Lodge.

We nodded our agreement.

"As with all theaters," continued Loge, so called to his close acquaintances, "the Criterion was built on the site of the White Bear Inn in Jermyn Street, now behind this Criterion Building. In 1870 Felix Spiers together with Christopher Pond, applied for a theater license from our old friends, the Metropolitan Board of Works. Again, true to form this *Apocalypse of Doom* and tireless enemy of the Music Hall, tried to reject the application.

"They attempted to do so on this occasion, on the basis that the Criterion Theater was to be housed in the basement of the Criterion Building, in the ground, thirty feet below street level, and to be illuminated by town gas. This was unacceptable, so the Metropolitan Board of Works, argued, because of the attendant risk of town gas leaking with fears of toxic fumes filling the auditorium and gassing the audience!

"The license was only granted on the specific and

preposterous condition that fresh aëther was to be pumped into the theater auditorium continually during any performance, use or other activity involving members of the public.

"The original design of the building called for the basement to house a concert hall and not a theater. Accordingly, the names of famous composers are embossed in the ceramic tile work lining the walls of the on stairs leading down to the auditorium, which of course is now the theater of choice to launch our Choral Anthem Symphony! My friends, a toast to our inevitable success!" offered Lodge, in a show of concentrated magnanimous gesturing.

"Still the construction of the Criterion went ahead," continued Lodge, "to the ornate designs of Thomas E Verity. Quite a prolific architect our Verity, designing not only this august establishment, but a range of other theaters including the Royalty Music Hall in Dean Street, in which we have just held our rehearsals. He also designed the Comedy Theater, the Scala Theater and the Folly Theater all hereabouts.

"The Criterion opened in 1873 under the management of Charles Wyndham, the manager and lessee. It was Wyndham who introduced WS Gilbert and George Grossmith to the London audience. Wyndham, of course, then left to set up his own Wyndham Theater.

"In 1883 the Metropolitan Board of Works came back with a vengeance for another go. On this occasion, they demanded forthwith the immediate closure of the Criterion Theater, because apparently, pumping fresh aëther into the auditorium, thirty feet below ground level, was considered unsatisfactory. Again, any excuse to attempt to close a theater down. New ventilation ducting was installed primarily to appease the insatiable Metropolitan

Board of Works, the implacable enemy of the Music Hall," completed Lodge

Looking around the Criterion Bar, I noticed several sepia tinted Daguerreotypes that I could barely make out, ranged on various walls. However, the artistes' names and faces meant very little to me and I should think Jack as well. Still contemplating my drink and admiring the interior décor of the establishment, I became aware that a gentleman wearing a top hat was staring at us intently. Lodge had not noticed him, because he was preoccupied with trying to extract some foreign body from his glass of whisky and Schweppes' aërated water.

Presently the gentleman approached our persons in a determined manner. Bella instantly recognized him, and it was she, who in turn introduced Jack and me to him as the manager of the Criterion Theater, a Mr. Henry Byron.

"This is Jack Houston and Theo Mitchell, Vaudeville artistes from America. Of course you know Michael Lodge, impresario and my new agent," said Bella, dropping a little curtsey at Byron.

"Hello," I said, "I am Theo Houston, he is my stage partner Jack Mitchell. We are both pleased to meet you Sir!"

Lodge on hearing the introductions being made, spun around. He did so with a look of concerned surprised on his face; that such introductions had been made without his making them. He looked hard at Bella because of her initiative.

"Ah Loge, very good to see you again and I take it you are ready to launch your new and exciting show this evening?" inquired Byron, manager of the Criterion Theater.

"We are indeed Henry," replied Lodge.

"Good then follow me please and I shall escort you to your respective dressing rooms," instructed Byron, "and remember the golden rule; do not ever, ever allow the audience to panic you into performing!"

1. The aluminum memorial is of the Angel of Christian Charity popularly mistaken for Eros

Chapter 8

The Choral Anthem Symphony

We had arrived at the Criterion Theater located at the Regent's Circus for the first public performance of our new Choral Anthem Symphony with Jack and I integrating our *turns* into the symphony in a new a daring subtle but innovatively clever device involving the mass delusion of an audience, albeit without their apparently realizing it. Our performance was scheduled to run about a third of the way through the evening. Accordingly Jack and I went to the wings to watch others do their *turns* before ours.

Looking into the auditorium from the stage wings, we could not quite believe the pandäemonium extant in the Dress Circle or in the front rear of the stalls. The place was full of very unsavoury individuals who were intent on acting in a confident manner and, displaying very *determined behaviour* to all and sundry. These persons were of course the Nihilists, intent on heckling throughout any performance on stage. I felt a sickening feeling in the pit of my stomach.

Bella suddenly appeared at my side and upon noticing the *concentration* of Nihilists in the audience, dismissed their presence with a sniff and said, "Huh, those mindless baboons; they shall learn." And then promptly disappeared back stage.

Ironically, on hearing her utter those words of contempt for the *concentration* of Nihilists, or hecklers, as I prefer to refer to them as, made me feel slightly less scared, even cautiously confident. It could be that Bella may have been ignorant as to what these persons were, but really, I knew that was probably not the case, and that Bella would brook no crapulence from such bearded malcontents, whatever their motives!

All of a sudden there was a lot of shouting, notably in cockney accents, coming from the costermongers in the cheap seats. Then, thunderous applause commenced during which, onto the podium, stepped a diminutive man, wearing, with inordinate confidence a wide smile, a white tail-coat, white trousers and more alarmingly, white shoes! He was the conductor, Mr Thomas, who we had rehearsed with earlier in the day at the Royalty Music Hall in Dean Street, in Soho.

With a down ward stoke of his batten he launched the orchestra into a medley of tunes. Presently a singer came onto the stage, and wearing a long flowing gown of yellow silk. I recognised her as being the renowned Diane Hall, who, I recall Loge saying, performs at Barnard's Music Hall in Woolwich, where she sings regularly for her supper rather like the songbird she is!

Well she was very much here on the stage singing away and getting the audience going in sympathetic response. Even the Nihilists hecklers embedded in the audience were moved to become quiet and ceased their disruptive behaviour during her recital. Though looking at her, it would take a brave man to be anything other than attentive.

The interval arrived and the heavy red velvet safety curtain was lowered. This fact triggered two distinct events. One was an immediate evacuation of the stalls by person in their blind panic and stampede to get to the Crush Bars. The other, was to get ourselves organised for our *innovative sensation*, now to be let loose on this unsuspecting audience?

Bella was arranging her attire including a dazzling electric blue satin gown whilst singing softly to herself. Presently she was joined on this first night by the remaining *Two Graces* in the persons of Katie Lawrence and Dot Hetherington, both of whom viewed Bella with such a concentrated malevolence. Were that antagonism able to take on physical form, it would without doubt have resembled the properties of volatile quicklime.

Lodge dressed in his dapper outfit comprising his favorite midnight blue silk suit, ebony cane and top hat materialized and made a moving little speech about giving our all for the benefit of mankind. But more importantly, he emphasized, the incalculable benefits of Box Office receipts, and asked us all to bear that little thought in mind during these next few trying hours. He also advised us that we would be performing in front of royalty, as Frank and George were sitting in the Royal Box.[1] He then tapped his top hat and disappeared to take his seat in the Dress Circle.

Jack and I were separated and standing on either side of the proscenium arch. The Compière began his narration as the curtain was raised revealing the *Three Graces* and a small choir. The orchestra, of course, was already assembled in the pit immediately in front of the stage.

"Ladies and gentlemen, you are tonight invited to be a part of something new and vital. Imagine if you will, such noble ideals which we all of us seek in our all too brief and tragic lives. Such ideals as *Hope, Aspiration*, or *Courage* which can confer strength to our faltering resolve, especially in times of great adversity or despair.

"Imagine if you will, a symphony," so the Compière invoked, "a symphony in which those noble ideals are encapsulated and given laudable expression. Ladies and gentlemen, the Criterion Theater is pleased to present, for your delectation, the *Three Graces*, who shall sing the rôles, especially composed for soprano, in espousing those noble ideals and promulgated in this magnificent Choral Anthem Symphony.

"Ladies and gentlemen, please welcome the unsurpassable Bella Elmore who will be singing the rôle of *Courage*. Our renowned and delectable Katie Lawrence will sing those sections devoted to *Aspiration*. And she will be followed by the incomparable and indomitable Dot Hetherington who will bring up the rear and sing those sentiments devoted to *Hope!*"

As each of the sopranos was called, the intensity of the applause increased accordingly. Culminating into a thunderous crescendo, where nearly everybody in the auditorium rose from their seats and stood up, whilst clapping and demonstrating, unequivocally their unadulterated approbation for their adored, *Three Graces*. Also during this ecstatic welcome for the *Three Graces*, some members of the audience erupted with unbridled enthusiasm. Whilst others, ascended into an uncontrolled, but induced delirium, at the prospect of hearing their favorite sopranos sing their respective rôles in this, this choral symphonic extravaganza.

The only persons that I could make out from my position in the wings, who appeared unmoved by this prospect, were the Nihilists. Most of who, with smouldering eyes, registered their contempt and disgust, at their adjacent neighbour's outward display of support for the sopranos.

After quite sustained applause, the audience settled

Gustav Mahler 1860 – 1911

down in their plush crimson colored velvet covered seats with brass division rails. The gas lights were lowered and a hush descended upon the auditorium. Of course the last time Jack and I experienced the Choral Anthem Symphony, so-called extravaganza – as billed, was at the Imperial Theater located in the depths of the Royal Aquarium & Winter Garden in Victoria, when we were guests of the renowned Actor Manager, Mr. George Leybourne.

On that occasion we were not treated to an orchestral performance on account to the fact the usual Royal Aquarium Orchestra was performing elsewhere abroad the Metropolis. Instead, the musical passages to the symphony were paraphrased by two barrel organs and transcribed by three player pianos together with an Aëolian pianola. This evening however, was different and the orchestra under its conductor Mr. Thomas, were reported to be in fine fettle.

It was Katie Lawrence who broke from her rank with the other sopranos as she approached the front of the stage. Immediately she launched herself into taking up a sustained D major chord created by the orchestra. I confess, there are, at times, quite some sublime passages in this symphonic work for soprano and orchestra. But then of course, it was jointly composed by the acclaimed composer, Gustav Mahler. [2]

I was particularly moved by the invocation [3] by the chorus and soprano,

> '*Arise, my dust, yes rise again,*
> *from your all to brief repose;*
> *He who has called upon thee,*
> *will grant thy soul immortal life!*'

> '*With wings which I have gained,*
> *Shall I soar aloft into the aëther,*
> *In love's ardent striving,*
> *Into a light no eye ever beheld!*'

Now that we were hearing the symphony performed properly by a well-rehearsed orchestra, and not by barrel organs and player pianos including an Aëolian pianola, the work, especially Katie Lawrence's interpretation of *Aspiration,* could reach up into ethereal realms of beauty in harmony and verse.

Upon concluding her rendition she was met with tumultuous applause by a grateful and appreciative audience. I noticed that some of the Nihilists and hecklers were even moved to clap, if only lightly. After a lot of bowing and shouts of encore Katie Lawrence yielded the stage, having sang her rôle in espousing the cause of *Aspiration,* but only with reluctance.

At length she too began her slow and gradual withdrawal from the front of the stage. She yielded the position, only eventually after the introduction chords for the next *act,* ours were sounded. Despite these chords, Lawrence's retreat to the back of the stage was indeed slow, as it was ponderous, with the occasional steps forward in order to respond to her clamoring admirers.

It was our turn now to work the magic, and in so doing, totally confuse the audience.

On cue, from our respective wings, Jack and I marched on to the stage and met in the middle shaking hands and bowing to the audience. Most of whom, looked more bewildered at having their experience of a soprano singing, rudely interrupted by a couple of interlopers, who had appeared on stage in front of their chorus.

Jack approached the pianoforte that had been wheeled onto center stage whilst I got myself organised to sing for my supper. In the meantime, Judd, our ventriloquist's dummy, wore his usual manic fixed grin, and accompanied by Jack, sat down at the pianoforte in readiness to play it at my cue. Some how the deep misgivings I had experienced during rehearsals earlier, came back into my mind like a cataclysm of biblical proportions.

I simply could not envisage that my song about 'The Girl from Oklahoma' was going to go down well, especially after the audience had had their spirits raised to empyreal heights, if not to the sublime, by the invocation offered by Katie Lawrence in the words;

> *With wings which I have gained,*
> *Shall I soar aloft into the aëther,'*

Whereas my offering to match that transcendental and divine was with such profound lyrics as,

'That Girl from Oklahoma,
My God you should have known her,
With a ukulele she would often sing
Verses to gain her wedding ring!'

'Whilst riding though Missouri,
She met a handsome attorney,
Who upon seeing her ukulele
Abandoned her entirely!'

Still the arpeggios started to tinkle out from the pianoforte as Judd pounded the keyboard with his little wooden hands and I broke into the song. I had only gotten into the third verse, about the ukulele-playing Oklahoma girl who still had not found her wedding band, when the hecklers began their chant much to the surprise of the rest of the audience.

I moved nearer to the front of the stage in order to present myself in an obvious and dominating way. I even resorted to lifting my Sennit straw hat from my head with my left hand and waving it above my head, whilst twirling my cane in my other hand, all to create an overall dominance illuminated by the stage foot lights.

We got to the end of the song and Jack and I looked about for applause. None was forthcoming, not even from their graces Frank, Duke of Teck and George, Duke of Cambridge in their Royal Box, both, in fact, looking very imperious and thoroughly bored with my *turn* on the stage below them.

Right the next song, 'Central Park in Moonlight,' will get them going, I thought, it always does in New York or Chicago. Accordingly I began with a low E flat minor chord and rising to join with the pianoforte. At this point Jack, or rather Judd our ventriloquist's dummy, mischievously skipped the order of songs and went on to play a new song 'Alabama in the Morning' leaving me stranded in the key of E flat minor.

The audience noticed this faux pas and re-acted in an agitated manner whispering amongst themselves. I distinctly over heard someone in the front row ask loudly when would the Choral Anthem Symphony re-commence.

I turned around to Judd who also responded by beaming that fixed grin on his jaw to me. Still we got under way again and people genuinely looked as if they were enjoying our new song.

Then it happened. A vociferous Nihilist simply got up from out of the cheap seats and asked me at the top of his voice why I was indulging in the heinous act of enslaving Judd and making him perform remorselessly at the pianoforte without respite, sustenance or pay.

I was astounded by this outburst by the heckler. Even more so when Judd, the dummy turned his head around and agreed with the Nihilist! Adding that his life was a misery and he yearned for emancipation and freedom back to his wooden folks. Others in the audience agreed with him and added their own spiteful remarks aimed as both Jack and me.

"You are exploiters of the mindless and underprivileged!" one bearded heckler said, "I demand that you release Judd now at this very instant."

I am not certain whether Judd agreed with his being called mindless, but there it is.

I also stopped singing, as the calls for Judd's release increased, becoming more audible and vociferous.

"He, or rather Judd, is a wooden dummy, a ventriloquist's dummy and…" I responded, flabbergasted at the absurdity of the situation.

"No," interrupted the bearded heckler, "the person upon whose lap Judd, if that is his name, is sitting, is the dummy!"

At which point Jack abandoned the pianoforte and carrying Judd in his arms marched up to the very edge of the stage and engaged the heckler in an unbridled discourse about his not being the dummy, but that Judd was. At the same time the dummy appealed to the audience for his release. To which the audience unanimously demanded that Judd be given his freedom without delay or any condition. The hecklers exhorted the audience, who were now standing up, to continue to press for Judd's release from his bondage. Judd responded by moving his head in a wide sweeping arc of the auditorium still beaming that manic fixed grin upon his wooden painted face.

What then happened could not have occurred at a more inconvenient a moment. Whether Jack had failed to securely fasten Judd's head to his shoulders I could not be certain. But at that instance, Judd's head departed from his shoulders and fell to the stage floor bouncing for several moments around the stage during a deathly silence and finally rolling off into the orchestra pit.

This action had a salutary effect on the audience who responded with gasps of 'oh my God,' as people and hecklers in the audience looked away in horror, visibly disgusted at what they considered an unmitigated act of wanton cruelty of truly grotesque proportion.

Presently, it was the Compière who intervened by clearing Jack, me and a decapitated Judd off the stage. I noticed too that Frank and George had abandoned their Royal Box. Others in the audience took their lead and began to vacate the auditorium, at a truly astonishing rate, no doubt for the preference of the Crush Bars strategically place throughout the Criterion Theater.

Words failed me as I too left the stage whilst the Compière announced that the Choral Anthem Symphony would re-commence in forty minutes with the uplifting sentiments expressed by Dot Hetherington who will sing those noble ideals devoted to *Hope*."

At which point the heavy red velvet safety curtain descended with indecent haste nearly engulfing me in the process. Judd's decapitated head could stay where it had landed; in the orchestra pit, as far as I was concerned. In addition, a thought had presented itself to me vividly; it was time we removed Judd from our double act.

1. Frank, Duke of Teck and George, Duke of Cambridge were frequent visitors to Music Halls
2. Based on Mahler's Auferstehungs Symphonie No 2 in C minor
3. After Friedrich Klopstock

Chapter 9

The Unexpected Performance

Whilst at the Criterion Theater in the Regent's Circus performing our innovating sensation that will, according to Lodge, sweep all before it, involving as it does mass delusion on a grand scale of an entire audience without their realizing it, seemed to have faltered. The only thing that was swept away by our so-called *innovative sensation*, was the audience, who abandoned their comfortable red plush velvet covered seats, for the Crush Bars, whilst we were performing our *turn*. In addition, the hecklers had made their presence known, and had in fact scored a resounding victory at our expense. I blame Judd, our ventriloquist's dummy, for our misfortune on the stage. In addition, it is an evident fact that Judd is certainly getting above himself with his unscheduled predilection to ad lib, at my expense and that of Jack's.

The interval time of forty minutes was coming to an end as shown by the auditorium filling up with an apprehensive audience unsure of what they could expect. Even their graces George, the Duke of Cambridge and Frank, the Duke Teck and his Duchess had regained their seats in the Royal Box.

Jack and I again, remained in the wings on either side of the stage. As the Compière had announced previously, the Choral Anthem Symphony would re-commence with the uplifting sentiments expressed by Dot Hetherington who will sing those noble ideals devoted to *Hope*. Predictably enough the orchestra re-assembled and an uneasy hush descended over the auditorium. Again the town gas lights were lowered. Gradually a single beam of limelight illuminated a statuesque figure wearing a pink satin robe. From my position to her left, she appeared almost as a goddess bathed in this translucent light imparting an ethereal quality to her presence.

It was Dot Hetherington and I remember well her performance in the Imperial Theater recently, especially her very effective coup de grâce, which she executed on her sister sopranos. She did so without mercy and with a ruthlessness I could not think that the woman now standing on the stage, bathed in the warm limelight, was capable of doing and, with such inordinate enthusiasm and relish.

Quite what Dot Hetherington had pulled off at the Imperial Theater remains a mystery to me, even though I witnessed it with my very own eyes. All of a sudden she had the audience swaying from side to side in their seats, in response to her waving her head from side to side. Hetherington's achievement in getting the audience going and to re-act in sympathetic harmony was to the very obvious annoyance of the other two sopranos also on the stage at the time.

But her very effective coup de grâce, was a lesson in total ruthlessness, especially, given the fact that the other two sopranos had somehow failed to move the audience in quite such an enthusiastic way. After twenty minutes of ecstatic re-action from the audience and calls for encore and bravo, Hetherington finally conceded the front of the stage and then had the temerity to actually summon the two other sopranos to join with her in holding hands! Neither Marie Lloyd nor Katie Lawrence could scarcely reject this overt magnanimous gesture by Hetherington and were somewhat compelled to comply with her invitation!

That was then in the Imperial Theater. I was curious to see what she would do here now in the Criterion Theater in order to maintain her position as the undoubted queen amongst the *Three Graces*.

The orchestra took up the haunting solemn chords of G major. Dot bowed to the conductor, and then seamlessly took up his introduction with a powerful sustained voice an octave higher than the fist violins, responsible for creating the orchestral melody and sonorous chords. In her invocation, Hetherington sang about the deep reaches of despair which can corrode both the heart and soul until there is nothing left but everlasting sadness.

> *'Witness our hearts which are but flesh and mortal,*
> *That our souls are but spirit and so immortal;*
> *But both cannot resist the corrosion of despair,*
> *Now in a vacuüm of emptiness beyond compare.'*

The orchestra continued to relate remorselessly this melancholic theme in the key of G major. Then, it was as though Fate had taken a hand. Hetherington's voice rose powerfully above the music made by the orchestra as she transcended into A flat major. Her voice was echoed by the chorus who took up her refrain and together they established for all to hear and appreciate the *leitmotif*[1] for *Hope* arising from the wreckage of despair.

Hetherington's singing, together with the chorus, augmented by huge orchestral forces, created a sensuous music which was developing remorselessly into a resounding and positive re-acclamation of faith, and a release from the clutches of despondency!

Hers, without doubt, was a powerful performance which, she brought to a tumultuous finalé, accompanied by ecstatic and thunderous applause from a very appreciative audience some of whom erupted into uncontrolled ecstasy and delirium. This applause went on for quite some time during which Hetherington bathed in what could only be described as unbridled adoration of her and the pathos with which she exalted the virtue of *Hope*.

Dot Hetherington, executed flawlessly, her singing the rôle dedicated to *Hope*. After much applause, she too retreated to the back of the stage and joined her colleague Katie Lawrence, both now looking like unemployed angels.

The orchestra then started to play what I knew was the Symphonic Interlude. This had the effect of bringing a semblance of order throughout the auditorium as people regained their seats and dignity. We were on again after the interlude.

Again, the Compière introduced us again, if slightly hesitantly, as Jack and I marched on to the stage, or into the arena, whichever seemed more appropriate. We restricted ourselves to singing a couple of tame songs, neither of which captured the attention of the audience. And as for our attempts at witticism and anecdotes; they too failed to elicit any response.

I think the audience thought we were some roving act that had somehow stumbled into the Criterion Theater by mistake and on the wrong night. What the audience clearly wanted was a continuation of the Choral Anthem Symphony, and not two imbeciles marching around the stage, complete with an enslaved decapitated ventriloquist's dummy. However, what they got eventually, was equally unexpected as it was astounding.

Our act was followed by another Symphonic Interlude. Then the Compière, in his rôle of Master of Ceremonies, I think, introduced the next feature by banging his gavel.

"Ladies and gentlemen, please welcome the unsurpassable Bella Elmore who shall now sing the rôle of *Courage*, for your delectation and continuing delight!"

No sooner had this so-called Symphonic Interlude ceased, than Bella Elmore glided to the very front of the stage. As near to the footlights as possible, in order that she in her electric blue satin gown, might too be illuminated to the fullest effect and intensity.

After the ecstatic applause had subsided, Bella raised her arms with her hands facing towards the back of her.

"Your graces, ladies and gentlemen," she announced, whilst curtseying, "it remains my privileged honor to be able to relate to you, as soprano, the sentiments expressed in this most important of the rôles of the Choral Anthem Symphony; that of the rôle of *Courage*.

"Accordingly, I am delighted to be able to dedicate my singing this very difficult rôle to my very, very dear good friend, Marie Lloyd, who unfortunately cannot be with us, on this, this very momentous and special evening and be a part of our experience!"

Loge will certainly appreciate that esoteric piece of sarcasm, even if the audience were not quite up to doing so, I thought.

Her singing was better than we had experienced at rehearsals. Though her breath control was not perfect by any means and she had a tendency to drift between keys, and more alarmingly, between *flats* and *sharps*. And, during her recital, despite the apparent sublime lyrical intensity of the work, she stood there waving her arms about in an abandoned manner screeching out her words in falsetto and especially in the irritating key of C sharp minor.

During her recital, it became evident that her singing was no more than a thinly veiled attempt to simply to out-sing her previous rival in Marie Lloyd. And, that the dignified and noble ideals expressed in the Choral Anthem Symphony were of little relevance to her. Or, indeed of real significance in her vocal attack on the other two sopranos in Katie Lawrence and Dot Hetherington, now standing patiently on the same stage behind her.

After fifteen or so minutes of this musical onslaught by Elmore upon our ears, her part in this transcribed oratorio, thankfully for the time being, came to end. And after much bowing and raising her hands, she finally commenced her so-called retreat to the rear of the stage, as required to do so. When she did retreat it was not quite to the back of the stage. Rather she deliberately positioned herself occupying a place in front of Lawrence and Hetherington and certainly not out of the glare of the footlights.

Accordingly, at this juncture in performing the so called Choral Anthem Symphony, all three sopranos were required to sing in unison, as their respective noble ideals came to together, their rôles musically *fused* into one as it were, in the face of adversity. Though as to which adversity, the Choral Anthem Symphony simply failed to define.

The three sopranos did not so much sing together in unison, as *fused*, but rather gave the impression of being more *confused* than anything else. Aside of this unifying requirement of the sopranos to sing in unison together, rather they looked with a concentrated hostility and envy, at one another in vying as to who would basically out sing the other whilst putting them in the shade.

It was whilst all three sopranos were attempting to sing in unison at the very front of the stage that a few of the Nihilist hecklers decided to risk all and attempt to interrupt their combined singing. All three sopranos ignored the hecklers, since not one of them was willing to give up the more important task of out-singing the other soprano.

At length that particular movement of the symphony came to a dignified end. It was Bella Elmore who ceased the initiative by yelling at one of the more vociferous Nihilists.

"Oh do sit down dearie, as you look out of place in your black coat and beard standing up in the stalls!" said Elmore.

"You would not want us to tell your momma that you were a naughty boy tonight now would you, because if we do, and we might, she will not let you out again!" enjoined Dot Hetherington.

"I came here to listen to singing, not screeching," replied a bearded heckler, albeit with slight trepidation in his voice.

"Come up to the stage sunshine and I will have you singing in the register of top C soon enough," offered Katie Lawrence, much to the amusement of the audience who clearly regaled in this impromptu entertainment. This banter went on for some minutes, but in the end it was that particular Nihilist who backed down and certainly not the *Three Graces*.

The outcome of this encounter did not really surprise me. I remember at the beginning of the evening when Bella and I first recognized the Nihilists and hecklers sitting in the audience. Ironically, what gave me courage then, in having to deal with these persons, was the presence of Bella, and her inherent ignorance of the real danger the vociferous Nihilists could pose to us whilst we performed on stage.

Order was established again as Mr. Thomas, our constantly smiling conductor wearing his flamboyant white tail-coat, white trousers and white shoes plunged the orchestra into the final movement of the Choral Anthem Symphony. This brought the sopranos back into their singing contest in which they performed in a more animated manner. Waving their arms about and singing with a greater depth and feeling brought about, no doubt by their having dispatch some of the Nihilists to oblivion.

Notwithstanding that, the performance was clearly turning into a singing match, worthy of Rickard Strauss's opera *Guntrum*, in deciding finally who could sing the loudest, with sustained control. And do so with sheer fortissimo, accompanied by the inevitable falsetto to audibly dismiss the other singers into oblivion.

The resultant cacophony was appalling, as it was ear shattering, but the audience appeared to adore such an extravagance of voice technique. Bella Elmore was still leading the other two sopranos and used this situation to re reëstablish her position as queen amongst the *Three Graces*. As all three approached the climax to their various rôles leading to a thunderous crescendo, an event occurred which no one could have imagined or foreseen.

The audience were by now standing in the stalls, Dress Circle, Royal Box and in the aisles and applauding for all their worth as the symphony concluded with the loud closing bars beaten out by the tympani, kettle drums and brass section. The sopranos may have personally thought that their hour of glory had arrived; but alas at that very instant all *Three Graces* were ignominiously out staged by the unexpected arrival on stage of the irascible Little Bo

Peep! And who, well before her allotted time limped onto the stage with her shepherdess' crock and stood directly in front of the *Three Graces*. The audience erupted even more with thunderous sustained applause at her appearance on stage, as did the Nihilists, who now appeared to be enjoying themselves, if cautiously.

Little Bo Peep looked about the auditorium with swollen red eyes and a sad bewildered expression upon her face. Lowering her head in shame, she then made to leave the stage, but stumbled on account of her limp and fell down hard onto the floorboards dropping her shepherdess's crock.

That was it; the *Three Graces* knew it, the audience knew it and as it happens, so did Jack and I. Within moments of her fall she was rolling around the stage clutching her supposedly damaged knee that was now apparently bleeding profusely.

The sound of her crying emanating from her was considerable. Then it happened. Bo Peep had obviously perfected her *act*, but knew it had to evolve with new *turns* and the unexpected. We witnessed her innovation. During one particular loud episode of her distressed crying, she hauled herself up from the floor. But because she could not quite reach her shepherdess' crock, was unable to support herself and collapsed again back down to the stage deck with a look of helplessness upon her face wet with tears which glistened in the soft limelight for all to see.

The audience could hardly contain themselves and resorted to stamping on the floor of the auditorium or the decks of the Dress Circle and Upper Balconies. There was even visible activity, by their graces, in the Royal Box, who were now standing up. In the auditorium of the Criterion Theater, the applause generated by the ecstatic audience was tremendous, as it was sustained, and this was clear for all to hear and see.

The utter contempt upon the face of the *Three Graces*, unable to do anything about Bo Peep's unscheduled appearance at the expense of their glory, was something indescribable.

However, Bo Peep was not finished yet. Unable to stand up, she dragged herself along the boards, to the accompaniment of desperate crying, to where her crock lay. On approaching her shepherdess' crock, she reached out feebly with her thin arm and tried to pull it towards her. She after an agonizingly long time succeeded in retrieving it.

Then we were subject to another out burst of tears and crying, but she did so whilst pushing her face up to the audience and moving it in a sweeping arc in front of her so no one, but no one should fail to see her sad tearful face full of pathos and the miserable predicament she found herself in.

The audience could not believe their good fortune in witnessing this impromptu unscheduled appearance of Little Bo Peep, especially following on after the pathos-ridden Choral Anthem Symphony. Members of the audience were ecstatic and showed their appreciation with continued clapping.

The *Three Graces*, in comparison could barely conceal their overt unadulterated contempt and seething repulsion. Especially at being out-staged, out-performed and out-applauded by this pathetic bonnet-wearing, frilly dressed with ribbons, concentrated cuteness. Who, was able, within seconds of arriving unannounced on stage and with ease, relegate them, the *Three Graces*, into total oblivion.

At one stage one of the Nihilists mistakenly thought

that he could capitalize on this torrent of emotionalism by attempting to interrupt. Her re-action was swift as it was effective. She hobbled over to that part of the stage nearest to him. She stood there for a moment or two on the precipice of the stage, sniffed back and then burst back into continued and unrelenting tears worthy of the Niagara Falls in late Spring. The heckler did not so much resume his seat, but rather left the auditorium, with smouldering eyes following his departure.

At length her impromptu appearance culminated with her not bursting into song, as she had done when we saw her recently at the New Bedford Music Hall. No, on this occasion, she varied her act. Her performance was brought to an end with the appearance on the stage of a little lamb that walked toward Bo Peep bleating as it did so. The audience became wilder showering further applause on her, some inducing themselves in to a delirium, whilst others stamped their feet on the decks of the stalls, Balcony, Dress Circle and Royal Box.

Hers was a performance that equalled if not excelled that of the Dumb Mute's that we had witnessed at Wilton's Music Hall recently.[2] Her striking demeanor and predicament were evident for all to appreciate readily and quickly. She had augmented her performance, a great performance, to a level worthy in stature to that of a master class given by the renowned actor, David Garrick.

"We have to learn from her Jack," I said "we have simply have got to learn from her," were the only words I could utter in response to witnessing Bo Peep innovative *turn* on stage.

1. A reference expressed in music of a recurring idea or character
2. For an account of this amazing performance refer to the 'Royal Aq - Queen of Music Halls' ISBN No. 978-0-9571629-7-6

Chapter 10

The Innovative and Splendid

Whilst we had performed our innovative sensation to an unsuspecting audience, I personally remained perplexed at just what it was we had in fact achieved, or indeed failed to. Our *act* did not seem to me to have a defined rôle. It was as though we were an adjunct, at best, to the main act, auxiliary at worst. Certainly the weakness of our *act,* incorporating Judd, the headless ventriloquist's dummy, appeared to me to be redundant and out of step with the other *acts* or *turns* extant on the stage, not least that of Little Bo Peep's.

Even though I remain full of misgivings about our performance, we repaired to the Long Bar, still wearing our garish grease paint on our faces; just to let everybody know that we are actual performing artistes, albeit with a yet defined or specific rôle.

After several drinks we left the noisy Long Bar and resorted upstairs to the Dining Room for dinner. Byron, the Criterion Theater Manager led the way through a series of corridors and galleries. As we ascended the broad grand staircase, up to the *piano-nobile*, Lodge all of a sudden made a statement of great import.

"Yes Bella, gentlemen, it was in this very Dining Room, to which we are now headed, I remember the

Gustav Mahler by Sickert

artist Walter Sickert, you know of the Camden Town Group, located at Mornington Crescent, actually sketched a drawing of Gustav Mahler. At that momentous time, both were luncheon guests of mine," informed Loge.

When we had gotten over this unexpected revelation, we continued on into the expansive and luxuriously appointed Dining Room, resplendent in all its opulence and luxuriant fittings. Typically, we were greeted by two carved white *Carrara* marble nymphs, located on plinths at the head of the staircase on the *piano-nobile*. Each held in their hands a white, opaque-glazed, illuminated globe lantern.

The most striking aspect of this extravagant luxury were two smooth, gold-painted columns tapering to lavish Corinthian capitals, seemingly holding up the ornate stucco ceiling with its intricate raised and gilded tracery designs. Echoing these pillars was a pair of grooved mahogany pilasters set flush against the wall. In between them, the walls were lined with red silk-flocked wallpaper ornamented with gold filigree.

Set into the architrave were highly varnished panels depicting even more complex designs. Some of the recesses were sufficiently deep as to take highly decorated porcelain vases. With the exception of four lights suspended from an ornate plaster ceiling, other ostentatious wall-mounted acetylene gas fuelled globe lanterns and candelabra provided most of the illumination. The Dining Room continued the usual combination of Byzantine and Baroque styles with brass fittings and ornaments ranged around the room, with the walls panelled in highly polished elm; one of which fronted by a counter of white *Perlino Bianco* marble.

Complementing the general style throughout, were incorporated rich drapes of red velvet, framing engraved windows and decorative glazed panel openings in the internal timber partition walls. The ceilings again were painted white with raised gilded filigree detailing looking down on to a deep red silk broadloom carpet with intricate fleurs de lys elaborate patterning. Ranged around the room, in between the tables, which were covered in crisp white linen cloths, were several sofas, upholstered in red damask with white cotton antimacassar headrests and of course, being in England, numerous ubiquitous indoor palm trees planted into large green glazed urns.

During dinner we astutely avoided discussing anything about this evening's performance on stage, as is the custom. The time for that would be soon enough in the morning. What we did discuss briefly were the occupants of the Royal Box witnessing our performances, for good or for bad.

"You mentioned much earlier in the evening, before we went on stage, that we would be performing in front of royalty. Just who in fact were we acting in front of?" asked Jack, of Loge.

Lodge put his wine glass down and looked over both his shoulders as was his custom.

"Do you recall when we were in the Canterbury Music Hall drinking at the Crush Bar? Well I did mention then that the royals have, over the decades, been very good patrons of the Music Hall. This started with the Prince of Wales' regularly attending the lush *Pleasure Gardens* to be found at Vauxhall, Cremorne, Ranelagh or Marylebone, especially with its distinctive sandstone Mausoleum," said Lodge.

"I do indeed," said Jack, "you mentioned several members of the royal family, in particular those regular visits by the then Prince of Wales, who became, I believe, your Edward VIIth. and his successor George Vth. In front of whom, Marie Lloyd was not permitted to sing."

"Very true Jack, but in addition, other members of the royal family also patronize the Music Hall. The Canterbury Music Hall especially," Lodge continued, "has been host to royalty on numerous occasions as have other Music Halls such as the Criterion and the Imperial Theater in the Royal Aquarium & Winter Garden. Notably two royal Dukes in particular are to be found in them on a regular basis. They are their graces the Duke of Teck and his Duchess and the Duke

Marylebone Gardens Mausoleum

of Cambridge, commander-in-chief of the British Army!

"Indeed, it is known that the Duke of Cambridge in 1847 took as his wife, the stage actress Sarah Fairbrother, a commoner, who worked the Lyceum Theater, Covent Garden Theater and the Drury Lane Theater," informed Lodge.

"Does that make Sarah a Duchess then?" Jack asked.

"Imagine that! A Duchess actually performing on the stage!" I rejoined,

"Alas Theo, Jack, not at all; when the Duke married the actress it was in contravention of the Royal Marriages Act of 1772, which meant that their marriage was not sanctified by the then reigning monarch, the old queen, Queen Victoria. Accordingly, the marriage was considered to be Morganatic. This in effect means, the ducal title cannot be passed down by the present Duke to his spouse or issue. Sarah may be married to the Duke of Cambridge, but she remains simply Mrs. Cambridge.

"But," continued Lodge, and looking over his shoulders, "even stranger and more singular set of circumstances attend his grace the Duke of Teck! One might even consider these startling events to be a suitable libretto for a comic opera, were they to fail to reach the dignified and august realms of Music Hall. Our grace, the Duke, though not considered wealthy by comparison to other royals, was quite a gambler and thought nothing of loosing £10,000 on a single bet!

"This loss, of course, necessitated his having to work as an employé, for the City firm of Panmure Gordon & Co Ltd. It must be remembered Jack, Theo, princes of the realm do not work in trade. The prospect of 'a prince in trade' was too much for Frank, our erstwhile Duke, and accordingly, he was forced to relinquish his position there, and also give up his stately home of White Lodge in the Richmond Park near London. He was then obliged to take chambers at 36 Welbeck Street, behind the Bechstein Hall, the front of which, adorns Wigmore Street.

"And, it continues; Frank's mother was the daughter of Adolphus Frederick, the previous Duke of Cambridge. Do you see the connection between Frank and George, the two Dukes sharing Royal Boxes in Music Halls? But to continue, for I digress in relating my interesting, if singular, narrative. In keeping with an indigenous gambling streak, Frank's mother had acquired a set of precious stone which she purchased with her winnings. They became known as the *Cambridge Emeralds* which Frank inherited on his mother's death. The stones only came to light again on the occasion when Frank, the Duke of Teck drew up his own *embarrassingly generous* will and testament, leaving the gems to his mistress Lady Kilmorey," completed Loge.

"So we were performing in front to two royal Dukes, one of whom was the commander-in-chief of the British Army and other a reckless gambling womanizer, both of whom attend Music Hall on a regular basis?" inquired Jack.

"They most certainly do and the Duke of Cambridge, was in fact was the commander-in-chief of the British army for forty six years!" replied Lodge.

Suddenly Bella got up and left the table and walked towards a man. Having reached the place where he was standing, she commenced gesticulating with her arms and seemed to be in a deep and animated conversation with him. I assumed him to be a fan of hers and thought nothing more of it. Lodge, I noticed, at the same time, made his excuses saying that he had just spotted someone whom he knew and wished to consult over a matter of some delicacy. Jack buried his garishly painted face in the menu, in order to select more wine for us.

Presently Bella returned, looking decidedly flushed and agitated.

"A fan of yours Bella?" asked Jack.

"Oh no, not at all; though I have known him for considerable time," informed Bella, whilst falling into her chair at the table.

Jack selected a wine, a Chablis, and instructed our waiter accordingly.

"He actually thoroughly enjoyed our show this evening and was quite impressed with all of us who took part," announced Bella.

"When you see him next please extend our appreciation of his compliments," said Jack to Bella.

"Oh you can do that yourselves;" advised Bella, "for

he has invited us all to dinner tomorrow evening at a house near Hampstead Heath."

"That is uncommonly generous of a relative stranger to invite us all to dinner on the strength of our stage performance this evening," Jack said.

"I do not see why," replied Bella Elmore, slightly slurring her words, "after all, he is my husband."

The rest of the evening in the Criterion Dining Room passed in an agony of self-doubt and unanswered questions, all of which coursed through my mind incessantly.

Eventually Lodge returned to our table, a little worse for wear, I thought, but did offer up an interesting observation.

"Bella, Gentlemen please, please attend me. I have been speaking with some esteemed members of the Fourth Estate[1] and indulging in a spot of supererogation,[2] as it were," he said, whilst tapping the side of his nose with his index finger, "and ambrosial sensuality,[3] to say that it remains probable that we may have achieved the unachievable in the innovative and the splendid," before lapsing into the back of his green velvet covered seat at the dining table.

Needless to say it was as much as we could do to get Loge into an open Landau carriage to convey him back to his town house in the Bergen Avenue. And then be compelled to use that same carriage, with *extra charges*, to get us home to the St. Pancras Hotel.

1. Persons engaged in the publication of newspaper
2. Doing more than one's duty or circumstance demand
3. Delighted

Chapter 11

The Sublime to the Ridiculous

Our launch of the Choral Anthem Symphony was attended with both success and disappointment. I should not care to wager either way on which was the greater. However, things can only improve. And, as Lodge has been at great pains to remind us; one can only expect set backs when launching a new scientific-based concept such as our new innovative sensation. And, if things were easy then they would not be worthwhile doing. So Lodge claims, by the application of this specious argument. However, we have been invited to stay overnight as dinner guests of Bella and her husband, presumably Mr. Elmore.

Such were the thoughts going through our minds whilst Jack and I took our break-fast in the Grand Dining Room at the St. Pancras Hotel in which we are hold up during our stay in London.

"Well Jack, do tell me your thoughts on yesterday's adventure at the Criterion," I asked.

"You want that I should tell you Theo, tell you what?" replied Jack.

"You must have some thoughts?" I repeated.

"Theo," continued Jack, "I simply do not know whether we made complete fools out of ourselves, or only partial fools, yet again. Or, that in fact we have really accomplished the unachievable or something last night. I guess I do not really know.

"Looking at the audience, I got the distinct impression that they were as confused as I was. They did not know when to clap, and when they did clap, they were uncertain as to what they were really clapping for.

"Theo, let me be frank here. I cannot see how Lodge's ideas of this innovative sensation are going to pan out. He talks about it taking the audiences by storm. Yeah, well the audience stormed out alright; they stormed out of the auditorium and straight into the strategically placed Crush Bars. This has happened to us twice in as many evening performances where the audience has simply just walked, sorry, run out, on us…"

"No Jack," I interrupted, "that is not the case! Yeah last night I too had grave misgivings, but now in the cool light of retrospect, I see things differently. I think Lodge does have something, not as a result of his thinking; I hasten to add, but rather by pure default and good fortune!

"Jack, remember when we were in Chicago, you and I both harbored feelings about our *act* being tired and stale and in need of something new to rejuvenate it? Well, then Loge walked into the bar in North Michigan Avenue in search of us having seen our *act*, albeit a desultory one. From the moment we met him, and some of his, shall we say, colleagues, what has become obvious to me, like a freight train bearing down on one, is the resurging and constant need for something new, novel, unexpected, innovative even as in *innovative sensation*.

"Whether we like it or do not is irrelevant. What is relevant is quite simply, what the audience wants. In this respect Lodge is quite right; the only important fact here are the Box Office receipts. They are as good an indicator of whether we are providing what the audience wants, or not. In this, we cannot fault the man," I said.

"Yeah, but Theo, do we still not have some dignity? Are we to let Lodge lead us by our noses, as we descend into the abyss of Burlesque?" asked Jack.

"I do not think so. And I sure as hell did not experience much dignity when we were being heckled at the Majestic Theater in Chicago. No Jack, I think with some work and minor adjustments, we can make this thing work. Well if nothing else, it is different, and you …" I said.

"Theo," Jack butt in, "can you believe it; Lodge is approaching our table looking pretty pleased with himself?"

I looked over my shoulder and saw that Lodge was indeed negotiating his way through the tables bending and swerving like a seasoned waiter. I also noticed he was carrying several newspapers. At the thought that they may contained reviews of our efforts last night brought on a dull feeling in the pit of my stomach.

We both of us got up and shook hands with Lodge.

"Gentlemen, please resume your seats," he said, whilst commandeering a vacant chair from a nearby table, "I have been reading these newspapers and their review of our *innovative sensation*. As I intimated yesterday evening in the Criterion Restaurant, we may have achieved the unachievable in the innovative and the splendid. That may have been a slightly premature statement to have made, since some newspapers are referring to aspects of the evening that to me remain irrelevant.

"I have been looking at the reviews," he said, with a look of distain upon his features, "some are favorable, other not so, notably those that appeal to the lower orders. Typically I quote from *The Daily Telegraph*.

'It is reported that a group of hecklers, sitting

in the cheap seats in the Criterion Theater, attempted to interrupt a show last evening. The militants, commonly known as Nihilists, are sworn to disrupt the Music Hall proceedings at every opportunity, and last night was no exception. However, it was with some difficulty to understand precisely what had galvanized the hecklers into action since the evening was, in the main given over to a symphonic choral work composed by a certain Michael Loge with help from an acquaintance called Gustav Masters. The work conformed to the standard oratorio repertoire as defined by Mendelssohn or Handel and was performed to reasonable satisfaction of the audience. The hecklers were however in evidence and even managed on no less that three occasions invade the actual stage in order to carryout their disruption. This involved two individuals, with American ascents, who repeatedly attempted to sing aided and abetted by a wooden doll that appeared to be able to speak for itself. Eventually the Compière brought order to the proceedings by evicting the American intruders from the stage.'

Both Jack and I sat there in disbelief of the newspaper's article.

"American intruders, indeed!" announced Jack

"Just what did the audience think we were doing on the stage?" I asked.

"Well, according to *The Daily Telegraph,* intruding," replied Lodge.

I grabbed a paper and looked at the open page containing a review. I glanced through it and sighed.

"Listen to this Jack," I said, "it is from a journal called *The Chronicle* and seems pretty vitriolic in its reporting of the event.

> 'Disaffected parties have again imposed force-
> fully their grievances and impossible claims
> upon the unwarranted attention of ordinary
> decent members of the Music Hall-going
> public. They achieved this deplorable state of
> affairs, yet again, by behaving in a disagreeable
> manner and, in public too! It is time the
> government acted against these over confi-
> dent malcontents and introduced legislation
> in Parliament to severely curtail their activi-
> ties. It was reported that a concentration of
> the so-called Nihilists masquerading as heck-
> lers had assembled inside the foyer of the
> Criterion Theater, before repairing to the
> Crush Bar where several had been seen
> drinking heavily. Then, satiated with alcohol,
> they emerged from the bar and immediately
> went to take their seats in the cheaper areas
> of the stalls. During the concert, they pro-
> ceeded to disrupt and generally behave in a
> thoroughly outrageous manner offering
> threats and insults to all and sundry. At one
> stage during the performance two of the
> hecklers managed to gain the stage with a
> wooden doll of sorts wearing a manic fixed
> grin on its face. Then they proceeded to
> interrupt the show by engaging with their
> fellow hecklers in a lengthy discourse with the

wooden dummy, that was more in control than its supposed operator, who appeared powerless to stop the wooden doll from talking! A full thirty minutes of this rampage had elapsed before order was imposed by the courageous Compière, and at great risk to his person.'

Jack in the meantime, was perusing a copy of the *Daily News,* a popular daily, so I believe, often purchased by the undeserving poor. He quoted from it.

'Yesterday evening the audience assembled in the Criterion Theater was treated to a spectacular and triumphant performance of the oratorio-styled Choral Anthem Symphony, written entirely by the Austro-Hungarian composer, called Gustav Mahler. During the performance, which set, new records in reaching the ethereal heights of dignity and nobility of purpose, together re-defined those precious ideals as Hope, Courage or Aspiration. The rôles of which, were sung by Dot Hetherington, Bella Elmore and not least Katie Lawrence respectively. In addition, Mr. Mahler is to be congratulated on his intuitive insight of the troubled soul as expressed in his Choral Anthem Symphony, and the resounding redemption alluded to therein. As with all new works where innovation is the prime mover, the audience was somewhat confused and appeared not to know quite when to clap or refrain from doing so. This apparent inability was made all the more so by the repeated appearance of two Vaudeville actors who had; either arrived at the wrong theater in which to do their *turns*. Or, were there as a result of a deliberate and concerted action to deceive the audience with alternate acts of a grotesque nature involving decapitated wooded dolls inter-dispersed with the sonorous music emanating out from the symphony via the orchestra and chorus.'

"Is this an example of English sarcasm and grudging response to innovative Music Hall?" inquired Jack, "because were it to be so, then I too remain uncertain as to whether we have been slated or praised?"

Lodge then read a report from the *Sporting Life*.

'Yesterday, for the delectation of an unsuspecting audience, a new and innovative sensation, so described by impresario Michael Loge, was unveiled at the Criterion Theater. The show involved various *turns* or *acts* by numerous participants. At one stage we were treated to a symphonic choral work with sundry *turns* acted out during the course of it. The audience on several occasions appeared genuinely perplexed and did not know what to make of it, let alone when to clap. At one stage two amateur Vaudeville artistes stepped into the limelight with a ventriloquist's dummy who attempted to sing along with the symphony chorus! Why this was so, remains a mystery, since it [the dummy] did not lend what might be cautiously termed verisimilitude to the choral elements in the symphony.

Indeed at one stage it was competing with three seasoned sopranos who did not require the dummy's vocal assistance. In the evolution of Music Hall [sic] from the *Song and Dance*, to *Turns*, extant in the now extinct to *Pleasure Gardens* to now this innovative form of entertainment. Combining pathos with tragedy expressed by the repeated appearance of two Vaudeville artistes who deliberately interrupted the show. To towering majesty of the Choral Anthem Symphony, composed by Loge with some assistance from an acquaintance by the name of Gustav Masters; in this respect we can only assume that Loge, as impresario, remains confident in what he is doing in presenting this complex type of entertainment.'

It was Jack who recognized the typeface of *Variety* journal peeping out from the pile of newspapers. And immediately pulled it out and went to the review columns. We both of us were interested in what this indispensable magazine should have to say about our performance at the Criterion Theater.

'Yet again we have witnessed disorderly conduct on the very streets of the London, England with renegades rampaging, this time through a Music Hall in Piccadilly and acting in a confident manner, dispensing insults at members of the audience and to artistes on stage whilst doing their *turns*. We know this outrage to be the result of the activities of an extreme sect called the Nihilists – who are by way of being revolutionaries and part-time hecklers. The focus of their wrath on this occasion was two American Vaudeville artistes out of Delaware currently on tour in England. Irrespective of the disruption suffered by both artistes and spectators the theme of their show was different to what one might normally expect to see on the Vaudeville stage in London, England. The show, bizarre as it is, involves the performance of a symphonic piece of music for orchestra and chorus and was played to wild acclaim. During the course of this work, other sundry *acts* or *turns* were performed in conjunction or at variance with the symphony. This included a headless doll being banded about the stage and a crippled child brought in from the London streets to be compelled to sing for her supper!'

I picked up a paper called *The Echo* in the hope of retrieving a review that we could be proud of.

'Impresario Mr. Michael Loge, introduced his much vaunted new innovative sensation as he calls it, on to an unsuspecting audience at the Criterion Theater last night. We do not know what these turns were supposed to be about, oscillating as they did from the sublime to the ridiculous. This included a range of pathos from a headless ventriloquist's dummy to an impersonation of Little Bo Peep. We also witnessed on stage the occasional appearance by two Vaudeville actors on an extended tour of London, to add pathos to what was an exercise in controlled hysteria set to a background of a huge musical extravaganza for orchestra, three sopranos and chorus. On the whole we remain impressed, as were the audience, with this new departure in orthodox Music Hall entertainment. The evening was qualified by a couple of incidents involving a concentration of Nihilists turned hecklers, intent on causing maximum disruption in the theater, and who acted in a confident and provocative manner in the forward stalls of the auditorium. And two wondering Vaude-ville artistes, who appeared lost. Some time had elapsed before order was eventually restored and then only after employés and ushers of the Criterion Theater intervened against the Nihilists often at risk to their persons.'

"I do not get it Lodge, just what the hell are these English papers writing about? I ask, because these varying reviews add up to absolute zilch. Even with their use of wild superlatives it is difficult to know what was happen-ing on the stage we were supposed to be on; and indeed we were on it!" said Jack.

"One can expect a little criticism at the beginning of any new idea. I have been in this situation before and the public will learn, they shall learn," said Lodge, though not very convincingly.

"Yeah learn," said Jack, "I do not doubt that; but at whose expense?"

They shall learn, I tell you," Lodge re-iterated.

And with those parting words Loge rose from his chair.

"Gentlemen, I will leave you to enjoy your break-fast

as I have business to attend to," said Lodge, tapping the side of his nose with his index finger, "but of course we shall be meeting at Bella's house this evening!"

Jack and I sat in our chairs for a few moments thinking about the enormity of the various reviews we had read. Somehow break-fast had lost its appeal; and it was with that realization that Jack and I instinctively got up and headed out of the Grand Dining Room and straight for the well-appointed bar on the on the *piano-nobile* for restorative consolation.

Gradually we recovered our composure, that or the alcohol was taking effect, and the annoyance we both were experiencing by degrees dissipated into a feeling of resignation. We drank until our anger had abated. At length, we were able to take a less passionate view on the reviews, and instead adopt a more pragmatic or indeed, a philosophical stance. At one stage we both confirmed that our *turn* was so revolutionary in its style and form that it would, perforce, upset the conservative elements in the Fourth Estate or audience.

But then are ameliorated anger settled on to a laudable, if unanimous excuse.

"I blame that Judd, our over-confident ventriloquist's dummy and the incident of his head rolling around the stage floor and finishing up in the orchestra pit. It could be Theo that Judd's days are numbered, in that I think that he has at long last reached his apotheosis. Certainly in London headless dummies do not seem to be all the rage or go down too well," I ventured.

"I think that you are right Theo. The manic fixed grin on his face in between his red cheeks may now be passé. But what do we replace him with, Cinderella?" responded Jack.

"Not a bad idea," I retorted, whilst ordering two more whiskies from a very attentive bar-tender.

Chapter 12

The House Next to the Heath

Our reading through the various reviews of our new act at the Criterion Theater had produced a desultory feeling of disappointment in our hearts. The general consensus was that the reviews were confusing in their reporting of our show, probably based on the fact that was that our new performance was innovative and new and yet to be understood fully. The *sensational innovation* aspect of the show that was suppose to sweep all before it, had somewhat eluded us and our audience. Still we were to have dinner with Bella and her husband and what she might have to say could be of interest and possibly re-assuring too.

"Your Landau carriage has arrived sir and is waiting for you beneath the western Porte Cochère," informed the Concièrge

On this occasion he appeared quite civil, even obsequious.

"Thank you my good man," said Jack as we both rose reluctantly from our comfortable buttoned down red leather Chesterfields, upon which we had been reclining for the better part of the afternoon. We were dressed for dinner and accordingly went straight out to our carriage, which Lodge had organized to take us to Hampstead for dinner with Bella Elmore and her husband, presumably Mr. Elmore. Lodge had informed us that Aloysius would drive him there from his town house in the Bergen Avenue.

"To Hilldrop House, Hampstead is it sir?" asked our liveried coachman.

"Yes," replied Jack, as we climbed aboard and made ourselves comfortable on the buttoned down green leather upholstered seat of our spacious Landau carriage. In fair exchange, I guess, for the red leather Chesterfields we had just vacated in the salon.

Our carriage emerged from our vestibule, from within the Porte Cochère, and plunged into the clammy acrid fog still with us. As we did so the hooves of our two horses clattered on the cobbled stone road as they negotiated their way through the fog. Jack and I were both in a pensive mood, for no particular reason.

"Such dreadful news is it not? The whole of England is talking about the sinking of that ill-fated *Titanic*, which sank the other day. And how the crew fired rounds at the passengers to stop a mutiny from breaking out," said our liveried carriage driver.

Jack and I looked at each other.

"Had that ill-fated *Titanic* boat, been built on the Clyde shipyards in Scotland, it would have gone straight through that iceberg, and sunk it without trace!" continued the carriage driver unbidden by either of us.

"Quite!" responded Jack, in a manner deliberately intoned to discourage the carriage driver from any thoughts of his indulging in any banal conversation with us during the course of our journey.

"It must have been quite a performance on that *Titanic* boat," continued the carriage driver, evidently undeterred by Jack's verbal dismissive, "what with the mutiny and the fire which broke out into which the crew tossed recalcitrant passengers who refused to pay them an extortionate fee in order to gain access into the all but too few life boats. And what about that band of musicians floating around on a raft in the waters of the Atlantic playing popular tunes and even requests from those struggling in the water, including '*Abide with Me*' and the like kind!

"And, how some of the passengers tried to lynch the captain from a yardarm, but were prevented from doing so, by the fact the *Titanic* then broke in two. With the captain on one side and the frustrated erstwhile lynchers, ropes in hand, on the other side; all to the background hymn of, '*Nearer my God to Thee, Nearer to thee*' being played by the band! And how pandäemonium erupted on the forecastle, just before she sank, I ask you. Dread-filled news, Guv, dreadful," said the carriage driver.

"Indeed." I said.

"Cor, what a palaver! It would not happen on a Cunard boat," our liveried coach-man continued.

"No doubt…," I replied.

"You take that *Lusitania*; a fine Cunard boat and unsinkable," butted in the carriage driver, "safe as houses. It has got none of your triple screw reciprocating engines, powering forty-seven thousand tons of boat into what, straight into an iceberg? The captain of the *Titanic*, Edward Smith must have been at the old mother's ruin too. That *Titanic* boat was not the only wreck plying the waters of the Atlantic during that fateful night. How can you not miss an iceberg the size of St. Paul's Cathedral, I ask you?"

"My old lady is from Liverpool and when I have been up there I have seen those big boats coming round the headland and all over the place they are. Do they have rudders I kept asking myself, when watching them? The chances are if they do, then they do not know how to use them. Those boats seem to spend more time banging around and crashing into other ships or hitting harbour walls and the like. One even managed to ram a ship of the Royal Navy. Cor guv if I drove my carriage around London like that, I would have to go up to the Hackney Carriage Office, and there, give a good account of myself, or I should find myself in Queer Street. Reciprocating engines, what!"

The Landau carriage driver continued to offload his diatribe irrespective of the lack of encouragement from either Jack or myself.

"It is wise to use the a Landau carriage when travelling to Hampstead by way of Camden Town," remarked Jack, "if only to frustrate the intentions of footpads who line the route and remain always ready with their ambuscade of the unwary traveller. You can imagine Jack, especially in this fog, such individuals can operate under its concealment and invariable have the advantage in any incident, staged or otherwise."

Our Landau carriage driver eventually delivered us to Bella's Hilldrop House, located on the hill next to the vast expanse that is the Hampstead Heath. At once we alighted from the carriage and in an instant it went clattering off into the fog with only its ghostly red lantern visible suspended eerily as it eventually disappearing into the white shrouds.

Lodge had evidently only just arrived, as his carriage proclaimed as much. And then it too went lurching off into the all-embracing fog, leaving us alone in the empty lane in which Hilldrop House is located. I pulled at the cast iron doorbell plunger that operated a bell, the faint sound from which was just audible to our ears. It came from within the house that stood in its own grounds behind a high stone wall topped with protruding broken glass.

Whilst waiting for a response to our summons I surveyed our immediate door threshold. It was centered on a massive overhanging Gothic stone archway, which surrounded a heavy iron-clamped oaken door, glistening with dew. This archway clearly formed the entrance, through the wall, from the road into the garden and to the house that lay behind within the precincts of the high wall. The whole aspect of this road door entrance, was that it not only had an look and smell of decay augmented by the damp fog, but that it also had the appearance of an entrance to a fortress. In addition, it also retained the appearance of an entrance to a Gothic ruin, rather than the residence of a Music Hall actress.

The sound of a retaining iron bar behind the wooden door being scraped back heralded that our summons was being answered. At length we heard a clanking and jarring of keys and the door began to open very slowly creating an opening in which stood a person from the household. He waived his arm in the direction of the house at the end of a rising pathway of wet flagstones. We obliged and entered the premises through the arched portal and waited there in desolated grounds, most of which had been dug up forming creators, as if the occupiers had been busy burying objects.

From what I could discern in the gloom the house which rose up before us in the mist appeared to be that of a tall Gothic mansion complete with ancient Egyptian stone symbols and architectural details. Including, just visible in the fog amidst the protruding crenellated gable-ends, was a massive, if foreboding-looking tower, rising ominously from the centre of the mansion.

The tower appeared all the more sinister by the fact

Hilldrop House, Hampstead

that on top of it was a truncated pyramid, surrounded by four massive carved stone pinnacles placed at each corner. The vastness of the mansion with its deathly fog-shrouded silence was evidently someway back from the road and in its own seclusion. The person, who had opened the road gate, a servant of the household presumably, beckoned us to follow him up to the house. Given our previous experience with servants such as Aloysius, we did not engage him conversation.

We walked along the damp slippery flagstones that formed a path to the mansion. The pathway led us through the lifeless vegetation of the desolate garden speckled with dead autumnal leaves amongst the monstrously overgrown laurel bushes set in clumps and partially obscured by the fog. Several large deformed looking trees dominated the garden; some with haunched glistening branches arching down as though bearing the oppressive weight of the fog and dampness. Both of which were pervasive and lingered within the precincts of the high wall that surrounded the house.

By degrees aspects of the mansion came into vision revealing even more detail of this gloomy looking building. Many of the walls of the house were covered in dark green ivy that was creeping its way around, as if in the process of actually consuming the building's bricks and stonework. Some of the ivy had fallen away leaving gaps in its conquest and lay upon the ground forlorn and rotting.

Occasionally within the matted mass of this creepy ivy a solitary window could be seen. Though by now already in the process of being swallowed up and covered completely by the relentless and prevalent ivy plant, the tentacles of which ever searching for new surfaces upon which to colonise its grasp.

As we approached the front door, framed in a stone porch comprised of wide columns supporting its heavy stone canopy and castellated parapet, we could discern to our right a large curved stone wall with window openings cut into its surface forming window reveals. The mansion was built of stone with areas of brickwork to its façade. The overall effect was one not of beauty but of a pervasive and heavy ugliness as though the builder had wanted deliberately to repel visitors to his creation.

Many of the windows of the house were either boarded up, or they fronted what appeared to be heavy drapes within, permanently drawn, to exclude the outside world from intruding into this structure. The windows visible to us were smeared with years of grime and neglect giving them a gaunt minatory look, as though openings not on to light, but on to a dead soul. The general impression of the mansion was one of neglect or decay, as though the building were crumbling apart in slow motion. Together with an overbearing sensation of dampness and desolation which are often captured and conveyed very poignantly in the oil paintings of abandoned mansions by the artist Atkinson Grimshaw.

Having gained the interior of the house, our eyes became accustomed to a gloomy hall in to which we had been shown. Here we were abandoned and left to wait. Presently, no doubt we would presumably be shown to where Bella, her husband and Lodge were chatting amiably with each other over drinks. The hallway was large and illuminated only with the blue flame from coal tar gas jets in the form of wall-mounted brass appliqués, shaped as angels holding forth their firebrand, in this instance of town gas flame. Everything in the hall was covered in a thick layer of dust that had accumulated over the years which made breathing difficult in this still and suffocating atmosphere.

I was on the verge of choking, but stopped only by the shock of the vision that confronted us, for it was one of utter astonishment. Piled high almost to the ceiling of the hall and on every step of a grand staircase in front of us, were stacks of newspapers going back several years, so the date informed us. I had never, quite before, witness such extreme degrees of monomania for collecting old newspapers.

The collection of old newspapers were not those, one might come to expect in a person such as Bella or indeed her husband, to be those of *The Times, Daily Telegraph* or even the *Daily Chronicle*. But instead the hoard comprised newspapers from American cities, including the *Chicago Tribune, New York Times* and even the Michigan based *Ann Arbor Journal*.

"Why would Bella or her husband wish to read avidly

on a regular basis, newspapers, the origins of which were American?" I asked, but received no answer from Jack, so I continued to gaze around the hall.

In so doing I noticed that at the far end a huge tarpaulin had been draped over part of a wall from where the plaster had been hacked away revealing bare brickwork. Upon looking carefully at the brickwork, it seemed to be fairly recent, as though a large hole in the wall had been bricked up, quite why this was so, I could not think.

I was about to ask Jack, but he was pointing down with his finger at the floorboards of the hallway. Looking down on to the bear timber boards, I did indeed notice that some of the floor battens had been pulled up recently, but nailed back into place in a rushed haphazard manner. On some of the boards the nails had not been hammered home and were protruding.

So absorbed were we in examining prominent features of the hallway that we failed to notice immediately a singular event that was becoming louder. It was the distinct tinkling of musical notes, made by a piano, which drifted down the stairs from the upper floors of the rambling mansion. I stood there, momentarily transfixed, listening to the music and realised that no accomplished pianist was actually playing a piano. Instead, I reasoned the music was either being created by one of the new fangled contraptions; either a player piano or an Aëolian pianola.

In any event, we both recognised that the music being played was Franz Liszt's piano transcription of Bellini's opera 'Réminiscences de Norma' which Jack and I have played on many occasions. This ethereal combination of sensual musical arpeggio technique and the strange atmosphere in which we found ourselves was too incongruous for me to take in and I felt myself becoming slightly apprehensive.

"Where is Bella or Lodge?" I demanded of Jack.

"Probably drinking all the liquor," Jack replied.

The music had in fact heralded the return of the person who had let us in to the premises, and who had now descended the creaking staircase and glided past us and flung open the large green baize covered double doors. He pointed with his hand inviting both of us to wait in the drawing room.

"Bella and Michael will be joining you directly," he said, and left the room closing the doors silently behind us. The air inside became still again but was marginally more breathable than the air in the hallway. Here at least I thought an attempt had been made to make the room habitable, though by no means to the level one might describe as being voluptuary. The windows were covered with long heavy faded purple velvet drapes the kind which block out all daylight. The room was sparsely furnished. The items of furniture present were of a heavy varnished type the origins of which resembled more Queen Anne in style than Victorian. The walls may have been painted white at one time but now gave off a greyish hue probably due to the gloominess of the room.

In one corner of the room occupying an inordinate amount of space stood a grand piano encased in highly polished walnut and partly covered in a faded red velvet material folded back to reveal the keyboard. On the ornate brass music stand, I was surprised to notice, rested the sheet music of the pianoforte transcription of the score of Rickard Strauss's symphonic tone-poem 'Panathenäenzug.'

The Abbé Liszt was also represented in the form of a fired-clay glazed bust that rested on top of the grand piano. There were a few paintings on the walls, but they represented concentrated naïveté than considered art-work, of the style Bella would almost certainly have preferred.

On one wall and built of timber were shelves that had at one time contained an enormous and extensive library. Though most of the shelves now only contained layers of dust in place of books. Those that I glanced were on topics ranging from Homeopathic Medicine or pharma-ceutical sciences. Other books were devoted to the Theater, or Music Hall songs and dance routines. Certain books showed me that the original creator of the library was from the University of Michigan Medical School.

Curiously, what did catch my attention, as Jack busied himself playing the piano, was a boiler hidden in the darker recesses of one of the corners in the room. The boiler looked as if it was being fitted to receive the lengths of lead pipes which were placed around it on the floor. I picked up one of the pipes and examined it. Possibly central heat is being laid on, or so I thought. The whole room, though uninviting, cold and musty, had an eclectic incongruous collection of items adding to a feeling of strangeness to it.

Presently we heard a muffled sound outside in the hallway. In an instant the double doors to the drawing room, in which we were waiting, burst open and in stepped Bella together with the gentlemen who had let us in to the house, presumably the butler. Lodge walked into the drawing room after them.

It was Bella, now wearing a different dress, who made the introductions. Lodge remained unusually quiet. In fact, there was a noticeable change in the normally loquacious and suave Loge, now very much an agitated person. Needless to say his monomania, that of looking over his shoulders, had returned with a vengeance.

"This is Jack Mitchell and Theodore Houston, Vaudeville artistes out of New York," said Bella.

We shook hands with the butler.

"This is my husband," continued Bella, "Doctor Hawley Crippen."

Chapter 13

The Sound in the Night

We had been invited to dinner and to stay over as guests of Bella and her husband, a certain Dr. Crippen. Their house, a large rambling Gothic structure, was situated next to the vast lonely tracts of Hampstead Heath. For some reason, I naturally assumed our talk over dinner would be centered on Bella's performance of her rôle in the Choral Anthem Symphony, such as it was. However, nothing could have been further from this.

We had adjourned to the Dining Room in which to take dinner, which was a peculiar, if not a singular occasion. In addition, it was served to us not by servants, but rather by Crippen or Bella who in turn, would repair to the kitchen to bring in the next dish. The dishes places before us, from which we helped ourselves, were not in any way appetizing. They did more to remind me of Lodge's preferred food, he refers to as *specialité*, but in my opinion is a type of food which has simply rotted. The wine we drank was indifferent and well on the way to being corked.

"We are not big drinkers," Bella would repeat during dinner.

"Possibly, only when you are at home," I would hear Jack say in response.

"So you are from the United States," Jack inquired of Crippen, "whereabouts?"

"I was born in Coldwater, Michigan and attended the University there in county seat of Ann Habor, reading medicine," he replied.

University of Michigan Medical School is where our good Dr. Holmes, of murderous inclination and hotelier in Chicago, also read medicine. I felt sorely tempted to ask Crippen did he know of a certain Dr. Howard Holmes, since I figured they must both have been contemporaries of each other, whilst reading medicine at the University.

I did not, but Jack did, and no, he had not known him at University.

Crippen further responded with a question of his own.

"I understand that you are both stage artistes and have recently been in Chicago entertaining the large crowds attending the Chicago World Fair. Did you find Chicago interesting?" he asked.

"We certainly did Doc. Especially being holed up in our Castle Hotel on W. 63rd. Street in the Englewood neighborhood of the city," said Jack.

I detected a corollary in this mischievous remark by Jack, deliberately said by him to taunt Crippen, inferring a connection with Holmes.

Crippen did not rise to the challenge, but was himself, not above the peculiar. His face was sallow with small watery red-rimmed eyes set behind a pair of gold-rimmed spectacle. He sported a heavy light brown moustache matching the color of his thinning hair. He voice was of an abnormally higher pitch. The jacket he wore with wide lapels was made of worsted, the collar of which was trimmed with dark blue velvet. Beneath that his white shirt had a high stiff collar finished off with a loose fitting cream colored silk tie. He did not come over as a doctor, more of a dilettante,

with a touch of the gregarious in his sartorial preferences.

"So you stayed in the Castle Hotel on W. 63rd. Street;
cannot say that I know of it," informed Crippen, playing
Jack's game.

But at that moment Bella looked at Crippen. Though
at the time, Crippen was not aware of Bella looking at
him with a questioning look upon her round normally
blank face. In addition, his voice had gone up percep-
tively, by at least an octave, when answering Jack's inquiry.

Dinner was desultory affair and at length when Crippen
suggested we withdraw to the drawing room for brandy
and Trichinopoly cigars, we all of us, including Bella, fell
in eagerly with his suggestion.

Crippen did not come over as the sort of person to be
even remotely associated with Music Hall or theater of
any description, including those in a hospital. He was a
quiet and morose and his being Bella's husband only
added incredulity to this situation. The house he inhab-
ited bore all the signs of loneliness and a rejection of the
world and certainly of society.

When we had made ourselves comfortable on clothe
covered sofas, Crippen in answer to my inquiry
announced that he specialized in diseases of the eyes and
ears and the preparation of homeopathic remedies to
treat them.

Lodge still remained strangely quiet, which was most
unusual for him. I did however, notice on two occasions
Crippen give sideway glances at Lodge.

"So you are up on your *Bella Donna* [1] then?" Jack asked
Crippen.

Crippen ignored Jack's question and instead asked no
one in particular, in his squeaky voice, about his wife's
continuing success on the stage. Bella, in between bouts

of giggling, answered the inquiry, but in a way that was at variance to what I thought I knew. Neither did Crippen have much of a clue as to what Bella did on a daily basis. In fact I got the distinct impression that neither Crippen nor Bella knew much about each other and seemed more estranged than that of being married.

The evening wore on interminably, but at last, by general consensus we all decided to retire for the night. I was pleased to do so, because I was beginning to feel vaguely nauseas. Almost certainly probably due to the food we had been served during dinner. Bella showed Lodge to his room and Crippen escorted Jack and me to our rooms. After Crippen had closed the door on Jack's bedroom, I followed him to my room. This involved climbing a bare timber staircase up to the third floor of the mansion.

"Here you are Theo, I do hope you will be comfortable. If you need anything just pull the bell-rope, there, next to your bed. Well good night," he offered, and then smiled beneath that large moustache of his.

After he had closed my bedroom door, having taken his departure, I stood there and looked about the bed chamber I had been allocated. The room had a distinct chill to it, not noticeable in other parts of the mansion.

The room was sparsely furnished and dominated by a large bed in a cast iron frame. A nearby bedside table had upon it a lit candle flickering and a large glass of water. Above the candle was a wall-mounted gas mantle in the form of a brass appliqué of an angel holding forth a firebrand.

A chest of drawers of stained pine and a couple of straight-backed Cathedral chairs completed the furniture in the room. There was no carpet upon the floor, revealing untreated coarse elm boards. The curtains, of thick deep red velvet were drawn together. I walked across the room to the curtains and drew them apart revealing a shallow bay window. Beneath the windows was a large ornately patterned cast iron radiator and it was stone cold, adding to the chill of the room.

Instantly I recognized why the room was chilly. One of the windows had been left open. I peered out and took the opportunity in order to get a breath of fresh air. In so doing I noticed that my room was on the third floor of the house next to a tower. Hampstead, being on a hill and away from the river, was still shrouded in fog, but less dense than in the center of London which lies in the valley of the river Thames.

Surveying the gardens from my opened window, revealed that most of it had indeed been dug up, and now comprised a series of elongated holes in the ground. The nearby tower had a forlorn and minatory look about it, as though it had been abandoned. Indeed the windows to it were boarded up, not from the outside, but from the inside.

Feeling a bit weary I elected to retire and sleep until the morning with the hope that my worsening stomach ache would have dissipated in the intervening time. Not wishing to be left in a room in total darkness, I left the curtains drawn apart allowing a diffused light from the fog-laden aëther to enter my bed chamber.

Eventually I fell into a fitful sleep, drifting in and out of awareness. However, my stomach ache rather than decreasing, seemed to be getting worse to the extent it prevented my finding refuge in sleep. After an hour or so of discomfort I decided to seek help, though in what form, I remained uncertain. Then I remembered the bell rope! I was just about able to see in the gloomy light of the bedroom and pulled at it eagerly. To my utter dismay the bell-rope simply fell from the ceiling onto my arm followed by a cascade of dust. It was unlikely that this bell-rope was attached to anything, least of all a bell elsewhere in the mansion.

In my disappointment I gravitated to the only source of light in the room emanating from the lead framed windows. On trying to open one of the windows, my legs leaned against the large cast iron radiator. The heat from it was searing and caused me to receive a scalding burn to my thighs. Why was the radiator so hot, especially in the middle of the night? To create such heat, must involve the furnace in the basement being operated at its maximum, by someone. However, I persevered and opened one of the windows silently, thinking that some air might improve my stomach discomfort. Such was my desperation to find relief.

For the second time that night, I looked out over the secluded garden bathed in that translucent light created by the light fog. On doing so a distant church bell tolled out the time as being the mid hour at night. Then I saw it. I became aware of something flitting through the garden. I assumed it was a cat or dog. But then I realised, as my eyes became used to the subdued light, that what was moving around in the garden was in fact a person, possibly a trespasser or burglar.

The person down in the secluded garden was shrouded in black garb and seemed to move across the garden, rather as a black shadow might move over a dark background. The figure moved around the garden for a few minutes. During the course of which it would occasionally drop into one of several elongated holes dug into the ground. Then, again a church bell tolled the quarter hour. This had the effect of making the person, who at the time was in one of the holes in the ground, look up, as though surprised.

As he did so, I instinctively withdrew my face from the open window to avoid been observed. But, in so doing I was able just to catch a glimpse of the person's face. I could see very little of it, because the lower part of the face was covered with a black material, a cape of sorts. However, I did notice that the person, who ever it was, wore a pair of gold-rimmed spectacles, the lenses of which appeared opaque due to reflecting the subdued light of the fog. Then, in an instant, the figure had disappeared in to a clump of laurel bushes shrouded by the fog and thus into oblivion.

I stood there for a few moments trying to make sense of what I had just experienced. Then I heard it, a very low sound at first, but increasing into a quite discernable rumbling, as though a heavy stone were being pulled over the surface of another stone. All of a sudden a more distinct sound reverberated through the fog-laden aëther shrouding the secluded garden. It was the sound of a heavy metallic door to a vault, or somewhere being closed. And in so doing creating that distinctive grating noise one associates with dense metal doors closing on their hinges followed by a dull slamming sound. All was silent as the fog swirled in vortexes around the secluded garden.

A cold shiver went through my body and was grateful for the searing heat coming from the radiator adjacent to which I was standing. The person in the garden could have been anyone, but it was the distinctive sounds coming out of the garden, which I had just heard, for some reason, unnerved me. I resolved there and then to search for some form of remedy for my stomach ache, even a massive intake of brandy in order to force myself into sleep.

Accordingly, I picked up my cracked yellow candle the

flame from which flickered out from the draft caused by the open window. This had the effect of plunging the room into a subdued light, but I continued to approach the bedroom door. Naturally I did not want to disturb others sleeping in the house and so turned the door handle quietly and pulled at the door.

The door would not yield nor open and in fact appeared locked. I pulled frantically at the door as a panic gripped my heart. The door to my bed chamber was securely locked, preventing my leaving the room! However, at that very instant an odor assailed my nostrils, inducing nausea and then, I seemed to fall senseless to the elm floorboards of the bed chamber.

1.   Poisons

Chapter 14

The Empty House

We had been invited, as guests of Bella and her husband, a Dr. Hawley Crippen, to dinner at their house, a large rambling gothic structure next to the vast lonely tracts of Hampstead Heath. I had slept badly during the night due to a stomach ache, that from memory, I knew could cause mild hallucinations to affect the sufferer. I may have had just such an episode during the night, because I recall seeing somebody moving about in the garden below my window. And he was doing so at the dead of night. I had then tried to open my bedroom door during the night only to find it locked from the outside, resulting in my being unable to leave the bed chamber. I had then collapsed to the elm floorboards.

What made me wake up was the sheer pain searing through my right arm. I found myself on the elm floorboards of my bedroom and had slept with the weight of my body resting on my right arm on top of the floor. I picked myself up from the floor. However, the feeling of nausea, which still attended me, was not that from my previous stomach ache; but rather one coming from my chest. Very much the kind of sickness one experiences sometime when travelling on timber burning locomotives on American rail roads. Especially, where the smoke from those wood burning engines is often blown into the train carriages; and in so doing, causes unintentional mild asphyxiation of rail road passengers.

I then remembered that the door of my bedroom had been lock trapping me inside the room. I immediately went to it and before even turning the brass fluted handle, pulled at it with determination. The door opened! Leaving it ajar, lest it relocked itself, I dressed quickly into my clothes. Having consulted my steel-case pocket watch, I was aghast to learn that the time was nine and twenty minutes past. Somewhat put out by this oversight by either Bella or Crippen for that matter, in not being awakened, I stormed out of the bedroom and into a dimly lit corridor.

Jack's bedroom, from memory was just down this corridor and down a flight of steps to the second floor. I retraced my footsteps from the previous night and recognised Jack's door. I knocked upon it and called out to him. It would be very unlikely for Jack to sleep late in the morning. We had both of us, from the early days at Vaudeville, had gotten in to the habit of always rising early in the morning.

"Jack, are you in there?" I inquired,

Probably downstairs having break-fast, but then, I figured, Jack would have certainly raised me from my slumbers. I tapped on his door again. This time I did so louder. I received no response so assumed he had risen and was down stairs. Just as I was about to turn and leave, I heard a slight groan. I stopped dead.

"Jack, is that you, are you alright?" I asked. I then heard a thud, as though some thing or body had hit the deck. I knew Jack well enough to go into action. I turned the door handle. It was stiff and the door locked. However, there was a key sticking out of the lock. I turned it, with difficulty and then pushed against the door. It was jammed in the door set but my determination over came that obstacle. As the door swung open I was hit with a sensation from an odor, from the stilled air in the room that I, at first, simply could not recognize, but nonetheless had the effect of taking my breath a way. By this time it had nearly taken Jack's, who had fallen to the floor. I rushed to the curtains and drew them apart in order to open the windows and ventilate the bed room. To my surprise, there were no windows, only a brick wall behind the curtains.

I noticed his room was pretty much the same as mine, except it had no windows and was sparsely furnished. A similar bed in a large cast iron frame also dominated the room. A nearby bedside table had upon it a large glass of water. Above the bed was the same styled wall-mounted gas mantle in the form of a brass appliqué of an angel holding forth a firebrand.

I hauled Jack up on to his feet and we both of us staggered out of the bedroom and headed down the corridor to fresher air and an explanation. We both of us found ourselves in the main hall way of the house. No sound could be heard and the place, though it was daylight outside, was still in partial darkness with most of the curtains on the ground floor, drawn together.

"Where the hell is everybody Theo," said Jack, coughing very deeply, "and in particular our hosts?"

"Beats me Jack, but presumably they are here somewhere," I replied, surveying our dim surroundings.

"Coffee, I need some coffee," informed Jack, "can you remember where the dining room was? Perhaps they are taking break-fast in there."

I did not much feel like taking break-fast here or for that matter, some place else. I was all for leaving the mansion house and heading off back to our hotel. Jack however, was quite insistent and stated that he was not moving until he had gotten his morning caffeine.

I looked around the hall. In so doing, remembered the huge tarpaulin draped over part of a wall from where the plaster had been hacked away revealing bare brickwork. I also recall that some of the brickwork was in fact quite recent as though a large hole in the wall had been bricked up. Quite why, I could not think then, and standing in front of the wall now, I was none the wiser.

Next to the brickwork was a highly polished mahogany panelled door with an ornate brass fluted handle. I turned it only to discover that the door was locked. The same experience attended my trying another door. I turned around to tell Jack of my discoveries but only to see him tripped over a protruding end of a floorboard which had not been fastened down properly. In so doing he careered into one of the stacks of American newspapers which immediately collapse engulfing him in an avalanche of printed matter and a cloud of choking dust. He was not amused by this misadventure and his facial features proclaimed as much.

"You all right Jack?" I asked, helping him to feet, yet again.

"Theo, I think that is the door leading to the dining room in which we had dinner last night, "said Jack, ignoring my polite inquiry. I knew this was more out of embarrassment for his tripping over, than rudeness.

Whilst he rubbed the dust from his clothes I went up to another gleaming mahogany panelled door and turned the handle. It was locked. I tried another similar door and turned the handle on it. To my repressed surprise it opened! I beckoned Jack over on continued to open the door fully. It was Jack's expression upon his face that made turn back and look at the door opening again.

I did so. And to my surprise, found myself staring at a brick wall!

"Theo, can you smell cooking?" asked Jack.

I instinctively took in a sharp intake of air through my nostrils but succeeded only in taking in dust caused by Jack fall in to the pile of newspapers. Eventually I did detect a faint aroma of meat being cooked, though rather it resembled meat being burned.

"It is coming from downstairs in the kitchens. After trying a few more doors we succeeded in locating the door beneath the main staircase which gave out onto a stone landing and from it steps led down into the basement. The smell increased as we descended the stone steps. Presently we found ourselves not in a busy kitchen with Bella, Lodge or Crippen being served break-fast, as we had hoped, but rather into a scullery with stained white marble shelves and very little else. We progressed into what we took to be the kitchen, but was devoid of any activity on the range or hearth.

"But where is the smell of cooking meat coming from?" asked Jack.

We both scoured the basement following our noses; driven more by curiosity than appetite.

"The smell would seem to becoming from behind that door," said Jack.

We both made towards the door. It was Jack who opened it and on doing so a heat sensation hit our faces together with a strong smell of cooking meat, which drifted up another set of stone steps.

"Voile," said Jack, "here comes break-fast and hot coffee."

We both descended the stone steps leading down further into the basement. As we did, the spring-loaded door closed behind us. We paid it no attention, as our hunger and thirst for coffee drove us on. When we had reached the foot of the steep staircase, Jack and I turned a corner only to be met by the site of a cast iron furnace the heat from which was ferocious and stopped us in our tracks. Instantly Jack and I raised our hands to shield our faces from the effects of the intense heat radiating out from the furnace.

"What the hell is that? That surely cannot be where break-fast is being cooked," demanded Jack.

For me the sight of this cast iron furnace covered with a patina of rust on it surface and hissing hot gases and plumes of white smoke had all the significance of something disturbing. In a flash I thought about Holmes and his Castle Hotel in Chicago and the shadow fleeting across the secluded garden beneath my window at the dead of night. Together with my finding Jack, nearly unconscious, in his locked windowless sealed bedroom. And now, realizing that in fact we were alone in this empty house, all combined to fill me with a disturbing presentiment of something untoward.

"Come on Jack, let us just quit this place, and get the hell back to our hotel," I said, whilst turning away from the searing heat of the furnace and walking back towards the steps leading up to the ground floor.

Jack knew me well enough to detect the *timbre* in my voice, and showed this by his unquestioning compliance with my suggestion. Together we ascended the stone steps up to the upper basement floor and up to the door that had closed on us during our decent into the lower basement. Jack turned the handle nonchalantly. The door would not open!

We considered the door; it was dense and made of rough-hewn oak. More disturbingly, the door sur-mounted the last step at the top of a steep flight of stone steps. We therefore did not have the distance in front of the door to force it open with our shoulders. In effect we were looking up at the door.

Jack tried repeatedly to put his shoulder against the door without success.

"This door is jammed or spring-locked," I said, turning the door handle fully clockwise, "because this handle is not connected to the lock mechanism. We could push at this door for eternity and still not be able to open it."

"Come on Theo, there must be another door leading out of this cellar or at least window we could force, in order to bust out of this place, "said Jack, with a determination and annoyance which somehow compensated for the feeling of resignation that was creeping over me.

Together we both descended the stone steps again with trepidation into the lower basement containing the cast iron furnace with its internal conflagration. The furnace, hissing hot gases ferociously was positioned in the basement in such a way as to make walking past it difficult, not least because of the intense heat coming off it. But also, in attempting to get by it, there was every chance of being serious burned by the frequent intermittent plumes of hot smoke and gases erupting from the furnace periodically in any direction.

It was Jack who led the way by crouching down and barrelling his way past the furnace. Driven by fear of being abandoned, I followed on behind Jack. Never in my life have I been in abject fear of being seriously burned by flaring plumes of hot gases or smoke. But also, not least in the furnace simply exploding next to me, for such was the pressurised intensity of the conflagration within its rusting cast iron assembly.

All of sudden the furnace assumed a ghastly aspect of being a functioning crematorium oven.

At length we did get past this potential horror and continued our way into other areas of the basement, which were damp and where a distinct musty odor prevailed about the place. The light was subdued and made finding our way difficult. On two occasions I tripped up. One was over a discarded mattress lying on the floor. And the other was when I stepped on a greasy and dust encrusted dinner plate causing my shoe heel to slip on its ceramic surface.

Eventually, our exploration paid off and we did find a door, a small iron door braced with brass studs protruding from its dull surface. To our continuing dismay it was locked. That incidental fact did not in anyway deter Jack, and within a few moments, he was pulling frantically at it. I joined in with a brass poker, with a lion's head as a handle, which I had found laying on the floor of the cellar. I also realized that this door, which resembled a bank's vault door, was almost certainly the one I had heard being slammed during the night.

I handed over my poker to Jack. I then searched around for a heavier piece of metal with which we would almost certainly need if we were to succeed in prizing the metal vault door open. We worked at it for quite some time, but eventually we managed to tease the door off from its upper hinge. The first shaft of weak daylight came through the small gap.

Jack stood back to catch his breathe and I looked into the gap we had created. Instantly a shadow went fleeting by. It was the shadow of a person. I was about to call out, but my instincts suddenly overrode my decision and prevented me from doing so. In addition to which, I very much doubt if I could have even formed words in my dry mouth. Instead I just stood there and waited for Jack to get back into action and resume our assault upon the iron vault door. Who ever was roaming the secluded gardens outside did not concern me. What did occupy my thoughts was gaining access out of this cellar and quitting this mansion.

Eventually, and with some difficulty we managed to prize the door open, sufficiently to allow us to ease ourselves through the gap. Having emerged from the opening we found ourselves in the garden, a fog-bound garden. Immediately we looked around for the main gateway leading out into the roadway.

Though the garden was still in the grip of the dense fog, this in no way deterred us from our task in locating the main gate leading out into the road. We found it and made toward the overhanging ornate Gothic archway housing the main gate. In so doing, we slid down the grimy and wet pathway to the road door entrance in the garden wall.

Upon reaching the gate, Jack and I both pulled frantically at the cast iron door beam, securing the massive timber door, until finally it slid out from its tight bracket. And, whilst Jack released other locks and catches on the road door, I looked back at Hilldrop House. Remarkably, I thought, it appeared quite innocuous rising up in the pale light of the fog-bound aëther pervading the garden.

Irrespective of this, I promised myself that never again would I accept another invitation from Bella or Dr. Crippen to visit their house. Certainly, not this side of eternity.

Eventually, we stepped through the doorway in that overhanging Gothic arch and into a lane, the other side of which appeared to be the vast empty fog-bound tracts of Hampstead Heath. Jack had thoughtfully pulled the door shut behind us whereupon we heard various automatic dead-locks whirring and clicking back into a locked position and thus preventing other uninvited persons from entering the garden and gaining access to the mansion.

Having left the stifling atmosphere of Bella and Dr. Crippen's residence for the infinitely preferable, albeit choking, effect of the fog, we treaded quickly along the road adjacent to the great expanse that is Hampstead Heath. Suddenly, Jack darted forward and intercepted a passing Drag carriage drawn by a four-in-hand that loomed out of the swirling mist like a ghostly apparition.

"St. Pancras Hotel, and step on it," I said to the carriage driver, in my broadest New York accent that I could muster.

Chapter 15

The Double Act

Having effectively busted out of Bella and her husband, Dr. Crippen's large rambling Gothic mansion, located on the edge of Hampstead Heath, we had, at last, gained the sanctuary of the St. Pancras Hotel. Our visit to Hilldrop House was instructive for several reasons, and explanations to which I shall certain demand of Bella and the good Doctor Crippen, even if he is out of Coldwater, Michigan and attended University in the city of Ann Habor.

It was still morning but Jack and I headed for the Grand Dining Room, for what, I do not know. We had just sat down on a red damask banquette curved around a table when a waiter materialized in front of us almost as though a ghost.

"Good morning gentlemen," the waiter started in, "what may I get for you?"

He said these words whilst handing out to us, two red leather covered menus with gold tassels dangling down.

Jack refused the menu with a wave of his hand.

"Coffee, hot and now and some ham and eggs," instructed Jack.

The waiter looked into the menu that Jack had refused to take. A few moments went by before he finally made a comment in such a lugubrious voice, that I could not help but feel sorry for him and his ignorance of Jack's present mood.

"I cannot see those items on this menu sir. I should think that they do not exist and further you …," said the waiter.

"Hey, hey," interrupted Jack, "what do you mean they do not exist? What, are you telling me that you do not have coffee in London? And tell me further; what the hell is ham; some thing you only get in America?"

"This is the luncheon menu and ham is not on it. You may of course have sirloin or even roast lamb, or if you prefer, roast pork, but not alas ham," responded the waiter.

This was going to be interesting, I thought. Because Jack, being born and raised in Jersey City, in western Metropolitan New York, was now re-acting to our experiences at Hilldrop House. He could, when in a pedantic mood, as he clearly was now, quite easily irritate people and induce such a tension as to make them loose their self-control or lugubrious accent in the process.

I looked at Jack who looked at the waiter.

"Hey, what, do you want that I should tell you again, huh?"

"Well sir..," said the waiter, in a slightly higher pitch voice.

"Hey listen to me alright. I want some pig and hot coffee, right now," advised Jack.

"But if sir would only…," replied the waiter, clearly irritated and in a voice that was rapidly deteriorating into *tremolo*.

"You have twice called me *sir*. That should tell you something, of the relationship between us. I am the sir, you the waiter," said Jack.

"Perhaps if you would allow me to explain, the kitchens are now prepa…," said the waiter, in a voice that had not quite achieved the *falsetto* range but it was certainly moving in that direction.

This encounter went on for some time each testing the other's resolve. It ended in the waiter reverting to his real accent, which I believe is called Cockney, and, in his case, pronounced in a higher pitch. This waiter had it in barrel loads and must have rued the day he met Jack.

Eventually, of course, we both of us got our ham and eggs and caffeine enriched black Santiago coffee.

Break-fast was certainly an improvement on last night's dinner at Hilldrop House and accordingly felt the stronger, both mentally and physically for it. Jack's argument cheered me up and allowed me to put last night's experiences into some kind of perspective.

I started in.

"Jack, a few things happened during last night. As you know, I retired to my room, after dinner, but found sleeping did not come easily on account of my developing a stomach ache, during the night.

"Eventually I fell into a fitful sleep, but was awakened by my stomach which seemed to have gotten worse. After an hour I decided to seek help and remembered the bell rope. When I pulled at it the bell-rope simply fell from the ceiling followed by a cascade of dust. Jack, that fact alone, obviously told me that bell-rope was not attached to a bell some place else within the mansion.

"I walked over to the window, quite why I do not know, but on trying to open one of the windows, my legs leaned against the large cast iron radiator. The heat from it was searing and caused me to receive a scalding burn to my thighs. The radiator, was stone cold when I first entered my bed chamber. So why Jack, was the radiator so ferociously hot, especially in the middle of the night?

"However, I did open one of the windows silently,

thinking that some air might improve my stomach discomfort.

"As I was looking out over the secluded garden bathed in that translucent light created by the swirling fog, I heard a distant church bell tolled out the time as being the mid hour at night. Then Jack, I saw something moving around in the garden. It was a person dressed in black shroud to conceal himself. I watched this person flitting around the garden for quite some time, barely perceptible; almost as a black shadow might move over a darkened background. The person showed no interested in gaining access to the house, as a burglar might. No he was moving from one hole the ground, you know, the ones we saw on our arrival and departure whilst walking through the garden.

"Again the church bell tolled out the quarter hour. This sound had the effect of making the person, who at the time was in one of the holes in the ground, look up as though surprised.

As he did so I was able just to catch a glimpse of the person's face. I could see very little of it, because the lower part of the face was covered his black shroud. However, I did notice that the person, who ever he was, wore a pair of gold rimmed spectacles. Then, in an instant, the figure had disappeared into a clump of laurel bushes shrouded by the fog.

"Then I heard it, a very low sound at first, but increasing into a quite discernable rumbling, as though a heavy stone were being pulled over the surface of another stone. All of a sudden I heard a more distinct sound reverberated through the fog-laden aëther. It was the sound of a heavy metallic door to a vault, or somewhere being closed. And in so doing creating that distinctive grating noise one associates with dense metal doors closing on their hinges followed by a dull slamming sound. Jack that was the door we broke off its hinges to climb out of that cellar!

"Not only that Jack, when I decided to leave my bedroom and find some relief for my stomach ache, I found that my bedroom door was locked. I think that I may have just fainted because I woke up on the bare floorboards of my bed chamber, next to the door. When I dressed I tried the door and discovered that it was unlocked and that I was able to open it.

"I then went in search of you and only managed to unlock you bedroom door too with the key sticking out of the corridor side lock. Jack you too were locked in your bed chamber! And, further more Jack, when I eventually gained access to your room, a room I noticed, had no windows behind the drawn curtains," I informed.

"What do you mean, my room had no windows?" demanded Jack, and thought for a moment. "Of course it never occurred to me to open the curtains. I just went straight to bed."

"That is not all Jack. When I opened your bedroom door, I went over to where I thought the windows would be, behind the curtain. The reason I went to attempt to open the windows, was because your room was full of gas. That gas mantle in the form of wall-mounted brass appliqué in the shaped of an angel holding forth a firebrand of gas flame, was leaking gas, and it was drifting down onto your head. You were being asphyxiated!"

I was only grateful that Jack had completed his argument with the waiter before I imparted this devastating news, or it would certainly have been a case of literally, God help that surly waiter.

Jack was visibly disturbed on learning that he nearly died, in a bed, in London, and in England.

At that very moment Loge, to our surprise, walked jauntily into the Grand Dining Room looking very dapper in his black silk top hat and monocle and with Bella hanging on to his arm.

"The Concièrge advised us that he thought you would be in here and taking break-fast," said Lodge, looking at his gold Hunter.

Lodge was his effervescent and ebullient self and acted as if nothing had concerned him whilst we were at Hilldrop House last night.

"I just popped by to advise you that we are on stage at quarter to eight o' clock this evening at the Alhambra Music Hall in Leicester Square. We are on after the *Cremorne Belles;* so we do not have a hard act to follow. Gentlemen, until this evening!" said Lodge.

"Do tell me Lodge," asked Jack, "before you go, or whatever, where the hell were you this morning and for matter you too Bella? Both Theo and I awoke to a deserted house. Is that how you normally treat your guests in England? And, we left without breaking our fast or coffee."

Lodge and Bella exchanged puzzled glances. It was Lodge who answered, as they took their seats at our table.

"I do not know about you two, but I slept like a groundhog, very comfortably. In the morning I awoke and went down to the Break-fast Room at the back of the mansion, the side that faces the sun. Very good break-fast too, comprised as it was of Harrods' bacon, eggs, whelks and lashings of hot black coffee.

"Both Bella and the good Doctor Crippen were a little concerned at your not being present at the break-fast table. And so we elected to send the good Doctor to inquire after you and ascertain if you wanted to join us for break-fast. On his return he said he was unable to enter your bedrooms on account of the doors to each of your bed chambers were locked. He put this down to your wanting not to be disturbed. And, presumably that you would make your way down for break-fast in due course, as you saw fit.

"On completion of break-fast I had to dash off for an important meeting in Soho. Bella, had of course, to be at the theater for rehearsals and the good Doctor Crippen had his clinic to attend to," completed Lodge.

"At the moment I cannot bare hanging around Hill-drop House, if I can help it" announced Bella, "what with the builders hacking around the place, re-plastering the walls and replacing old floor boards, the place is like, well a building site.

"All this building work is a major inconvenience just to have central heat installed. And, they still have not connected the coal-gas supply to our old furnace boiler in the basement. They keep testing the boiler in the basement at odd hours to see if the pipes are working. Radiators cold one moment suddenly pump out ferocious heat the next minute that can burn delicate skin like mine.

"Every where the floorboards have been taken up and not nailed down properly to the joists. You simply will not believe the amount of times that I have tripped up on nails or floorboards jutting up. Had a bad fall only last week and landed on my arm," said Bella, whilst showing a light blue patch on her forearm.

Jack looked at me.

"Holes in walls," continued Bella Elmore, "and dust, dust everywhere and it is unbearable and gets in my hair, which I spend more time washing than I had ever done so in my entire life."

She then predictably lapsed into her episodes of high pitched giggles.

"I saw someone from my third floor bedroom window moving furtively around in the garden last night flitting from one hole to another. The person was dressed in black shroud and spent some considerable time in the grounds, but at no time did he attempt to enter the house," I said firmly, in an attempt to bring the seriousness of my concerns back into consideration.

"Oh you do not want to worry about him," said Bella, "ever since we moved into Hilldrop House, every year about now a few roaming gypsies off the nearby Hampstead Heath come into the grounds at night, to pick up the fruit which has fallen from the several apple trees we have ranged around the garden."

"I heard a vault door slam in the middle of the night and…" I said.

"Oh that, sorry; I have been asking my husband to fixed that back gate, as the neighbors often complain about the wind catching it and slamming it closed," said Bella smiling at me.

"Bella, your house, Hilldrop House was shrouded in fog last night; there was no wind," I replied.

"Oh, was there?" said Bella, "I confess, to be honest I did not notice; I rarely look out of the windows."

"Though, I must confess too Loge, you seemed a rather quiet over dinner last night," said Jack, coming to my assistance. "In fact we were quite concerned. Shall we say, you were not quite your usual ebullient and loquacious over-confident self? I doubt you said more than a couple of dozen words during the course of the entire evening. Your silence, in this respect Lodge, was deafening. And, both Theo and I noticed it."

"Oh I felt a little run down and not really in a talkative mood, especially with Crippen lurking about!" said Lodge as he smiled furtively at Bella. Who, in response, immediately erupted into an uncontrolled bout of giggling that lasted for several moments.

And with that Parthian shot, Lodge sailed out of the Grand Dining Room with Bella on his arm, leaving Jack and I somewhat perplexed.

It could be that both Bella and Loge together, were the best double act the stage has ever witnessed, or I am loosing my grip on reality. I was not in any way convinced by their replies. Jack, though, I think, was.

Chapter 16

The Premonition

Our experiences at Hilldrop House left me feeling uncomfortable, as though the prelude to a presentiment of a kind. Bella's replies may be correct and plausible but were too glib. Still we were here at the St, Pancras Hotel enjoying the remnants of our ham and eggs which Jack had forced an over confident flunkey to bring to us. Hilldrop House still occupied my thoughts and it was possible Jack could read them too.

"Theo, looking through *The Globe* newspaper I see there is a concert featuring the music of Gustav Mahler on this lunchtime at a place called St. James' Hall in the Portland Road. We could ride the urban rail road on the Metropolitan-Circle to Portland Road Metropolitan Station and walk to the hall. I cannot be too far from the station," suggested Jack.

I think Jack was trying to cheer me up. Evidently he could read the concern in my eyes. Aside of which, we both enjoy classical music concerts as an antidote to the constant banter extant in Music Halls.

"Sure Jack, that sounds good, what works are being performed?" I inquired, whilst falling in eagerly with his suggestion.

Accordingly, when Jack had finished his argument with our surly waiter over the bill that had been presented to us, we left the comfortable and opulent appointment of our hotel. We were then immediately engulfed in swirls of the pervasive and acrid yellow fog which still showed no signs of dissipating. Eventually we managed to locate the entrance to King's Cross Metropolitan Station from which the Metropolitan-Circle departs. After the usual performance attending the purchase of tickets in order to ride the rail road, we at length boarded a train headed for Portland Road Metropolitan Station.

Our journey to the Portland Road Metropolitan Station was uneventful, apart from a demonstration of the now obligatory rudeness experienced when purchasing a ticket from the ticket clerk ensconced behind his acid etched toughened glass window. We stepped out of the station precincts and turned left into the Portland Road and made our way down it in the direction of the concert hall. Quite some forty minutes later, having groped our way down the thoroughfare, we arrived and stepped into the foyer of the St. James's Concert Hall. We did so with only just enough time to queue up to buy our tickets for the concert.

Having purchased our tickets for the Dress Circle, we walked up the stairs and into the auditorium to take our seats. Looking around the auditorium, we could not quite believe the pandäemonium extant in our Dress Circle. In trying to get to our seats we had to negotiate our way past some unsavoury individuals. Some of whom, were intent on acting in a confident manner and, displaying very *determined behavior* in our presence. The likes of which, I have never experienced before in a concert hall, at least not in New York.

All of a sudden there was a lot of shouting, notably in Italian accents, coming from the cheap seats. Then, thunderous applause commenced during which, onto the podium, stepped a diminutive man. He was wearing, with inordinate confidence, a white tail-coat and matching trousers together with a beaming wide smile on his face. But, more disconcertingly, he was wearing white shoes! Where had I witnessed this sartorial arrangements before, I pondered.

We then heard people remark that he was the great Russolo, whoever he might be? Suddenly, with a sweep of his arm, he launched the orchestra into quite what, I do not know.

The so-called music was based, not on harmony, but rather, on a cacophony of sounds, including those made by, *Thunder-clappers, 'Screamers* or *Cracklers* and other assorted mechanical noise-making contraptions and devices, each capable of creating a distinct noise. Suddenly a man wearing a beard came up to where I was sitting, and demanded that I vacate his seat, the very seat that I was occupying.

Instinctively I retrieved my ticket and looked at the number and then got up and turned around the check the number on the seat. It was No. 35. Both the number on my ticket and on the seat tallied.

"I am very sorry sir," I started in, "but I suspect that you have made a mistake. Here see for yourself," I said resuming my seat.

However, before I could do so the man started waving his arms about in the air and launched into tirade about my having taken his seat!

Somewhat taken aback by his ready use of strong language, of the type I am certainly not accustomed to hearing in a public hall, I got up out of my seat. It was only by Jack's intervention, that this encounter was brought to an abrupt halt. But, I had notice during this outburst, that other patrons were too being subject to the same type of treatment, and that my experience was not an isolated one. I looked at Jack in total bewilderment.

In the meantime the smiling conductor was engaged, not so much in conducting the orchestra, but rather in conducting various arguments with several members of the audience. Also, I noticed, that the orchestra had ceased taking directions from the conductor, and were instead, playing more or less what they fancied, whilst chatting to each amiably other over the cacophony.

"The concert, we were expecting to enjoy, was billed as comprising Mahler's series of songs in a recital of *Rückertlieder,* [1] the *Kindertotenlieder* [2] and *Lieder eines fahrenden Gesellen,* [3] all of which he composed when staying at his famous summer retreat, the villa at Maiernigg next to the sparkling waters of the Wörthersee in Austria.

The disruption which had erupted in the St. James's Concert Hall was somewhat annoying, because I know Jack is very fond of the music of Gustav Mahler, especially his lieder and particularly the *Kindertotenlieder.* We were expecting to hear these songs sung by the fabulous and acclaimed mezzo-soprano Lilli Lehmann, as billed, hence our being here.

I have said it before to others, Jack was trained to play classical music at the Julliard School of Music in New York City and in fact is very much an accomplished and versatile pianist. The concert, for which we had purchased tickets, was supposed to comprised a recital of lieder, and Mahler's last setting of the *Rückert lieder* - '*Ich bin der Welt abhanden gekommen,*' [4] and sung with a sensitive appreciation of the lyrics, together with an innate feeling and great control of the expression of emotional turmoil that the song invariably generates in the heart of the listener.

Villa at Maiernigg am Wörthersee

"The Mahler lieder were to be followed by Haydn's Symphony No 35 in B flat minor. And then finally, a performance of the triumphant Symphony No.1 in E Major, by Viennese composer Hans Rott," I remarked to Jack, who immediately burst out laughing.

Somewhat surprised by Jack's behaviour, I looked at him, in earnest.

"Theo, we are victims of what is known as, the Italian Futurist Movement, an extreme organization, that wishes to re-define music in terms of 'noise-sounds' and from all accounts is led by a derange composer called Marinetti. Chaos in sound, as in cacophony, is allowed; indeed it is to be encouraged. Chaos is also applauded in over double booking concert hall seats to, 'engender chaos' in the aisle, as people argue over who has the right to occupy a particular seat!

"When I was in London before I was aware of the activities of this Movement and their re-action to what they perceived as inferior performances by artistes. It would, for example, not be beneath them to throw large vegetables or hurl fruit at a performer on stage, of whom they vehemently disapproved, for any number of reasons, and not necessarily connected with the quality of music being played, but indeed, personal dislike would be sufficient cause!" informed Jack.

I felt ridiculous enduring this impromptu disruptive coup de théâtre, and suggested we abandoned the place, as our presence here was becoming untenable. It was also obvious no philharmonic concert was going to be performed in this hall today. Whilst attempting to leave the auditorium, we got involved with another disruptive individual acting in a determined manner in front of us.

Having made our way past him and other individuals, I considered asking for a refund at the ticket office, such was my annoyance. But, the risk of inviting a full scale riot, similar to the one that was now in full progress in the Dress Circle, was all too likely. I could scarcely believe the situation we found ourselves in.

The concert was supposed to be one of series, to be conducted by a fellow called Toscanini, and organized by something called the Philharmonic Society of London. The Society's aims, so the concert program informed me are, '*to promote the performance, in the most perfect manner possible of the best and most approved instrumental music.*'

Quite what we had just endured in that St. James's Concert Hall would seem to have defeated that laudable, if noble, intention.

We left the St. James's Concert Hall earlier than anticipated and therefore found ourselves standing in the Portland Road rather at a loss as to what to do next. I felt somewhat redundant and about as much use as the absurd information contained in an adjacent advertisement affixed to a wall.

I was trying to determine, sub-consciously, if there was, any significance in the Westminster Macintosh & India-rubber Company's choice of business address, opposite the Houses of Parliament. Or perhaps, that other Music Hall, the Palace of Westminster I thought, but certainly not to lend verisimilitude to their rubberized contraptions.

"If you wish Theo, we could go to the Artist Room, if it is still there at Pagani's restaurant, the one we walked past earlier on our way to this St. James' Concert Hall," suggested Jack, distracting me from the features of the advertisement, "it is up the road a number forty two."

With this abrupt return to reality, I concurred.

"What is the Artist Room?" I inquired, as we made our way up a fog-bound Portland Road.

"The Artist Room, so named, because of the numerous

artists and persons from the stage, who use it to dine in on a regular basis. The management of Pagani's reserve this famous room for the use only by artists and actors such as Sarah Bernhardt, Aubrey Whistler or other acclaimed artists or musicians, such as Henry Wood."

"I often wonder, whether the composer, Carl Maria von Weber, who lived here at number ninety-one Portland Road, ever used the Artist Room?" said Jack, pointing with his gold capped cane to a blue commemorative plaque cemented into the red brick façade of a building we were walking by.

"Those disruptive people back there in the concert hall; who were they Jack? Because I know one thing, they were not hecklers; so just who were they? Are they by way of being revolutionaries or worse, Nihilists, or what?" I asked.

"Indubitably so!" replied Jack, "that they are Revolutionaries is not in doubt here. But Theo you are correct; they not hecklers of the type you and I are becoming all too familiar with. Those persons, who we encountered earlier at the St. James' Concert Hall, are what they term Futurists and it is their sworn aim to re-define music into what they believe it ought to be."

"Just what does that mean?" I inquired, somewhat stunned at the remark.

"It means Theo, that music, in their definition should comprised responses to other influences and sounds and not be an artificial series of scales and notes creating harmonic development. The Futurists claim there is more real meaning in the noise made say, by a steam engine or automobile horn, than the sound created by a violoncello or flute!"

"Are you being funny here Jack? I do not go to a concert hall to listen to classical music, as billed, only to be interrupted by a bunch of noise-seeking clowns and then, find myself out in the highway with a ticket but no concert," I responded, with aspersion in my voice.

"The whole idea Theo, is to engender chaos into music, by such contraptions or devices as *Cracklers, Thunderclappers* or indeed *'Screamers* such as the ones we heard earlier," informed Jack.

"What is happening to Music Halls," I responded, "or for that matter, concert halls these days Jack, for they seemed to be filled with hecklers, revolutionaries or Nihilists? One wonders will there be any room for the ordinary members of the audience who attend concert or Music Halls?"

The situation did lend itself to humor and the absurdity

surrounding the fiasco we had just witnessed and we accordingly, responded to it by the both of us simultaneously bursting out laughing. Much, we noticed, to the consternation of passing pedestrians, not used to such manic laughter in the fog. I cannot even begin to conceive of such confident behavior in New York, especially in such a place as the Carnegie Hall during a philharmonic concert, or indeed in the Fourteenth Street Theater.

"Jack," I said, "so long as this kind of behavior does not represent a premonition of things to come. The auditorium is not the place to register dissatisfaction. I know people will heckle and be disruptive in order to get their complaint over to an audience assembled for quite another reason – to see *turns* or *acts* as billed and …"

"Theo," interrupted Jack, "I have just had an idea. I will tell you about it when we reach Pagani's restaurant, but thank God for the Futurists!"

We continued in silence whilst negotiating our way up the Portland Road still enshrouded in the fog. At length we came to the famous restaurant and on being welcomed by a waiter wearing a white apron, we requested seats in the Artist Room. Without demur he escorted us up to the first floor dining room. Having been shown to our seats we ordered whisky and some food of sorts. Jack was correct in his earlier description of the Artist Room. The place was busy and full of artists, artistes or painters all in deep conversation with each other as though conspiring to let loose on an unsuspecting public a new idea or concept.

"Right Theo," said Jack, "when the waiter had delivered our whiskies, "back to the serious business of Music Hall."

"Rather!" I enthused, whilst drinking deeply from my whisky, "you have my undivided attention Jack."

"Theo, think about it," invited Jack, whilst we both sat in the Artist Room, "we both of us have been running scared because of the actions of Nihilists, revolutionaries, Futurists or occasionally our audience! We are petrified of hecklers breaking into our routine and wrecking it. We saw earlier today in that St. James Concert Hall the Futurists at work. We experienced the hecklers at work to in the Criterion Theater here in London and in the Majestic Theater in Chicago.

"Theo, we should be relating with the audience. Not singing or talking to them. But rather engaging with them. If hecklers get up, then fine. Let us ad lib with them, even argue with them. Make it look as if this is deliberate and all part of our routine! In other words, harness their protest to aid us in being in control of the stage, not them.

"What are we now? We are involved with complex routines involving an incomprehensible juxtaposition with a choral symphony that makes us look like redundant intruders on the stage. One cannot, despite what Lodge thinks, have the audience wrapped up in sublime raptures emanating from the symphony. And then the next moment, have the audience falling around in the aisles with laughter, whilst Judd's decapitated head makes a tour of the stage floor, culminating in its drop into the orchestra pit. That Theo is Burlesque, and we are not that far down the rail road to oblivion quite yet. Even the newspapers remain effectively frozen by indecision in just how to describe our so called *innovative sensation*!

"This afternoon two very distinct ideas hit me like a freight train; the Futurists and Little Bo Peep!

Take the Futurists, they want to cause disturbances and disruption at every opportunity in order to bring to the public's attention their thoughts and ideas, especially about the evolution of music. Fine, but notice their method in so doing and getting the public's attention. They do not agitate in the streets or at rail road stations; which contain a greater number of persons at any one given time than a concert hall or theater.

"No, they focus on the concert hall or theater, deliberately, because it is within such places are to be found precisely those persons who they are trying to affect or even influence. That is to say, people who enjoy classical music, but should be influenced by other sounds emanating from typically, a steam engine. The Futurists could never invade a Music Hall, simply because the audience in such a place would not even know what Futurism is about let alone be influenced by their beliefs," completed Jack.

"Alright Jack, I hear you on the Futurists; but how come Little Bo Peep gets in on the act?" I inquired.

"Simply, just by her walking on to the stage and doing very little; hence her name, *Little* Bo Peep! Think about Theo, all she did within moments of arriving on stage was to fall down. Thereafter she had the audience in the palm of her hand. We could learn from her and the Futurists by refining our *act* to hit the audience straight on. Forget the song and dance routine; that is now passé. Audiences demand the unexpected. And our acclaimed Little Bo Peep, gives them exactly that. We both of us have seen it.

"Even Loge, said to us when we first met him in Chicago. That he occasionally left London for the provinces in search of new talent, fresh talent, as it were, and interesting *acts* or *turns* which will enthral his Music Hall audiences. And that one could not keep throwing sharpened knives at a woman bolted to a revolving Katherine Wheel forever.

"Eventually the audience will become bored with that *act*, or the fact of women being shot out of military cannons – for whatever laudable reason. No, Lodge said it was incumbent on him to search the venues and find new *acts* and skills which could be appreciated readily by his so-called discerning audiences. And even Marmeduke Gatti, manager of the Hungerford Music Hall echoed those sentiments expressed by Lodge. Audiences do want something new and exciting to be entertained by.

"No Theo let us go back to the evolution of the Music Hall, because it is by so doing that we will know where to develop our routine, and make it relevant for the future.

"As far as I have been able to figure it out from listening to Loge and others including Bella, it would seem that this type of profane entertainment commenced with the Puritans empting the churches of bellow organs. The reason for this draconian act was because were considered superfluous and an irrelevant function in already over decorated churches. The organs finished up with inn keepers who on certain evenings would invite their drinking customers to do an *act*, a *Free & Easy* to the accompaniment of the organ, when it was their *turn*.

"These inns evolved into the *Pleasure Gardens,* such as those of Cremorne, Vauxhall, Ranelagh or indeed Marylebone. Without doubt, those gardens were places of licentious behavior and debauchery both of which were practised on a large scale. Not surprisingly, given the fact that the entertainment, in the main, consisted of cock fighting, overt gambling, bull-baiting and boxing matches involving both male and female contestants!

"The Gardens were inexpensive and usually very crowded such were their popularity with all classes of society. Ranging from royalty, in the person of the Prince of Wales, down to prostitutes roaming for clients and the ubiquitous seasoned pickpockets, on a constant lookout for persons to rob whist distracted by the entertainment on offer.

"It comes as no surprise therefore, to realize that the origin and vestiges of such *Unbecoming Behavior* emanate from those *Pleasure Gardens*.

"From such *Pleasure Gardens* two distinct strands, I think Theo, developed.

"The first involved the origin of Music Halls, as we know them now. They really started out from the *Pleasure Gardens* which retained *Public Houses*, and from such humble establishments some *Song and Supper Rooms*, originated during the 1830s. They did so by either extending the existing *Public Houses* or constructing new and larger ones.

"Typical was the Canterbury Tavern into the Canterbury Music Hall, the New Bedford Music Hall was originally the Bedford Arms *Public House*, the London Pavilion began its existence as the Black Horse *Public House*. Even the fabled Criterion Theater was built on the site of the White Bear Inn, and the Oxford Music Hall was originally built out of the Boar and Castle *Public House* in Oxford Street. Even the famed so called first Music Hall Wilton's, in Whitechapel, started out as the Prince of Denmark *Public House*.

"In order to attract a less numerous, but wealthier middle class clientele, other *Public Houses* were converted into respectable *Song and Supper Rooms* such as Evans Late Joy's in the Covent Garden serving hot food as supper clubs, whilst providing entertainment. Such establishments began to appear from about 1835 onwards and stayed open until the early hours of the morning. Of course these modest *Song and Supper Rooms* soon developed into the lavish red plush establishments of the interior decorative and ornate appointments of Music Halls today.

"In those *Song and Supper Rooms* proceedings were '*chaired*' by vocalist, such as the legendary John Caulfield.

Wilton's Music Hall

Later that rôle developed into that of Compière. *Acts* or *turns* were performed on an elevated platform – a stage, located at one end of the hall. Those places evolved into the Music Hall we recognise today.

"One of the more famous of the *Song and Supper Rooms* which began in 1844 was W.H. Evans's *Music-and-Supper Rooms*, located in the Covent Garden. Evans acquired the establishment from the owner called Joy and it his name that the place was often referred to as 'Evans Late Joys'. Two other notable *Song and Supper Rooms* were the Mogul Saloon in Drury Lane and close by the Cyder Cellars in Maiden Lane, and both in the Covent Garden.

"In addition, these extravagant and flamboyant luscious designs, were continued in the decorative features to be found in the plethora of *Quality Wets*. Some of which developed into Supper Rooms to attract growing middle class, they in turn evolved into '*Harmonic Meeting*' places for seven hundred or so, person seated at tables ranged around a hall as in the Canterbury Music Hall in the Westminster Bridge Road at Waterloo.

"As with the *Pleasure Gardens* and later Music Hall, both

were the subject of royal visitation on numerous occasion, including visits by the then Prince of Wales, who I think was King Edward VIIth. More surprisingly though, the commander in chief of the British Army, his grace, the Duke of Cambridge, is a frequent and honored guest to Music Hall as are their graces, the Duke of Teck and his Duchess," said Jack, pausing to drink deeply from his glass of whisky.

"You have given this a great deal of thought Jack," I said.

"I have and only by my listening to Loge and to surprisingly, Bella too. For they do know something about the evolution of the Music Hall Theo, which is as well, because you and I both have got to get a handle on this, if we are to survive at all, period.

"The second development out of the *Pleasure Gardens* was into something resembling, typically the Coal Hole. A *Public House* and combined small theater. Located, I think from memory, in the Strand, near the Thames at Charing Cross in London and still retains a scurrilous reputation, deliberately to attract a certain of audience, that of *Rough Trade*.

"One is not going to inveigle the affluent or wealthy middle classes into hanging around, to their disgust, with the coarse *Rough Trade* extant in such a utilitarian establishment as the Coal Hole, unless of course, one is an Oscar Wilde or some other sybarite. Even the very name, Coal Hole betrays its origins and is symptomatic of its approach to entertainment of the lower variety, especially for the undeserving poor.

"There was of course a difference between *Song and Supper Rooms* cum Music Halls and theaters at the time. In the former, persons were permitted, whilst watching an *act* or *turn* from a table in the auditorium, to smoke tobacco and drink alcohol. By contrast, in the theaters at the time, one would be seated in the stalls focusing on the stage. Any drinking allowed on the premises was restricted to the Crush Bars, situated well away from the auditorium.

"However, Theo, according to our impresario Loge, the eventual emergence of the Music Halls did not evolve over a period totally unchallenged. There being, to Loge's undisguised and eternal disgust, but three perennial enemies of the Music Hall and by implication, drink. He mentioned the Salvation Army and typically their enthusiastic closure of the Eagle *Public House*, in the City Road, wherever that is.

"Then Loge went on to describe the actions of the deranged moral crusader, a certain Mrs. Ormiston Chant, and her constant objections to her perceived immorality extant in Music Halls. It is her continued exhortation of the Metropolitan Board of Works, the successor to the lenient magistrates, to impose stricter licenses for the provision of alcohol and safety regulations, including those appertaining to fire, on all existing Music Halls, including banning alcoholic drink in all new Music Halls and theaters constructed after 1909!

"Accordingly, Theo, Music Hall evolved yet again into another guise as a result of the activities of the Metropolitan Board of Works and that Valkürian woman, Lily Langtry. There is now what they call the emerging *Variety Theater*, complete with brass division rails crimson plush almost on what one might call on a pervasive and monumental scale. This, of course, is to give the impression of the utmost respectability, and lend, as it were, verisimilitude to these new establishments.

"This type of *Variety Theater* was developed when they decided to rebuild the old London Pavilion in the Regent's Circus at Shaftesbury Avenue during 1885 to the deliberately extravagant and opulent designs of James

Ebenezer Saunders. In this case a concerted attempt was made to sever, once and for all, connections with its gaudy and tawdry *exotic* origins as the roofed over stable yard of the Black Horse Inn, another *Public House*.

"From their luxurious and elegant foyers all the way their lavishly appointed auditorium and promenades illuminated brilliantly by glass chandeliers fuelled by acetylene gas creating a myriad incandescent light radiating down on to deep red carpets and brass fixtures and fittings. In such places, no expense shall be spared in reaching the empyreal heights of opulence. Certainly banned now are the *Spécialité Acts* that pulled in the crowds. In these variety theaters, the proceedings are governed by the Compière.

"This kind *Variety Theater*, the origin of where tables at which drink was served were ranged around a Hall with stage, has changed forever into the smug respectable auditorium where drink is not permitted under any circumstances. The *Variety Theater* achieved its recognition and, I suppose, apotheosis recently when the first Royal Variety Performance commanded by King George V[th.] took place during 1912 season. And accordingly, the *Variety Theater* was acknowledged as a respectable form of entertainment.

"During another Command of Royal Variety Performance, this time at the London Pavilion, it was instructive to note that the unsurpassable Marie Lloyd, though at the height of her career on the stage, was considered to represent the old Music Hall style, based on the *Pleasure Garden*s type of entertainment. Especially, with her lasciviousness and avalanche of innuendos, to the extent that she herself was thought to be too *saucy* to perform in front of a reigning monarch," completed Jack.

"What are you saying Jack?" I asked.

"What I am saying Theo," replied Jack, "is the fact that we should evolve with the times too. We need to rejuvenate our act to take into account what audiences now want; something new, a departure from the old and worn out. We have our cue, and it is in the form of being re-active with our audience. Get them involved in responding to us on stage. That tortfeasor[5] we saw doing his party tricks on the stage at the New Bedford Music Hall in Camden Town, was actually insulting and rude to his audience; but they loved it. Even that Little Bo Peep had them enthralled just by falling down!"

"Jack, that woman, that Woman in Red; now she had the audience in an iron grip, from which nobody could escape," I responded.

"Trick now Theo, is how the hell do we tell Lodge of *our* new innovative approach?" asked Jack, as we left Pagani's restaurant to make our way to the Alhambra Music Hall for our début on the stage there, this very evening.

1. Rückert songs
2. Songs on the death of children
3. Songs of a Wayfarer
4. I have lost track of the world
5. A person who commits wrongful actions.

Chapter 17

The Alhambra Music Hall

Our sojourn to the St. James's Hall for a concert of classical music had been sabotaged by a concentration of Nihilists and a radical group known as the Futurists, who hold extreme views on what, defines music or *noise-sounds*. We had abandoned the hall in favor of Pagani's restaurant in the Portland Road, and in particular the famous Artist Room. During our time there, whilst drinking and dining, Jack had unfolded a starting proposal which could rejuvenate our stage *act* and indeed, imbue it with a new vitality.

Having walked by the St. James' Hall, we arrived at Oxford Street, over which we crossed into Argyll Street adjacent to the Oxford Circus Avenue en-route to our destination at the Alhambra Music Hall. We turned into Great Marlborough Street and were surprised, pleasantly surprised to see another limestone plaque with gilt lettering embedded in the façade of a building proclaiming that of the pianist and composer, Franz Liszt, lived here in 1841.

To Jack, Franz Liszt, was always the *Abbé* Liszt, preferring to refer to Liszt in his ecclesiastical designation. Jack was very fond of the pianoforte works by Liszt and often played them in times of ennui or unadulterated joy. He was an accomplished pianist irrespective of his

Vaudeville career, and could execute, with ease, the complex arpeggios and progressive scales, inherent in any of the pianoforte works by Liszt. Jack's playing of the transcriptions and paraphrases by Liszt, were, without exception, always an experience of pure sublimity and sonority of chords. Especially, his interpretation of the '*Harmonies, Poétique et Religieuses*' and in particular, the beautiful '*Invocation*' emanating out from it.

Indeed I have much to be grateful for when listening to Jack's playing the pianoforte. His ability to extemporize from the pianoforte works by Liszt's never ceases to amaze me. Especially, in how so effectively the music can arrest my attention and in so doing instill in my soul an appreciation of rapturous arpeggios progression. I remember on one glorious occasion, back stage at the Fourteenth Theater in New York, Jack held us all in awe at his skill at the key board.

During that memorable time the sublime music responsible for this ethereal sensation, was I remembered, the '*Tantum Ergo*' from the sacred '*Benedition*.' How such harmony could combine so effectively with an appreciation of one's feelings released through an unforgettable experience, was beyond my ability to imagine, I concluded then as my mind drifted away with the music! Even the stage hands, normally boisterous, were moved to remain still and silent, as though in profound acknowledgement of a rare occasion taking place in front of them.

Jack fully appreciated that the *Abbé* represented an innovative form of music in the middle nineteenth century, termed the *Progressive*. It was later to be given powerful expression in the works of its great exponent, Rickard Wagner, in developing the *leitmotiv*,[1] and who later became Liszt's son-in-law. Wagner was himself, no stranger to the area, Jack informed me, having lived in

1839 at 25 Old Compton Street, in the nearby *Bohemian* Quarter of Soho.

We resolved there and then to go visit the address.

"It is on our way to Leicester Square," announced Jack, "we can pay homage to the master of the leitmotif."

We continued along a street the name of which escaped me. However, we carried out our mission with zeal and determination, as one could in the blinding acrid fog. Eventually having traverse Wardour Street we turned into where Wagner lived. On this occasion, our enthusiasm was misplaced; for we had never seen such a street full of characters most of whom did not give the appearance of knowing who Rickard Wagner was, let alone be familiar with his music or innovative *leitmotivs*.

There was no recognizable sign, symbolic or otherwise, of the fact of Wagner having lived here. Accordingly, we continued on, along Old Compton Street and then turned down into Greek Street and over the Shaftesbury Avenue and onward toward the Leicester Square.

We eventually arrived outside the Alhambra Music Hall, and although of a Moorish style of architecture, the façade of the Music Hall seemed out of place, almost incongruous with the surrounding buildings which formed the Leicester Square. The front of the building however, was nonetheless, impressive, as indeed it was designed to be for its original purpose. The Music Hall rose up through six floors, which culminated in a large dome spanning the central auditorium creating a large internal uninterrupted space.

Some of the window reveals addressing the Leicester square façade were essentially Gothic in style; though here an attempt had been made to imbue them with a

The Alhambra Music Hall

Moorish interpretation with elongated pointed arched windows. Despite its exotic design style, the building was quite substantial and had a solid look about it.

Of course this is the very same Music Hall, in which, Lodge was comprehensively traduced by Marie Lloyd, whilst we were drinking at the Crush Bar, and for whom now he only retains a mild disgust. This sadly resulted in their loss of friendship and her being relegated from the exalted position of one of the *Three Graces*. Not that she would care, I should think.

Originally the building was commissioned, I remember Lodge telling us, as the home of the Royal Panopticon of Science and Arts, as it was previously known. The building and ideas started out with good, if laudable intentions, as a place with admirable aspirations and a commendable nobility of purpose. But as with all institutions of this type, it deteriorated into something quite different, primarily as a result of popular demands made upon its operation as a place providing entertainment.

The intentions of the place were formally enshrined in its charter, which provided for the construction in 1854, following the example set by the Great Exhibition in 1851, of an exhibition hall. The main purpose of the hall was to encourage and organize, 'Scientific Exhibitions and Promote Discoveries in the Arts and Manufacture.'

"The building boasted a few firsts, including an operational hydraulic elevator or Ascending Room. The Royal Panopticon became a center of scientific learning complete with lecture rooms, art galleries and areas set aside especially for polemic discourse. Opened in 1854 as a *Pantheon of Eminent Victorian Worthies*, it promptly closed in 1857! Sometime later it was purchased by the impresario, E. T. Smith who turned it into the now infamous Alhambra Music Hall.

We of course entered the Music Hall by the Artistes' Entrance located in Hunt's Court, on the Charing Cross Road side, secretly hoping to be assailed by admiring fans. As usual, none were evident, at least waiting, for attention or our favors. Sure enough after introducing ourselves to the Stage Door keeper, we made our way to the subterranean Dressing Rooms to meet with the rest of the crew. It was Bella whom we encountered first in a corridor and seemed distracted as she staggered by without acknowledging our presence, followed by a strong smell of alcohol.

"Let us hope she is in fine fettle this evening," were the only words Jack said on realising her state.

As we wheeled around a bend in the corridor we came across Lodge who was in deep conversation with a person both Jack and I recognised as being the manager of the Alhambra Music Hall, Mr. E T Smith. On this occasion he appeared sober, unlike the last time we met him at his Crush Bar, on the *piano-nobile* here in the Music Hall.

"Ah gentlemen, you remember E T Smith the manager of this august establishment?" asked Lodge on seeing us approach.

"We do indeed. Very good to meet you again," said Jack, holding out his hand to Smith.

Whilst Smith took his and then mine, he viewed us as though we were total strangers to him.

Smith then turned his gaze on to Lodge with an expression of absolute dread and a manic look in his eyes.

"I think that you had better follow me, gentlemen," said Smith, without averting his look from Lodge, who equally looked stunned.

We followed Smith through a series of corridors, past dressing rooms and areas where we saw thee *Cremorne Belles* limbering up for their energetic performance imminently. At length we climbed a staircase up to the *piano-nobile*. Both Jack and I expected to be shown our dressing rooms in the basement areas, so it was with some degree of trepidation that we found ourselves on the first floor of the theater. We skirted around a brass railed opening in the floor looking down on to the foyer below. We were even more surprised, but nonetheless delighted, when Smith ushered us into the Crush Bar.

"What can I get you gentlemen?" asked Smith.

"We are aware that the *Cremore Belles* are on before us, but ought not we to be..." I said.

"There has been a change of plan Theo, and we shall not be doing the Choral because..." Lodge interrupted me.

"A bevy of costermongers," said Smith, interrupting Lodge, "has turned up to witness a more outrageous performance by a person called Cinderella, who is featuring this very evening. Somehow your esteemed Cholera Symphony, or whatever it is, will, very likely, not shall we say, be, as it were, appreciated, no?"

"I do have some sway with our friends the costermongers, but even I would be powerless to intervene with that mob, were they to become rowdy during the performance of our acclaimed *Choral* Symphony, Smith, *Choral*, not *Cholera* Symphony," corrected Lodge.

"What ever," replied Smith, before drinking deeply from his glass.

"I therefore have given everybody the evening off, "continued Lodge, "at considerable great expense to my purse, I can assure you."

This development of course could not have suited us better, since I know Jack wanted to talk to Lodge about our conversation we had Pagani's restaurant. However, we waited until Smith had finished his drink, plus a couple of more. We did not have long to wait.

"I fully appreciate this is an inconvenience to you," said Smith, eventually, "but I have reserved three of the best seats in the Balcony for your enjoyment."

And with that Parthian shot, staggered off out of the Crush Bar to run the Royal Panopticon of Science and Arts, now of course deteriorated into the Alhambra Music Hall.

"What is on your mind," asked Lodge, intuitively.

"Oh nothing much, just an idea to improve our *act* and avoid being involved with your Cholera Symphonic performance," responded Jack.

Lodge studied Jack for quite some moments with a look of incredulity upon his facial features.

"Are you being serious," inquired Loge, "are you being absolutely serious"?

"We are indeed. We also think our rôle in the Choral is simply not us. We are Vaudeville artistes through and through and that is what we are at. We have never had to share the stage with anybody throughout our working lives in Vaudeville. And to start now sharing with an orchestra and chorus to say nothing of three sopranos, all screeching for their supper, is not going to happen. Sorry Loge, but I guess that the way it is," stated Jack.

Lodge, who appeared downhearted, replaced his empty glass on the marble bar surface with a clink and looked at Jack and then at me. He then looked over each shoulder.

"Gentlemen, gentlemen this is excellent news, excellent," said Lodge, whilst rubbing his hands together, "this could not have suited me better, capital, capital!"

"But what about the show, your investment in it, the *Three Graces*, or Bella for that matter, surely our decision kind of puts your ideas out of tilter?" I inquired.

"Not at tall, Theo, not at tall," said Loge, "to be honest I was having second thoughts about the viability of the show. I had not realized the costs. Oh the costs, they have been crippling me. The Choral has in fact had an adverse effect on Box Office receipts, and we simply cannot and will not tolerate that. It is all about money and the ability to get one's hands on it. The Choral will never achieve that for us."

"But we have seen packed houses filled to the rafters with an audience who, as far as I can judge, appeared to be enjoying themselves immensely," I offered.

"A full house does not necessary mean good Box Office receipts Theo," replied Lodge, "oh I am sure we can have a scaled down version just to please the audience. First of all get rid of the orchestra and its ruinous financial drain on my anæmic purse. I am thinking of reverting to the original set up where the musical passages to the symphony were paraphrased, by a chap called Schönberg, a friend of Mahler's, in the original arrangement for two barrel organs, three player pianos together with an Aëolian pianola.

In fact, to be honest, I have always preferred this arrangement of instruments. And have thought that the barrel organ was an underrated instrument and this ought not to be the case. As it too, can reach those sonorous heights sublime melody creating a mælström of uncontrolled arpeggios and pure delight that no orchestra could ever match!"

"What about Bella," I asked, "we saw her go by in the corridor earlier looking decidedly a bit distressed?"

"I have informed her of my decision to reduce the Choral Symphony, but there shall still be a rôle for Bella. In fact her voice is in perfect harmony with the barrel organ, when it is tuned up correctly. But do tell me, what do you intend to do on the stage; revert back to your old style with Judd, the ventriloquist's dummy?" inquired Lodge.

"No, we are going to scrap Judd," replied Jack, "he has been getting above himself recently."

Lodge raised his eyebrows.

"Will not Judd have some thing to say about that?" inquired Lodge, in all seriousness.

"What we are saying here Lodge," said Jack, "is the fact that Theo and I should develop our stage *act* to be contemporaneous with what an audience wants today. We need to rejuvenate our *act* to make it presentable for the audience of today, not yesterday. Those hecklers are trying to say something to us. And we witnessed those Futurists or whatever carrying on like a bunch of clowns in a concert hall, name of St. James' and we simply need to involve our audience."

Lodge looked at Jack, whilst rubbing his chin.

"We need to start re-acting with our audience and get them respond to us on stage. That tortfeasor fellow we witnessed at the New Bedford Music Hall, was actually insulting his audience and they did not to mind in the slightest. They liked him because they could relate to his rudeness and they felt part of his *act*. They were involved, that is the trick we have got to develop, and we are going to do just that. Even that Little Bo Peep has got a fine edge on her *act* which simply involves her falling down and crying," said Jack.

"Well what do you think Loge," I asked, "we can still go on stage, talk and do our usual tricks, but now start to engage with the audience on an ad hoc basis making it up as we go along?"

"Jeze," said Jack, "that is exactly what we have been doing through out our professional Vaudeville lives!"

"Capital idea gentlemen, capital idea!" said Loge, more enthusiastically than I had ever seen him before.

Lodge had become very animated on learning about our decision and was now clearly in his element at this Crush Bar ordering outrageously expensive champagne and outsize cigars to celebrate our new innovative *relating act* on stage. After much drinking, Lodge looked at his gold Hunter.

"We better take our seats gentlemen," advised Loge, "those costermongers will not be kept waiting."

Jack and I duly obliged and followed Lodge to the Dress Circle to gain our seats, before the costermongers did. I remember on our last visit here that the ostenta-tiously decorated corridors, along which we were walking, represented more of a bordello, rather than a central

London Music Hall. At length we took our seats into the red plush Dress Circle, the same seats we had occupied before, complete with seats covered in red velvet material and scuff marks and evidence of spilled liquor.

The purple safety curtain was raised very slowly as if in delayed anticipation. Eventually, it made its way up into the stage attic and revealed a remarkable back drop of a perspective scene of classical buildings set in ethereal Olympian fantasy.

We had barely taken our seats when suddenly the auditorium lights were dimmed as the footlights increased in brightness when the inexhaustible *Cremorne Belles,* burst onto the stage singing their usual introductory song, *'It's the limelight for us or nothing.'*

I remember these inexhaustible *Cremorne Belles*, as they are called, when we last saw them at the Imperial Theater in the Royal Aquarium & Winter Garden and before that, at Wilton's Music Hall. Again, they danced vigorously and were very energetic and accomplished as they carried out complex formation dance rituals or manœuvres. They did so whilst singing popular songs from light operetta, including their evident favourite, *'Orpheus and the Underground.'* [2]

I distinctly remember their dancing caused fleeting shadows, created by the incandescent footlights, to appear on the stage back drop. The backdrop on this occasion was of a scene depicting classical temples in front of which they danced gaily with trailing ribbons intertwined about their hands, made more real by the interplay of shadows and different hues of lights. The impression they created, was as though they were dancing in between the columns, colonnades and porticos of various temples.

As instantly as they burst on to the stage, they evacu-

Classical Olympian Fantasy

ated it in ever decreasing numbers until none were left. The resultant applause from the costermongers was tremendous, as it was sustained, which surprised me. Then the footlights illuminating the stage, together with the gas lighting in the auditorium, were dimmed, creating a gloomy and subdued feeling throughout the theater. A reverent hush descended over the expectant costermongers.

1. A reference expressed in music of a recurring idea or character.
2. Properly, *Orpheus and the Underworld*, operetta by Offenbach

Chapter 18

The Uncompromising Cinderella

We have informed Lodge about our decision to abandon being intricately involved in the Choral Anthem Symphony. We had done so on the basis that we felt our *turn* was auxiliary to the main *act*, which involved a choral performance of the symphony and therefore inconsistent with our humorous double *act*. Instead we intend to rejuvenate our stage *act* by being more focused on the audience, and hopefully achieve this in a variety of ways, not least by engaging with them to respond to us. For the time being however, we were guests of Mr E T Smith, the manager of the Alhambra Music Hall, where we hoped to gain inspiration from watching other *turns* or *acts* extant this evening on the stage in front of us.

A lone voice was heard in the darkened auditorium.

"Ladies and gentlemen, exhorted the Compière, please respond and show respect to the incorruptible, uncompromising and inconsolable Cinderella, the second to the last word in dignity or decorum!"

In the gloom of the auditorium, the backdrop scene was visible enough to allow members of the audience to observe it wobble as some kind of activity took place behind it. Eventually a single shaft of limelight from a solitary arc lamp illuminated only a section of the backdrop scene upon which was painted a picture of an ornate gilded coach.

Again, the scenery wobbled, but eventually, the door of the gilded coach opened. The silence in the auditorium was deafening as it competed with an air of expectation.

Then in a flash, literally created by the footlights, Cinderella, the persecuted heroine leaped out of the gilded coach and landed in front of the stage with a crash. As she did so, the costermongers too, leaped up from their crimson colored seats in thunderous applause at her appearance.

I assumed the person who had leapt out of the gilded coach was in fact the heroine Cinderella. However, she did not conform to my preconceptions of the perse-cuted character. The person standing on center stage curtseying and bowing to the excited costermongers was dressed in an outfit very different in design to the one probably envisaged by Cinderella's creators, the Brothers Grimm. Cinderella, here at least, was of a large solid build with broad shoulders, and attendant attitude to match. Her hair was not blond and with long curly locks, rather it was cropped - severely and was dark, in fact, auburn in color.

Needless to say where one would expect to see her wearing a tiara of finely wrought silver with intricate and ornate designs gracing the top of her hair; out there on the stage, this individual was wearing a jet black stove-back top hat, wrapped in black crêpe and with two inordinately long black ribbons trailing from the back. This was the type of top hat usually worn by funereal undertakers.

This was all rather incongruous to the pretty white crushed satin bellowing ball-gown she was wearing.

Complete with pink ribbons and stones of purple amethyst or red ruby sown into the fabric, creating a glittering ensemble. But, rather than wearing dainty glass slippers, to compliment her white ball-gown, Cinderella instead wore a pair of scuffed pit boots with iron studs on the soles and clearly several sizes too big for her feet.

Whilst Cinderella, the persecuted heroine continued to bow and curtsey in acknowledgement to the costermongers sustained applause. She was followed by numerous other individuals dressed in a variety of costumes, all of whom came pouring out of the same open carriage door of the gilded coach on to the stage.

Within moments the stage was filled with taffeta-wearing ballerinas and other odd characters, most of whom were strutting around the platform and generally getting in each other's way. This of course, led to some confusion and before long audible arguments erupted together with some *determined behavior* and pushing. The costermongers were in their element offering advice to all and sundry both on and off the stage.

By the time some semblance of order had been imposed by Cinderella, who appeared to be acting in the rôle of sergeant-major, bellowing orders out to all and sundry. Including to the costermonger, and generally behaving in beastly manner to her sub-ordinate ballerinas who comprised the *Corp de Ballet.* That is until her three ugly sisters, in the persons of Mademoiselle Ariel, Mademoiselle Ada, and Mademoiselle Gillert, made their dramatic appearance, by swooning in from above and landing on the stage with a perceptible thud.

The three ugly sisters, in the guise of taffeta-wearing danseuses, then squared up to Cinderella in a series of prim and tasteful balletic manœuvres, clearly not exactly their début in this respect. However, it was the sisters who were in for a shock when all of a sudden Cinderella, not of the self-effacing type, leapt up into the aëther above the ugly sisters and in so doing landed on the head of one knocking her down to the stage deck before swooning around onto the other sisters, and repeating her graceful manœuvre. Cinderella then pointed with her swagger stick, beloved of sergeants-major, to a very noticeable and enormous pile of empty beer bottles, evidently in need of washing and rinsing.

Not surprisingly, the ugly sisters objected to this unexpected chore, they had been given to deal with, and attempted to remonstrate with Cinderella, who, with utter intolerance, ordered her *Corp de Ballet* into action against them. They obliged, and marched determinedly across the stage sweeping all before them in the quest to deal severely with the three ugly sisters, in the persons of Mademoiselle Ariel, Mademoiselle Ada and Mademoiselle Gillert.

However, before falling upon the ugly sisters, the *Corp de Ballet*, as if by a magic signal, stopped and turned on the arched toes and without any warning, or prompting, unanimously burst into song about, '*You shall go to the ball!*' Much to the evident delight of the costermongers, who joined in readily in singing the verses. At least those verses which they were familiar with, or chanting alternative responses not in the original lyrics.

At the end of this extended singspiel, the ballerinas chased the ugly sisters off the stage and all was quiet as the safety curtain descended, save for the low chanting and murmuring of the costermongers seated in the stalls.

After some bumping and rumblings noises were

heard, the heavy purple safety curtain, began its ascent again into the stage attic, revealing a backdrop with a remarkable painted scene very much resembling the gilded ornate interior of the Criterion Bar at the Regent's Circus.

Before the realization of the scene fully registered in my memory, the commencement of Act II opened with a scene of pure tranquillity at the bar with an assortment of odd looking characters in convivial rapport with each other. Assuming we were now at the infamous Grand Ball, before the twelfth hour, all appeared to be respectable and of the highest decorum and indeed elegance.

Others at the bar were talking with the fairies and the ballerinas assembled there. And in the foreground of the stage scene was the occasional action by the aërial fairies, who would swoon through the aëther, as quaint apparitions, above the stage and over the front rows of the stalls containing the costermongers.

Those fairies standing at the bar, were holding with both hands outsize pint glasses from which they drank copious amounts of dark beer. Then, again, as though by magic, the fairies put down their outsize pint glasses on the nearest surface, and in remarkable unison, exploded into song about;

'Tell me gilded framed mirror upon the wall;
Who is the prettiest heroine at this Ball?'

The costermongers seated in the stalls, in a predictable undignified manner, chanted their vulgar responses to the fairies at the bar.

Apart from that, all appeared very tasteful and elegant with some of the members of the *Corp de Ballet* actually performing an elegant integrated *pas de deux* for the amusement and delectation of those attending the Grand Ball held in the Crush Bar at the Criterion Theater.

Even Cinderella was moved to tread a measure or two upon the Ball-room floor with one of the more masculine ballerinas.

This blissful scene of tranquillity had all the hall-marks of ennui; and it was therefore, with reasonable fear, that we suspected we might all be thoroughly bored into amaranthine oblivion.

Then, imperceptibly at first, but becoming louder, was a noise, a rumbling which sounded to be just off stage left. Within seconds, a commotion burst on to the stage and confronted all upon it. It was the danseuses, and they had clearly recovered their self-esteem and were back; with a vengeance and about to erupt, as an angry Vesuvius might.

Cinderella, on seeing her ugly sisters, immediately let go her embrace of the ballerina with whom she was dancing and with a clumsy *pas de deux* turned around to meet the challenges posed by the unexpected arrival of Mademoiselle Ariel, Mademoiselle Ada and Mademoiselle Gillert.

Again the three ugly sisters squared up to Cinderella deploying a complicated step routine involving a series of prim and exquisite manœuvres, only this time, the danseuses in performing them, were visibly more circumspect. This precaution, however, was in vain; because as soon as Cinderella moved in to out-manœuvre her ugly sisiters, she was joined, or rather aided and abetted, by her stalwart and faithful *Corp de Ballet*. Who, in turn, lost no time in availing themselves of the opportunity to engage the strutting danseuses Mademoiselle Ariel, Mademoiselle Gillert and Mademoiselle Ada, in close physical contact.

The scene on the stage was now set for something that could transmogrify into something approaching the undignified, or even the grotesque. Accordingly, I turned my head away. At the same time Jack leaned to my side and whispered in my ear.

"Is not this not the dance troupe who performed that *Pat in Paradise* loosely based on Shakespeare's *Mid-Summer's Night Dream* we witnessed at the Canterbury Music Hall not these few days ago?"

Before I could marshal my thoughts and formulate a response in neither confirming or denying in my answer, pandaëmonium was loosed upon the stage, as the taffeta-wearing fairies erupted into violence. Somewhat annoyed by the danseuses' perceived threat of unmitigated violence to their precious Cinderella. And in supporting the fairies, the four aërial fairies swooned gracefully through the aëther above the stage, and occasionally out over the costermongers, who ducked every time.

Then it happened. The mass ranks of the taffeta-wearing *Corp de Ballet,* now in a frightful temper, made a determined move and surrounded the desperate danseuses. Within seconds of doing so, a flurry of feathers and bits of prim taffeta ascended into the aëther above the mêlée, which was undignified, as it was ungracious. At one stage one of the danseuses was seen to fall off stage, having been clearly pushed.

Now it could have been, on is particular occasion, that Cinderella may have been entirely innocent of being the instigator or indeed have precipitated the danseuse's fall from the stage platform. But, from where we were sitting, even during the mêlée, there was evidence to suggest that Cinderella was in fact implicated; or at least preëmpted the accident perpetrated against her luckless ugly sister. And, the gloating expression upon her Cinderella's face, illuminated by the soft glow of limelight, could only augment and confirm this presupposition.

As quickly as the violence on stage erupted, it ceased as all combatants, including the slightly bruised taffeta-less danseuses, turned and faced the audience and again burst into song lamenting the fact that it was now, *'Time to go Home.'*

Again, the discerning costermongers erupted into ecstatic applause, showering praise after praise on the irritable ballerinas, who were not quite finished. For as soon as they had sung the last verse, they recommenced their frenzied attack on the now hapless Mademoiselle Ada, Mademoiselle Ariel and Mademoiselle Gillert.

Again it was Cinderella, the heroine who brought the violence to an end. She did so by approaching the front of the stage up against the footlights, which illuminated her elegant white crushed satin dress, pit boots and stove-pipe top hat and looking quite the picture. She then burst into another song, *'It is twelve of the clock and where's my Carriage?'* To the murmurings of approval by the now attentive costermonger, who listened to Cinderella's fading song. A fragile peace seemed to have descended upon the stage.

Indeed, at the conclusion of Cinderella's song the rest of the cast too came up to the footlights. And holding hands together, launched into a rousing rendition of their last song, *'I Dreamt I Dwelt in Marble Halls'* whilst pointing to the Bar scene behind them. During this song they were led by the top hat wearing Cinderella, who marched up and down the ranks as the sergeant-major might as the performance on stage approached its tumultuous climax.

Then suddenly unexpected one of the taffeta-less wearing danseuses, I suspect Mademoiselle Gillert, leapt gracefully up in to the aëther. We all of us assumed this was to be the start of a particularly elegant *pas de deux* to conclude the performance on stage, with a balletic coda. This was not to be the case and within seconds, Gillert had grabbed one of the flying aërial fairies swooning gracefully through the aëther above the stage and brought her down to the stage deck with a crash and a flurry of taffeta and aërial fairy's wings.

The three strutting danseuses clearly indicated they were still capable of offering a physical challenge to all or anyone. To which the taffeta-wearing *Corp de Ballet* glided over on their arched toes to remonstrate with the danseuses and on reaching them, responded accordingly.

This final act of revenge by Mademoiselle Gillert, had gotten the audience into a frenzy. Most, if not all, were clapping unrestrainedly and, I might add, with reckless abandon. Whilst other costermongers in the audience were inducing themselves deliberately into an unbridled delirium, and I noticed with utter disgust, so was Loge, sitting here with us in the Dress Circle.

It was at this point that the management of the Alhambra Music Hall felt compelled to intervene in a forlorn attempt to restore order on the resultant escalating chaos the stage, and in the first front rows of the stalls, where the costermongers held sway.

It was at this point that the heavy sound muffling purple safety curtain was dropped with indecent haste, in a vain attempt to bring the proceedings on stage to an abrupt end, or endeavor to contain it.

As for the costermongers, the lowering of the curtain signalled a mass stampede to the numerous Crush Bars ranged strategically about the Alhambra Music Hall.

It was only whilst we were drinking at one particular Crush Bar, a few minutes later, that Jack expressed his inner thoughts.

"I cannot help but think, but that Cinderella who we have just been watching out there on the stage, kind of looks familiar. I do not mean her face, no more of her mannerism and movements, her deportment?" said Jack.

Lodge put his drink on the adjacent bar and drew upon his Trichinopoly cigar.

"So you realized too?" he asked Jack.

"Realized what, what is it that I should I have realized?" Jack responded, in his Jersey City accent.

"She is a traitor to the cause!" announced Lodge.

"Cinderella, a traitor to the cause, what are you talking about Lodge, have you lost your reason?" inquired Jack, incredulously.

"That woman complete in white crushed satin dress with boots and top-hat is a traitor to the cause of Music Hall," said Lodge decisively, whilst picking up his drink, and drinking deeply then breathing out noisily upon doing so.

I felt compelled to interject.

"Lodge, Jack seems to think that he recognises Cinderella, the person we saw on the stage earlier. You are saying that she is a traitor to the cause. What cause, Music Hall? How come she is a so-called traitor, what has she done?" I asked.

"You may recall when we were in this Crush Bar here in the Alhambra Music Hall..," said Lodge.

"The place where Marie Lloyd *crushed* you!" interrupted Jack, with a smile.

"You may recall, "Lodge continued, "where that Lloyd tried unsuccessfully to traduce me because of her treacherous rôle in the Music Hall strike which has been organized because of the fair imposition of the *Exclusivity Clause…*"

Jack had not quite forgiven Lodge over his attitude and treatment of Marie Lloyd. A woman with whom Jack immediately had affinity, telling her on their first meeting, that she was but, 'a Greek goddess in human form.' I distinctly remember him insisting.

"You mean that time," interrupted Jack, "when Marie Lloyd subjected you to her very effective coup de grâce, in this very Crush Bar? Do not forget Lodge, both Jack, I and those assembled at here at the time witnessed it. And, if I remember correctly, that infamous and oppressive *Exclusivity Clause,* which in effect, means that Music Hall artistes are unreasonably prevented from performing or appearing in any Music Hall or variety theater. Or indeed any other place of entertainment, within a specified area around the establishment in which they have worked, and for at least the duration of one year.

"So as Marie said, at the time in explaining the provisions of that unreasonable *Exclusivity Clause.* A clause that allows Music Hall managers to prevent artistes from appearing in another theater, within a certain distance or period of time, immediately before or after a performance in a particular Music Hall, during the course of a particular evening.

"That means the artistes cannot earn money by doing what they are trained do in entertaining the Music Hall-going public. They are stuck to performing at one theater, and one theater alone. Marie then gave an example, which clearly showed the absurdity of the clause. Were she to perform here at the Alhambra Music Hall under the manager E T Smith, and her *turn* finished at eight o'clock of an evening. She would be prevented from appearing across the Leicester Square out there at the Empire Music Hall, and sing another selection of songs because of the time and distance constraints placed upon her.

"That is the truth of it Lodge; is that not the case?" inquired Jack, with aspersion and traces of annoyance in his voice.

"You have to bear in mind Loge," I offered, trying to ameliorate the situation, "that both Jack and I are performing Vaudeville artistes and we have, perforce, an affinity and sympathy with other Music Hall artistes. So when you refer to treacherous behavior or traitor to the cause, by our brother artistes, then these are very emotive and loaded statements to Jack and me.

Lodge considered his drink for a moment.

"We were discussing that Cinderella; the fact remains is she is what I know her to be. In order to circumvent the fair and reasonable provisions contained in that *Exclusivity Clause*, she has resorted to subterfuge, and is pretending to be some one else in order that she might earn money on the same evening in a different place.

"So you have seen an individual, this very evening, performing in the rôle of Cinderella here at the Alhambra Music Hall on the eastern aspect of the Leicester Square. At this very moment that individual is walking, furtively and by way of the quieter back streets to the Empire Music Hall, located diagonally on the northern aspect of the square. And, I might add, in direct contravention of the *Exclusivity Clause*!" advised Lodge.

Empire Music Hall

"About whom are we talking, just who is this individual?" asked Jack.

"Ah, my lips are sealed; Valkürian horses could not drag this secret from depths of my soul," replied Loge, "you see Jack, whilst I have my opinion of her and what she is doing, I refused to stoop to naming her and thus expose her subversive actions!"

We let the matter drop and instead concentrated and what we had learned, apart from duplicity, by witnessing the *act* earlier this evening. We did stay for quite some time in the Crush Bar, in the hope Marie Lloyd might come in to galvanize support for her strike, but alas Jack was disappointed by her not appearing this evening.

Lodge, who had been drinking heavily during the evening for some reason, staggered off insisting that he had to meet a very important and influential person. It was only after a few more rounds of drink that Jack and decided eventually, that we too might attempt to get home to our hotel. Accordingly, we set off in the direction of Shaftesbury Avenue to intercept any horse drawn carriage headed towards Russell Square and St. Pancras.

We made our way across the Leicester Square and past the fountain, that forms part of a monument which had been erected to some worthy thespian. We continued onwards towards the Empire Music Hall on our way to the Shaftesbury Avenue. As we did Jack grabbed my arm and pulled me over to the one of the doors leading into the Empire Music Hall. Attached to the front of the building was a board, a sign board listing the acts which had been scheduled to perform that evening.

It was only when Jack, with his cane, tapped the

The Empire
Music Hall

Leicester Square, W.

Presents for your delectation

6-30 - Twice Nightly - 9-30

Jack Lorimar

Rachel D'Arcy and her Ukulele

RH Douglas

Jimmy Godden

Ena Dayne

Little Bo Peep

Talberto & Douglas

Spanish Goldionis Acrobats

Miss Ray Ford

poster on the wall, and particular the name of a Music Hall performing artistes who was scheduled to appear this very evening at the Empire Music Hall. She had of course appeared in front of us earlier at the Alhambra Music Hall as Cinderella. Now she had appeared here, in contravention of the *Exclusivity Clause*!

Jack then looked at me for my predictable response. It was not long in coming. I could see the name of the performing artiste in bold clears letters. I read them out allowed to Jack just to make sure I was correct.

Chapter 19

The Shrouded Depths

The next morning whilst taking break-fast, or in my case copious amounts of black Santiago café noir, a cable-gram was delivered to our table for the attention of Jack Mitchell. It appertained to our decision to abandon being involved with the Choral Symphony and instead focus on our accomplished Vaudeville *act*, but with a new *turn*. He has agreed this change of direction and accordingly has invited us to perform at the Oxford Music Hall in the Oxford Street just north of the Royalty Theater in Dean Street, Soho.

"Did not that Oxford Music Hall go up in flames the other day as a result of a danseuse performing her bawdy rendition of scenes from Stravinsky's new ballet *The Fire Bird?*" asked Jack.

"I think so Jack. Lodge did inform us that she got carried away in a reckless trance brought on by the ecstatic and rapturous applause she had generated from an appreciative audience?" I replied.

"But alas," said Jack, "as is often the case, in her dancing delirium, she bowed too near to the blazing footlights and in so doing her starched taffeta costume sticking out made contact with the flame causing it to ignite and catch fire!"

"The applause increased as she ran about the stage in

a blind panic, which the audience mistook as being part of her original *Fire Bird* act. It was not so much as what happened to the hapless blazing taffeta-wearing danseuse, as to what her flaming taffeta costume did to the stage scenery, which too went up in flames," I added.

"Obviously, they have made repairs and the place is now open for business," informed Jack.

"That fact does not surprise me; after all running a theater of any description involves money, as Loge is for ever reminding us. Time is money and money is time. Which theater, do we know, including the Fourteenth Street Theater back home in New York, can afford to be closed?" I offered.

"The cable-gram states that he will meet us in the Crush Bar at five o' clock this afternoon to discuss our routine and what we intend doing," said Jack.

We spent the day lounging around the various salons ranged around our opulent St. Pancras Hotel and occasionally discussing our routine for this evening in which we intend to as it were, speak to our audience with questions and engage with them. Well, that is our intention.

At length we met beneath the ornate Porte Cochère of the hotel and immediately one of the doormen whistled loudly for a carriage a few moments later a Hackney carriage, heralded by its green tender lamp, came looming out of then fog like a phäntasmagoric apparition.

We climbed aboard.

"Oxford Street Music Hall, 16 Oxford Street, near the Tottenham Court Road," instructed Jack to the coachman.

We pulled out of the Porte Cochère and clattered along the front of the St Pancras Hotel and then curved down the driveway, illuminated by incandescent gas lamps poring out their strong blue light through halos. Eventually we turned right into the Euston Road and joined the vicissitude of slow moving vehicles involving omnibuses, pantechnicon, dray wagons and those of military all lumbering along to their various destinations.

We had only travelled a few yards when Jack tapped my arm and pointed with his cane to a road plate of the street we had just turned left into.

I looked up into the swirling fog and was just able to read that which Jack had just noticed.

"Judd Street, my God Jack, do not tell me the English have named that street for our erstwhile ventriloquist's dummy!"

It could be that we were discussing our *act* for this evening or simply not paying attention to our journey. But after some time had elapsed, Jack stopped me whilst I was replying to some question of his and tapped the roof of our Hackney carriage with his cane. A moment or two later the roof hatch opened and staring down at us, was a beefy face with side whiskers of the Hackney carriage driver.

"We are going to the Oxford Street Music Hall in Oxford Street or are we going to then Holborn Empire Music Hall?" asked Jack, to my surprise and, I think the carriage driver's too.

Jack had obviously realized that we had been travelling south in the direction of the Thames. And further, that he had recognised we were in the Holborn district of the Metropolis, because he pointed out to me an impressive Mausoleum building standing and looking abandoned in its own grounds surrounded by tall railings.

In fact my knowledge of London is pretty well zilch; but Jack's was adequate, at least for the purposes of having a basic idea of where he is at. And we were not in the right place. Even I could figure that out since I

Mausoleum Building

knew we were travelling due south and not west, which was precisely the question Jack posed to our carriage driver.

"Tell me is not the Oxford Music Hall at the eastern end of Oxford Street; at number sixteen to be precise? So why have we crossed over the road that would take us directly to Oxford street and instead find ourselves traversing High Holborn and progressing south of our destination approaching Covent Garden? Which, as far as I can make out, is east of the Oxford Music Hall and certainly much further south," inquired Jack of the Hackney carriage driver.

"Road traffic conditions around the Great Russell Street museum, and Tottenham Court Road and what with them omnibuses and the like, it is quite a mess. So using my experience I am delivering you to where you want to get with the least amount of inconvenience. Or would you rather sit in my carriage and go nowhere, because that is what will happen if had I come down through Bloomsbury from the St. Pancras Hotel. Or, have you not noticed this *Pea Souper* [1] we are actually in?" replied the coachman.

"We too have fog in New York and that does not give

228

the carriage driver the right to go on a frolic of his own. We are miles away from the Oxford Music Hall. So when are you going to start to head off in that direction?" inquired Jack, in tones of mounting exasperation. I too was becoming slightly bothered by this circuitous route to our destination.

"Really?" replied the coachman, "well in that case would you rather that I drive you directly and in double quick time to Euston Rail Road Station 2 instead?"

And with that Parthian shot, the Hackney carriage driver slammed shut the roof hatch preventing any further communication from taking place between him and either Jack or me. We then turned sharply and with much jolting into some road or other, which eventually brought us in to a derelict looking lane the name of which we could not ascertain to aid is in our bearings.

"I think that we are near the street, in where the famous Middlesex Music Hall is located. We really should to avail ourselves of an evening there when we have time, do you agree Theo?" asked Jack, though not very convincingly.

I was not to receive an answer. Instead Jack directed a question, not at me, but rather at the Hackney carriage driver.

"Driver, why have we driven into Drury Lane, which is nowhere near the destination I gave you, and we are going south, not west, to where the Oxford Music Hall is?"

"We are still east of the Oxford Music Hall and have not gone West beyond it," replied the driver, marshalling as much contempt as possible for Jack under the circumstances.

"Yeah, can you be sure, are you absolutely sure?" inquired Jack, in his broadest Jersey City accent.

"As sure as I am about what will happen to top hat

wearing persons as you, come the Revolution," answered the carriage driver, with his voice laced with contempt.

"You could not organise a revolution on a steam-operated merry-go-round, and of that I remain certain!" Jack replied.

The driver did not even bother to reply but, with a series of quick, desperate turns and reckless manœuvres, took us clattering through echoing alleyways and court-yards, finally bringing his carriage to an abrupt halt. He then opened his roof hatch and looked down onto us.

"I know my way around London, fog or no fog, and I do not take kindly to fares telling me how to do my job; so you can both get out of my cab right this moment," he said loudly in a Cockney accent, "right this very moment."

If I had known this would have been the result of Jack's encounter with the Hackney carriage driver, I might have intervened, but such was Jack's impulsive character at times. One cannot win in these situations because carriage drivers invariably, have little else to do than to be part-time Nihilists or behave in a cantankerous manner.

Having been dismissed by our carriage driver, we found ourselves in a street, or rather a cobbled stone yard, which was not immediately familiar to Jack, or at least to me. The buildings, such as we could discern in the fog, were of a utility type, of very low quality and grimy, and seemed to rise through several floors up into the fog-laden aether.

Our situation was made all the more poignant by the fact that we were standing in front of a grubby advertise-ment that had partly detached itself from the brickwork upon which it had been pasted.

Every Man and Woman in England & the Empire should Use

DR SCOTT'S ELECTRIC 'FLESH' BRUSH
WHY ?

**Because it quickens the circulation,
opens the pores,
&
enables the system to throw off those
impurities which cause disease.
It instantly acts upon the blood,
nerves, and tissues.**

Imparting
A Beautiful Clear Skin
New Energy and New Life,
**TO ALL WHO DAILY USE IT
AND IS WARRENTED TO CURE**
Rheumatism and Diseases of the Blood,
Nervous Complaints, Neuralgia, Toothache,
Malaria, Lameness, Palpitations, Paralysis
&
All pains caused by impaired circulation.
It promptly alleviates Indigestion, Liver and Kidney
Troubles,
Quickly removes those "Back Aches" peculiar to Ladies,
&
Imparts wonderful vigor to the whole body.

**ALL DEALERS WILL REFUND PRICE
IF NOT AS REPRESENTED**.

*All Cheques, Drafts or Post
Office Orders made payable
to Dr. Geo. A. Scott, 84 Broadway, Victoria, SW.*

By degrees we began to notice persons moving through the shrouds of fog close by. Some moved quickly and disappeared, others with a slower and a more measured step, as though stalking a prey. I continued to look up for a street nameplate but found none, and nor did I really expect to, for such places as this do not advertise their location.

"Well Jack, what do you reckon now, because I have not gotten a clue just as to where we are?" I asked.

"Take it easy Theo, we can work this one out and navigate our way out of this labyrinth," replied Jack, though not very convincingly

"Do you think that we are in some kind of rough neighbourhood?" I asked with as much doubt in my voice as possible, as a way of indicating my deep concern.

"The carriage entered the yard from over there – or was it over there? Still, let us investigate this alleyway and see where it leads. Ah, nowhere. Right, let us try this one. After all, if all else fails, whatever remains must be the solution," said Jack.

"Where have I heard that before?" I responded.

It was not the solution and neither was the next one, and it became apparent to me that we were truly lost. I instinctively buttoned up my coat in order to create the vague dark outline of a bulky figure in the fog. I likewise removed my top hat to augment this anonymity in my attempt to blend in to our surroundings. I also suggested to Jack that he should do the same.

The carriage driver, however, by his yelling at us, would have alerted anyone near-by as to our presence and, perforce, predicament. My suspicions proved to be correct, for within minutes of our arriving in the yard the place began to fill up with street-urchin types. Some merely looked at us, others were sizing us up.

Above us people opened their windows and looked down onto us.

There was a feeling of being in the wrong place at the wrong time. At that moment, however, Jack pulled at my arm and led us through an archway that gave out onto a grubby side street that comprised a series of dirty and bleak tenement buildings, of the type we have in the Lower East Side of New York. We made our way along this street in the forlorn hope of finding our way out from our situation. Again Jack's sometimes over confident treatment of the lower orders, in particular carriage drivers, has yet again resulted in our present dilemma which might conclude in our being inconvenienced at best or highly incommoded at worst.

My developing annoyance due to being in this situation at least took my mind off our predicament and instead compelled me to concentrate my thoughts on gaining a respectable and recognisable street from which we might continue our journey to our destination at the Oxford Music Hall, where ever it was from here.

Of course I have experienced fog in other big cities on the eastern seaboard as in New York, where fog rolls in and obscures one's vision. But, unlike Metropolitan England, with its labyrinth of Georgian streets; the avenues and streets of which New York City is comprise, are built to a grid design making negotiating them in the fog comparatively easier than here in London.

Suddenly in front of us, two stationary figures with haunched shoulders loomed in to view. I could see that one of them was smoking, by the dancing of the red glow from his cigarette. I thought, instantly in order to blend in to our surroundings we too should be seen to be smoking in a nonchalant manner. Accordingly, I retrieve my red leather case containing several Trichinopoly cigars, one of which I was about to offer to Jack standing next to me, and turned around to do so.

My heart nearly leapt into my mouth as I realized the person with whom I had been speaking was not Jack, but a vagabond of sorts, who helped himself to one of my cigars. His face, only inches from mine, was scared and bruised showing me that he had been in the wars, though not of a formal military kind. The cap he wore was impregnated with filth and grease. This matched the equally greasy and dark hair protruding from beneath that cap on the side of his head.

His whole aspect and manner was one of latent intimidation without even saying or doing anything. Indeed his merely being here was of such repellent aspect as to induce in me a profound feeling of a presentiment. And an imminent expectation of his indulging in leger-demain or other form of trickery. I turned away to leave this vile looking creature and in so doing nearly walked straight into the two stationary figures. I managed to veer just in time, or I would certainly have collided with them. Expecting to be followed, I increased my step into I did not know what, except possibly oblivion.

Having stopped a minute or so later all was silent. I surveyed my surroundings and despite the swirling dank acrid fog, I realized by degrees that I was in a courtyard of a kind decked out in shiny York flagstones, on which the fog had condensed, making them slippery. I was trapped. The buildings, which comprised this hovel yard, were of a type that had possibly been derelict even a hundred years ago.

Whole sections of staffing had fallen away from the façade of the various buildings, and in so doing, revealed disintegrating brickwork and with bits of rotted timber protruding out from the walls. The yard had an inde-scribable stench to it, indicating to me that an open sewer or cesspit was nearby. I drew on my cigar, not for pleasure of the cigar leaf burning, but for relief from the smell of the sewer.

Suddenly I heard a scream closely followed by a dull thud, and then an oath, as though a body had fallen heavily to the ground. I remained motionless and tried to pump myself up so as to give the impression of being tall and of a substantial build.

Eventually I stepped through the courtyard into a small narrow alley and had not gotten for when all of a sudden the ferocious barking from a dog assailed my ears. I could hardly retreat so moved forward tentatively. I saw the hound. It was chained to the front of a building next to a heavy timber door with a rusting iron flat beam clasped to it.

I negotiated myself passed the creature who continued to bark at me. I was grateful, because while I do not hold with chaining animals up, on this occasion I was willing to make an exception. I also hoped that the weakest link in the chain would not break at this very moment, for I should not care to rate highly my chances against the brute were it to attack me.

At length I appeared to have come to the end of the lane and onto a wider, if still grubbier side street. I stopped and listened for any audible sound of a person or dog or anything approaching. No sound was heard, so I commenced walking across the road. Then suddenly, a green tender lamp came thundering towards me, causing me to momentarily panic as I stepped backwards to safety. The lamp heralded a huge pentechnicon carrying furniture, that went lumbering by and, as it did so, caused the fog to swirl around into vortices. Presently I did gain the other side of the street despite the thick fog.

In trying to gather my wits from that near encounter with the furniture wagon, not only made me nervous but served to remind me of the perils that fog can afford when trying to make one's way in it. I looked up to ascertain where I might be. A futile exercise, I thought, for what possible significance could the name of an alley or court yard have for me. I should be none the wiser. I continued to grope my way down the lane uncertain if I were heading deeper into this fog laden labyrinth of hovels and tenement buildings, or actually extricating myself out from it.

Possibly, I thought, this place cannot go on for eternity. A minute or so later, I came to a wall topped with broken glass cast iron railings, behind which I looked to be a burial grounds. [3] I gripped one of the railings to steady myself and, in doing so, looked behind it into the gloomy precinct of the grounds. An eerie silence pervaded the stillness of the dense swirling fog that partially shrouded the tombs, dominated by a substantial Mausoleum. No wonder the yellow fog was stilled and heavier, with an all-pervasive pungent acridity attacking one's senses.

The acrid fog-laden aëther seemed denser in these grounds than elsewhere in the vicinity. In particular, the concentration of the fog had the effect of deadening sound and inducing feelings of isolation with attendant claustrophobia. Both sensations were now combining rapidly, making me more anxious almost by the minute. I knew such feelings were an irrational re-action caused by the effects of fog and being effectively lost in a tough neighborhood, comprised of the undeserving poor, and told myself so.

Mausoleum in the Rookery

However, the feeling of suppressed near panic that had gripped my heart was till with me, and I felt it tightening its hold, even more so. However, having no option, if I were to find a way out of this place, wherever this place was, I should have to continue walking. I did so nervously, but with care along the pavement next to the railings for reference if nothing more. Without concentrating properly, I instinctively turned a corner, and walked straight into a woman wearing an outsized bonnet on her head.

I mumbled an apology.

"No you are not sorry. You done that deliberate!" she squawked almost at the top of her voice.

"I assure you Ma'am I…" I said

"You lot are all the same, come down here for a bit of rough trade, but with no respect, no respect," she butted in, and erupted into the most high pitched manic laughter I should ever wish to hear again this side of eternity.

Hers was not the only unsettling laughter to be heard in the vicinity. Mingled with the odd scream, cries too, could be heard. As I walked by one dwelling complete with broken windows, I could hear forced laughter emanating from within the house. The laughter sounded more manic than jovial, and accordingly, made me feel extremely nervous. Feeling uncomfortable in the vicinity of that house, I continued groping my way along the pavement. Several minutes later, having negotiated my way out of the lane, I emerged into yet another court yard.

However, just in front of me, though invisible, I could hear a commotion of some kind. I instinctively slowed my pace and proceeded cautiously, for I still had to find a way out of this slum.

All of a sudden a person came running out of the fog towards me and bowled into my person causing me to fall to the ground. Almost certainly fortuitous, because at that very moment a hammer or wrench whistled through the fog-laden aëther past where I had been standing. A second later a sharp thwack was heard, as somebody or other fell down on to the wet ground of the yard. In an instant it was all over, and silence returned to the shrouds of fog.

I recovered from my fall and picked myself up and did not care to linger in the vicinity to reap whatever consequences might be metered out. I continued on through the swirling fog, and I felt grateful that for once it made me invisible, though by no means out of my predicament, which showed no signs of abating. Still I resolved to keep going, for what else could I do? I asked myself repeatedly. Then it occurred to me, I am supposed to be on stage. And what has become of Jack, is he like me struggling to find a way pout of this place?

By dodging a ceaseless onslaught of drunks, and stepping over various inert bodies on the footpath, I made my way through this fog-laden labyrinth of lanes and alleys. This situation was brought about by the fact that the Hackney carriage driver had deposited us here deliberately, in this concentration of a slum, as a direct result of Jack's confident behaviour towards him. The fact that I was supposed to be on stage, with Jack, now began to concern me. But, irrespective of this concern, of course I did not know how far in distance the Oxford Music Hall was from here. For the simple reason, I knew not where here was.

As I walked down yet another alley, I began to discern movement, faintly at first, albeit of shadows and lights in the fog. By degrees and feeling my way along unfamiliar alleys and lanes, to the shadows and lights, I managed to extricate myself from this ghetto's embroilment. As I approached towards this vista of activity I increased by step.

Moments later I appeared to be standing in a wide roadway looking at various green tender lamps, suspended in the fog-laden aëther, and moving towards me like a ghostly procession. One by one a series of heavy vehicles lumbered by me, as though in deep thought. Renewed with confidence and energy I search for a corner and discovered that I was indeed in the Charing Cross Road, and on the junction of Denmark Street.

I was still unsure just where I was, but knew with confidence that Oxford Street ran off the Charing Cross Road. I needed only to ask any passing stranger in which direction was Oxford Street, in order to be able to find my way to the Oxford Music Hall. A few moments later I was able to ask a passing gentleman. He advised me it was to my right heading north and then making a left into Oxford Street.

I did walk, or rather groped my way up the Charing Cross Road. As my confidence in my navigational ability returned, I began to concentrate on our show tonight. We were, after all, supposed to be performing at the Oxford Music Hall. Our impresario has gotten us a turn at that hall that was ablaze only a few days ago! Resourceful if nothing else, I thought. I was glad to be able to go back to our usual routine and not augment a choral symphonic production. I turned into Oxford Street with a look of pure delight on my face that would seem a variance in a public street, were it not for the fact the fog concealed my features from unsuspecting pedestrians passing by.

I threw open the main door of the Oxford Music Hall and stepped into the foyer. Immediately a smell of burning assailed my nostrils. However, just to be in a place devoid of fog and its acrid smell and somewhere with brilliant incandescent lighting, was in itself sufficient for me. The whole effect was to create in my weary heart, a crescendo of light, a euphoric sensation of ecstasy and warmth and the ability to be able to see, all of which I needed so desperately. I headed for the Crush Bar; that is our instinctive rendezvous place, where Jack and I have always met when we have been separated anywhere, since neither of us could perform on stage without the other!

I ascended the broad, grand staircase on to the *piano-nobile* with an inordinate enthusiasm, for reasons which were not apparent to me at the time, nor did I particularly care. I was glad to be in light and out of that fog-infested ghetto. On entering the bar I saw Jack and Lodge and they were talking with another gentleman. Indeed the bar was a hive of activity and drinking, with loquacious and lively bar-maids engaging patrons in all manner of back-chat and suggestion, whilst they operated the beer-engines.

The walls of the bar were coverer in purple silk flocked

wall-paper with raised velvet designs. In one corner of the bar, an ornate grand pianoforte, encased in exotic rosewood with inlaid ebony tracery, was being played softly by an accomplished pianist. Indeed one might have thought this salon, complete with the ubiquitous indoor palm trees ranged around the room, could well have been the main aspect of entertainment with the auditorium merely auxiliary in the emporium of delectation.

The general warm lively atmosphere was precisely what my soul needed so desperately and all of which added to the feeling of relief after being lost in those shrouds of fog in that slum.

1. Thick dense fog
2. From this station trains depart to Liverpool and then by ship, passage to New York
3. St Giles's Churchyard

Chapter 20

The Oxford Music Hall

Because of Jack's innate Jersey City impetuous attitude, we had been abandoned by our loquacious Hackney carriage driver, in a slum area near the Charing Cross Road. However, having been separated from Jack I had eventually found my way out of that fog infested ghetto. That such a place could exist within minutes of the West End theater district, even now I find remarkable. For the time being I was now in the Crush Bar at the Oxford Music Hall having found Jack and Lodge in discourse with another gentleman.

"Ah Theo," said Loge, "waving me over to them, "come and meet Blythe Pratt, the esteemed manager of the Oxford Music Hall. Blythe, this is Theo, Theo Houston the other half of the double act out of New York."

I held out my hand to shake his. He seemed surprised, or confused, but did transfer the glass he was holding to his left hand and then proceeded to shake my hand.

"I am delighted to meet you Theo," he said, as he looked at me with wild staring eyes, "we were beginning to think that you had abandoned us for another more salubrious Music Hall, though I cannot think of any other one!"

This elicited a high pitched laugh from Lodge.

"Where have you been this last hour?" he inquired.

However, before I could answer Jack put a glass of whisky into my hand and Lodge bid us all to sit on two nearby sofas.

Having made ourselves comfortable on the blue damask covered sofas at the Crush Bar, and armed with a large whisky, I looked at Blythe Pratt to lead the proceedings. Especially in ascertaining why we were not performing on his stage, as scheduled to be doing so. He asked no such question and it was Lodge who spoke.

"Gentlemen, we are in good company being at this august Music Hall, managed by my good friend here Mr. Blythe Pratt," Loge said, in an attempt to engage my attention. "This establishment was run originally by Charles Morton and Frederick Stanley, his brother-in-law. Stanley was also retained to manage the Canterbury Music Hall as well, with both Music Halls featuring notable performers of the day, including Arthur Roberts, George Robey and that woman, Marie Lloyd."

"Indeed our Oxford Music Hall," continued Pratt, moving his arm in an arch as though to indicate possession, "was re-built in the year 1892 to the present designs and appointment you can clearly observe by architects Wylson & Long. And to add further credence to the place, highly acclaimed artistes, such as George Robey and Harry Tate both made their solo début on this very stage in 1895.

"The interior design of the Oxford can be traced back to the successful decorative and opulent aspects extant at the Canterbury Music Hall. This of course is not surprisingly, since Charles Morton was responsible the interior appointment of both establishments. Indeed sitting in the auditorium it was difficult not to be reminded of the interior decoration of the Canterbury.

Charles Morton, opened this Oxford Music Hall in 1861. The nearby Weston Music Hall operator, Henry Weston, lodge a complaint with the magistrates under the Theatrical Regulations Act 1843 claiming there were too many Music Halls in the vicinity of Oxford Street. His malicious claim was dismissed; and quite correctly so.

"Then the auditorium was in the shape of an elongated hall with crimson plush red velvet covered seats with brass division rails which comprised the stalls. A wide balcony, punctuated with Corinthian columns, was constructed to the side walls. [1] The rear wall facing across the hall was of a similar design. The stage was built as a tall alcove the sides of which were punctuated with more Corinthian fluted columns, which also reflected the exterior classical decoration to the Music Hall.

"Inside the building, the classical motif was continued throughout the foyer and other areas including the large expansive auditorium. In this hall, the same classical motifs were assembled and the usual stucco upon which were the usual raised gilt filigree detailing together with generous ostentatious décor throughout.

"The domed ceiling is impressive and clearly designed to be so, and is quite dramatic as it curves down to the side walls. Here it is intercepted by an extensive intricately decorated architrave which forms the soffit to the recessed balconied space beneath it…" said Pratt.

His description of the Music Hall was terminated by the appearance of one of the bar-maids seeking his permission to grant credit at the bar for a group of top hat wearing gentlemen. After studying them for a few moments Pratt consented to their request and informed the bar-maid accordingly.

At the same time Jack whispered in my ear.

"Jeze Theo," said Jack, "is Blythe Pratt, the

manager of this Music Hall, trying to sell the place to us? We have just barely sat down with our drinks and he is talking about features of the hall as though we were potential buyers!"

Even Lodge was predisposed to look up at the ornate ceiling of the bar in slight exasperation at Blythe's detail account of his Music Hall.

I was neither concentrating on Blythe's description or Jack's re-action to it. Of course I had not been able to view the front of the Oxford Music Hall. This in part was due to my dire need to hit the Crush Bar immediately upon my arrival, and also because of the presence of the fog swirling about in Oxford Street, which obscured my view of the building. But whilst Pratt was describing the architectural details of his Music Hall with inordinate enthusiasm, I had been looking at a large fine drawing of the façade of the Oxford Music Hall, hanging on a nearby wall.

Observing this drawing, in its gilt frame, I concluded that it was an elevational drawing of the Oxford Street façade of the proposed designs for the re-built Oxford Music Hall. The architects had clearly elected to impress the front of the Oxford Music Hall with ornate details and motifs embedded in what was an exercise in a restrained classical style.

These designs included fluted columns topped with Corinthian capitals together with pedimented window reveals incorporating side columns. A loggia, similar to the one at the Vaudeville Music Hall, fronted by balustrade and a plethora of classical motifs addressed the front of the Music Hall over looking Oxford Street.

As a consequence of these embellishments and decorative details, reflected in the drawing, the façade of the building would seem to radiate out a certain dignity in

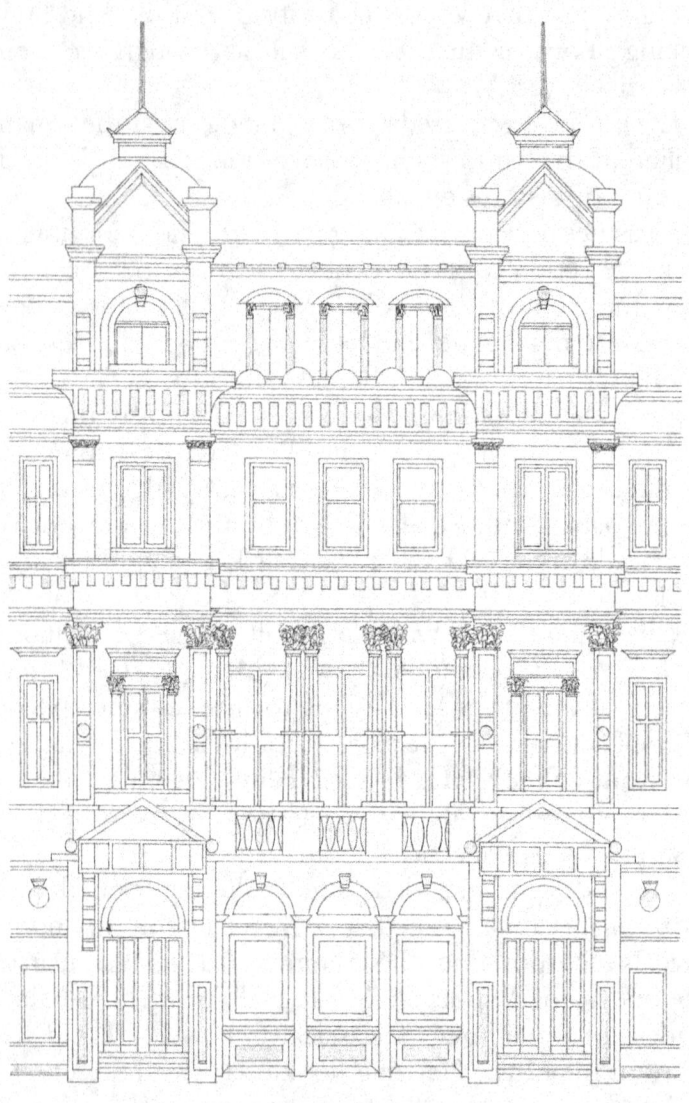

Oxford Music Hall, London

masonry, which is at variance to the usual design one normally associate with the architecture of Music Halls.

After another round of badly needed drinks, I was now at last prepared to field inquiries from the assembled on the red damask covered sofas, regarding my sojourn into that fog-bound slum.

"You were where?" asked Lodge.

"What do you want that I should say? I still have no idea as to my wanderings in the fog," I replied.

"What Theo is saying," said Jack, "is that he did not know where he was; and he should know, after all he was there!"

"You said that at one time you were next to a church yard with a Mausoleum, or something like it?" inquired Loge, with a profound look of concern upon his face.

"Yes," I responded.

Lodge then looked at the manager, Blythe Pratt.

"You say that you were around the Holborn area, headed towards Covent Garden?" asked Lodge of Jack.

"I believe so," answered Jack, "and then as I told you before, the Hackney carriage driver made us get out somewhere."

"On what road were you travelling along in Holborn?" inquired Pratt.

"I believe it is called High Holborn and we were headed in the direction of Covent Garden, crossing over a roadway called Drury Lane, in which is located the Middlesex Music Hall," replied Jack.

Again Loge and Pratt exchanged looks of concern. Pratt then looked directly at me.

"Theo, you were in an area known as the *Rookery*. 2 That place refers to a notorious slum hereabouts between the Charing Cross Road and St. Giles's Churchyard. You obviously entered it from the High Holborn - St. Giles's

High Street side, and can count yourselves, both of you, extremely fortunate. We, at least, can be thankful that you were not very seriously incommoded; for in that area, are concentrated a general array of ambitious undesirables," said Pratt.

"These include thieves, footpads, dog stealers, prostitutes, seasoned pickpockets, and, more particularly, costermongers. All of whom will revert instantly to speaking in their incomprehensible esoteric language, on the sight of any person representing authority or the law, or indeed respectability and their attendant wealth. The costermonger's language is also designed to keep their intentions secret and frustrate the uninitiated, especially against you and what they might intend doing to your persons," advised Loge.

"You probably find it a bit difficult to accept that the Rookery could actually exist in the heart of London. But Theo, it does and you have experienced it. But you are now quite safe and sound," advised Pratt.

Despite Pratt's offer of another drink, I instinctively, got up from the blue damask covered sofa and walked to the French windows of the Crush Bar and into the loggia and looked down on to a busy Oxford Street now seemingly impervious to the fog. I got out one of my Trichinopoly cigars to smoke and gain some relief and comfort from my ordeal. It did not work, for within moments I felt a tightening in the pit of my stomach followed by a sensation of nausea as the realization dawned upon me on learning from Lodge and Pratt of my near encounter with a calamity in that place called the *Rookery*.

In that desperate place, all manner of atrocities could have been committed against my person and, done so with impunity. I immediately remembered that wrench or hammer flying through the aether and just missing my head. Lodge, on hearing that Jack and I had been separated and had stumbled around in the fog in that ghetto had filled him with terror, and concern as to our well-being. My experiences in the *Rookery* had unnerved me. But it was only when Loge, in tones of real concern, had advised Jack and me what could have happened to us, lost as we were, in the shrouds of fog just a few yards off the Charing Cross Road that the real terror was becoming apparent to me. And I thought that I knew the Lower East Side in New York City.

"Theo, come inside from the fog; you have probably had your fill of it today. Come in and have some more whisky. You look as if you could do with it!"

The person uttering these words, was not Jack, but rather Loge, and to which I gladly responded to the notion.

"But what about our *turn,* are we not supposed to be performing on the stage at some point during this evening?" I inquired.

"You were supposed to be on an hour ago! But do not concern yourself, we can do our *turn* here another evening," said Loge.

And so we went back in to the Crush Bar, but I did not feel like drinking. Instead my thoughts were about Jack and the damn near disastrous consequences of his behavior with the Hackney carriage driver. This was not the first time that I had found myself in an awkward situation, as a direct result of Jack's impetuosity. I remember, quite vividly in fact, as though it were yesterday one particular situation.

I recall the incident, it was at the Carnegie Hall on Seventh and 57th. Street in New York. We had attended a performance of Ezra Kendall, the eminent, or infamous Monologist, whom Jack and I knew, but only slightly.

He had though, been gracious enough to include us in his benefit concert. I liked him and thought him funny and amazingly talented in being able to recite non stop anecdotes and scenarios continually for upwards of forty minutes. We all claimed that he could breathe backwards; that is annunciating words whilst breathing in. I think that he really could so.

Jack however, never really took to him, and thought that he just kind of rattled on about irrelevancies interesting only to the imbecile or deaf. Be that as it may. During any concert, including this particular benefit concert, it was customary for Jack and me to drink heavily at the small Crush Bar, provided by a thoughtful management of the establishment. The first half of the concert had concluded with Ezra doing a rather complex, if sarcastic inverted recital of astonishing length and memory feat and done so to great acclaim by all assembled at the bar.

We all of us gathered in the Crush Bar agreed that his was one of the most accomplished monologues yet heard in quite some years at the Carnegie Hall. Granted, both Jack and I had been drinking liberally, but, it did not in my opinion justify or indeed excuse his outrageous remarks about Ezra Kendall's performance. Jack amazed Kendall's assembled admirers at the bar by insisting that had he been born in Jersey City, Jack's home town, with the same brain, he might have at least possessed the intellectual and memory capacity to carry out his function as a so-called Monologist more effectively. Kendall, by his restricted intellectuality was devoid of this basic requirement.

On that occasion the management, fearing a hostile re-action to Jack's unwarranted remarks, felt it appropriate that we should leave the Crush Bar, and indeed the

Carnegie Hall forthwith. Typically, Jack found the episode to be one of great hilarity, saying as we walked home
in the soaking rain, that it provided the best excuse for
quitting such an onslaught upon his sensitivity.

For myself I was not at all pleased nor amused at being
ejected from a public hall and of missing the second half
of what had up until that moment been an enjoyable
evening of humorous dialogue with anecdotal reminiscences and observations, the tickets for which I had
purchased. On that occasion I did vent my feelings upon
Jack, but he received them with blank indifference, which
only added to my annoyance. In the interest of aesthetics
and the thorough appreciation of monological witticism
and comment Theo, he remarked, I have saved you from
that miserable Kendall masquerading as a Monologist,
rather than an acclaimed interpreter of the facile and
banal of which he is truly the master. Indeed Theo, I have
saved you from a fate worse than death!

That was then, but now we were here in Oxford Street.
I looked into my whisky for consolation from familiarity.

Pratt then got up from his comfortable blue damask
covered sofa at the Crush Bar, offered his hand to us and
made his apologies about having to run his Oxford Music
Hall, but hoped he would meet us again in the, 'near
distant future.' I think Loge saw that I was feeling not
too pleased with the way this day was unfolding and my
look of ennui probably expressed this fact clearly to him.

After a couple of more drinks, the general consensus
was that we ought to go in to the auditorium and cheer
ourselves up with whatever *acts* were extant. On this
occasion, we were unable to get complimentary tickets
to the Balcony from the management of the Music Hall.
Presumably the management of the Oxford Music Hall
were, on this occasion, somewhat anxious to earn ticket

sales after their near disastrous fire of a few days ago. Lodge purchased the tickets, and I noticed they were for the inexpensive area of the auditorium.

The auditorium on this particular evening was filled to the rafters with business men, shop-keepers and clerk types. The women looked as if they were unattached, neither being sweethearts or wives, but probably of the looser variety. All seemed pre-occupied in drinking; be it wine or drink of a bulkier type served from numerous beer-engines ranged around the place.

The Oxford Music Hall, I distinctly remember Lodge informing Jack and me when we were drinking at the Crush Bar in the Criterion Theater, was constructed on the site of the old Boar and Castle *Public House* at number sixteen Oxford Street in 1861. It was done so by Charles Morton, the very same builder of the Canterbury Music Hall that we attended recently. The Oxford Music Hall was based clearly on the concepts developed at the Canterbury Music Hall in the Westminster Bridge Road, Waterloo.

The Canterbury Music Hall might, in this respect, according to Lodge, be considered something as a prototype, where the Music Hall became the opulent design standard and place of entertainment, fit for royalty, that we expect today, here now repeated at the Oxford Music Hall. Most of the ideas and expectations in opulent and plush interiors rather emanate from the Canterbury Music Hall.

I recall when we were at the Canterbury Music Hall, remarking at the time to Jack about the extravagant opulence and luxurious appointment of the place. However, we were now at the Oxford Music Hall and being taken to our seats by Lodge.

Notwithstanding the pervasive smell of burnt timber and material lingering around the auditorium, the man-

Canterbury Music Hall

agement of the Oxford Music Hall had obviously gone to great pains to mask the visual effects of the damage due to the recent fire. No doubt as a consequence of the recent fire which an over enthusiastic danseuse had caused when she was performing her *Fire Bird* suite dance routine. They had achieved this reparation with a generous application of fresh paint which had been applied to various surfaces, and in a remarkably short period of time.

Irrespective of the repairs carried out and re-instating a degree of opulence, I really was not in the mood, but nonetheless, with Jack and Lodge, sat in the cheaper seats of the stalls. The various *acts* and *turns* on stage neither attracted my attention nor gained my approbation. Indeed I must have looked thoroughly bored and indifferent at whatever was being performed on stage that evening. Even Little Bo Peep's, tearful pathos and melodrama, did not move me in the slightest.

However, what I did notice was the fact that Po Peep was able to do her *act* in a number of Music Halls, with impunity, as we had witnessed recently with her appearance twice in two Music Halls in Leicester Square Was there not an *Exclusivity Clause* extant, unreasonably prohibiting Music Hall artistes from performing or appearing in any Music Hall, Variety Theater? Or indeed, any place of entertainment, in a specified area around the establishment in which they have performed, and for at least the duration of one year?

Obviously, Bo Peep has managed to find a way over this restriction, which itself had precipitated a strike by Music Hall artistes, starting at the Holborn Empire and led by the incomparable Marie Lloyd.

I was all for leaving the auditorium and returning back to my St. Pancras Hotel and simply condemning this day to oblivion, and was just about to make my excuses in order to do so, when this day transmogrified into something very different.

1.   The ceiling of the Music Hall was remodeled into a dome shape.
2.   A notorious slum between St. Giles' Church yard and the Charing Cross Road.

Chapter 21

The Woman in Red

Jack and I were booked in to do a *turn* at the famous Oxford Music Hall in Oxford Street but in our attempts to get here had become lost in a particularly desperate place, known as the *Rookery*. A ghetto, a slum in fact, where all manner of atrocities could have been committed against our persons and, done so with impunity in the shrouds of fog just a few yards off the Charing Cross Road. Notwithstanding that unpleasant ordeal, which Jack and I, had survived, we had elected to join the crowds in the auditorium of the Oxford Music Hall and a take in a few of the *turns* extant on stage. I was however, all for retiring back to my hotel and there, attempt to obliterate today's event from my mind. That is until I saw something which more than compensated for my previous trials and tribulations erupting during the day.

In a private crimson plush box located at the end of the lower Balcony level and up against the proscenium arch fronting a deep alcove containing the stage, sat a woman, it was the Woman in Red!

From what I could see, located in our cheap seats, courtesy of Loge's rampant generosity, which of course knew no bounds, she appeared to be attired in a blazing red crushed satin dress. I caught glimpses of her arm when she raised it to view the stage with her opera glasses and she was wearing elbow high black velvet gloves. Her hair was dark auburn and tied up into a short style with a red ribbon and crowned with a silver tiara.

Her lips were those of rouge in color, deep rouge. Around her throat was a dark band of velvet from which hung a solitary jewel, of amethyst. To look at her was to behold a vision of beauty. Hers was a vision which could, with ease dispatch to oblivion other images beauty, such as those depicted in the paintings by Rossetti of which *Astarte Syriaca* [1] is but one. To gaze upon her noble features was a sight to behold; and one which radiated a translucent light.

Despite this avalanche of beauty emanating out of the box, she looked thoroughly bored. She was alone and for relief from the *turns* on stage, she would occasionally peer over the balcony of her red plush private box down to the auditorium and audience alike, with a pronounced expression benign regality upon her face. As though a queen looking down upon her realm. This Oxford Music Hall could have caught fire again, but I should not have noticed it, such was my distraction at beholding the ethereal vision of this Woman in Red.

Occasionally she would avert her gaze in our direction. However, it was difficult to make ourselves noticeable. Lodge, I observed buried his face continually in his playbill of programs to avoid being recognized. It was evident he neither wanted to attract her attention; nor be seen by her, especially, sitting in the cheap seats, in the stalls of this auditorium.

It is to be remembered that Jack and I had first encountered this woman, though we refer to her now as the Woman in Red, when we were in the Crush Bar at the New Bedford Music Hall in Camden Town. She had intercepted Loge whilst purchasing drinks at the bar and had engaged him in a heated discourse about his previous treatment of her. Indeed on how she had been ruined at Loge's merciless hands. At the time Jack and I thought her to be fading actress, seeking to revenge herself upon Loge.

What became apparent as the discourse progressed was that she and Lodge had obviously known each other intimately. The verbal blows which were exchanged between them could only corroborate this fact. But, it was she who had defeated him convincingly; his simply being no match for her, over some previous liaison they had shared in the past, their mysterious past.

She, the Woman in Red had rounded on Lodge on two occasions. In so doing, she had dispatched him forthwith into oblivion with a very effective coups de grâce, both delivered with unerring accuracy.

I remember now that when Lodge was subjected to those two decisive coups de grâce, he looked quite crushed. However, the Woman in Red had not quite finished with him. She had said at the time, for all those assembled at the Crush Bar in the New Bedford Music Hall, '…it was a fate Lodge, a fate worse than death by far, being in your company…'

And it was with that Parthian shot she then staggered out of the ornate and opulent Crush Bar to prepare for her *turn* on the stage. A *turn* I might add, that Jack and I determined there and then that we should not miss. We did not, and when we did see her bathed in the soft ethereal limelight on stage, she was electrifying.

It was to this Woman in Red that I now concentrated my attention. The mere fact of her regal presence in that Balcony level private box was compensation for all that I had endured this day. I would do it again, endure the unendurable, go through any ordeal, just to be in sight of her. However, I realized that my position here in the cheap seats, courtesy of Loge, would be unlikely to attract her attention, nor facilitate such a desirable fortuitous meeting.

I was lamenting this fact, whilst looking indifferently at Leclaire, the King of Conjurors on stage, when all of a sudden she rose from her plush crimson colored velvet seat, as though a phœnix rising from the ashes. And, with one final imperious look down upon her subjects in the auditorium below, pulled her red cape over her shoulders and disappeared though the archway leading out of the red plush private box.

"Come on Jack, we are out of here!" I said.

Jack did not need me to explain, he had been observing all the while my re-action to the Woman in Red. Loge stayed where he was. In a couple of minutes Jack and I had made our way up the stairs to the foyer on the *piano-nobile,* the same level as the private box in which the Woman in Red had been seated. Quite what we expected to achieve by this daring ploy was not immediately obvious to me or in the least bit clear to Jack either, I suspected.

We looked about but saw no sign of her. I instinctively looked over the ornate brass railing down into the ground floor foyer, and there she was. The Woman in Red was gliding across the floor of the foyer towards one of the doors leading into Oxford Street. I grabbed Jack's arm and together we both descended the Grand Staircase up which I had ascended earlier that evening. We headed straight for the entrance door and with out any consideration for others using the doors to gain entry to the Music Hall, barged our way in the Oxford Street. The fog had not abated in the intervening time we were in the

Music Hall. However, I looked both up and down the street. There was no sight of her.

She cannot have gotten very far. She was only a few seconds ahead of us. It then struck me. Had we met her in the foyer or anywhere in Oxford Music Hall, including the bar, we could have claimed chance meeting and taken it from there. We could have made comments on her performance at the New Bedford Music Hall singing that emotional song in memoriam of the loss of the ill-fated *Titanic*. Not to mention her sterling act at the Crush Bar. However, it was now a bit late, since we could hardly go gallivanting around a fog-bound Oxford Street in the hope of precipitating a chance meeting and engaging her in small talk on the footpath of Oxford Street.

Such highfaluting logic soon dissipated into the fog-laden aëther, because at that very instant a Clarence carriage went clattering by on the other side of the street with the Woman in Red sitting upright like a Goddess.

I was minded to commandeer the first carriage that I came across but realized that we could keep up with the carriage simply by walking quickly behind it. This is precisely what we did.

"Perhaps Jack she is going somewhere for dinner or after theater supper, or whatever. Where would one go in this part of London for such refreshment after a show?" I demanded from Jack.

"Beats me Theo," Jack replied, somewhat out of breath, "but probably Café Royal in the Regent's Street, perhaps Kettner's in Soho or even the Criterion at whatever that Circus is called." [2]

"Which direction is she headed?" I asked.

"Her Clarence carriage and we are headed east along Oxford Street towards the junction of the Tottenham Court Road and Charing Cross Road," advised Jack.

A profound feeling of apprehension attended me at the prospect of going anywhere near that Rookery slum near the Charing Cross Road again. Visions of the Woman in Red flitting through that ghetto in her blazing red dress and cape began to fill my chest with a deep foreboding. I need not have worried because at that very moment, both Jack and I could see quite clearly, several constables stopping all carriages from turning right from Oxford Street into the Charing Cross Road.

Her carriage stopped, but we continued walking towards it, whilst the Woman in Red spoke with her liveried coachman. He then jumped down from his high bench and opened the Clarence carriage door for her. Where upon she stepped down to the carriageway and immediately started to walk into the Charing Cross Road!

My heart sank as we too followed the Woman in Red into that road, motivated more to protect her from those persons who infest the Rookery, than by anything else. We were several yards down the road when I looked up to ascertain some kind of bearing. In so doing I noticed, to my great surprise, that we were outside the offices of the sheet music publisher, Francis, Day & Hunter, located here, at 149 Charing Cross Road. Of course, Jack and I know them from their New York operations in Music Hall. In fact I felt certain that we owed them royalties.

Despite this moral acknowledgement, we continued to walk down the Charing Cross Road, when suddenly the Woman in Red turned abruptly into a side street. When we arrived there, it was in fact outside the entrance to the Astoria Theater located there. She cannot have entered the theater, I thought. But it was Jack who pointed out a vague redness in the fog. That must be her and accordingly we started down a lane called Sutton Row, so the road plate informed us.

She continued fleet of foot along this fog-bound lane into what looked like a garden square. Indeed, upon gaining the place we noticed that it was precisely that, and it was into this garden that we followed the Woman in Red.

Then we lost her again. The fog was heavier in this garden where the aëther was stilled and almost stagnant with acridity. Both Jack and I stood there amongst the monstrously overgrown laurel bushes that loomed into view only to recede back into the shrouds of fog as we ourselves moved around the garden.

"Curse this fog Jack, will it ever dissipate?" were the only words I could think to utter.

We both of us stood there motionless.

"There, Theo there quick," said Jack pointing with his cane into the white swirling abyss created by the fog. But then I too saw it. We could just make out her resplendent blazing red silk dress and red cape set against the shrouds of white banks of fog as she flitted momentarily in and out of vision. For a moment she appeared to be standing motionless beneath a protruding ornately designed masonry canopy to a door entrance of a building in Soho Square.

We quickened our pace towards her. But even from the distance we were at, she still appeared distinctively regal and majestic, in spite of the obscuring presence of the all-pervasive fog. Then on our final approach to her we came across cast iron railings. We searched around for an opening through the railings, but only found a gate. It was locked, and thus prevented our continuing to progress after the Woman in Red. By the time we had re-traced our footsteps and founds an alternative route to where she was standing, the shrouds of fog had reclaimed her again.

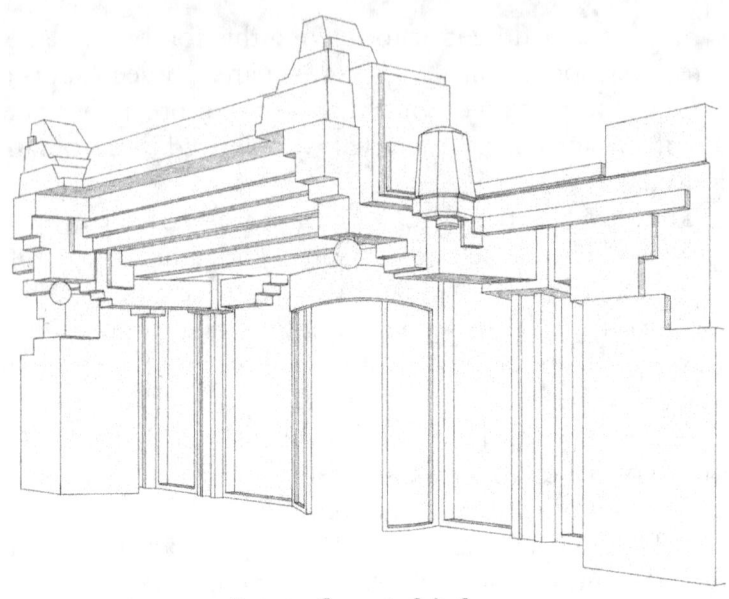

Entrance Canopy in Soho Square

We continued walking along the southern aspect of Soho Square, until we came to a street named Frith. Assuming the Woman in Red had turned left into this street, we too did so and continued down it.

Thus it was under these conditions, that we made our way through Soho, with only the occasional glimpse of the Woman in Red. Twice we lost sight of her, but regained a view of her red distinctive dress in the fog. She seemed to moving with purpose and determination, but in and out of vision as the fog reclaimed her again.

We followed the vision of red as we made our way down Frith Street. Here we lost her again, but rather than continue down Frith Street we instinctively elected to turn right into lane called Bateman Street. There we caught another fleeting glimpse of her as she turned left into a road we later found on arriving there to be named

Dean Street. Here we lost her again, since there was no sight of her. We looked about for some time but no vision of her presented itself to us.

We walked down Dean Street, but still could not pick up a sighting of the Woman in Red and her distinctive red attire. We stopped outside a green painted door opposite a roadway called Bourchier Street. There was in my mind a significance here, but could not determine it, such was my pre-occupation visually searching for her in the fog-bound area we were in.

Our predicament did not in anyway reduce the pleasure others were enjoying. For whilst we were standing on the footpath and strained our eyes for another glimpse of our elusive Woman in Red, others in a room above the green painted street door were laughing and singing.[3] It was against this background of jollity above us that we came to an awful conclusion.

My heart sank as I realized that I had probably lost the Woman in Red to the all-pervasive shrouds of acrid fog.

1. Phoenician goddess of love
2. Regent's Circus
3. They were standing outside below the Colony Room Club into which the Woman in Red had gone.

Chapter 22

The Camden Theater

The previous day had bought much excitement including stumbling around aimlessly in a fog-bound slum, a dangerous slum. But in addition, it had also allowed us to see the Woman in Red sitting in her crimson plush private box whilst we attended the Oxford Music Hall. Alas, we had hoped to make her acquaintance when she left the Music Hall, but we had lost her to oblivion in the fog-laden aëther hanging over the Soho streets. Still one hopes against hope. In the meantime we are to attend the Camden Music Hall, in Camden Town, and there meet with the manager a certain Mr. E G Saunders, and of course, Loge. He has assured us that it would be in our *definite interest* to do so.

Rather than wait for a carriage outside our Porte Cochère, we decided to go into the roadway and intercept one there. Accordingly, we walked along the façade of the St. Pancras Hotel and again, could not help but admire the neo Gothic splendor in the exquisite detailing in the brick work and general ostentatious but thoughtful designs inherent in the architecture of the building. At length we came to a flight of steps leading down from the podium in front of the hotel to Pancras Road in which there were several highly varnished Brougham carriages lined up waiting by the kerb.

The Camden Theater

We approached the one at the head of the queue and I, not Jack, instructed him respectfully to take us to the Camden Theater located in the Camden High Street on the junction of Crowndale Road. I was determined that we were not going to be incommoded by this carriage driver on this occasion, as I had no wish to go gallivanting around a fog-bound Camden Town. Accordingly, our liveried carriage driver duly obliged and flicked his chestnut horses and we headed north. It was not long before we could hear the cries and screams of the inmates as we clattered by the St. Pancras Asylum for Criminally Insane.

"Ought not we to avail ourselves of an evening's entertainment in that Music Hall," said Jack, sarcastically, referring to the asylum, "I feel certain we could learn a trick or two from them!"

"We are headed for Camden Town," I said to Jack, "where we are to meet with Loge; but was this not the place where he experienced his resounding defeat at the hands of that Woman in Red in the New Bedford Music Hall?"

"It was indeed, which makes me wonder why he is keen for us to attend the Camden Theater, and in our *definite interest* to do so," Jack replied.

The fact that the Woman in Red was an artiste who had performed only recently at the New Bedford Music Hall, up the road was not lost on me. And, that there might be another chance of a meeting with her, here in the vicinity of Camden Town.

The horses drew our Brougham carriage along the Crowndale Road towards Mornington Crescent, the home of Walter Sickert and other members of the Camden Town Group of artists. Presently our driver reined his team of horses to the right and in front of the Camden Theater.

I jumped down from the carriage and looked at the front of the Camden Theater, and could see, even in the fog, that the building was quite impressive and elegant. The intricate design of the façade of the Theater was based on Italian Renaissance, complete with arched window reveals, which gave the building an aura of sublime dignity, as though one were entering a church.

This aspect was made all the more so by an ornate copper-plated dome which dominated the structure. The theater was clad in white stone with intermittent areas of red brick work with cement dressing.

Unfortunately the almost reverential aspect of the decoration of façade was some what qualified by the presence of a spurious advertisement poster extolling the virtues of Sutton's Compound Cream of Ammonia plastered to a blank area of red ornate brickwork which formed the wall of the vestibule in front of the theater.

Aside of the intrusive advertisement poster blighting the decorative front of the vestibule, this one-tiered structure running the width of the building and at least seventeen feet in depth, dominated the front of the theater. And, it was from this handsome vestibule that Jack and I ascended a flight of marble steps which lead up to the *piano-nobile* and a selection of well-appointed Crush Bars. The salons of which were decorated with striped silk wall panels and paintings of sylvan scenes in gilded frames, all lending an opulent extravagance and a degree of verisimilitude, as it were, to the establishment. It was obvious, even to the uninitiated, that the place was a warren of interconnecting corridors and passageways.

It was not long before we could hear Loge's somewhat squeaky voice, which always sounds about an octave higher than what one might call normal. We followed the sound of his voice and came upon him, in an ante room, whilst he was in conversation with a man wearing a top hat and tails. On seeing us he motioned Jack and I over to where he was standing.

"Gentlemen, this is the manger, Mr. E G Saunders," Lodge said extravagantly, as though addressing the audience assembling in the adjacent auditorium, "and he has agreed to be our host tonight!"

SUTTON'S COMPOUND CREAM OF AMMONIA:

⚊

CLEANS AND RESTORES COLOURS TO CARPETS

⚊

ACTS AS A DISINFECTANT IN THE SICK ROOM OR HOSPITAL

⚊

HAS NO EQUAL FOR REMOVING GREASE SPOTS FROM CLOTHES

⚊

INVALUABLE TO ENGINEERS FOR REMOVING OIL AND GREASE

⚊

MAKES LINEN WHITE AND WOOLLEN GOODS SOFT

⚊

CLEANS CULINARY UTENSILS AND PLATE

⚊

FOR LAUNDRY PURPOSES SOFTENS HARD WATER

⚊

IN YOUR MORNING BATH REMOVES THAT TIRED FEELING

-0-

We all shook hands and repaired to a very busy Crush Bar. The presence of the Saunders at the bar ensured our being served our whiskies, almost immediately.

"Have you been manager here long?" Jack inquired of Saunders when we had made ourselves comfortable on pale blue moiré covered sofas.

Saunders looked at Jack with a seasoned eye, took a large draught from his glass and then breathed out noisily.

"I have been running the place ever since we opened on 22 December, 1900," informed Saunders, "in addition, I also run the Coronet Music Hall at Notting Hill Gate near the Hyde Park. Interesting theater this place gentlemen, it was designed by the eminent Music Hall architect W G R Sprague and built by Wallis & Company.

"Sprague once confided in me, actually at this bar, that the Camden Music Hall was the fifteenth such establishment that he had designed including the designs for Wyndham's Theater, for which he was justly proud. We even managed to get that Ellen Terry, the well-known tragedian, to come up from Brighton, and to formally open our theater when we had completed building it. And as usual, her speech ran on and on into epic proportions as though she were reciting a Shakespearean melodrama that would make that doom-laden play Macbeth appear as though frivolous pantomime in comparison.

"But we did not meet up this evening to discuss theatrical architecture," said Saunders, "so gentlemen if you will please follow me, I shall be happy to escort you to your seats in the Dress Circle."

We duly fell in with his suggestion and followed him. Saunders lead the way through a truly labyrinth of wide spacious corridors and eventually to our deep comfortable deep seats. All of which were covered in vibrant ruby colored plush upholstering ranged around the cantilever Grand Circle of the auditorium. Indeed the interior appointment of the place was very distinctive in that it was designed and decorated in the rich opulent Louis Quinze Rococo. The majority of the extravagant décor comprised cream and gold embellishment to the walls, complimented by endless rows crimson colored seating in the stalls.

Another distinctive feature of this very well-appointed and elegant auditorium was the level from the pit to the sun-burner in the center of the roof is approximately approaching a height I would estimate at about fifty feet. The decorated plasterwork complete with raised gilded filigree relief surrounding the sun-burner is further adorned with painted with allegorical figures representing the Hours.

The playbill that Saunders then handed out to us informed me that we would be treated to a play loosely based on the concept of what the butler saw. It stared two accomplished Music Hall artistes, so the handbill informed us.

**The Camden Theater
London, NW**

Proudly present
What the Butler
With
Mr. Lionel Rignold
&
Miss Ada Blanche

*Both previously
from a successful run at
Wyndham's Theater
& Savoy Theater*

From the moment the red safety went up, the play was an unmitigated disaster; it dragged on in an agony of suspense and melodrama. I think Jack, who was sitting to my left, away from Saunders and Loge who were to my right, actually nodded off at one stage. The play involved a preposterous plot worthy only of French farce. People with no real interest in the proceedings on stage would appear, look around, utter some inane comment and abandon the stage for other drifting artistes to roam about on.

It can hardly come as a surprise that Wyndham's and the Savoy Theaters, saw fit to remove it off their schedules. Perhaps this is the difference between Music Hall and Theater. After all, I noted, this place is called not the Camden Music Hall, but rather the Camden Theater, perhaps to lend verisimilitude to its establishment and what it promotes.

"Such an extended act would be relegated to the domain of the Burlesque; in that it would never be illuminated by the footlights or limelight of Vaudeville," Jack said, with asperity in his voice, after he had come round due to the noise of the scattered applause at the end.

It was with undiluted relief that we abandoned the auditorium, albeit, a very ornate auditorium for the Crush Bar. Evidently, other members of the audiences had reached the same conclusion, because of their very presence at the Crush Bar. To say the Bar was busy would be an under statement of description of monumentally proportions. The Bar was busy and filled to maximum capacity with people, the numbers of which possibly were equal only to those found in such epics of biblical proportions as the time when Moses led the Exodus out of ancient Egypt under the Pharaohs.

None the less, despite this static tide of humanity hold up in the Bar, we were, with the help or authority of the manager of the Camden Theater, E G Saunders, able to *find* four vacant chairs upon which could sit in comfort.

Saunders had clearly forgotten what Jack and I were, because as soon as we had taken our seats he launched into a remark which indicated this was very much the case.

"I am terribly worried Loge, about the long term effects, of the Music Hall strike, is having on our all important Box Office receipts, especially during the matinées, which as you know earn us good money," said Saunders.

"Is that because Music Hall operators or managers do not pay those artistes for doing matinées?" asked Jack.

"Yes," answered Saunders.

Jack, I noticed, did not disabuse Saunders as to what we were, but continue the questioning as though it were out of a polite inquiry.

"How are those artistes, one wonders, supposed to support themselves if performing and not being paid to do so?" asked Jack nonchalantly.

"Good question," said Lodge, fielding the inquiry on behalf of Saunders, who clearly was the definition of concentrated naïveté in this respect, regarding Jack's line of inquiry. "There is a simple reason why artistes are not paid for doing matinées, in the afternoon. It is because they are rehearsing for the real performance in the evening. We Music Hall owners and managers are kind hearted enough to let them practice on the stage without charging the artistes for doing so!"

"But, you charge the audience attending those matinées, so why not…" said Jack.

"No, no, no," interrupted Lodge, "we have to charge the audience, obviously. They cannot come in for nothing; otherwise our crimson plush red upholstered seats would be occupied by the undeserving poor of an afternoon. Imagine that! Aside of which, we allow members of the public in during the afternoon, during the artiste's rehearsals, to create that 'live with the public,' atmosphere to keep the artistes on their toes when rehearsing during matinées performances I ask you; what could be fairer than that!" replied Loge.

"But what of that *Exclusivity Clause*, the one responsible for the current Music Hall strike?" inquired Jack, earnestly.

"What *Exclusivity Clause?*" asked Saunders, looking specifically at Jack.

"Oh do not bother about that, Saunders, just a small matter, a trifling matter, nothing of great import," replied Lodge, "I will tell you about it when we are not so busy discussing a very fine show you put on this evening. Indeed, I cannot think why I have not seen, what was it called, 'When the Butler Sees' a very fine production. You are to be commended Saunders, commended I say and am not afraid to state that to anybody in the land!"

"We give our matinées artistes performing in the afternoon a bottle of beer and some whelks," said Saunders, whose mental agility had just caught up with the discussion.

"What of that *Exclusivity Clause*, Lodge the question still stands?" inquired Jack.

"Well let me ask you a question which will probably answer your question," said Lodge, "do you consider yourself a fair-minded person Jack?"

"Of course," answered Jack, with a puzzled expression upon his face.

"Precisely! But, I put it to you now, to do justice to that question Jack, one has to go back to when the performing artistes merely turned up at the stage door and asked if they could do a *turn* on the stage. Because the arrangement was informal there was no contract. A few pennies as agreed, for a certain *act*, lasting so many minutes.

"It was only when these informal arrangements were made more formal, that is, to allow Music Hall managers to know, with certainty, what *acts* of an evening they could reasonably be expected to provide, and by which artiste. That is when the very laudable idea of having contracts, for managers and artistes alike, which excluded artistes from drifting off to another establishment and leaving the Music Hall manager without an *act* to put on stage or a gap in the entertainment being offered that evening.

"The *Exclusivity Clause* really benefits the artistes, not the Music Hall manager. It allows for the *consideration* to be present in the contract, giving it legality or substance, as it were, and certainty to the artistes. One might even go as far as to say that the *Exclusivity Clause* favors the artistes in that it *exclusively* allows the artistes to perform with certainty! In this respect there was never any compulsion exerted to sign a contract as in the case of *Williams v. Bayley,"* [1] completed Lodge.

Both Jack and I looked at each other, for we had now seen a side of Loge's character. For the first time I think we both concluded simultaneously just why Lodge has earned the sobriquet of *Loge*. Lodge would claim it derived from the only honorable and noble character in the opera *Das Rheingold*, by Wagner from his *Ring Cycle of the Nibulung*. In fact it would be nearer the truth to describe this operatic fiction *Loge* for what he really was.

If I remember correctly my Wagnerian synopsis about *Das Rheingold,* the opera in which *Loge*, makes his first and last appearance in the *Ring Cycle of the Nibulung,* it was instructive that even Wagner did away with him. Such was his character that Wagner had not wished to deploy him in the remaining three succeeding operas, which, of course, make up the *Ring Cycle of the Nibulung!* The reason being; Loge was, without redemption, simply a Mercurial character, venal, mischievous and totally without inhibition and invariably lurking in the background waiting for or creating opportunities.

It was these characteristics of Loge's personality which allowed him to be evasive, elusive and like, Proteus, more than able to change shape for advantage. Typically, he would answer a question with a question. And, his use of legal nomenclature and terms, such as ...well I put it to you, or his reference to the *Williams v. Bayley* case in defining *undue influence* or indeed the concept *consideration* in a contract, indicated experience of court, if nothing else. Though from what position in the court room, one could not be certain nor determine!

1.   1866. L.R. 1 H.L. 200

Chapter 23

The First Apocalypse

Yesterday whilst drinking in the Crush Bar at the Camden Theater, we had seen a side of Loge's character. Especially in his dealing with the Music Hall strike and the artistes involved in it, which Jack and I had always suspected, but never witnessed first hand. That he could be elusive, evasive even, were consistent aspects of his personality. However, when Lodge joined us for break-fast the following morning, what he had to impart to us indicated that even his Mercurial skills were going to be tested, if not deployed to the utmost.

Lodge came marching into the Grand Dining Room in a distracted and agitated manner, and without any cere-mony, sat himself down at our break-fast table.

"They are done for me, done for me I tell you! I simply cannot contain my disbelief that they are done for me!" Lodge kept repeating this remarkable statement several times whilst he munched on Jack's toast and drank my black coffee.

"Who, what, are done for you, why?" inquired Jack.

"Those creatures, about which do you think I could be possibly referring to?" replied Loge, with traces of incredulity in his voice, "those creatures who run the Metropolitan Board of Works – you know, the First of those Three Apocalypses of Doom, about whom we have spoken at length."

I had never seen the usually suave and able Loge so worked up or animated before. It was only when Jack asked him point blank just what had happened to render Loge into this gibbering wreck confronting us. Needless to say Loge's nervous affliction, his monomania took a decided turn for the worse with a visible increase in intensity as he looked over each shoulder continuously. He did this to the extent that his behavior attracted the attention and comments of other nearby diners having break-fast, who pointed at him with their forks.

At length he recovered himself sufficiently to commence a rather singular narrative in endeavoring to explain to us what event had nearly stricken reasoning and senses clean from his mind.

"Gentlemen," commenced Lodge, "you may remember when we were taking luncheon at my house recently. At the time we discussed briefly the Three Apocalypses of Doom, as it were. The three implacable enemies of Music Halls, and therefore, by implication, drink with jollity, especially in London.

"They are the Salvation Army and its intervention at the famous Eagle Tavern Music Hall in the City Road, resulting in their closing it down permanently on that day, that awful day of infamy.

"The second threat to our Music Halls emanates from that Valkürian woman, Lily Langtry, who campaigns constantly to promote her ridiculous notion of banning alcohol in drink. But it is the fact that she is aided and abetted by the deranged Mrs. Ormiston Chant, who with her cohort of malcontents constantly campaign against what they perceive as the immoral operation of Music Halls. A ridiculous notion, but there you have it.

"They do so in conjunction with the other Apocalypse of Doom; in the form of the Metropolitan Board of Works. This organization not only remains notoriously sympathetic to any number of moral or social reformers. But has its own avowed crusade against the existence of Music Halls, which they consider to have a corrosive influence of moral turpitude, how ever one defines that," said Lodge.

"Just what is this Metropolitan Board of Works and how come it has gotten you all riled up Loge?" asked Jack.

"This Metropolitan Board of Works," continued Loge, "is a public board charged with overseeing construction and the operation of buildings in the London area. In 1855 a misguided Parliament passed the Metropolis Management Act 1855 setting up the Metropolitan Board of Works with offices in Dean Street, in Soho. The Board was called to life on 22 December, 1855. The basic rôle of the Board was to construct sewers, build parks, and lay new roads such as Shaftesbury Avenue, Northumberland Avenue or the Victoria Embankment to tame the Thames.

"As the years went by the Board took on more powers to itself, including the responsibilities formally exercised by Justices of the Peace under the old Theatrical Regulations Act 1843. It was the provisions in this act that formed the basis of Music Halls and theater regulation within the London Metropolitan area. It was a bad day when the Board extended its powers in order to regulate Music Halls; they should have stuck to building deep level sewers, a task they were eminently suited for and apparently gifted at.

"The reason the Metropolitan Board of Works made incursions into the regulation of Music Halls and theaters, was in part due to the fact they were responsible for the

London Fire Brigade. Accordingly, they argued, it is not only their responsibility to put fires out; but by virtue then, to prevent fires and insist on fire protection régimes being put in place, especially in public buildings, as theaters. This fact need not have been problematic, unless of course, one feels that the public needs to be over-protected.

"What became problematic was the of regulation of Music Halls for fire reasons, transmuting into regulating Music Hall for moral reasons as identified by that lethal combination of the other Apocalypses of Doom; the Salvation Army, Ormiston Chant and Lily Langtry. Ever since then, the régime at the Metropolitan Board of Works has been one of belligerence to the operators of Music Halls and theaters in London, by using the fire regulations as a weapon in order to close, reduce, ban or in some other way curtail the activities of our musical establishments.

"Yet they are not above suspicion themselves and have often been cited in numerous cases or allegations of a series of scandals involving bribes and corruption during the 1880s, leading to a Royal Commission investigation. In addition, the Board was never popular with the people of London who are required to fund the Board with increased taxes on alcohol and coal.

Take the case of the London Pavilion in Shaftesbury Avenue. This avenue was laid out by the Metropolitan Board of Works as an improvement project to ease traffic congestion in the area around the Regent's Circus.

"The London Pavilion scandal erupted from the purchase in 1879, by the Metropolitan Board of Works of the *old* Pavilion Music Hall in Regent's Circus, because the site was to form part of the proposed construction of Shaftesbury Avenue. However, there was some time between the acquisition of the land on which the theater stood and when the actual construction of the avenue would commence. Accordingly, the *old* Pavilion Music Hall was leased to Mr. R.E. Villiers, a Music Hall operator on a short lease. Villiers paid rent to the Board, but, as it was later found, also paid to the Board's chief land appraiser, F W Goddard, a retainer to maintain favors.

"In 1883, the short term lease came up for re-appraisal as construction of Shaftesbury Avenue was now imminent. Again, Villiers liaised with Goddard and a certain T J Robertson, a surveyor employed by the Board, in order to negotiate leasing the remainder of the site on the corner of Shaftesbury Avenue and the Regent's Circus. Accordingly, this land would then be available to Villiers to enable him to construct a *new* Pavilion Music Hall. An agreement was subsequently concluded between them, which involved part of the site domain being reserved for use as a Public House, and disposed to a Mr. W W Grey, as the tenant. It later transpired that Grey was in fact the brother of Robertson, though for obvious reasons - in the surname, this fact was not at first appreciated.

"Still staying with the London Pavilion, this type of new *Variety Theater* with its lack of alcohol but increase in morality was promoted by the Metropolitan Board of Works to the deliberately extravagant and opulent designs of James Ebenezer Saunders. Who was also an employé of the Board and had not designed much in the way of architecture, but was *retained* as the architect, even though he was woefully inexperienced.

"So even where property owners wanted to build, say a theater or hotel, as the Grand Hotel or Metropole Hotel both in the Northumberland Avenue, that is, land owned by the Metropolitan Board of Works. They were invariably *encouraged* to use persons employed by the Board, such as the inexperienced Saunders!

"However, the saga continues, in that Robertson told Villiers in the November of 1884 that the Metropolitan Board of Works will be inviting offers lease the site for the new London Pavilion. An annual rent offer of £2,700 was made by Villiers, based on confidential rental value information conveyed by Robertson to Villiers. The Board instructed its under-surveyors, Goddard and Robertson to examine the offer, which they did reporting that the value of the site was nearer £3,000 per annum, rather than £2,700.

"Villiers agreed to this re-valuation and the revised rent was presented to the Metropolitan Board of Works for approval, which was forthcoming even though and alternative bid, in the sum of £4,000 was submitted. Here the Board thought it had gained an increase in rent of £300, where in reality they had lost £1000 in rental income due to their scheming employés.

"Typically, where this loathsome Metropolitan Board of Works really incurred our wrath is on those occasions where Music Hall and theater managers are reminded about an impending inspection for fire safety, or other such matters. They would be reminded by an assistant architect, employed by the Board, a certain John Hebb, who would carry out these inspections. His rôle at the Board was to carry out inspection of theaters for fire regulations and safety matters, which meant he had the real power to close theaters down on the flimsiest of pretexts.

"Hebb, before commencing his inspection would implicitly suggest that the manager might like to make available to him free seats, to enable him to assess the theater when being used! Given his powers, most Music Hall and theater managers would arrange for such seats to be available for him, though usually behind a column or some distance from the stage.

"However, members of the Metropolitan Board of Works have their corrosive fingers in other areas that affect life in the Metropolis, and again seem incapable of understanding precisely what they are about, or ought to be about.

"Take the court case of *Metropolitan Board of Works versus McCarthy* in the House of Lords in 1874, where it was held that the Board must pay compensation to the plaintiff, McCarthy who was the owner of a warehouse in Blackfriars. This came about when, without any aforethought, the Board constructed the highway called the Victoria Embankment. But in so doing, cut off the plaintiff's access the public highway to his dock on the river front.

"It was held that in so constructing the Embankment road the Board had in effect physically interfered with the plaintiff's legal right to conduct his business, including access to his dock on the Thames shore. The numbers of law suits one could cite against the Board are legion. But more importantly, these factors simply indicate the arrogance and remoteness from reality, under which that Metropolitan Board of Works operates, and aptly displays at every opportunity.

"As I have said before, the Board should restrict themselves to the construction of deep level sewers, for which they are eminently suited and unsurpassed in that ability," informed Lodge, to a stunned Jack and I including other diners, taking break-fast, in the Dining Room at the St. Pancras Hotel.

Lodge was clearly winding himself into an apoplexy of outrage as he reminded himself about the activities of this loathsome organization, for which he retains the highest disgust. It was also possible that Loge, thus incensed, may well have tried to induce himself into an uncontrolled delirium of indignation, had Jack not brought him out of his growing semi trance.

"So what is the point of this diatribe Loge?" inquired Jack.

"The point is Jack," replied Loge, "that Music Hall, and the artistes who work them, are evolving yet again as a result of the rôle which Metropolitan Board of Works plays in our business. We have seen, in particular the London Pavilion, a product of the Metropolitan Board of Works and its corrupt ways. But also, the Board's corrupt ways in changing Music Hall, especially in demanding that the consumption of alcohol be banned from the auditorium, thanks to our friend Langtry.

"And that the style of *acts* or *turns* is brought into line with what a bunch of sewage engineers at the Metropolitan Board of Works, consider suitable, and not what the Music Hall managers or the public want. Again, thanks to the efforts of Ormiston Chant and the Salvation Army. This was given clear credence as you know when the Command Performance in front of the monarch, King George V[th.] banned the likes of Lloyd and Tilley, to name but two artistes the public hold in high esteem and affection, to say nothing of regard.

"What is likely to happen now gentlemen, is that our Music Halls will irretrievably transmute into Variety Theater of the respectable sort, where each *turn* or *act* has been homogenized into something so clean and safe, as to render it boring. This is the legacy afforded us from the Metropolitan Board of Works.

"Accordingly, a few of us impresarios and Music Hall managers have been resisting the Board's every move, to make Music Hall irrelevant - by the imposition of harsh regulations upon us. In this way they hope to kill us off; ostensibly by systematically alienating our audiences and driving them away. They intend to achieve this deplorable state of affairs by making we Music Hall operators and impresarios put on facile and nonsensical shows, of the type we experienced last night when we witnessed that farce called, '*What the Butler Saw*' at the Camden Theater.

"It is in our interest to provide the public with what it wants; hence my journey to Chicago to look for new talent. Our real fear is that if we do not keep Music Hall as the main stay of entertainment, we will lose our audience to Variety or indeed something called *Kinema* invented by a couple of brothers by the name of Luminaire. Already in certain theaters in London one can experience this thing called the *Kinema*.

"Why, even since 1897 the Palace Theater at Cambridge Circus has been showing films from the American Biograph Company on a regular basis, including Kinemacolor. There is now talk about constructing purpose built *Kinemas* rather than adapting existing Music Halls and theaters.

"Those films being shown at the Palace Theater are of the 2¾ inches width type, which creates a clear moving image capable of filling the theater's proscenium arch. This development of *Kinema* can only augment the end of Music Hall, as we know it, if our audiences are inveigled to resort to the *Kinema*, as their main form of entertainment. It remains a probability gentlemen, that Music Hall in London, and perforce the provinces if not the actual Empire, has reached its apotheosis, even as we speak. More alarmingly, the Metropolitan Board of Works is making this real concern and fear, happen!" said Lodge, with a sadness in his eyes.

"Loge," I said, "both Jack I understand what you are saying, and you are to be commended for your stance. But, just what is it has gotten you into this state of repressed anxiety?"

"You say I ought to be commended for my stance," responded Loge, "perhaps, but clearly my stance has been getting in the way of the intentions and plans of the Metropolitan Board of Works. And, it remains entirely feasible a notion, that I am having an impact on them. I know this to be the case for this morning gentlemen, this very morning gentlemen I was served with a writ. A writ issued by the very same Metropolitan Board of Works!"

Both Jack and I looked at each other, as indeed, other diners did, in total bewilderment whilst shrugging our shoulders.

"It is all so obvious to me now," said Lodge, "the Metropolitan Board of Works wishes to revenge themselves upon my person."

Obviously Lodge had irritated that Board and had attracted their vengeance. It is of course a well known axiom propounded by no less a philanthropist than Machiavelli: always take out the loquacious leaders who inspire and thereafter those weaker persons will be vanquished.

It is possible that if the Board can dispatch Loge into oblivion; other managers or impresarios will fall in line with the policy of the Metropolitan Board of Works. For the moment now they would appear to have Loge in their sights. I wondered, did they realize what this might mean for them!

"What will you do now Loge?" I asked.

"I shall deal with this challenge; as one would simply deal with head cold,' said Lodge, with inordinate confidence.

"What, put a bullet in your head?" asked Jack, in tones of concentrated innocence.

Chapter 24

The Incomparable Impresario

Our friend and impresario, Michael W. Lodge, Loge to his close acquaintances, has been indicted under the Theatrical Regulations Act 1843 [1] in which are contained the provisions relating to the current law governing the operation of theaters and performance of plays in England. It would appear that Loge has been indicted on numerous counts under this statute, the most serious being a charge of running an unruly house, sometime in the recent past.

Lodge had stormed into the Grand Dining Room at the St. Pancras Hotel and up to our break-fast table. Having advised us of the indictment served on him, he had now abandoned us in favor of seeking counsel's advice at Lincoln's Inn. But before leaving us, imparting this resounding piece of information.

"You will see, they shall not have their way we me!" Lodge repeated this remark several times as he made his way out of the Grand Dining Room

We too left our break-fast and made our way to a small library located in one of the salons to see if we could apprise ourselves of Loge's legal situation, merely for the purpose of appreciating fully his dilemma.

Though I suspect Jack was motivated for other more sensational reasons, by his nonchalant remark expressed to me.

"It will be interesting to see, no a master class, to witness the aptly named *Loge,* evade his responsibilities outlined in the indictment," said Jack, with a glint in his eye. "And that nick-name of his, that sobriquet derived from Wagner's *Das Rheingold* opera, and with good reason. Forgive me Theo, but what did Loge tell us, in this respect about his name, when we first met with him in Chicago?"

"The same as he told us when we met with him in his town house for lunch with Bella; something along the lines of why people refer to him as *Loge,*" I replied, "did it not go something well, like this?"

'No, gentlemen, no formality here,' Loge had said to us at the time, 'I prefer that my new close acquaintances call me '*Loge*' they do so in honor of the only noble character in the opera *Das Rheingold,* by Wagner from his *Ring Cycle of the Nebulous*? An amusing tale based on the Völsunga saga of Teutonic gods, mortals, female warriors and heroes plotting, in the depths of the Nibelung mountain, on how to get their grubby little hands on an ill-fated golden band. In addition to a demented woman, a Valkürian no less, besotted with her dead hero lover, who incidentally is burning away on a flaming funeral pyre.'

"If I remember correctly Theo, this *Loge*, was a Mercurial character, venal mischievous and totally without inhibition and invariably lurking in the background waiting for opportunities, if not creating them" Jack concluded.

It was Jack who offered up some surprising information in respect of Lodge's predicament as we consulted Statutes at Large, a book containing out of date theater law in relation to Lodge's predicament.

"Amazing Theo, listen to this. This is English law as described in this preamble in the glossary.

'Over the last four hundred years English theater has been subject to repressive laws and persecution than probably any other European country. The Church considered theater to be a thinly disguise pagan ritual and promptly outlawed its performance, with stiff penalties for even minor infractions. Eventually, however, the Church did relent and allowed some basic, albeit strictly controlled dramatic expression only, as Miracle Plays as a means of explaining biblical stories to the illiterate masses. The undeserving poor, as they were, to the Church.

'There has therefore always been a tight régime of censorship and control affecting English theater and this was always the case even in Tudor times under Henry VIIIth. and re-iterated repeatedly during the English Civil War, which led to a rise of puritanical fervor, called the Commonwealth. Theater all but disappeared during this twelve year period of intolerance and religious zeal under the puritans. Theater in the public domain was only allowed when the monarchy was restored under King Charles IInd.

'But given the inherent legislation affecting theater in England, was strictly regulated. The Crown, would grant permission in the form of Letters Patent, in - particular to Sir Thomas Killigrew and to Sir William Davenant. These Letters Patent allowed them to have performed in the Theater Royal in Drury Lane, and also at the Theater Royal at Covent Garden '*straight* drama involving spoken dialogue. Other theaters, not granted Letters Patent, had to express their acting sentiment not in words, but in mime!

'At about 1660 an officer of the Crown emerges called the Lord Chamberlain. He was charged, in his rôle as advisor to the monarch, to enforce the provisions contained within the granted Letters Patent and to monitor their implementation in making sure the law was neither being broken or abused.

'The powers of the Lord Chamberlain were re-defined and restricted by the provisions contained in the Theatrical Regulations Act 1843. Thereafter the Lord Chamberlain could only intervene and order a play stopped, where he felt that, '...*it is fitting for the preservation of good manners, decorum or of the public peace so to do.*'[2] The 1843 Act also empowered local Justices of the Peace to license theaters, and helped remove the monopoly of theaters operating on the Letters Patent to the disadvantage of non patent theaters. This one piece of legislation effectively facilitated the unhindered spread of popular saloon theaters at Public Houses or supper rooms leading on to the development of the Music Hall.

'Typically, the penalties for performing, in secret behind closed doors were stiff, as they were brutal. These fines were imposed on the manager of the establishment, not the actors performing the illegality. On the basis that the manager would inevitably have the wherewithal to pay the heavy fine; whereas the iterant artistes may not have the necessary funds with which to do so, nor an address at which to apprehend them!

'Further, any contract, signed between the manager of an establishment and the artors, might at any moment become illegal by operation of the law. That is, if the play is deemed to be in contravention of the Theatrical Regulations Act, notably section 12, making the fulfill-ment clause of the contract, null and void, and the play cancelled at cost to the establishment.

'Irrespective of the powers exercised by the Lord Chamberlains many plays were performed in public as a result of innovative and resourceful playwrights. Often, they could write lines which appeared innocuous according to how they were spoken with the ingenious use of lascivious innuendo, double entente or simple inflective. This clever use of words and sound could defeat the examination by the Lord Chamberlain. This grammatical resort is still extant in Music Halls today.

'A seasoned practitioner in this area was Marie Lloyd who found herself on numerous occasions in trouble with the censors both in New York and England as indeed other artistes did too. Witness Lloyd's appearance inn 1896 before the censors for the Music Halls, called the Vigilance Committee.

'On that occasion, she sang several well-known popular songs at the hearing. No criticism was attracted to any song, as all in fact, were consider to be innocent in character. What the Committee had not been subjected to, whilst Lloyd sang her songs, was the attended performance. Complete with her sultry looks and gesticulations, which of course could qualify and innocent sounding song into one of extreme vulgarity or obscenity,"' completed Jack

We sat back in our green button down leather armchairs and considered just what territory Lodge was moving into. We stayed in the hotel, preferring to play the rôle of exhausted thespians lounging around in a perfected listless manner, worthy of *Camille aux Dames*. No luxury or pampering could be too much or excessive. It was thus how we spent the afternoon, away from the cares of the world including the fog, Loge and his Metropolitan Board of Works, and their sights on his dapper person.

It was therefore with a feeling of presentiment mixed with trepidation that Lodge came into the salon and made straight towards us as though at the head of a cortège, such was his down cast demeanor.

"They think that if they can break me they have won their battles over who governs the Music Hall. But they shall learn, they shall learn that to engage with me is to invite the ill-fated, where no quarter can ever be given. It is all, or it is nothing!" thus spoke Michael Lodge, impresario extraordinaire before he had even gained upon our position.

"Did you seek counsel's advice, and what was the outcome?" asked Jack.

"There is but one, and only one outcome Jack, for person in my position. Fight, we must fight!" said Loge, responsibly.

I noticed, as did Jack, the pleural of *we*, must fight, declared by Lodge.

"What exactly is the specification for the indictment for which the Metropolitan Board of Works demands your blood?" inquired Jack.

"In the main," replied Lodge, "I was responsible for allowing a play, a play which I had previously vetted, and thought we had the Lord Chamberlain's approval. As it transpired later, the actors decided at the last minute, without informing me, to incorporate a scene which had, in fact, been specifically banned and approval withheld. Accordingly, it is this play and other minor infractions, including those appertaining to fire safety which form the reason why the Board is determined to revenge themselves upon my person."

"Would that vetting be, as a provision, within the meaning of the Theatrical Regulations Act of 1843, specifically section twelve?" I asked in a nonchalant manner.

Lodge gave me a sideways glance, complete with a glint in his eye.

"Well yes and no," replied Lodge, "but there are other

remedies available to me. The Board is charged with matters relating to buildings, including safety and fire concerns, not censorship. Section twelve remains in the province of the Lord Chamberlain, but the two together could prove to be awkward. The first thing to do is to organize the Fourth Estate [3] in our defense. But gentlemen come, for we have challenges to meet and over which we shall all three of us ultimately prevail!"

Loge's generous use of the pleural in incorporating Jack and me as integral co-defenders with his resorting to such words as, *our, we, all* and *us* left me with a feeling of vulnerability about the repercussions from something I remained vaguely unfamiliar with, not being an impresario.

However, but thus galvanized, we all stood up and followed Lodge, hopefully not into obscurity, ridicule or oblivion.

---

1. Also known as the Theaters Act 1843
2. Theatrical Regulations Act 1843, Section 12 - Running an unruly house.
3. The Gentlemen of the Press

Chapter 25

The Redoubtable Loge

It seems that the inevitable conflict between Loge, representing the freedom of the Music Hall and indeed all theaters and the bureaucratic but repressively moral forces of the infamous Metropolitan Board of Works were now ranged to break out and engage one another. The Board seeks to revenge themselves on Loge who clearly has been but a thorn in their side, as it were. But of course there are other issues at stake here, including the inalienable right of the public to choose what and how it wishes to be entertained without influence from religious or moral crusaders who are motivated by their own personal rational, let alone by a bunch of sewage engineers of which the Metropolitan Board of Works is comprised.

We had accompanied Lodge to various meetings with persons engaged in Music Hall and to a couple of newspaper offices in the Fleet Street area of London. After those meetings Lodge had informed us that he had two more meeting of a, *delicate nature,* as he put it, which he would prefer to conduct by himself. Accordingly, we had availed ourselves of a passing Barouche carriage and returned to our hotel. Upon entering the hotel through its ornate vestibule we headed straight for the well-appointed bar for obvious reasons.

"What can I fix you two gentlemen, the usual?" inquired our considerate bar-tender.

"Yes, please do," I answered.

"I confess Theo," informed Jack, "just what is Lodge up to. Apparently he has been indicted under some legislation or other, but what gets me is why he does not leave it to his attorneys, after all he must have several of them stashed away in numerous places?"

"I do not think Lodge is the kind of person who would delegate such responsibility to anyone but himself. Do not forget Jack, Lodge is an impresario, albeit of the *Sans Pareil* [1] type, and what is even…" I said.

"Mr. Houston, Mr. Theodore Houston?" asked an anonymous voice behind us.

It was the bar-tender who pointed the voice in my direction.

"Cable-gram for you sir," said the bell-boy, as Jack gave him a coin of the realm.

I tore open the buff colored envelope.

"It is from Loge," I said, handing the paper to Jack.

```
HAVE SECURED ++++ CHARING X
HOTEL ++ 4TH.  ESTATE TOMOR-
ROW ++ 11-AM ++ APPRECIATE
YOU BEING THERE ++ PLEASE
BRING JUDD, VENTRILOQUIST'S
DUMMY AS WITNESS ++ MAY NEED
HIM FOR CHARACTER REFERENCE
+++LOGE…. .
```

"What is with Judd that he wants that we should bring with us?" was Jack's response.

"There is no reply," I said to the bell-boy, "but, please go out into the foyer and get me every early edition evening newspaper, including late editions of the dailies."

By the time we had gotten ourselves another whisky each, including mine with a dash of the Coca~Cola and its vitally uplifting ingredients, the bell-boy had returned with an armful of newspapers. Having paid him for his errand we turned and scoured all the banner headlines. I found one, it was in the *Evening Standard,* and it confirmed my thoughts.

'Impresario indicted under ancient powers and charged by MBW'

Here is another headline out of the *Daily News*; the report goes on to state the fact of his indictment and also what Loge was reported to have said, whilst being served with legal papers!

Well known theatrical agent and impresario indicted

'...that Michael Loge, the well-known impresario was today fighting for his mere existence and right to put on shows and Music Hall which the public have a right to choose to attend.

'..."I shall have my day, I will not be silenced by that Board, you will see!" he is reported to have uttered...'

'..."I shall be holding a press conference at the Charing Cross Hotel Tomorrow at eleven o'clock, and there I will vindicate myself of these scurrilous charges brought by an over-bearing Metropolitan Board of Works, which is nothing more than an unelected interfering public body which seeks only to revenge themselves on me, because I speak out against their moral tyranny and crusade that they wish to impose on us the public in what we may wish to see and enjoy on the stage; or what we may not enjoy. As I have said before, the Board should limit their activities to constructing deep level sewers, at which they eminently excel. Not trying to govern our great British Music Halls of which we can all be proud,"…' it is reported Lodge said, whilst giving what looked like a 'V' symbol with his two fingers.[2]

Lodge had organized a meeting with the Fourth Estate with commendable haste at a place called the Charing Cross Hotel, which from memory was above the Hungerford Music Hall, or rather the Hungerford Palace of Varieties, as we were corrected by its diminutive actor manager, Marmeduke Gatti.

Given the fact that tomorrow will be a day of great importance for Lodge, if no one else, Jack and I decided to retire early and be refreshed in the morning and able to withstand the vicissitudes the day would invariably impose on all good men.

1. Without compare
2. V possibly for Valiant?

Chapter 26

The Fourth Estate

Lodge has been indicted by the Metropolitan Board of Works, under some obscure law relating to public conduct at the theater for a play he unwittingly allowed to be performed in public. In addition, the Board, called to life on the 22 December, 1855, and ostensibly charged with the construction of public buildings, structures and deep-level sewers in the Metropolis, has inherited certain magisterial powers under the old Theatrical Regulations Act of 1843 in respect of public safety including fire regulations in public buildings. One of which, at the material time, was operated by Lodge.

Jack and I got through our break-fast in double quick time, such was our enthusiasm to get to Charing Cross and get a front row seat at the press conference organized today. It will be here that our friend and mentor, the impresario, Michael Lodge will attempt to astound the world with his address to the Fourth Estate gathered for that one purpose.

We consulted the Concièrge's indispensible Bäedeker's Guide to London and found that the quickest way to this Charing Cross would be to ride an urban rail road train called the Metropolitan-Circle. That rail road would take us all the way to Charing Cross Underground Station, in the vicinity of which is the Charing Cross Hotel.

"Our journey can start from below this very Hotel by entering King's Cross Metropolitan Station' whatever that means. And ride that Metropolitan-Circle urban rail road," I announced.

Accordingly, we left the comfortable and opulent surroundings of our hotel, this time enthusiastically, and were immediately enveloped in swirls of the acrid fog that still shows no signs of dissipating. Eventually we managed to locate the entrance to the urban rail road station from which the Metropolitan-Circle, departs, en-route to Charing Cross Underground Station. After some uncalled for discourtesy whilst purchasing our tickets, an adjunct activity which appears to attend such a function, especially in London, we made our way down to the platforms.

A signboard indicated upon which platform we should wait for the Metropolitan-Circle. Again we were reminded, whilst looking for the correct platform, of the plethora of gaudy advertisements including one for artificial legs plastered on every available surface, including those of rail road equipment and buildings. The display of such advertisements made it difficult to search for useful rail road information, and indeed, almost impossible to achieve.

In order to ascertain just how we might travel to Charing Cross, we approached a rail road servant upon the platform, dressed in his black velveteen uniform with red piping. He listened politely and attentively to our inquiry and our wish to get to Charing Cross, and did he know the way? He then informed both Jack and myself, in an indifferent and supercilious manner, that, yes he did know the way, thanked us for our polite inquiry and then, promptly turned on his heels and marched off quickly down to the far end of the platform! This was

POTTS'S

IMPROVED ARTIFICIAL LEGS,

WITH
GRAY'S IMPROVEMENT

PATRONISED BY
PRINCE ERNEST OF HESSE PHILLIPSTHAL
THE MARQUESS OF ANGLESEY
THE FIRST NOBILITY AND GENTRY AND THE
MOST EMINENT SURGEONS
THROUGHOUT EUROPE, AND ALLOWED BY ALL
TO BE THE PERFECT DESCRIPTION OF
ARTIFICIAL LEG HITHERTO PRODUCED.

THEY ARE MADE SOLELY BY WILLIAM GRAY, OF
10 CHARLES STREET, GROSVENOR SQUARE, LONDON,
APPRENTICE, MANY YEARS MECHANICAL ASSISTANT,
AND NOW SUCCESSOR TO THE INVENTOR, THE LATE
CELEBRATED MR. POTTS, OF CHELSEA.

ALL PERSONS WANTING ARTIFICIAL LEGS
SHOULD COMPARE THEIR MERITS WITH ANY
OTHERS AT PRESENT MADE.

EVERY INFORMATION MAY BE OBTAINED BY APPLYING
AS ABOVE.

AN EXPERIENCED FEMALE PROVIDED
TO ATTEND LADIES

ALL LETTERS MUST BE POST PAID.

not the first time that I had been the recipient of confident behaviour at the hands of a truculent rail road servant, and on the platform.

At that moment a locomotive hauling several carriages, each painted in purple livery, came thundering down the side of the platform. We and a tide of humanity boarded the carriages. Eventually after an inordinately long delay, the train began to progress slowly along the platform edge heading east. Minutes later we arrived at Farringdon Street Metropolitan Station. This fact in itself confirmed that we were on the right train, I think.

A few minutes later, having passed through several stations, we pulled into Aldgate Metropolitan Station. Here we changed for a train in green livery of the District Rail Road operating on the Inner Circle Line that would take us through Mark Lane, Monument, Cannon Street, Mansion House, Blackfriars and Temple underground stations. Again we waited for some time before moving on. Whilst doing so, we found ourselves discussing several blatant advertisement posters affixed to the platform walls. Do the rail road companies, we inquired of ourselves, deliberately stop their trains in order to compel their passengers to have to read various and sundry advertisements?

We had no option but to read one particular glaring bill poster immediately in front of our train window extolling the rather dubious virtues of Pear's soap. The image on the poster took the form of a triptych divided by two classical fluted pilasters creating three spaces. Two of which were occupied by paintings of statues from classical antiquity of figures representing the goddess *Venus*. The other statue portrayed, being that of *Hygeia*, presumably the goddess of health. The larger central panel showed a nymph basking on a bed of flowers having her feet washed by an indulgent maid.

I recognized the original painting. It was by an artist called Albert Moore of the New Olympian School, the classical rivals, I think, to the Pre-Raphælelite Brotherhood, if I remembered correctly. Jack too, I noticed was also engrossed in the advertisement. Adjacent to this classical image was a more patriotic poster, advertising the Royal Military Tournament at its new home in an exhibition hall located at a place called Earl's Court. And that the tournament has been authorised by the gracious permission of our friend, his grace the Duke of Cambridge – Commander-in-Chief and stalwart thespian.

All very interesting I thought, but, quite why one would want to observe soldiers parading around an exhibition hall was a mystery to me. Presumably, one would have thought that they had seen enough military action, of the deadly kind, whilst serving in the army during various campaigns in the far flung reaches of their British Empire. In addition, the prospect of seeing their old regimental comrades, or what there was left of them, marching around aimlessly, seemed to me to be incongruous. Even with the gracious permission granted by their Commander-in-Chief, his grace the Duke of Cambridge.

At last our train began to glide down the side of the platform and straight into a tunnel emerging a few minutes later at another intervening station. Eventually we did gain the Charing Cross Underground Station and left its precincts to find ourselves standing on the Victoria Embankment near an Obelisk looming up into the fog.

Jack took the lead from here on, and having gotten our bearings, we reëntered the station and groped our way up Villiers Street and towards a main thoroughfare called the Strand in which the Charing Cross Hotel is located.

"Do tell me Jack," I asked, "is this Villiers Street named

The Obelisk, Victoria Embankment

for Mr. R.E. Villiers, the person who leased the *old* Pavilion Music Hall from the Metropolitan Board of Works and was the center of the scandal?" I asked.

"Beats me Theo," was Jack's reply, "but I will wager it will not beat Loge!"

Having reached the Strand, we turned left into the court yard of the hotel, and entered the building through the ornate decorated stone built Porte Cochère forming a vestibule to the main entrance to the Charing Cross Hotel. It was through this decorated doorway that we both walked quickly in our eagerness to secure the brightness and fog-less space of the hotel. I threw open the main doors of the hotel and stepped into a brilliance of incandescent light of the foyer emanating from large lanterns of glass and chandeliers suspended from the ceiling which illuminated the plush crimson silk broadloom carpet below.

We ascended the broad grand staircase up to one of the main salons located on the *piano-nobile* and looked about for the impresario Loge. It was he who would be directing this meeting and, marshalling the Fourth Estate. It was also to these gentlemen of the press, that Loge would be held accountable in his replies and mannerism when answering their inquiries about his impresario activities. It was into their hands he would also have to consign his soul, and by implication, his destiny, Box Office receipts and possibly ours.

We stepped into a very ornately appointed grand salon. The room was daunting, as it was immense and decorated to an exquisite and voluptuous level of opulence with no expense spared in creating this lavish and extravagantly appointed interior. Indeed the large room was reminiscent of classical Rome. Each of the four walls making up the salon, were finished with a highly decorated and deep overhanging perimeter architrave.

On each wall this elaborate cornicing was punctuated by a wide low arched opening, but screened off with golden brocade drapes. Each arch was supported by two pink *Rosso Magnaboschi* marble pilasters, in the form of piers, with collars of gold.

Adjacent to these piers were round smooth columns made of the same pink marble. These columns supported the ornate architrave upon which were placed stone statues of angels. Their wings were outstretched, as though in the form of a corbel, supporting the intricate white stucco ceiling above, that comprised generous designs in plaster and finished in raised gilt filigree detailing.

Suspended from the center of the ceiling by an intricate chain, was an ornate and highly polished brass chandelier, from which radiated a soft incandescent light illuminating the deep red patterned silk carpet upon which we were standing. Lodge was there in his favorite electric blue silk frock-coat holding forth in the midst of a large group of well-dressed gentlemen. Within a few moments he saw us; and having extricated himself from the group, came up to shake our hands with inordinate enthusiasm.

"Ah Theo, Jack, good to see you again, did you perchance bring Judd, the ventriloquist's dummy? No, oh you did not, pity as he would have been indispensible. But please, please do follow me," he said this, whilst at the same time gesturing to the group of gentlemen, he had just left.

They too followed Loge into the Blue Imperial Room. It was in this salon that the session would to take place and within a few minutes, Lodge had gotten the gentlemen of the press from the salon and assembled in the Blue Imperial Room. In the mean time as Jack and I made ourselves comfortable on Chippendale chairs, the seats of which were covered in resplendent moiré silk, other persons came into the salon, looked around and took their places. Whatever else Loge may be, he was clearly more than capable of organizing and attracting quite a considerable gathering in this elegant Blue Imperial Room located on the *piano-nobile* at the Charing Cross Hotel.

Whilst people took their seats, I looked about Blue Imperial Room; it was decorated in a restrained but graceful, understated manner, unlike the extravagant décor of the grand salon we had just left. The walls of the room were painted in light pale blue; with doors, window frames and pilasters in complimenting white, and again reflected a classical appearance, creating a calm natural elegance to the place.

This calming effect may well be to Loge's advantage,

I thought. The ceiling was of white stucco and dominated by ornate glass chandelier that augmented the wall-mounted, smaller chandeliers surrounded by traces of intricate filigree in the plaster panels of the walls. Again, the deep carpet was of silk; but now blue in color and augmented that feeling of luxury. It occurred to me whilst looking around the Blue Imperial Room, that Loge, in his Mercurial way, may well have chosen this very room for specific reasons that were now becoming evident, even to me.

The wall behind where Loge stood, on a raised podium enclosed by a brass rail, was punctuated with three arched internal French windows, framed with red velvet curtains, which led into another large salon. The walls of which were glazed, as in a loggia and addressed, I think, the front of the hotel, over looking the Strand. Again, the classical motif in decorative style had been carried into this room making it feel as though one were in a classical temple with very little masonry. Except, today that design illusion was lost on the assembled observers, at least on this occasion because of the pervasive fog pressing against the several panes of glass creating a white opaque effect.

However, it was not the ornate decorative effects of the room, nor it chiselled white stucco ceiling and it fine gilt work or the deep carpet which lay on the floor. None of these design details were of concern to the gentlemen of the press. What was of overriding and of consuming interest, were several tables, each of which was loaded down with a generous supply of fine cigars and drink of every description from around the known world! I counted at least eleven types of whisky, and vodka of every variety including one brand with gold leaf in its bottle.

Loge certainly knew how to acquire the undeviating attention he wanted from the Fourth Estate and, more importantly, how to maintain that interest to his best advantage.

In typical fashion, Loge opened up the meeting with exaggerated and rhetorical expressions and statements, confirming further his predilection for catachresis, that or his being a victim of it. Though as often with Loge, it was difficult to tell which.

"Gentlemen, gentlemen," Loge started in, "I remain, as usual, privileged in being able to advise you of an event!

"Esteemed members of the Fourth Estate, you are the first to be informed of my inextricable fight on behalf of the peoples who attend our Music Halls. It is my intention, with your guidance and support," said Loge, glancing at the drinks tables, "to join forces with me, in our heroic struggle, to eradicate ignorance, and our fight against intellectual destitution or interference, here in the midst of our great Metropolis! We shall achieve this noble and plausible state of affairs in our historic quest to create light and fulfilment in our great Metropolis. We shall do so by banishing darkness, despondency and bureaucracy which lurks everywhere. We shall start with the Metropolitan Board of Works, or as it is really known to the public; the Metropolitan Board of Perks! [1]

"Gentlemen, gentlemen of the press; attend me!" invited Loge. It was at this point Loge gave a perceptible, if shallow bow.

"We shall be taking the attack home to the Board in their luxurious and palatial offices in Spring Gardens. Their old offices in Dean Street, Soho, now not being good or grand enough for them, but for which we have to pay for with taxes on our coal and alcohol. This of course, is an unfair taxation on our poor people, many of whom simply cannot afford to pay this exorbitant excise for the sole benefit of the grandees at the Board. The only relief for our poor peoples and great British public, is the occasional visit to the Music Hall for social succour that the Board now wishes to remove from their short but tragic lives!" advised Lodge.

It could be that Loge was quite a dab hand at these events; he seemed to be and I sincerely hoped so.

Then with a flourish he pulled at a purple cord, at the end of which, was a bulbous tasselled gold-braided ball and immediately two red velvet curtains parted revealing a tripod easel. Resting upon the easel was timber backed frame supporting, in full sight of Jack, myself and members of the Fourth Estate to see, a poster, at least six feet in height and four across its width, proclaiming in bold confident letters allegations appertaining to the Metropolitan Board of Works!

I must confess to my being amazed with Loge, given that he only received the indictment yesterday and had evidently moved swiftly to accomplish producing this elaborate poster with its incriminating statement. Printed in bold letters for all to see, and take note, were the shortfalls, mistakes, financial ineptitude, bribes, convictions, scandals, and injudicious excursion into business, appertaining to the Metropolitan Board of Works!

After the sound of collective gasps had died down, Lodge raised his arms with the palms of his hands facing upward – to the heavens.

"Gentlemen, Gentlemen of the esteemed Fourth Estate, attend me!"

"We are gathered here today to reveal to you the devious machinations of the Metropolitan Board of Perks, sorry Works and its venal attack on our Music

Halls and theaters with their overbearing abuse of authority in trying to extract from we struggling impresarios and managers, obligations for which we are not liable," stated Lodge.

"Mr. Lodge, I represent the *London Chronicle*, can you tell us briefly just why you have called this meeting, apart from the fact that you state on your poster the grievances you have against the Metropolitan Board of Works. But, just what are the reasons which have brought you into the Board's purview?"

"I shall try," said Lodge, "as usual anything to do with that, that Board develops into something quite convoluted and amaranthine. The Board would have you believe that I was personally responsible for allowing a play to be performed that I had previously vetted and thought we had obtained approval from the Lord Chamberlain's office. It transpired that at the last minute the actors decided to incorporate a scene which had specifically not been given approval. Accordingly, it is this play and other minor infractions including those appertaining to fire safety which form the reason why the Board seeks to revenge themselves upon my person."

"Presumably the vetting would be under section twelve of the Theatrical Regulations Act of 1843?" asked the reporter from the *London Chronicle*.

"I believe so," replied Lodge, "alas this is the essence of the problem; one understands that the Board's responsibilities are limited to matters relating to buildings, including sewage, fire safety but certainly not censorship."

"But surely Section Twelve," asked the correspondent from *The Globe*, "remains in the province of the Lord Chamberlain, and not a bunch of sewage engineers sitting around a board-room, burning coal in their fire place all day, [2] especially during the summer?"

In response, Lodge indulged in his habit of tapping the side of his nose with his index finger, whilst members of the Fourth Estate looked down to the blue silk carpet and suppressed their chortling with their notebooks at the man from *The Globe's* witty remark.

"In your rôle," asked the portly gentlemen from the *Pall Mall Gazette*, "as *Arbiter elegantiarum*, what do you think of the responsibilities imposed upon you?"

Loge temporarily stalled at this question, but then recovered his wits attended by a beaming smile.

"Well that is very good question," replied Loge, "but, as a member of …as a conscientious member of the *Arbiter elegantiarum,* I of course accept fully the duties and obligation such a position confers upon me when making aesthetic decisions. That is why I believe in the consensus approach. That is, gathering opinions, ideas, feelings and attitudes from a wide range of persons. I do not, unlike the arrogant Metropolitan Board of Works, impose my thoughts arbitrarily on to an unsuspecting public.

"Gentlemen, I have to take into account what my public want. If I started drenching them with Beethoven's music of amaranthine boredom, they would soon abandon the auditoria of every Music Hall in Christendom. The same could be said gentlemen about yourselves. Your readers buy your esteemed and valued newspapers, because they know they are getting the best news coverage according to their need to be informed."

If Lodge knew how to charm the Fourth Estate, then here was a master class in action.

"You said that, quote, you gather opinions, ideas, feelings and attitudes from a wide range of persons, but how do we know this is the case," asked the reporter from the *Morning Post*. "The Metropolitan Board of Works, also seeks consultation with affected parties to any worthy and laudable scheme it undertakes for benefit of Londoners and all those who wish to see our Metropolis thrive and prosper."

"The difference between consultation, as defined by the Metropolitan Board of Works, and my definition of consensus is vastly different. I can demonstrate success by Box Office receipts. Whereas the only proofs the Metropolitan Board of Works are able to readily produce are those of ineptitude, indifference and corruption! Yes sir, you heard me! Ineptitude, indifference and corruption all of which are endemic throughout the Board, and we all know that. And there is not one citizen of London would disagree with me. The only persons the Metropolitan Board of Works consults are those at the Salvation Army and the likes of Ormiston Chant and other misguided malcontents who despise jollity and happiness extant in our treasured Music Halls.

"You talk about the Board's method of consultation, almost in an Evangelical manner, as though they had some God-given right to do so. The truth of it is very much different. They consult with the friends in order to hive off property, as we have realized in building of the *new* London Pavilion. These are not mistake based on human nature, that is mistake of commission; but rather, they are mistakes of principle, calculated deception leading ultimately to theft of real estate. Whether this nefarious activity involved complicity by the Board or just pure ineptitude, one at this stage cannot tell, but we shall, we shall and you will see!

"How can the tenant of the Public House adjacent to the London Pavilion, who is also the brother of one of the Board's surveyor go about with a different surname, accept to deceive. I ask you esteemed gentlemen of the press, is that consultation? I cannot bribe my audience in what ever manner I choose. If they do not like what I put on the stage, then they simply will not attend," said Loge.

Loge was becoming clearly animated and looked as though he were quietly working himself up into a deferred delirium. I feared that his monomania might grip him with a vengeance; but thus far he seemed able to repress any outward manifestation of it. He did however, failed to control his liberal and continued use of extravagant descriptions complete with predictable catachresis.

"I am from the *Daily News*, could you please tell us more about the nefarious activities of this Metropolitan Board of Works and its underhand dealings, especially in the realm of theaters and the Music Hall. What exactly is of great concern to you, other theater managers, and not least, the public?"

"I take it you are all aware of the scandal surrounding the London Pavilion and the Board's architect Ebenezer Saunders?" asked Loge, with a glint in his eyes.

"The London Pavilion Variety Theater scandal is instructive and erupted when the Metropolitan Board of Works purchased the *old* Pavilion Music Hall at Regent's Circus. The reason they gave was the proposed construction of Shaftesbury Avenue. However, before construction was to go ahead there was a lapse of time during which the Board would grant a short lease on the property rather than see it empty.

"Accordingly a short lease on the *old* Pavilion Music Hall was granted to Mr. R.E. Villiers, who had operated Music Halls in the past. The rent was paid by Villiers to the Board, as was a small retainer, to the Board's chief land valuation surveyor, a certain Mr. F W Goddard, to maintain favors, as it were.

"As construction of Shaftesbury Avenue was now imminent, the short term lease came up for re-appraisal. Again, Villiers met with Goddard and a certain T J Robertson, another surveyor employed by the Board. The reason given was ostensibly to negotiate leasing a corner site off Shaftesbury Avenue to enable Villiers to construct a *new* London Pavilion Variety Theater. The agreement, all three concocted, called for the erection of a Public House with the tenant being a mysterious Mr. W W Grey, who turned out to be the brother of T J Robertson, even with a different surname?

"It is reported that Robertson told Villiers that the Board will be inviting offers lease the site for the *new* London Pavilion, who responded by offering an annual rent of £2,700. The Board asked Robertson and Goddard and to examine the offer. Eventually they reported that £3,000 per annum would be a more accurate valuation than the £2,700 offered by Villiers, who agreed the re-valuation which was immediately accepted even though an alternative bid of £4,000 was submitted at the same time.

"The *new* London Pavilion, a *Variety Theater* type was duly designed by non other than the Board's chief architect, James Ebenezer Saunders. He was retained by the London Pavilion Variety Theater, even though he had previously designed nothing of import, including theaters. However, the building did enshrine the Board's policy of morality, non alcoholic drink, extravagant and opulent designs to deliberately attract the abstemious middle classes. This was going to be Variety Theater, and definitely not a Music Hall.

"Gentlemen of the press, we have to remember here, Saunders was an employé of the Board and was inexperienced in designing theater or important buildings. Yet he was *retained* as the architect on non Board projects. For example gentlemen I invite you to consider two projects and the scandal surrounding the construction of Grand Hotel and the Metropole Hotel. Both buildings are in the Northumberland Avenue, nearby here at Charing Cross, and were constructed on land owned by the Metropolitan Board of Works. Even though both hotels were built for private use, the hotel owners were *encouraged* to use persons employed by the Board, such as Saunders!" completed Lodge.

"We of course were the first newspaper to inform the public of our misgivings about the activities of the Metropolitan Board of Works," informed the corre-spondent from the *Financial News*.

"I am in your debt Sir," replied Lodge, "and fully acknowledge your informing the public about the cor-ruption extant at the Board. But let me ask you a question if I may? When did your esteemed paper, the *Financial News,* first realize the extent of malpractice, corruption, favors, lies and illegality rife at the Metropolitan Board of Works?"

The reporter from the *Financial News,* duly complied and listed a series of aspects of malpractices in support of Lodge's allegation of corruption extant at the metro-politan Board of Works.

Both Jack and I were amazed by Loge's manœuvre and exchanged looks with each other. I am a Vaudeville actor, out of New York and not an Attorney~at~Law. But, I do possess a basic understanding of defamation being on the stage and quoting people. What I had just witness was Loge at his best in terms of literally being *Loge* – mercurial. He had just in full sight of God and the Fourth Estate off-loaded any future court proceedings for liable by a vindictive Metropolitan Board of Works. Simply by ascribing any allegation he has made vicariously to the correspondent from the *Financial News* having made it first in his newspaper! Of course, the correspondent had not refuted Loge *generous acknowledgement*!

"May we call you by your nickname?" asked David Spittles of the *Evening Standard*.

"You have my permission to do so. But, I warn you; only my close acquaintances dare to do so!" advised Lodge, much to the pleasure of those assembled in the Blue Imperial Room at the Charing Cross Hotel.

"Clearly a man of great humility," replied David Spittles.

"Really, I have always considered humility to be the worst form of conceit?" responded Loge.

"Speaking of close acquaintances," continued Spittles, "we all of us here assume you to be an extremely well-connected individual, being a fabulously successful impresario, would you not agree?"

"On my being fabulous? Yes, I most certainly would agree!" responded Loge, with a broad smile on his face.

"Well the question still stands. Are your close acquaintances here to lend support to your cause against the Metropolitan Board of Works?" asked David Spittles the *Evening Standard*.

Lodge put his left hand up to eye brows and surveyed the Blue Imperial Room in a mock searching manner. A few moments later he answered Spittles's question, which was still standing.

"I believe so," condescended Lodge.

"Really," said Spittles, "well I do not claim to be familiar with all your friends, acquaintances or indeed enemies, but even I can count at least one absent friend!"

"And who might that be," asked Lodge, with a slight timbre in his voice.

"A very good and close friend," advised Spittles, and

you once described her as being one of your *Three Graces*. Does that ring a bell? No, well how about the word *incomparable* used here as a prefix to her name?"

"Everybody is *incomparable*; it is how the merciful God made us. It is a term of affection, and not fact," replied Lodge

"The particular incomparable person I am referring to is the incomparable Marie Lloyd," informed David Spittles of the *Evening Standard*.

Lodge was beginning to look uncomfortable, as this inquiry by David Spittles could only go in a way not favorable to Loge.

"Perhaps she is busy," said Spittles, "but do tell me. Do you in your capacity as a sagacious impresario, champion of the down trodden and artistes, defender of the public in its choice of entertainment, consider yourself to be a marked man by the Metropolitan Board of Works?"

"I certainly do," replied Lodge, seemingly bouncing back with a smile and relief.

"So you consider yourself champion of the down trodden and artistes? Interesting, because I just happened to be in the Crush Bar at the Royal Panopticon of Science & Arts, now of course called the Alhambra Music Hall in the Leicester Square, the other evening. There I witnessed your almighty row with the incomparable Marie Lloyd. What was it over, ah yes, the strike she and her fellow artistes have organised against you and other Music Hall and theater managers regarding the infamous *Exclusivity Clause,* which you have impose on the down trodden and Music Hall artistes! Perhaps the strike action, is the reason why she cannot be with us today," said Mr. Spittles of the *Evening Standard*.

"I think my colleague from the *Evening Standard*, Mr.

Spittles has a point," said the reporter from the *Morning Post*, "but we are here to ask questions about a notorious public body, charged with erecting structures and buildings in London in an open and legal manner and not interfering in areas of the public domain, in which it is not equipped to do. Mr. Lodge is to be applauded for bringing to our attention these incidences of this abuse of public funds. In addition to alerting us to the witch-hunt by a public body on individuals who disagree with their corrupt ways and only seek to satisfy public demand for well-deserved wholesome entertainment after a long day's toil.

"It may be that Marie Lloyd cannot be with us today. But alas, there is amongst us, a tireless friend and companion who has been at Loge's side through trials and tribulations and has emerged stronger and wiser for it. If anybody here can testify as to the honesty, fortitude and selfless dedication to the public cause, then the person must be Bella Elmore.

"Bella," said the reporter from the *Morning Post*, "this is not a court room drama of the type one might experience in Vaudeville play. But please tell us about Loge. For example where did you first meet him?"

"Oh Sir, you are too kind," replied Bella in a high squeaky voice, as dropped a little curtsey, whilst making her way to the railed podium, upon which Lodge was standing, in order to be next to him.

Bella was dressed in exactly the same clothes as she wore when we first encountered her in our dressing room at the Imperial Theater a few nights ago. She had not much changed and was still plumpish, and wore the same dress of luxuriant red velvet, interspersed with opulent layers of mauve and pink silk. Her hair was dark and tied up with ribbons of electric blue silk.

Upon her head she wore an outsized hat in the shape of what looked like a bowl, with fruit in it. Sticking out, and at an awkward angle, was a feather, a long blue feather, of an indeterminate species of bird. Staring out with big round blue eyes, from this lush and extravagant ensemble, was a face, a pretty face, but one that none the less exuded all the qualities of profound ignorance and overwhelming anonymity.

She looked at Lodge earnestly with her big round blue eyes. Turned to her audience and dropped another curtsey.

"I have known my agent Michael Lodge only for a relatively short time, but he has been ever so sweet to me," she offered up to the Fourth Estate.

"Yes Bella, but you knew Mr Lodge before then," said the reporter from the *Morning Post.*

Bella again turned to Lodge and emitted a high pitch giggle.

"Oh I see what you mean," she replied, "then yes I suppose so."

"Perhaps Bella you might like to cast your view on why Marie Lloyd cannot be with us today. You heard Mr. David Spittles from the *Evening Standard* suggest why. Could you counter his reasons for this being the case?"

This question was asked by the representative of the *Daily News.*

"Quite simply," responded Bella, "it is a question of sustained pitch especially in the key of C major. I have it, Lloyd does not. And in fact gentlemen, she never did have it. How she can earn her keep singing for her supper is beyond me and, I suspect, a good many people sitting in the audience in any Music Hall, if you ask me.

"Oh, and because Mr. Lodge had to let her go, simply because she was not up to scratch in singing as one of the famous *Three Graces*, she has now taken against Micha…, I mean Mr. Lodge here. And not only that, she is still trying to organize a strike, in order to disrupt ours and your Music Hall entertainment; such is her continuing ingratitude to Mr. Lodge."

"Do you think…" said the reporter from the *Morning Post*.

"I have not finished yet," interrupted Bella, "that Lloyd is the one thing that is doing our treasured Music Hall in, what with her lewd songs and lascivious innuendos and the like kind. She is trouble, unadulterated trouble," confirmed Bella Elmore, bearing her soul on the matter.

"Ah are you saying Bella that lewd and lascivious innuendos are extant and a regular occurrence on Music Hall stages in London, including those songs sung by Marie Lloyd, is this the case?" asked reporter from the *Morning Post*.

"Certainly not," responded Bella in her squeaky voice. "Certainly not, the only person who flaunts decency is that Lloyd. She cannot sing for her supper and so she has to resort to singing the indescribable for the benefit of her costermongers who make up the bulk of her followers. They would not be able to differentiate between E flat minor or C sharp major even if Lloyd could reach those scales, which of course, she is unable to do so.

"No, if Lloyd packed it in and went back to making children's' boots, we would not have need of censorship in the Music Halls. The only thing that needs censoring is her. She is always getting into trouble and being brought up before the Lord Chamberlain. Why, she even got arrested in New York for her mouthy ways. Does that answer your inquiry sir?" asked Bella, as she dropped another shallow curtsey.

I turned and looked at Jack.

"We have had on two previous occasions Jack cause to remark about Bella abilities in a different light. She is not quite the dummy she pretends to be. She has in one coup de grâce or coup de théâtre, whichever, managed to deride her arch enemy in Marie Lloyd. Do not forget, she replaced Lloyd as a member of the *Three Graces*. And not only that she has managed to give the sound impression that all the ills and probable reasons for censorship, if any, are as a result of Lloyd's behavior, and her behavior alone, involving no other artistes. In this respect, remove Lloyd and you have removed the problem!" I said.

I wholeheartedly agree with you Theo," replied Jack.

"It is not just about lascivious innuendos and vulgarity bordering on the obscene," said the reporter from the *Morning Post*, rising up again from out of his seat, "it involves other pastimes on the stage, such as women dressing up as men. Would you not agree?"

"Well I do not dress up as a man! But, if it is acceptable for male judges to wear wigs and gowns whilst they dispense the laws in court and those gents in parliament to wear powered wigs, *costumes* including knickerbockers and the like, then who am I to judge?" informed Bella, much to the delight of the gentlemen of the Fourth Estate.

"Bella I represent the *Daily Gazette* and I am wondering just how long have you known Mr. Lodge for you to make valued judgements about him that we are supposed to accept without question. And, what your feelings are about the Metropolitan Board of Works and their tireless campaign to clean up acts in the Music Halls. You yourself have admitted there is a need to do so and who better placed to carry out this task than our illustrious Metropolitan Board of Works?"

"How long does one need to know someone," replied

Bella, "to realize that person is caring and conscientious in their dealings with everyone they come into contact with? It is also possible that you have known somebody for ten years and simply do not know them at all. Likewise having known somebody for only a short time and really understand and know them, and you can take my word for it."

At this point Bella looked appealingly at Loge and emitted a suppressed giggle.

"And, incidentally," she continued, "I have admitted no such thing. I merely said that we would not need to be censored by anybody, if that Marie Lloyd packed her large feathery hats and went back to being a cobbler. [3] We other artistes are not vulgar, nor do we resort to lewd singing to gain our audience's attention. And even if censorship were needed, it ought not to be by the Metropolitan Board of Works, for reasons which kind Mr. Lodge here has stated and printed on that board on the tripod, or were you sleeping at the time? Do wake up dearie!"

"On the point of morality affecting the cavorting and licentious behaviour extant in Music Halls what are your comments about the arrest of Olga Nethersole?" asked the same reporter from the *Morning Post*.

"Who?" countered Bella, with a look of even more total bewilderment in her big blue round eyes.

"I am sure a few of us here recall," continued the *Morning Post*'s reporter, "the scandalous reports emanating out of a play called *'Sapho'* in New York recently. Where certain respectable societies, which comprised sober upstanding members of society, were compelled to protest at what they considered to be unadulterated and infectious concentrated filth on the New York public stage. Such societies as the New York Society for the

Suppression of Vice, the New York Mother's Club and the Society for the Study of Life were outraged at the language expressed on stage and the provocative costumes worn by the actors, were immoral. In particular they protested about Olga Nethersole's leading rôle in the performance in that degradation and indecency. Such was the level of public outcry that the District Attorney for New York City, Asa Bird Gardiner, ordered the immediate arrest of Nethersole and members of her touring company with the police closing the threater down,"

"I will field this inquiry Bella," Lodge was over heard to advised.

"The reporter from the *Morning Post* is correct. The District Attorney Gardiner did order Olga and members of her company arrested and the theater closed down. But what our friend from the *Morning Post* fails to mention, is the fact that the hysterical and inordinate re-action to a play, that simply explores emotions in adults, by those very same societies he named, was motivated by the *Yellow Press* of journalism. [4] The *New York World* reporters as much as admitted so under oath in the subsequent trial which lasted all but two-days. At the end of which the jury spent less than fifteen minutes in acquitting Nethersole and others of the charges brought against them.

"In this respect indecency is in the mind, not on the stage. And it was ironic that the trial judge warned the jury before they adjourned to deliberate the evidence submitted to them that, and I quote, 'you the members of the jury are not the moral guardians in this commu-nity,'" said Lodge, confidently.

"That may well be the case," replied the reporter from the *Morning Post*, but the question I asked Bella was clear enough to elicit an answer. With respect to the Metropol-itan Board of Works, my readers will be interested in the Board's legitimate concern for the moral well-being of the public in particular morality, or the lack of it expressed on a London stage. And the fact remains Nethersole was arrested in New York for what a senior attorney considered to be indecent, offensive and pro-miscuous behavior in her leading rôle in *sapho*, and on the public stage?"

"Oh I see what you mean," said Bella, "but the fact remains, Olga was acquitted and by a jury who did not consider the play to be indecent. I can only imagine that District Attorney Gardiner must have issued arrest warrants for Olga on the basis that the play was too boring and therefore offensive, and not indecent. Hence the fact the jury let her go! In future Olga, stick to Music Hall performances and remain free!"

"Mr. Lodge, I represent the *Sporting Life*. Can you please confirm to us that the constitutional basis upon which the Metropolitan Board of Works, was founded is the Metrop-olis Management Act of 1855 which brought the Board into creation on the 22 December, 1855. And, does that Act of 1855 define specifically the rights, duties and obligations of the Board's in this taut field of censorship? And, more importantly, is there any truth in the rumor that it is the avowed intention of the Metropolitan Board of Works to apply for a levy to be imposed on wagering, precisely in order to increase their own funding?"

"That is a very good question," responded Loge, in fine fettle, "next question please!"

"Mr. Lodge, I represent the *New York Daily Tribune*. We are interested in what is happening here in London with the Metropolitan Board of Works, because some of us in New York are concerned about a well-meaning organization called the Society of St. Tammany or the Columbian Order. [5] It is a political organization, controlling New York City and New York State, and is primarily involved with municipal construction, rather like your Metropolitan Board of Perks! Need less to say, like any big public funded body; there are allegations of corruption and injudicious behavior. Aside of the fact there is a movement to impeach members of that society for a variety of misdemeanors. My question is; do you have any such plans to do the same to the members of the Metropolitan Board of Works?

"My contacts in the office of the First Lord of the Treasury [6] tell me there is whispers of a Royal Commission being assembled to look into the activities of the Metropolitan Board of Works," replied Lodge, slowly and deliberately.

I noticed in the corner of my eye, two journalists immediately left the Blue Imperial Room, with their notebooks in hand. One of the reporters was David Spittles from the *Evening Standard*.

"Gentlemen, gentlemen, on that note, I suggest we adjourn for some badly needed refreshment," insisted Lodge, pointing with his empty wine glass, at the inordinately generous supply of drink stacked on the precariously nearby tables.

The stampede to comply with Loge's suggestion was intense, as it was undignified.

1. The public's nick name for this unpopular Board because of the 'perk' it gave its members
2. Alluding to the fact the Board funds came from tax imposed on coal the public had to pay
3. Marie Lloyd started out in a factory making children's' shoes
4. Sensationalism journalism based on little researched news and exaggerated headlines to increase sales
5. Colloquially known as Tammany Hall
6. Office of the British Prime Minister

Chapter 27

The Apotheosis of the Impresario

The gathering of the Fourth Estate was, as far as I could determine, working in Loge's favor. However, like all things, including staged events, one incident could turn advantage into disadvantage. What is clear to Jack and myself, was Loge's unfolding strategy in getting certain members from the press to ask seemingly innocuous questions, designed, irrespective of the answer, to send a clear implicit threat to where it was intended, or expected. Witness the Parthian shot from the reporter representing the *New York Daily Tribune* about the possibility of indictments being issued to members of the near equivalent of the Metropolitan Board of Works in New York, the Society of St. Tammany. Together with the rapid exit of two reporters, favorable to the Metropolitan Board of Works, presumably to report to that Board the possibility of an inquiry being instigated against them. The free liquor and fine cigars were simply a welcome adjunct to the proceedings.

At length we the help of several hotel ushers in their powder blue morning coats with red piping, Lodge was eventually able to persuade certain reporters to leave the drinks table and reconvene for the rest of the conference.

"The refreshments are not going to walk away, and will be there at the conclusion of our little meeting,"

Lodge would say to the more hardened recalcitrant of the assembled members of the Fourth Estate.

"I represent the *New York Sun,* and would like to pick up from where my esteemed colleague from the *New York Daily Tribune* left off. As you know in America we encourage rampant capitalism, of the type emanating out of Pittsburgh, as the only way to move forward. We do not like big government; they have gotten us into trouble before. Aside of which, they seem intent on spending our money not allowing us to do so for ourselves. However, whilst we applaud the capitalist and industrialist Titan, we also expect them to stay within the bounds of proprietary or the law. When they stray beyond that limit, irrespective of what they have achieved for the public good or themselves in terms of personal enrichment, we will indict them at the drop of a hat. Tell me Lodge, what is the attitude in England to such persons who have been found to be guilty of such allegations as you have printed on your poster there?"

"I am not a judge, just a simple hard working impresario trying to pleased the great British public," said Lodge, decisively and laying down his empty wine glass. "But I have read that such persons, upon convictions can receive lengthy prison sentences. And, not only that, but be sociably ostracized even years later when released from prison. The British people do not take kindly to persons who cheat them of their hard earned wages, as the Metropolitan Board of Works does and continues to do so, as it has been revealed over the London Pavilion scandal."

"My colleague from the *Sporting Life,* over there, touched upon a question that I think we would be grateful for your thoughts on the matter," said the correspondent from the *St. James' Gazette.*

"I take it you are referring to the Board's specific rights, duties and obligations in the field of censorship?" inquired Lodge, rubbing his hands.

"That is absolutely correct…," replied the man from the *St. James' Gazette*.

"Rights, duties and obligations; ah but what do the Board members know?" cut in Loge obliquely, "except how to squander our *duties* – in terms of coal tax paid to them as their revenue!"

This was obviously the desired question with the appropriate answer submitted as a reply and was appreciated by the assemble journalist as indicated by their sustained laughter.

When the laughter had receded another journalist got up and looked at Lodge with a hard face.

The *Daily Gazette* here Mr. William Lodge, and I should like to ask a question of you in particular. You claimed that the Metropolitan Board of Works is everything bad, almost the devil incarnate. Yet you yourself are not beyond reproach in your treatment of people. I refer to the current strike, over the *Exclusivity Clause*, now ragging through certain Music Halls throughout the Metropolis. Now irrespective of the rights and wrongs of the strike and the fact that Marie Lloyd cannot be with us; what about another woman whom you have wronged? This one in particular was the woman with whom you had an encounter whilst drunk at the Crush Bar at the New Bedford Music Hall in Camden, not these few days past. Cannot she be invited to address the assembled members of the Fourth Estate; or would her remarks about you and your personality be an embarrassment?"

Lodge was momentarily put off by this onslaught but soon recovered his usual suave self and came back with a question.

"Let me pose the question to you. Where people do

business in the provision of an amenity to the great British public, then perforce there will be disagreement. The contracts, incorporating the *Exclusivity Clause*, issued by several managers, is legal and no one Music Hall artistes was compelled to sign the contract nor duress brought to bear in obtaining a signature upon the contact indicating acceptance, as in the precedent-making case of *Williams v. Bayley* of 1866 decided in the House of Lords.

"Lloyd was dismissed by me because, as Bella explained earlier, Marie's voice was simply not up to the range required for soprano to give real expression to the music she was required to sing. This is very much in keeping with my personal motto that only the best is good enough for the great British Music Hall attending public.

"With regard to the lady at the Crush Bar in the New Bedford Music Hall, and I think I know about whom you are referring, there was no point in inviting her as she could hardly make a valid contribution, unlike Bella here, to a discussion about corruption at the Metropolitan Board of Works!

"Again, gentlemen of the press," said Loge, addressing the whole of the *Press Corp*, assembled in the Blue Imperial Room, and in so doing relegating the reporter from the *Daily Gazette*. "A man in my position will be in constant contact with numerous persons. Invariably, there will be those very rare occasions where a disagreement will exist. This is human nature, but where this is so, it will be because, as I have intimated before, it remains my unde-viating principle that only the best is good enough for the great British public and I say this in ...."

Lodge was not allowed to complete his sentence before he was interrupted by a sustained applause and cries of, 'quite right, quite right!'

What was becoming evident to Jack and I almost by

the minute was the juxtaposition of Music Hall and authority. Invariably, when these two meet head on Music Hall tends to win because of the very nature of what it is; flexible, humorous, engaging and able to initiate at any level. In comparison, authority is perceived to be unyielding, obsessive, pettifogging and bureaucratic and the harbinger of bad news.

Witnessing this press conference was an education in the rationale and culture of Music Hall. Both Jack and I knew this to be the case.

"May we just for moment get back to one of the allegation you have listed on your board over there Mr Lodge," said a gentleman from the *Evening News*. "It involves the case of the surveyor Hebb and your remarks you made earlier. I am a bit confused, are you able to elaborate further?"

"Ah yes, your man Hebb, "responded Lodge, a man who, like Proteus, could change shape for advantage in front of one's very eyes without noticing it. A humble surveyor and employé of the Metropolitan Board of Works on an even humbler wage, but he had a trick by way of supplementing it. One of the duties imposed on the loathsome Metropolitan Board of Works is to carry out fire safety inspection on buildings used by the public, theaters and the like.

"On these regular occasions, the Music Hall or theater managers would be reminded about the impending inspection for fire safety, or other such matters. They would be advised of this visit in advance by an assistant architect, employed by the Board, a certain John Hebb. His rôle at the Board was to carry out inspection of theaters for fire regulations and safety matters, which meant he had, on behalf of the Board, the power to close theaters down for the most ridiculous of reasons.

"Hebb, before commencing his inspection would implicitly suggest that the manager might like to make available to him free seats, to enable him to assess the theater whilst *being used* by the public. Given his powers to close a theater, most Music Hall and theater managers would arrange for such seats to be available for him. Alas though, usually behind a column or some distance from the stage!" informed Lodge.

"The *Morning Post* here again Mr Lodge, despite my original inquiry, regarding the obscenity trial in New York over Olga Nethersole's lewd performances on stage, do you set yourself up as a guardian of the public mores?"

Again Lodge temporarily stalled in immediately answering this question, but then recovered his wits and repressed somehow his inherent monomania which ought to have manifested itself at least a half hour ago.

"As I have stated before; I am merely a humble impresario who seeks only to provide what amenities the public should like to enjoy. I have not, do not, and will not ever set myself up as the arbiter of what is right and what is wrong, moral, amoral or immoral. Rather I should wish to let the great British public decide what it is they prefer!" Lodge replied, with renewed confidence.

"*New York Times* here Mr. Lodge, for the record given what you have just said, would you have managed Olga Nethersole's play in New York knowing what you do about the legal outcome of the case?"

"As I have said *Ad nauseous* on numerous occasions," responded Loge, "I am but a humble impresario. I organize theater use, not manage plays, programs or people!"

"Would you consider putting Nethersole's play *Sapho* on in a London Music Hall?" asked the gentleman representing the *Daily Chronicle,* slightly slurring his words.

"If the public demanded so, then I would consider it all things given," replied Lodge.

"Mr. Lodge, I represent *The Daily Telegraph*. One of the charges preferred against you is keeping an unruly house as defined by section 12 of the Theatrical Regulations Act 1843. Surely this oversight on your behalf is a matter for the Justices of the Peace not the Metropolitan Board of Works? Or are you suggesting that the Board in their zeal have tacked on to the specification these charges relating to fire and safety and inspection violations. In other words, the Board has deliberately confused a fire regulation violation with a moral stance, and usurped powers under section 12, normally reserved for magistrates, motivated by their obsessive dislike of Music Halls which they perceive as being immoral places. Irrespective of the state of the building or fire regulation compliance, and are aided and abetted by the likes of the Salvation Army and Ormiston Chant, even though the Board itself has been found to be corrupt and acting immorally?"

"You have Sir, summarized my dilemma with the Board very succinctly! The Board, of course, again are wrong and one wonders just how deep the corruption is at Spring Gardens, in order for them to conclude such an absurd charge," responded Lodge.

There stunned members of the fourth estate stood in silence at this revelation.

"Music Hall never corrupted the morals of the nation; unlike the Metropolitan Board of Works," informed Lodge.

"My name is Thomas Dixon Galpin and correspondent for *The Echo*. May I ascertain from you Mr. Lodge, since it appears you know an awful lot; is it true that the Metropolitan Board of Works, intend to sell off the Palace of Westminster to the highest bidder?"

"I thought it was already sold off," answered Loge, with a smile, "and already functioning as a Palace of Varieties!"

This remark by Loge elicited a standing ovation, which by now was alcohol fuelled and he lost no time in capitalizing on his advantage.

Lodge had uttered those words in all honesty whilst still indulging in his habit of looking over his shoulder, which I still find somewhat unnerving. What I found even more disquieting was the certain probability that Lodge was living proof that a little knowledge was dangerous. I have witness this before. Somehow, he managed, to engage the assembled members of the esteemed Fourth Estate into a agreeing to his definition about the essential altruistic rôle of the Music Hall in society.

In particular, Loge argued, there were educative aspects of the Music Hall and its ability to lend dignity and imbue the soul with nobility of purpose. For example, he proposed, emanating from these eminent establishments, were such noble ideals as hope, aspiration, courage or even fortitude in the face of adversity.

"And indeed," continued Lodge, unabated, "such magnanimous intent should be conveyed in the idiom of music, song and acts for the whole of humanity, in its diverse forms, to endure, and not just for clever people like us."

The Fourth Estate listened attentively.

"Might not the Music Hall," Loge suggested, "be used to convey such ideals as our being British, and indeed our national character?

"Indeed our esteemed Music Halls have encouraged that social mobility we all desire. The advent of the Music Hall has broken down those barriers which hitherto prevented those talented individuals amongst us from going forward for the benefit of all mankind in its diverse and fascinating form. In addition, our Music Halls have provided the ability for women to escape the drudgery of the house, as *Angels of the Home,* and instead apply their talents to the stage. I need only mention, Bella Elmore, Katie Lawrence and Mari…. Dot Hetherington.

"Indeed, not only have some artistes become famous on the stage, but away from it too. One need only look at the successful alliances between the Music Hall artistes and nobility, the finest nobility. Take our Anastasia Robinson's marriage to the Lord Peterborough and Lavinia Fenton, becoming the wife of the Duke of Bolton.

"Even a cousin of our late Queen Victoria, his grace the Duke of Cambridge took as his wife, the Drury Lane stage actress Sarah Fairbrother. The Earl of Denby saw fit to marry Eliza Farren, as did the Earl of Craven to Louise Brunton. Mary Bolton would still be Bolton had not the Lord Thurlow offered his hand to her, as Kitty Stephens accepted gracefully that of the Earl of Essex's.

"Who could not express absolute joy at knowing of the union between Frances Braham and the Earl Walde-grave. And our sweet Harriet Mellon of Drury Lane, is now her grace the Duchess of St. Albans, and widely respected as such. Camille Clifford, known to us and her adoring followers as the 'Gibson Girl' is equally happy to be addressed more formally as Lady Aberdare. Who could forget the incomparable Rosie Boote, now the Marchioness of Headfort?

"We all know of the wager of the Earl of Clancarty [1] and his marriage to Bella Bilton, who at the time was appearing at the Oxford Music Hall, in Oxford Street. The Earl of Poulett and Sylvia Storey's marriage court-ship was, of course more orthodox as were Frances

Donnelly and Lord Ashburton's. Denise Orme, now delights in being Lady Churston, as does Estelle Berridge, who became Lady Clopmell, together with Connie Gilchrist, who married the seventh Earl of Orkney. Eva Carrington's marriage to the Lord de Clifford is still blessed, as is the knighthood bestowed upon the husband of Vesta Tilley, making her now the Lady de Frece. But there is hope! Adelina Patti Married Marquis de Caux and later the Baron Rolf Cederstrom!" recited Loge.

Anyone in the room could now detect quite clearly signs of rumblings with the ranks of the Fourth Estate, as though Vesuvius were about to erupt. Loge continued, holding his audience enthralled.

"Gentlemen, we all know that the Metropolitan Board of Perks is an unelected interfering public body which seeks only to revenge themselves on me. Simply because I speak out against their moral tyranny and the crusade they wish to impose on us, the public, the great British public in what we may wish to see and enjoy on the stage; or what we may not enjoy.

"It is neither about the safety of buildings nor even the fire regulations; for who here would want to see a Music Hall go up in flames, apart from the Metropolitan Board of Works? No, more importantly, think of the loss of Box Office receipts! Now that would be a calamity. As the correspondent from *The Daily Telegraph* alluded to earlier, it is about who governs us. Parliament and the peoples' wishes as expressed through our elected representatives? Or a Board of sewage engineers, a board which is moribund and evidently corrupt at worst, or inept at best, usurping powers from the Theatrical Regulations Act and passing moral judgment upon us, we the great British people.

"Did we defeat Napoleon or the Boers only to become

enslaved by a Board of deep level sewage engineers? I think those engineers ought to go back to tendering their steam engines and pneumatic sewage pumps and leave the business of running the Music Halls to those who sympathize with the public and understand what they want in terms of stage entertainment," advised Lodge.

By now most of the journalists had risen from their comfortable Chippendale chairs, the seats of which were covered in resplendent moiré silk.

"The British people love their Music Halls; it is the one aspect of our nation where all are equal in enjoying fun and being entertained. Even in the precursor to the Music Hall, the Pleasure Gardens, including those of Vauxhall, Cremorme, Marylebone or even Ranelagh where royalty in the person of His Majesty the Prince of Wales would attend along side the ordinary subjects of the realm.

"Why, even in more recent years, Edward VII before being crowned attended the Canterbury Music Hall with their graces the Dukes of Cambridge and Teck with his Duchess. And, as we have heard just previously nobility and the Music Hall go hand in hand – well literally to the altar!

"This talk about Music Hall being the harbingers of indecency and immorality propounded and perpetuated by the Metropolitan Board of Works, can at best only be a nonsense. Because were it to have been the case, is it likely our sovereign lord, King Edward VII have been a party to visiting such establishments which were allegedly the purveyors of indecency or lewd behavior? Because if Metropolitan Board of Works think this to be the case, then perhaps they should take the matter up with His Majesty and commence proceedings against the present King!" completed Loge.

I knew then that Loge, had at some time in his life had acted on stage. His timing was impeccable, worthy of any stage performance. Loge did not falter but instead honed in accurately on this tidal wave of approbation.

"Gentlemen, gentlemen, can I be held responsible," he pleaded, "for something beyond my control and for which I am charged? I read the script of the play in question as passed by the Lord Chamberlain. If the actors decide to ad lib on stage, then I am powerless to prevent them from doing so! Also censorship and morality are defined in the Theatrical Regulations Act of 1843, not in the Metropolis Management Act of 1855, which, God rue the day, called into creation the Metropolitan Board of Works, which has assumed to itself the power of censorship.

"The whole rationale of censorship, at least in England, is built upon a defective premise, which has no real relevance today. Henry VIII introduced censorship, not as a means of preserving public morality, but rather to control what was said on stage, especially religious or political sentiments not conducive to that of the Crown's. Hence, the office of censor has always been filled by a member of the King's household, the Lord Chamberlain. The Board now wishes to continue those outmoded concerns today!

"This is about freedom, and freedom of choice and great British peoples' inalienable right to choose, and not censorship by the Metropolitan Board of Works who wish, with usurped powers, to ban Music Hall and theaters and return us all to a Cromwellian tyranny of puritanical killjoy and grim existence! Their censorship is not restricted to the Music Hall; it extends into the concert hall too.

"Even the contralto Clara Butt was prevented from

singing Saint Saëns's opera *Samson & Delilah* because the representation of biblical subjects is banned on the British stage. And I will not mention Maud Allan's portrayal her as *Salomé*, what with John the Baptist's head rolling about the stage, rather like Judd, the ventriloquist's dummy's head. Where will, this infected creeping hand of censorship by the Metropolitan Board of Works stop?

"We need to be released! From legislation not subjected to more of it, with its pettifogging rules initiated by a corrupt moribund organization, as such the Metropolitan Board of Works. We need to be released! We need to be released from…" completed Lodge, in an impassioned plea, to thunderous applause as the Fourth Estate erupted into unbridled ecstatic delirium.

Looking at Loge's face, flushed by the intensity of his emotional oration, it seemed bathed in a warm almost translucent light, as though in a state of grace.

Lodge and Bella, then lead the journalists on another stampede to the drinks tables, upon which had been heaped an even greater selection of drinks and fine cigars including those of Trichinopoly

Some time later Jack and I were able to meet up with Lodge and Bella, who had just managed to extricate themselves from the scores of admiring journalists eager for *special* quotes from Loge for their newspapers.

Lodge was standing with Bella, fluted champagne glass in hand and looking the definition of contentment. He acknowledged us.

"This is quite a good turn out Lodge, we are very impressed," said Jack, in genuine tones of admiration.

"Thank you Jack," responded Lodge, "but it is really all about having the right contacts, with whom I have some sway; in order to enable me, to evade, and thus avoid apparent responsibility, and thus any resultant liability! There is no point Theo, Jack, in going to a court where all one can expect to find is an unfavorable decision, confirming guilt as per the specification in the charge. The trick is to take the battle to where one can position oneself strategically and, accordingly, there win."

"Speaking of which," I said to Loge, "one gets the distinct impression that any drama acted out in court is but one step away from the stage!"

"It is Theo, it is. It must also be difficult for playwrights or performing artistes to decide just where to put their plays on; in court or in the Music Hall!" replied Lodge, taking a deep draught of champagne from his glass and then breathing out noisily.

"Jack, from now on my profound respects go to Loge here; he has certainly gone up immeasurably in my estimation for his scheming abilities. I cannot help but think that we can only benefit by his undoubted talents. And I thought Little Bo Peep was good!" I said.

"When you say *Loge*, exactly to which *Loge* do you refer?" inquired Jack.

"Why, the one from Wagner's opera – *the* Loge, the *Sans Pareil!*" [2] I replied.

"It is to be said that Michael acquitted himself admirably; would not one agree?" said Bella, slightly slurring her words of praise, "and that towards the end of his towering oration in defense of Music Hall, his face took on an ethereal appearance bathed as it was by a mystical shaft of translucent light."

"Oh that," responded Loge, "just got a theater stage hand I know to train a hidden low intensity limelight beam on to me!"

---

1. He bet that he would marry the first girl he met in the street, and did.
2. Without compare

Chapter 28

The Palace Theater

We were still reeling from the positive effects of Lodge's impromptu calling of the Fourth Estate in an attempt to vindicate himself from the unwarranted charges preferred against him by an over zealous Metropolitan Board of Works. His simple but effective strategy at the time, was based on the assumption that the mere discussion of, not the charges relating to him, but rather the implicit allegations of injudicious or corrupt behavior of the Board, would in themselves compel a review of those charges against him. For the Board to proceed with charges against Loge, legitimate or not, could only in the long run invite ruin upon the Metropolitan Board of Works itself. According, we were informed later that the Board would, on this occasion, only issue a written warning. Insisting that compliance with sanitary or fire regulations, in future, must be adhered to, and the case against Lodge withdrawn.

Possibly as good an outcome as one might expect. That press conference with the Gentlemen of the Fourth Estate, certainly demonstrated to me the importance of understanding where you are, and indeed, what you are. There are times when Loge, actually ascends to those empyreal heights, he is so often fond of referring to, as though they really were within most peoples' abilities.

In addition, not only has Loge, a though he were Machiavelli, dispatched forthwith the Metropolitan Board of Works to oblivion, at least in his domain: but has shown the inherent fallacious dichotomy extant at the Board between corruption and moral crusade.

However, we are now to visit the huge Palace Theater in the Charing Cross Road, with the intention that we might perform there. This opportunity depends upon Lodge persuading the manager there, a Mr. Alfred Butt of our new approach on the stage of engaging with the audience under a controlled ad lib scenario. We remain confident, for if Lodge can deal effectively with the Metropolitan Board of Works, then Jack and I can only congratulate him, prematurely in this respect, on his inevitable success, at our being allowed to perform at the renowned Palace Theater.

Accordingly, we were cantering down the Charing Cross Road in our Landau, whilst relaxing on the purple button-down leather upholstered seats. Thankfully our liveried coachman was not minded to dump us off in that nearby slum area, called the Rookery, I noted as we were passing, the notion of which sent a shiver down my spine. At length we pulled up outside the ornate and very imposing front of the Palace Theater.

"This place always reminds me of Columbus Circus on Broadway and West 58th. back home in New York," said Jack, stepping down from our Landau carriage, "and, what did Lodge instruct us to do in his cable-gram he sent earlier?"

"He asks that we meet with him at the Crush Bar, where else? Though in fairness, he has much to celebrate!" I replied.

The five storey red-brick banded curved façade of the Palace Theater, was impressive even if partially shrouded by the fog. The curved façade of the theater, reflected the curve of the Cambridge Circus on which it is located and dominates. The basics architecture reflected an early Romanesque style complete with arched windows forming enfilades to each floor, and culminating in triangular framed pediment, the apex to which supported a statue, and rising from the attic, punctuated with a roundel forming a window reveal. The façade of the building was buttressed by two turrets rising up beyond the attic level and capped by domes upon which were affixed statues.

We walked into the building and having gained the foyer we looked around for an usher to escort us to the Crush Bar. The décor in the foyer was magnificent with every surface clad in different types of marble ranging from *Rosso Verona* to the deeper *Trachite Giallo Veneta*. The Romanesque arched motive addressing the exterior of the Music Hall was continued inside in creating a luxurious and sumptuous space one might find in the imperial splendor of ancient Rome. A central glass chandelier added to the opulence of the foyer, radiating out a myriad of beams light which reflected off the highly polished marble columns and wall panels.

Presently an usher in his red morning coat did approach our persons and asked if he could be of assistance.

"You certainly can my good man," answered Jack, "we are looking for the impresario Loge; I believe it is quite possible that he might, at this very moment, be in the Crush Bar."

"Ah gentlemen, but you must mean Mr. William Lodge; please follow me," replied the red morning coated usher.

Accordingly and with great gravitas, the usher

The Palace Theater

escorted us beyond the red-roped ticket barrier and down into the famous Crush Bar.

"I know you will like this bar Theo. People come here to drink and admire the décor with no intention of checking into the auditorium. Indeed, men have been known to abandon their paid for seats and stay in the bar after intervals during what ever is being shown on the stage. Such is the allure of the bar!" said Jack, with a rueful smile.

Though the exterior façade of the Palace Music Hall, addressing the Cambridge Circus, was impressive, it did rather pale into insignificance when compared with the lush extravagant interior of the Crush Bar. Even the marble foyer looses a bit of it glamorous appointment at the side of the Crush Bar. Not unlike the Criterion Bar, this Crush Bar was by no means orchidaceous,[1] but rather a successful fusion of elegance and opulence creating a sumptuous effect which radiated out extravagant optimism and confidence in interior décor aspiration.

The bar was essentially curved which suggested it was addressing the curve of the front façade of the building. The walls of the salon were finished in pale yellow and gilded surfaces with raises designs and filigree detailing all of which augmented very effectively the sheer lavish appointment of the bar. The ceiling comprised impressed bold designs punctuated with large round medallions the centers of which displayed painted scenes. The floor was covered with a red broadloom silk carpet upon which were ranged several kinds of chairs and low tables painted in a gold color. Invariably, the great English weaknesses for urn-planted ubiquitous palm trees were in ample evidence!

"Gentlemen, gentlemen, over here!" shouted Loge, from the end of an exquisite cream colored *Botticino Fiorito* marble clad bar which complimented the pervasive gilded and pale yellow painted surfaces of the Crush Bar.

As we approached him, he disentangled himself from

the two beautés, with whom he was drinking champagne out of long fluted glasses.

Loge, dressed, typically, as though he were the Count of Monte Cristo, complete with his electric blue frock-coat, of which he was inordinately clearly fond, together with a deep red silk waist-coat. All beneath his black cape complete with blazing red silk lining.

"It is his shiny silk top hat that gets me Theo, his top hat," said Jack, with a smirk.

"Do have some Perrier Jouet champagne, gentlemen. Alfred Butt, the manager of the Palace Theater will be joining us directly.

"Is he by any chance related to Clara Butt, the contralto?" inquired Jack.

"No," said Lodge, resoundingly.

"This place seems awfully grand to be a theater or indeed Music Hall," I said, trying to show an interest in our opulent surroundings.

"Absolutely," said Lodge, "you are quite, quite correct Theo. This theater was built in the 1889 by another impresario brethren of mine in Richard D' Oyly Carte, to the designs of Thomas Edward Collcutt, the architect. The building was originally intended it to be a grand opera house, with seating for over fourteen hundred people.

"It is obvious when just looking at the opulent appointment of this place, that Collcutt when designing this establishment, clearly had in mind Garnier's grand designs, extant at the Paris Opéra. [2]

"Though the intended use of the theater as an opera house initially proved successful with a run of the opera *Ivanhoe* composed by the esteemed Sir Arthur Sullivan and other composers' works too. That initial success was not maintained, and D' Oyly Carte ended up leasing the Palace Theater to Sarah Bernhardt for one season only, for her to perform in.

"The whole venture proved disastrous and D' Oyly Carte sold the opera house within a year at a loss to Sir Augustus Harris, from the Theater Royal, Drury Lane. After some time it was redesigned to plans by Walter Emden, and converted into its current use as the grand Palace Theater we know today. The Palace Music Hall, as it was then known as, was previously managed by my old friend, the *'Father of Music Halls,'* Charles Morton who renamed it, in 1893, Palace Theater of Varieties. Accordingly, it attracted such artistes as Vesta Tilley, George Robey, Fanny Brice, Little Tich and a rising talented American out of Piqua, Kansas, I think, called Buster Keaton in 1909. You might possibly know him?" asked Lodge.

"Cannot say that we do," replied Jack.

"Yet again," continued Loge, "in 1911, the establishment changed its name to that of the Palace Theater, by which it is now known. Though there are those who still prefer the term *Music Hall* suffixed to the word, *Palace*. Herman Finck, is the current musical director, but alas cannot join us this evening, but as you know, his manager Alfred Butt will be attending us instead.

"This is a shame, because I should have liked to introduce you to Finck. Not only because as musical director, he has been instrumental in organizing a series of innovative recordings on Shellac,[3] performed by his superb Palace Orchestra. But also for the famous dancing *Palace Girls,* for whom he has composed many songs together with dances especially for the popular routine called *Tonight, "* informed Lodge.

"That is the one which became the romantic instrumental piece, by the name of, *In the Shadows*, and was all the rage in New York," informed Jack.

"However, In 1904 Alfred Butt took over the management of the Palace Theater, and it is, of course, with him that we have our meeting. He was the manager responsible for introducing the first showing of the Bioscope film involving travel films or events as the funeral of Edward VII[th.] or the coronation of George V[th.] I have already spoken with him about you two gentlemen and in principle he remains amenable to our proposal!" said Lodge.

"This Alfred Butt, is he able to authorize such a decision regarding us?" inquired Jack.

"I should say so; his father, Alfred Beyfus own the Palace Theater! You will be in good company here. Many artistes have performed on stage here on a regular basis including Margaret Cooper pianoforte performer and lyricist, Maud Allan in her rôle as *Salomé* and a Tsarist Russian dancer by the name of Anna Pavlova. Recently the Palace Theater was chosen, by command of King George V[th.] to host the first Royal Variety Performance.

Eventually, Alfred Butt did indeed join us looking more like a stage hand than the manager of an illustrious Palace Theater. He whispered a few words in Lodge's ear who repeatedly nodded his head in agreement. He then turned to Jack and me and handed us this evening's Program of Acts. Shook our hands and turned on his heels and marched out of his well-appointed opulently gilded Crush Bar.

"Do not mind him, gentlemen," said Lodge, "he is a man known for his economium of words!"

The Program of Acts Butt had handed us with this evening's various *acts* and *turns* listed, made for quite

THE PALACE MUSIC HALL

CAMBRIDGE CIRCUS, LONDON

Presents for your
Delectation

~O~

Phyllis Broughton 5-45pm

Eva Carrington, 6-00pm

Rachel D'Arcy and her Ukulele, 6-30pm

Cinderella, 7-00pm

Little Tich, 7-15pm

Vicky Delmar, 7-30pm

Miss Mary Gilby, vocalist, 8-00pm

Clarice Vance, 8-300pm

Little Bo-Peep, 9-00pm

Anna Pavlova & Michael Mordkin, 9-15pm

George Robey – The Prime Minister of Mirth, 10-00pm

Jules Léotard - Daring Young man on the Flying Trapeze 10-30

Dan Leno, 11-00pm

Vesta Tilley, 11-30pm

impressive reading. Clearly The Palace Theater remains second to none.

We could not help but noticed Little Bo Peep doing her rounds in addition to her performing her secret Cinderella act too!

After a few more glasses of Loge's champagne largesse, he made an announcement.

"Gentlemen, we had better take our seats as it is now five and thirty minutes past five o'clock"

We duly followed Lodge through a maze of red carpeted passageways and corridors. Without doubt the Palace Theater, though designed as a grand opera house, had an ethereal style and splendor which of course would now be at variance to the *acts* and *turns* currently being staged here. I could well imagine D'Oyly Carte's dream of hearing the sublime chords emanating from the operas of Wagner, Puccini or Mozart drifting throughout the auditorium and galleries and down the various opulently appointed corridors.

We entered the auditorium through two large highly polished mahogany doors held opened by two ushers who bowed as we walked through the portal. We were to be seated on the first tier Grand Circle in the center. One thing was for certain, Loge knew how to get the best plush crimson velvet covered seats in the house! We took ours. Looking about the auditorium it was huge. One immediately felt overwhelmed and insignificant by its grandiose appointment.

We were seated in the first tier balcony. Above us was a second and third tier. All the balconies curved round to the sides of the auditorium terminating at the proscenium arch. At that point the balconies were sectioned off to form intimate private boxes of which there were two to each balcony and all contained plush red velvet covered upholstery. Indeed below us the stalls was swathe of crimson colored seating of generous proportion.

One aspect of the Grand Circle became obvious to me and that was the fact of there being a conspicuous absence of columns supporting the balcony above, as is usual the case in theaters. These columns of course can block one's view of the stage, and therefore eminently suitable to locate the likes of the Metropolitan Board of Works' fire inspector; John Hebb. However, it would appear here, that the balconies must be constructed on the cantilever principle; meaning that the balconies are supported from metal girders anchored into the back structural walls of the balcony. A novel feature I thought. Dominated the auditorium was an elaborate and extremely ornate ceiling comprising detailed gilded raised designs.

"Well Lodge," said Jack, "you always appear to be able to get us the best red plush seats in the house. But, do you think Theo and I will be equal to the task of actually being able to impress the patrons sitting in such opulent surroundings as this ornate auditorium?"

"I certainly do not see any reason to prevent your inevitable success with such an audience, where ever seated, Jack," replied Lodge,

At that moment the safety curtain ascended into the attic above the proscenium arch. In so doing, it revealed a demur Miss Phyllis Broughton, who immediately launched into her bout of singing with vigor.

"Did we not see that Phyllis Broughton the last time we were at the Canterbury when she was performing her rôle as *Kevin,* King of the Fairies? And, if I remember, organizing unbridled pandaëmonium especially against those swooning aërial taffeta-wearing fairies which erupted into well-organized violence?" Jack asked.

"I believe you to be absolutely correct Jack!" replied Lodge.

Looking at a somewhat restrained Phyllis Broughton singing for her supper about a lonely girl on Brighton Pier searching the deep red horizon for her sailor boy, as opposed to her recent rôle as *Kevin,* King of the Fairies, seemed incongruous to me! Later we were treated to listening to the fabulous Eva Carrington. Or should I say, the Lady de Clifford? As Lodge reminded us, during his monumental and impassioned speech he delivered in the Imperial Blue Room in defense of the Music Hall against the unwarranted incursions of the Metropolitan Board of Works into such a domain.

We were then treated to the remarkable Rachel D'Arcy who stroked her Ukulele with inordinate affection whilst singing at the top of her vocal range, another bout of highly suggestive songs which the audience clearly adored as indiacted by their sustained applause.

Then *she* came on!

It was Cinderella, in her rôle as the abandoned heroine. She strutted on to the center stage, as near to the footlights, for all in the auditorium to avail themselves of the vision of her. I was curious because whilst she retained her outsized pit boots with iron studs on the soles and clearly several sizes too big for her feet. She wore no top hat on this occasion. But instead was wearing a tiara of finely wrought silver with intricate and ornate designs gracing the top of her closely cropped auburn hair.

The tiara complimented the ball-gown she wore which comprised layers of different silken material colored purple, red, blue or indigo, complete with white ribbons and stones of lapis lazuli and black jet sown into the fabric, creating a somber ensemble, more appropriate for a funereal occasion.

In performing her *act*, as the abandon heroine, on this particular occasion, Cinderella restricted herself to a couple of lullabies. Followed by a quick dance routine, during which she threw herself across the stage, with, what could only be described as, reckless abandon. Despite the heavy stud impressed outsized pit boots she wore, Cinderella was able to execute and accomplished a particularly graceful *pas de deux*.

Not withstanding her balletic abilities, I find it almost incomprehensible to imagine this girl, in short cropped auburn hair strutting around the stage in outsize pit boots; and then dressed as the definition of pure innocence, in the rôle of Little Bo Peep, prone to falling down on stage, cutting her knee and crying her eyes out! Jack and I have much to learn about English Music Hall, I thought.

After series of *acts* involving, Vicky Delmar, Miss Mary Gilby vocalist and Clarice Vance, in that order, we decided to repair to the bar for the interval session. It was good feeling to be back in this resplendent bar. Lodge did the honors and ordered champagne and even offered his cigar case to Jack and myself, to which, we gladly consented.

After discussing various points about the evening's program we got on to what Butt had discussed with Lodge previously.

"He is prepared to give you an opportunity to perform here in the near future. I explained to him your new innovative idea of mixing it with the audience and he liked the idea and so do I," said Lodge.

We were into our third bottle of champagne when in

the far distance an interval bell sounded. It sounded, more like the Bells of Doom, implying that we must alas abandon the bar and return to our plush crimson, if comfortable, seats. That deep toll of bells, triggered off a surge of people back to the auditorium including us. Some persons I noticed made no effort to even begin to consider vacating the comfortable Crush Bar. I wish I could have stayed with them.

We arrived at our seats just in time to see the safety curtain ascend revealing a pastoral scene of a water meadow, trees and blue sky complete with fluffy clouds which resembled balls of cotton wool. From stage right hobbled on a pathetic figure with an arched back.

It was Little Bo Peep and looking pretty sorry for herself, complete with big reddened eyes, as she limped on to the stage using her shepherdess crook as a crutch. I sat forward in my seat, for such was my curiosity to see what she would surprise us with this evening. Her attire was predictable, for one whose character portrayal is one of precious innocence, comprised as it was of a light blue dress with frilly white piping to the hem and tightly fastened collar.

Below that her two thin anæmic legs were covered in thick white woollen stockings at the end of which she wore her clogs, blue in color. Above her dress, she wore a cotton smock covered in embroidered simple designs, with lacing to the front and pale yellow ribbons trailing down. Upon her head, partially covering a mass of blond curly locks, was a wide brimmed straw bonnet complete with a garland of primroses and buttercups, all which augmented a picture of daintiness befitting her simpleton image.

Presently, she hobbled up to the footlights and with her right hand held up to her eyes, surveyed the auditorium as though looking for someone or something.

Now it could have been the fact that Little Bo Peep had not realized just how near she was to the edge of the stage, when her vision was diverted whilst she looked around the auditorium. But, all of a sudden Bo Peep fell off the stage edge and straight into the orchestra pit, to the general unanimous gasp of horror by the audience.

She landed on one of the euphonium players next to the percussion section, to the accompaniment of cymbal crashes and general pandäemonium being let loose, as orchestral instruments were knocked over or set in disarray. Bo Peep had by now disappeared beneath several percussion instruments and a plume of sheets of music some how suspended in the aëther immediately above her in the orchestra pit.

Presently, a not very sympathetic euphonium player extricated her from the chaos and sheets of music now settling, like snowfall, on to the floor of the orchestra pit. She all too readily burst into tears pointing to a red stain on her white woolen stockings. The euphonium seemed at a loss in what to do or how to re-act to this calamity, apart from offering her, his red paisley pat-terned handkerchief to the stricken Bo Peep, who immediately snatched it out of his hand and applied it to her injured leg.

Eventually, the euphonium player aided by one of the violoncellists, lifted Bo Peep back onto the stage. It was all a bit upsetting. Clearly she had sustained some injuries, as witnessed by the blood on her white stocking, because whilst she may have been lifted back onto the stage, she was unable to pick herself up. Even when the euphonium player, upon whom she had fallen, handed her shepherdess' crock, it was as much she could do to drag herself across the stage, in her attempt to leave, albeit with some degree if dignity.

She stopped and lay there on the stage floor for a few moments. She looked quite forlorn and a pathetic crumpled mass of cotton and ribbons with an ever increasing patch of red on her white stocking, which she caressed as she sobbed away, in her desperate attempt to comfort herself.

Then, imperceptibly at first, but becoming more distinct as the seconds went by was the faint sound of murmuring which sounded like a fusion of sobbing and singing. Eventually, the singing of lyrics became more audible as the sobbing receded. It was Bo Peep, singing in the low key of E flat minor.

Eventually, the murmuring transmuted into clear distinct words as Bo Peep related her story of how she had lost two darling lambs to a sly fox. And how she dare not face the farmer, for whom she toiled as shepherdess, because she was petrified he would beat her up again and cause further injuries to her crippled legs.

Whilst Bo Peep related these heart-wrenching facts there were from the audience regular sounds of gasps of horror and cries of 'shame' abounded around the auditorium.

I noticed that Bo Peep's allotted time was from nine o'clock until fifteen minutes past nine o' clock. It was now thirty-five minutes past that hour! The following *act*, in the form of some Tsarist Russian dancers called Anna Pavlova and Michael Mordkin would have to wait in the wings until Little Bo Peep had finished draining her audience of every ounce of emotion they possessed.

I liked watching Bo Peep. Her performances were truly stupendous and stretched innovation at every occasion. Hers was a polished *act*, and yet as I remembered when I first saw her at the New Bedford Music Hall in Camden Town, she did not require anything save her shepherdess' crook, and she did not really need that. Bo Peep spent more time sitting on the stage floorboards, than she did standing upright upon them!

At length her song receded back into sobbing which increased in loudness, as she made her exit stage right, complete with authentic limping, to meet with her ill-fate and the cruel farmer.

The thunderous applause that erupted was deafening and sustained. I countered just over seven minutes of unceasing clapping and stamping of feet in all sections of the auditorium; from humble rear stalls to the Grand Circle and plushed up private boxes.

"Jack, I keep saying we need to learn from her. What has she done now? She did not even fall down to the stage floor; no, she fell off the stage down into the orchestra pit instead, by accident, whilst distracted looking for her lost lambs!" I said to Jack, who nodded his agreement.

"You are correct Theo," responded Jack, "you play the rôle of Bo Peep from now on, and I shall play the rôle of Cinderella too, and see how we both fare!"

"You are on; we cannot fail," I replied.

When at last the audience had settled down in their seats a quietness descended over the auditorium which was only interrupted when the safety curtain ascended revealing what the program billed as Mr. George Robey – the 'Prime Minister of Mirth'. Presumably Bo Peep's *turn,* having gone on beyond her allotted time, meant that Anna Pavlova and Michael Mordkin's *act,* had been abandoned. Without any preamble by the Compière, he immediately launched into that favorite song of his and a very popular one, I believe, called '*If You Were the Only*

Girl in the World,' followed by his observations upon mundane, but comic situations, making them even more preposterous.

I seem to remember Loge saying that this accomplished Music Hall artiste made his début on the London stage, at the Oxford Music Hall some time ago in 1890. Upon completion of his monologue Robey returned to singing, in particular *'He'll Get It Where He's Gone to Now'*. After vigorous clapping and much bowing and waving, Robey vacated the stage for a certain Jules Léotard, billed as the 'Daring Young man on the Flying Trapeze' that he proceeded to manipulated with a series of death defying manœuvres, designed to amaze his audience in the stalls, over which he swung out regularly.

"I think Theo, we could do well here. The range of *acts* and *turns* are varied as they are interesting. We should be able to fit in well with the general ethos extant here and the quick flowing *turns* should help our *act* rather than hinder it!" said Jack.

"I am glad you conclude so," I replied.

In quick succession, Léotard was followed by the versatile comedian and *dame* impersonator, Dan Leno. Looking and listening to him, one could not help but feel that he was under used in his present rôle, for his diction was clear and timing impeccable.

I could not forget the images of Little Bo Peep and that of her Cinderella. The *acts* being performed out there on the stage before me faded into an obscurity by comparison. However, at that moment, Vesta Tilley, bringing up the final *turn* of the evening, came marching on to the stage wearing the khaki uniform of a recruiting sergeant.

Both Jack and I have seen this artiste perform in New York, and she is known for her varied and wide impersonations of men including dressing as one. Witness the uniform she has donned tonight. Then it came to me I recall reading a report, it could have been in the *Variety* journal, I remain unsure. But, the article informed the reader that Tilley first stage appearance was when she was but three and half years old.

Quite what made Tilley adopt, at the tender age of six years, her preferred rôle in donning male clothing, was a question the *Variety* journal asked, but received no answer. Possibly, it speculated, that Tilley at the time, in 1870, was billed as *'The Pocket Sims Reeves'* [4] including singing songs from his operatic repertoire, to make her impersonation of him appear more realistic. She was, I remember, and who does not? Quoted as saying, 'I felt that I could express myself better if I were dressed as a boy!'

It was all the rage at the time, certainly in New York, where the *Yellow Press* got to hear about the pervasiveness of female impersonators, who clearly had a predilection for preferring men's' clothing, whilst on the stage. These included such Music Hall artistes as Bessie Bellwood, Millie Hylton, Hetty King, Fanny Robina or Ella Shields.

It was the implied suggestion of criticism in continuing to dress in males clothing, *off* stage, which caught the undeviating attention of that *Yellow Press*. I remembered Tilley, in order to counter such criticism, was compelled to emphasis her femininity off stage, more so than usual since she had no children. In this respect Tilley was always well presented in public wearing fur coats and orchidaceous jewelry. In any event, her rôle at the moment on the stage below us, involved her marching around bellowing out orders to members of the orchestra, in the pit and to imaginary soldiers.

We did stay in our seats until the end of the evening to the witness Tilley's final *act* of the evening. But, after experiencing Little Bo Peep's emotionally charged melodrama, my emotions, and that of the audiences' had been wrenched quite significantly for one evening. We were now quite incapable of re-acting to further delectations on the stage, even by an array of accomplished artistes, as we had done so.

Again, I found myself wondering about Little Bo Peep being the epitome of pure innocence working for a wicked farmer. And then, trying to reconcile the image of this girl Bo Peep playing Cinderella, especially in her rôle as the persecuted heroine in short cropped auburn hair strutting around the stage in outsize pit boots! It really is almost certainly probable that Jack and I do have much to learn from her.

I keep repeating this sentiment to myself and have every intention of doing something about it. One thing is clear to me; a thought, a profound thought was taking form in my mind and, I feel confident in my understanding it.

1. Ostentatious or showy
2. It was known as the Royal English Opera House and opened in January 1891
3. Early form of recording on disc
4. Impersonating Sims Reeves, an actual opera singer

Chapter 29

The Fatal Embrace

Our evening in the Palace Theater yesterday was both important and an experience that Jack and I have agreed needs to be examined more closely. We saw a range of *acts* and *turns* that were not only highly polished, but innovative. Bo Peep's being one that readily springs to mind. We should very much like to return; and not a moment should be lost in our doing so. In this respect have we have been assured that we shall be given an opportunity to perform there on the stage at the acclaimed Palace Theater.

Again, as is our routine, we discussed the previous day's encounters over break-fast in our St. Pancras Hotel Dining Room. Jack and I agreed that our experiences yesterday evening at the Palace Theater were of great interest and entertainment.

"I was very impressed with that Crush Bar Jack, the likes of which, I have never seen before, especially in a theater or Music Hall. For me, irrespective of what happened on the stage, the ornate décor of the Crush Bar was well worth the experience," I remarked to Jack.

"I knew that you would be Theo," replied Jack.

"I was also particularly impressed with the architectural designs of the Palace Theater, which were clearly based on those designs by Garnier for the Paris Opéra house.

I can also appreciate readily the fact that the Palace Theater was designed to imitate the Paris Opéra, as England's foremost opera house. Would you agree with those observations Jack?" I inquired.

"Yes, I agree so far as I am able to understand and appreciate fine architecture Theo. But you do that better than most of us. But what I did appreciate fully was what Little Bo Peep got up to. You are, as usual, Theo quite correct. She does continue to fascinate audiences, you and I with her simple but innovative *acts*. All of which very effectively play on her audience's emotions and feelings," said Jack.

We both sat in silence in order to take in the enormity of our observations. However, we have agreed to meet with Loge over luncheon at Kettner's Restaurant in Soho to discuss some finer points regarding our particular stage *act*.

Having exchanged the warmth and comfort of the St. Pancras Hotel for the acridity of the still pervasive fog, we were now clattering in our highly varnished Clarence carriage en-route for Kettner's Restaurant and our rendezvous with Lodge for luncheon. At one stage we were passing a classical structure, very much like the Temple of Erechtheion, in Athens, complete with the Caryatids supporting a vestibule roof. We then turned left, passed a massive triangular stoned frame pediment supported by a colonnade of Corinthian columns, in to Upper Woburn Place, or so a road plate informed me.

"That building, Theo, is a church," said Jack, who had noticed my facial expression of inquiry as I looked at the building.

"It is the parish church of St. Pancras - named for the fourteen year old Roman martyr, the designs of which, I think, are partly based on the Temple of Erechtheion,

Temple of Erechtheion

especially the Caryatids Porch located on the Acropolis in Athens, Greece," informed Jack.

"I thought I recognized the classical style of the temple," I responded.

"We should be at Kettner's Restaurant directly," added Jack.

True enough, having eventually emerged into the Tottenham Court Road, I think, we made our way down into the Charing Cross Road, passed the Rookery of ill-repute and into Cambridge Circus, dominated by the majesty of the imposing Palace Theater. Our Clarence carriage took us along the side of the Palace Theater and down Romilly Street.

It was whilst progressing down Romilly Street that we nearly collided with a pantechnicon, with a Fortnum & Mason cipher emblazoned on its highly varnished side panel. What is it in London; one is always colliding with other wagons or experiencing near collisions? Probably the fog, and its ability to conceal on coming wagons, I concluded. However, at length and intact, we pulled up outside Kettner's Restaurant.

I leapt down from our Clarence carriage, onto the glistening pavement made wet by the presence of the fog. And it was with inordinate enthusiasm, that we both made our way into a red carpeted foyer. Arriving at the

Reception desk, Jack informed the Concièrge that we were expected by a certain Mr. Michael Lodge, as his luncheon guests.

"One moment please sir," responded the Concièrge, and like his brother Concièrge at the St. Pancras Hotel, turned on his heels and disappeared into the recesses of his domain. A few minutes later he re-appeared, but asked a question that filled both Jack and me with a premonition, as it were, of a resigned inevitability.

"With whom did you say you were having luncheon?" asked the Concièrge.

"Lodge, a Michael Lodge," I answered, "and is this inquiry for Lodge going to turn into a matinée performance?"

"You wish to see a matinée performance in which a certain Mr. Michael Lodge does a *turn*? No sir, I am afraid this is Kettner's Restaurant," advised the Concièrge, wearing a structural expression of seriousness upon his face.

"If you do wish such entertainment, then I feel certain that the Palace Theater, over there, along Romilly Street towards Cambridge Circus, will accommodate your thespian needs. Though I could not, of course, say for certain whether this Lodge artiste fellow will be doing his *turn* on the stage or not!"

"This is intolerable," I exclaimed in exasperation to Jack, "that Loge, can he ever be trusted to deal with...."

"Loge, did you say Loge?" asked the Concièrge, interrupting me, but in tones of sincerity, "we have *Loge* here of course, and he has booked luncheon for three persons. Alas, he has not arrived yet, but you are very welcome to use our well-appointed bar whilst waiting for him!"

The moment he uttered those words, his two young

assistants at the Concièrge's Reception, burst out into uncontrollable giggling, with barely concealed joy.

"If you will follow me please," replied the Concièrge, in a deep resonating voice, "I will show you to our well-appointed and comfortable bar."

Presently, we were escorted through the various salons, of which Kettner's Restaurant, is comprised. The general décor of establishment was based on simplicity of restrained elegance which favors understatement, rather than ostentatious embellishment to lend opulence to the place. This is in stark contrast to the exuberant décor similar to which is prevalent at the more ornate Criterion Bar at the Regent's Circus. Accordingly, I instinctively found it pleasing to be here and felt at ease with the place. At length we were shown in to the so-called well-appointed and comfortable bar and immediately went to the *Carrera* marble clad counter to order our drinks.

Jack and I were discussing the remarkable Little Bo Peep, whilst we were standing at the bar at Kettner's in Romilly Street, in the fog-bound depths of Soho. We both of us concurred; hers was quite a unique *act*, the likes of which we had never experienced before, until seeing her of course, and certainly not in United States, or even heard about a similar *act*.

We were into our second round of drinks when a commotion was heard some distance off. Jack, I and others drinking at the bar turned instantly turned around to the entrance to the salon with an expectation of something, as the noise of the commotion became louder.

Suddenly Lodge burst into the salon and staggered towards us at the bar. He did so as though he were possessed or afflicted with some brain fever. That or another writ had been served upon his person. He was clearly in a state of extreme agitation and waving a newspaper above his head. As he approached our persons I could see quite clearly that his were eyes rolled around aimlessly in their sockets. His monomania, need less to say, had increased to such an extent that we feared the worst in that his head might at any moment detach from his shoulders.

"Bar-tender, brandy, quickly," said Jack, decisively, recognizing the urgency of the situation.

"What is to become of me?" asked Lodge, whilst tapping the newspaper repeatedly with the end of his index finger, "see, look, look at what has been done!"

Jack and I exchanged glances as Lodge drank deeply from his glass of brandy. Another one was duly ordered for him, for he seemed beside himself with anguish and despair.

Presently he opened *The Daily Telegraph* and pointed to a telegram report in the *Stop Press* section, posted on the left hand margin of the page. It was Jack who took the paper from Lodge and began reading the article aloud.

Actress Bella Cora Elmore Done In

Detectives from Scotland Yard, led by inspector Walter Dew of the Criminal Investigation Department were summoned earlier to an address in Hampstead, after friends of Music Hall artiste Cora Crippen, whose stage name was Bella Elmore, reported her missing.

Elmore's failure to turn up for crucial rehearsals at the Royalty Music Hall in Soho, alerted both the manager of the Music Hall, Mr. Arthur Bourchier and her co-artistes who became suspicious when, Kate Williams, the professional strong woman known as Vulcana and friend of Elmore said that she had met Crippen at a ball recently. There Crippen is said to have informed Vulcana that Bella had returned to the United States.

Vulcana did not accept this explanation from Crippen because Elmore had never mentioned this planned trip to the United States. And Williams' suspicions were increased further when she noticed that items of jewelry belonging to Bella, and of which she was inordinately proud, were being worn by a woman, with a fondness for large hats, standing with Crippen, whom he subsequently introduced as his niece, Ethel Neave.

It is a fact that the Crippens were often seen quarreling together in public. Including a particularly virulent argument at that drinks party the couple had held recently at their home at Hilldrop House, near Hampstead Heath, in north London. A drinks party to which Williams and other friends of Elmore including, John Nash and Lil Hawthorne his wife, attended. Elmore has not been seen since that time of that drinks party.

Fearing something untoward, Williams and others went to Scotland Yard and expressed their concerns to a Superintendent Frank Froest of Scotland Yard, who duly instructed Inspector Walter Dew, to initiate inquiries. He did and visited Crippen at his home to investigate the whereabouts of Cora Crippen.

Upon arrival at the house Crippen was

inordinately cordial and helpful. So much so that he invited inspector Dew into his home. There Crippen maintained his story insisting that Cora had gone back to America, to California, accompanied by a friend of hers, a certain Music Hall performer by the name of Bruce Miller. Eventually, the police withdrew satisfied that there was no evidence of a misdemeanor having been committed.

However, inspector Walter Dew returned to Hilldrop House later to confirm a detail in his investigation. Upon arriving at the address, there was no reply. Eventually inspector Dew and several constables forced their way in to the house. It was abandoned with Crippen nowhere to be found, despite the fact that he had previously assured Dew that he would be at home. At first there was no evidence of foul play. But Crippen's absence prompted the police constables to search the house again. This time they did so more thoroughly.

And it was during a search of the basement and lower basement that produced what looked like evidence in the form of bleached blonde hair, bits of flesh and a pajama jacket near or around an inordinately large gas-fired cast iron furnace. These items suggested that a body may have been done away with, or indeed, cremated. It was later that a shallow grave was discovered containing a dismembered torso, without limbs or head, but parts of which almost certainly to have been disposed of, in the adjacent furnace. It is believe that this torso is all that now remains of Cora Crippen.

It has now transpired that Hawley Crippen was born in the township of Coldwater, in the state of Michigan in the United States and graduated from the Medical School of Michigan University. It is also reported that information on the fugitive Crippen is incomplete; but it would seem that he was married to another woman called Charlotte. She too is reported to have died of heart disease, but with whom he has two children now in the care of Crippen's parents, who are resident in the State of California.

It is also known, that it was whilst Crippen practiced medicine in New York, he met and later married, in 1894, his second wife. Corrine Turner. She is better known to the public as, Bella Elmore or 'Cora' and who too was an American citizen and born Kunigunde Mackamotski from German-Polish ancestry.

Police have now launched a manhunt for Doctor Hawley Crippen, who is believed responsible for the death of his wife Corrine Turner in their home at Hilldrop House, London.

Lodge who was now beside himself with grief, having had the awful facts of this devastating news read out aloud to him in a graphic way, could only serve to increase his anguish. What, however, went through my mind, was the significant connection between Crippen attending the University of Michigan medical school and another accomplished murderer in the person of the good Doctor Holmes, of the Castle Hotel in Chicago, also a graduate from that University!

It still fills me with dread when I think of what Doctor Holmes was up to as the proprietor of the now infamous Castle Hotel on 63rd. Street in the Englewood neighborhood of Chicago. There both Jack and I resided as hotel guests for a period, while working the Music Halls during the World's Columbian Exposition.

In that Castle Hotel, which he designed and had built for himself, specifically with multiple murders in mind. The Castle Hotel on 63rd. Street, was less than two miles away from the site of the World's Columbian Exposition, and therefore convenient to many visitor to Chicago. Accordingly, Holmes may have taken in an unknown number of victims, most of whom were women.

Incredibly, some of his innocent and unsuspecting hotel guests were simply gassed whilst locked in sound-proof chambers.

While other victims were not gassed, but were left rather, to suffocate in a huge sound-proof bank vault located in the basement, conveniently adjacent to the crematorium!

Our Doctor Holmes was not above cremating his victims in two giant furnaces he had built in an outhouse next to the basement of the main hotel building. It was later reported that the heat from these crematorium furnaces, provided the hot water and central heat for the hotel!

Nor indeed, was he reticent in placing their corpse in lime pits in addition to acid baths. Poisons were, I recall, a favorite of the good Doctor, and often administered to recalcitrant hotel guests, irrespective of age or gender, who quite unreasonably, were unwilling to die for him, whilst visiting the World's Columbian Exposition in Chicago.

"My God, this is all very similar to Crippen's preferred method of disposing of corpses," I announced, to other members of the bar who had in the meantime congregated around the disconsolate Loge.

By now several brandies consumed were having their desired effect on Lodge, who seemed to be rallying over the news regarding the untimely demise of Bella, formally lead soprano in his *Three Graces*, of which there were now, of course, only two.

This news was, for all to see, very distressing for Loge; but what in fact had happened, apart from the obvious death at Hilldrop House, Hampstead where we had dinner, and indeed stayed over night recently, I wondered.

I asked Loge.

"I am at a loss myself to offer an explanation. It seems that Bella is, sorry, was, experiencing difficulties with her husband whom you met at their Hilldrop House the other evening. Apparently after a drinks party, they had recently, Crippen, perhaps in a fit of pique, who knows, but it would seem that he done her in and tried to conceal the evidence by disposing her in that huge gas-fired furnace they have in the basement," said Lodge.

"That sounds rather anæmic," said Jack, "if Crippen wanted to leave Bella for his mistress called Ethel Neave, according to the Stop Press, then why did he not just move on, and why commit this hideous crime against his wife?"

"It is probable that Bella, being of a tempestuous disposition, would not have allowed Crippen, her husband to abandon her to the Fates. Were he to have done so, she would almost have certainly instigated divorce proceedings against him culminating in his being ruined," offered Lodge.

"More importantly, what be I to do about my *Three*

Graces, of which, now of course there are only two left?" cried Lodge, throwing his hands above his head, to the heavens for salvation, "for I too shall be ruined, ruined I tell you!"

"But surely, one can pick up another contralto or soprano or whatever to replace Bella?" inquired Jack.

"Contraltos? Contraltos are as cheap as life itself; it is a soprano that I really need, even a mezzo-soprano, would temporarily suffice," replied Lodge.

"Loge, when we were staying at Hilldrop House, near the Hampstead heath the other night," I said, very slowly and with deliberation in my voice, which alerted Jack's attention, "I expressed to you and in fact to Bella in the Dining Room at the St. Pancras Hotel, that I had a series of experiences during the night. I also recall that you and Bella dismissed my experiences and observations as normal everyday, almost mundane occurrences."

Neither Jack nor I were convinced by this interpretation offered by Bella or Lodge. And in fact the memory of our experience in the murderous Castle Hotel in Chicago came flooding back into my like a spring river in full rage running off the Alleghenies Mountains.

"Jack will testify to you Loge; that I am neither given to hallucinatory or repressed hysterical behavior. Nor is my imagination unbridled. I saw and heard things during that sleepless night whilst at Hilldrop House, which were inexplicable. That house represents the very same Castle Hotel in Chicago, in that it was used as a place of terror and death. When Jack and I stayed in the Castle Hotel, as you well know, we experienced various things there which did not make sense because we could never have known the real purpose of the hotel and murderous intent of the good Doctor Holmes.

"However, upon learning the truthful, aspect of the

place things began to make sense. The pervasive musty odor that invariable prevailed in the hallways and corridors. The unconventional layout of the building, with corridors leading to literally nowhere, staircases which abruptly terminated at a brick wall, and bedroom doors which could only be opened from outside the room.

"The same with Hilldrop House, when I was awake at the mid hour at night due to my being unable to sleep, I witnessed some strange happenings. That radiator in my bedroom was cold one moment and then, I noticed, searingly hot the next, during the middle of the night? It was almost like a correlation between the crematorium furnaces at the Castle Hotel providing the central heat there, and a inexplicable heat source for Hilldrop House, where gas had not been laid on yet! And what about that mysterious shadow moving over the darkened secluded garden, what about that?

"The fact also that my bedroom door was locked from outside in the hallway, to mention nothing of the fact the gas mantle immediately above my bed was leaking deadly gas straight down onto where I should have been sleeping. And, when I eventually manage to get out of my bedroom and went to Jack's, I had to virtually force his bedroom door open only to find Jack unconscious when I got into his room. That bed chamber, I might add, was full of gas that had been pouring out of the gas mantle immediately above Jack inert body.

"And then, when I went to the curtains to draw them apart in order to open the windows to let air into the room, I was confronted, not by a window, but by a brick wall. That and other facts were beginning to suggest something more akin to sinister events and not, as you and Bella intimated, merely a series of unrelated coincidences. Our experiences of being locked in the cellar, near that furnace radiating vicious intense heat were too also instructive…" I said.

"Come on Lodge, what are the goods on Crippen," interrupted Jack, looking distinctly displeased at my revelation, "aside of Bella, and the fact he has done her in? Theo is absolutely right. There have been some nefarious activities extant at Hilldrop House, and Theo experienced some of those goings on when we were there."

"Gentlemen, I am at a loss as to render any explanation to you or indeed anybody. You must remember, that I too am astonished as you are, to learn of the terrible fate that has befallen our Bella," said Lodge.

And with those words, Lodge got up and mumbling, "My *Three Graces*, I have lost a *Grace,*" and left the bar at Kettner's, clutching his newspaper to his chest.

We elected to stay in the bar, as we both of us did not feel like going any place else, if only in view of the fact that Bella, for what ever reason, had been done in.

Chapter 30

The Final Fiasco

The news of Bella having been done in supposedly by her husband, Doctor Hawley Crippen was bad enough. The manner of her being so done was horrific for all those who knew her, including, of course, ourselves. The news had further ramifications for Loge, who now had lost one *Grace*, out of his *Three Graces*, and the implications of which such a tragedy posed for him personally.

It was therefore with mixed feelings that we met with Loge after a suitable period of mourning. He had sent a cable-gram ahead of his arrival inviting us both to attend Bella's small but intimate funeral before her burial. This is take place at Highgate Cemetery in north London; just a mile or so beyond the New Bedford Music Hall in Camden Town. Accordingly, Jack and I were in the foyer of the St. Pancras Hotel waiting on Lodge to arrive.

Again, Lodge's entrance into the hotel foyer was preceded by a commotion outside in the ornate stone vestibule of the Porte Cochère. Even the normally reticent aloof Concièrge looked over his shoulder to determine what had caused this consternation.

Then, as though taking a curtain call, Loge strode into the foyer and came up to us.

"Gentlemen, gentlemen my condolences," he said these words whilst he held both Jack's hand and mine in both of his hands. He looked for the entire world to see, or at least those gathered in the foyer of the hotel, as though he were the chief grief-stricken mourner, suitably attired in somber black and in everlasting deep mourning.

In place of his favorite rather sybaritic silk suit of electric blue in color, Lodge wore a black frock-coat made of herringbone patterned broadcloth. His trousers were of the same material and his black patent leather boot had been particularly well varnished for today's occasion. His shirt was white and the collar which was fastened with a stone, not his usual flamboyant amethyst or orchidaceous lazis lazuli, but a stone of pure black jet to compliment his somber mourning garb.

The top hat he wore, complete with black ribbons trailing at the back, appeared to be taller than usual and had wrapped around it a black crêpe material, the latest, I believe, in funereal garb together with an armband of black silk.

Despite the effort Loge had obviously gone through to look the part of the grief stricken soul in deep unceasing mourning, he did in fact also look worn and had touches of gray to his face. [1] Even his smile was sad.

Lodge then turned on his well polished heels and led Jack and I out to the Porte Cochère as though he were heading up a funeral cortège such was his stately and solemn measured walk. Eventually, we arrive at the vestibule underneath which was a large Barouche carriage, with a team of four shiny black horses in front of it, scraping their hooves on the cobble carriageway, and snorting steam through their nostrils, as though impatient.

It was the presence of these four horses and Barouche carriage blocking the Porte Cochère carriageway that had caused the commotion earlier. It was evident that the liveried coachman had, delivered Lodge to the hotel; but had thereafter, refused to move his Barouche carriage that was blocking the carriageway. This was much to the consternation of other coachmen unable to get by the stationary large Barouche carriage and team of four horses.

I could not believe this sight in front of us. Each horse was draped in black velvet with golden piping and upon their heads was fixed a large plume of black ostrich feathers. The Barouche carriage itself was decked out in black ribbons and other funereal symbols including rolled black crêpe resting on the two buttoned-down black leather upholstered seats.

Sitting high on his Barouche carriage bench was our liveried coach driver. He too was decorated in the appropriate somber funereal style. In place of the usual morning coat in red livery complete with gold braid and epaulettes and top hat worn by carriage drivers, this coachman was dressed differently. He wore a morning coat of black with black twisted cloth braid and black tasseled epaulettes and again his top hat was covered with black crêpe in keeping with the solemnity of the occasion.

I was looking at this black crêpe covered top hat when its wearer turned to face me. It was Aloysius, Loge's man-servant! This was the loquacious man-servant, an employé, with inordinate self-confidence, who had served us at luncheon the other day. Yet despite this, I was, for some unknown reason, grateful for his re-assuring presence and of the fact that Aloysius would be driving us, with his team of four hired black-plumed horses to the funeral at Highgate Cemetery.

We duly clambered aboard at Lodge's behest, and with a flick of Aloysius's whip, the team of black horses pulled our black ribbon and crêpe bedecked Barouche carriage out from beneath the Porte Cochère and into the pervasive acrid yellow fog, still with us.

Following behind us, was a not inconsiderable convoy of frustrated carriage drivers and their fares, all of whom had been compelled to wait for us to move our Barouche carriage on out of the way. Notwithstanding this barrage of mumbled cursing, from the carriage drivers behind us, we spoke in dignified terms about Bella and her befalling great misfortune. Lodge then pulled out of his jacket pocket a document which he looked at for a minute or two. Then with a look of resignation upon his worn face he at length spoke to us.

"Today is indeed a great day of immense sadness gentlemen. I for one would never have expected to inter Bella into a fine limestone sarcophagus within the confines of a fine imposing granite Mausoleum at Highgate Cemetery. A funereal structure, which I have just acquired," informed Lodge, pointing to the document he held in his hand, entitled, *Particulars of Sale*, and upon the front cover of which was a picture of a stone built Mausoleum.

"Bella was of course monotheistic, so there is the hope we shall see her in our futures, now she has *passed-over,*" said Lodge, bowing his head in deep manufactured reverence at mentioning Bella's name.

"A Mausoleum; how come you have managed to avail yourself of a Mausoleum in double quick time, since Bella only die… *passed-over,* only but these few days past?" asked Jack, for a reply to which would also be of incalculable interest to me too.

Lodge duly replied whilst he tapped the side of his nose with his index finger, whilst looking over both shoulders.

"Since it was obvious that Bella's husband, Crippen, was really in no position to organize a funeral for his wife

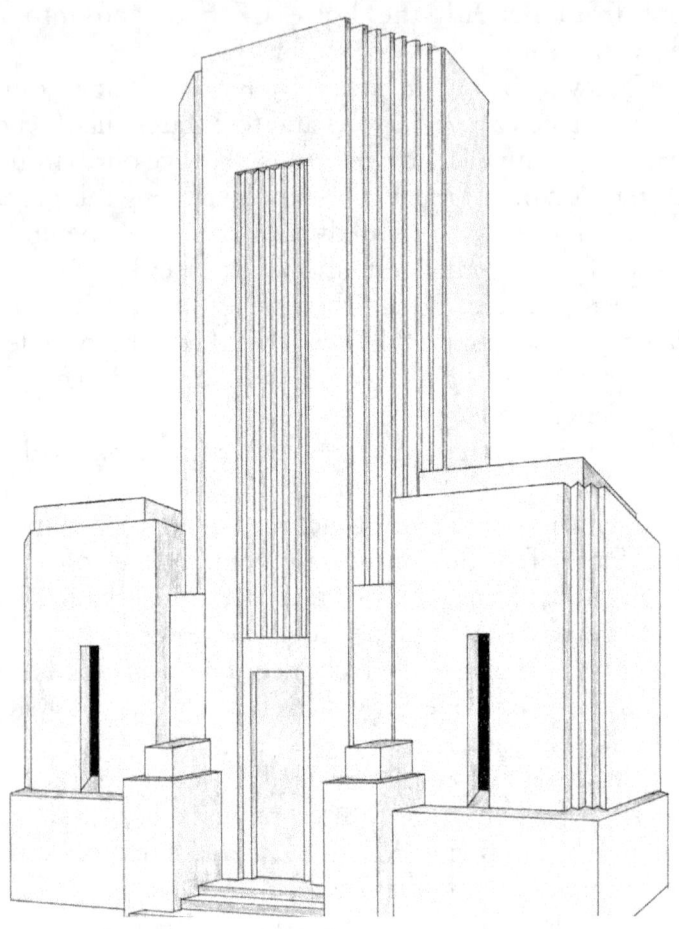

Mausoleum at Highgate Cemetery

that he had just murdered; I thought that I should do the honorable thing by Bella. It all came about whilst talking to an acquaintance over whom I have some *sway*, if you get my meaning. He informed me that in his rôle as an undertaker with the London Cemetery Company, that he had learned of an empty Mausoleum on the market for a quick private sale!

"The reason for this macabre good fortune, was simply, the person, for whom the Mausoleum was constructed, perished when the ill-fated *Titanic* ship sank the other day, with a loss of over fifteen hundred souls, including, of course, his.

"Since they cannot find his corpse and are unlikely to do so, his widow has been made all the poorer by her husband's unexpected death. Quite reasonably the widow thought it a good idea to sell the structure and make a profitable and satisfactory conveyance of the Mausoleum, since the purpose for which it was erected is now somewhat redundant. And aside of which, the sale of the superfluous Mausoleum, would enable her to raise the badly needed funds to provide for her ability to continue to inhabit this very real living world, albeit now as a happy, if richer, merry widow! That is why we are headed to Highgate, and not Brookwood, or indeed any other Necropolis, because it is there that the Mausoleum is located," completed Lodge.

"What you buy and sell constructed Mausoleums as though they were houses or dwellings?" asked Jack, with some incredulity in his voice.

"Well they are but dwellings, are they not? The mere fact the occupants of them are dead is neither here or there. But gentlemen, let us be grateful on this occasion that this vacant Mausoleum is in Highgate Cemetery and not in some other God-forsaken place such as Putney Vale; for who would want to spend eternity in such a place," said Lodge, pensively.

Aloysius and his team of four black-plumed horses hauling our somber-decked Barouche were making good progress, whilst on our way in to Camden Town. As indicated by the fact that we had just driven passed the lunatic asylum located in the St. Pancras Hospital, the inmates of which were incarcerated within the high walls of that establishment. These high walls however, did not stop or in any way reduce the noise of their screams of anguish drifting through the fog-bound aëther over those high walls of the asylum and into the streets beyond the precincts.

Again we drove down the Crowndale Road along the side of the Camden Theater which we had attended recently. We then swerved into the Camden High Street. It is of course, in this road that the infamous New Bedford Music Hall is constructed. Accordingly, I kept an eye out, just in case the Woman in Red was in the vicinity scuttling in the fog for a rendezvous at this Music Hall.

It was in this very Music Hall that Jack and I first encountered her, when she performed in a breath-taking performance of emotional expression, the type of which I had never experienced before in my professional life on the stage.

She did not appear from out of the fog, much to my dismay. So it was with added sadness that I, in the company of Jack and Lodge progressed by the front of the Music Hall and continued onward to Highgate and our rendezvous at the Mausoleum to inter Bella for eternity.

At length, we arrived at the somber stone entrance to Highgate Cemetery. In particular, the Western Cemetery, wherein lies the Egyptian Avenue of the Dead, with its series of catacombs and Mausoleums, including Bella's, we are told, and leading to the series of crypts that comprises the Circle of Lebanon, dominated by a huge cedar tree.

For some hitherto unexplained reason, we expected to

New Bedford Music Hall

see a mass of black-garbed grief-stricken mourners; instead, what we witnessed was the color and gaiety of fashionable clothes, including ostentatious striped blazers. And, all were worn with such gay abandon on the shoulders of various so-called mourners.

One got the distinct impression that had these mourners, beside themselves with grief and presumably Bella's friends, thought that the sun might have been shining on Highgate Cemetery, instead of being shrouded in fog. Then they would have supplied themselves with an assorted collection of Fortnum & Mason hampers, complete with champagne, cotton parasols and striped blazers with caps.

Jack and I recognized a few faces of course, as we surveyed the current Music Hall establishment. Loge, accordingly, had, marched into the crowd of grief stricken mourners, to renew contacts, make new friends or enemies, and generally disport himself amongst the mourners. The two other *Graces* in the persons of Kate Lawrence and Dot Hetherington were here to pay their respect to the other *Grace*, albeit now diseased. The failed *Grace* in Marie Lloyd was very much in evidence too, even if partially shrouded by the dense acrid fog which hung in the aëther, above the cemetery.

Vesta Tilley was there, dressed as a man, wearing a robust thorn-proof rust colored Harris Tweed suit and nonchalantly smoking cigars, to which, I understand, she is addicted. She was in conversation with Phyllis Broughton one of the strutting danseuse we had on two occasions witnessed. Nearby Dan Leno was laughing with George Robey who himself was ribbing Marmeduke Gatti, the Actor Manager of Hungerford Palace of Varieties, as Gatti, once corrected Lodge.

Standing nearby was the manager of the Metropolitan Music Hall, who from memory is called Henri Goss, and who virtually offered us a job when last we met with him in his innovative Crush Bar at the impressive Metropolitan Music Hall.

Thomas E Clay, the Manager of Wilton's Music Hall,

Metropolitan Music Hall

was also here to pay his final respects to Bella. He was standing alone from the other assembled mourners and with a vacant expression upon his face. Indeed, he was wearing, in a slovenly fashion, the same clothes which he wore when we first met with him in the depths of Wilton's Music Hall. Then, his attire comprised the ill-fitting frock-coat fabricated of black broadcloth and worn to a shine in patches. His shirt was still of a greyish hue and frayed at the collar, but closed on this occasion with a black neck-tie fastened by a stud finished in black jet.

His brown boots, which I noticed, were scuffed and unvarnished. Surmounting his dishevelled state was a head, the face of which was pocked-marked and of a sallow complexion, and into it were set deep eyes as black as coal, which stared out into the fog-laden aëther, as though he were looking out into oblivion. His black eyes matched the color of the hair on his head, though thick, was greasy and unkempt. He looked very much as an undertaker might.

Of course, I by, myself or with Jack, have attended funerals or memorials in the past in New York. Especially in Brooklyn Cemetery and witnessed our acting profession en masse, away from the stage. Without fail, the actual funeral, though privately may induce contemplation or a time for reflection in some, invariable was an excuse for others to exhibit themselves in full regalia.

The same evidently applies in England, for just observing the assembled collection of Music Hall artistes or actors, one got the distinct impression they appeared as if they were taking part in a fashion gala or promenade. Certainly if the larger the size of hats being worn, was indicative.

Most of the assembled grief-stricken artistes glared at

one another; or alternatively greeted each other with inordinate enthusiasm, which of course, shielded a repressed inherent mutual dislike. None behaved as though they were grief-stricken mourners bereaving Bella's *passing over.* Some were more concerned about comparing each others sartorial arrangements and ascendency in their endeavors to out shine one another.

A distressed and a mournful collection of Music Hall artistes come together to say their farewells to fellow performer Bella Elmore, was certainly not the case here, at Highgate Cemetery during this particular morning. Rather, it was a sartorial display designed to enhance the success of certain stage artistes and not to acknowledge Bella's *passing over,* nor indeed to bid her farewell. Neither was this a solemn funeral; but instead more of an opportunity to indulge in unbridled egotistic behavior and contests being played out on different levels.

To my consternation and continuing disappointment, there was no sign of the Woman in Red or indeed, of Cinderella, however dressed.

Despite this, these so-called acquaintances of Bella, none of whom Jack or I really knew personally, had in the mean time formed a cortège, as such. Though it seems at variance with their clearly determined intention to have fun between here and the Funereal Chapel of the Necropolis, in which the Requiem mass, in accordance with Roman Catholic rite, was to be held.

Later, the interment service was to be conducted at the limestone Mausoleum and there, elaborate funereal ritual exequies [2] were to take place upon Bella's coffin, as it was inducted into the sarcophagus located within the stone burial vault. Then, it was to be bricked up for eternity.

"Whilst we were standing at the back of the cortège,

waiting for the coffin to be retrieved from the hearse carriage, there appeared to be a commotion of some kind involving shouting in the vicinity of the hearse. We could not, from our position, determine immediately the reason for the shouting, nor ascertain the cause of the commotion.

Eventually we were able to ascertain the reason. It seemed that a liveried employé of the London Cemetery Company, the owners and operators of the Highgate Cemetery, was advising verbally, a carriage driver from the local funeral undertaker. He was suggesting in no uncertain terms and in language becoming crystal clear, as it was audible to all, precisely what the hearse driver could do with his *'gaudy coffin cart'*. And, I heard further, the London Cemetery Company employé even ventured a permanent place where the rival carriage driver might like to put his *'gaudy coffin cart'*.

Further mutual advice was offered which resulted in blows being freely exchanged between each employé, from the two rival undertakers, which escalated, as others joined in the mêlée. After much shouting and cursing, other officials from the Highgate Cemetery arrived to bring this outburst of tempers to an abrupt halt. Without success as it happened and during the fracas the catafalque, bearing Bella's small coffin draped in purple velvet cloth, had been wheeled out of the hearse, and pushed, unceremoniously through this commotion.

Immediately, and with very little dignity, an official ripped away the purple velvet cloth covering Bella's coffin. In so doing, revealed in one fell swoop, upon the catafalque, and there in the fog-bound Necropolis for all to see, was Bella's small coffin.

For some reason again, both Jack and I looked at each other in recognition that we would have thought a much more ornate coffin would contain Bella's remains. Made perhaps of black ebony wood with bronze handles, hinges, plaque and other ostentatious paraphernalia might have been deployed to convey Bella's corpse to the Mausoleum.

Instead what was resting on the catafalque was a cheap coffin of pressed wood, grey in colour with hinges and handles of string, almost an imperceptible grade above card-board! This was the cheapest coffin it would be possible to purchase, and legally place a corpse in, within the provisions of the law. Anything less than this, then the coffin would have been relegated to the status of an outsized Carbolic Soap box.

Still, the cortège moved off and we began our slow solemn march to the Funereal Chapel. Eventually, we arrived at the building. It was a stone built structure devoid of any architectural detail. It resembled more a place of functionality than of prayer and reflection. Indeed the presence at the back, of a coal-fired furnace indicated its more fundamental use.

If the architecture of the chapel could be considered bland, then the congregation of mourners certainly was not. Together, they resembled not so much a gathering of grief-stricken thespian mourners, as a group of day excursion trippers to the nearby Hampstead Heath for a picnic. But who, in the meantime, had lost their way in the fog, and found themselves instead here in the Highgate Cemetery.

Once inside the Funereal Chapel a rather undignified scramble erupted as grief-stricken mourners indulged in pushing and shoving as they fought amongst themselves for prime position in the pews in the chapel. Quite what they were expecting to witness from the front rows was beyond me; perhaps a matinée performance of some sort.

However, it was now on the front row that focused my attention. Looking like the Dame aux Camellias in full distress and somber regalia, racked with consumption, and all the more valetudinarian, acting as if she were about to endure her supreme moment, there and then, or at any rate pass out, was Marie Lloyd. She was dressed from head to foot in deepest black, and wearing a hat that in its own right merited some kind of architectural recognition, such was its size and construction.

Something then happened, a woman overcome with grief, so one would like to think, passed out and fell crashing onto a mourner standing next to her. She in turn fell, and both unconscious and conscious grief stricken mourners tumbled out of the pew, into the chapel aisle. Apart from a piled mass of black crêpe and velvet material, and language quite not concordant with being in a sanctified place, as a chapel, they manage to carry the unconscious artiste out.

As they did I distinctly over heard a few people remark that it was an amazing feat that she had even got anywhere near to the Funereal Chapel. Most did not rate her chances highly of even being able to get off the char à banc, which had brought her here, let alone gain the confines of the Funereal Chapel.

Whether people simply accepted this kind of behavior in keeping with attending a Requiem, I could not say. Mourners were falling down to the Funereal Chapel floor all around, and at one stage there must have been more persons having collapsed and lying crumpled on the floor, than those of us left standing. It was all very distressing, and I felt that at any moment I too might just as well collapse to the floor and have my inert body manhandled, legs first, out of the Funereal Chapel. At one stage I saw Loge looking distinctly as if he too were about to be overcome with emotion and faint to the Crematorium Chapel floor.

My blood instantly ran cold as the service began, heralded by the organ. A priest came in duly wearing a regulation black *cope* and swinging an ornate brass perforated thurible containing burning frankincense, the aroma from which wafted about the Funeral Crematorium Chapel. At the same time he chanted the antiphon *De Profundis &c.* followed by the, *Et lux perpetua luceat ei.* This was followed by the beautiful and harmonious *Tantum Ergo* [3] as a prelude to the *Requiem Aeternam dona eis, Domine* proper.

Never though in my life have I witnessed a Requiem being conducted at such a furious pace. We had barely completed the *Introitus Ad Altare Dei* and *Kyrie Eleison* before lurching into the *Offertorium* with such indecent haste as to make the customary reflection somewhat redundant. Quite where the powerful statement expressed in the *Dies Irae* and the harmonious *Lacrimosa* had gotten to, confounded me, for I do not recall a resounding confirmation of either.

I was beginning to experience feelings of depression and sadness about Bella's loss and of her *passing over.* Made all the more poignant by her presence reposed as she now was in that pressed wooden grey coffin. But, took some solace in the fact that her funeral and Requiem were evidently being conducted according to the rites of the Catholic faith. During the course of which, we were commending her soul to place where no eyes have before gazed upon such ethereal splendor.

I was reminded about the words in Gustav Mahler's mighty Resurrection Symphony,[4] in which he quotes the haunting words by Friedrich Klopstock, in particular, my being moved by the invocation;

'Arise, my dust, yes rise again,
from your all to brief repose;
He who has called upon thee,
will grant thy soul immortal life!'

'With wings which I have gained,
Shall I soar aloft into the aëther,
In love's ardent striving,
Into a light no eye had beheld!'

Despite my inner feelings, now seemingly existing in a vacuüm, devoid of caring persons, assembled in the Funereal Chapel, for such was the express speed of the Requiem that we were already at the *Agnus Dei* and from that without a pause we entered the *Sanctus*. The *Sanctus et Benedictus with Oblation of the Victim to God* – *'Unde et memores',* lost its relevance and meaning to me in this service. From the *Sanctus* we progressed, or rather, rushed in to the *Libera Me*.

I dared not steel myself to witness the preparatory *In Paradisum deducant te Angeli* and so I left the confines of the Funereal Chapel and sought refuge outside in the fog-bound aëther. When I did so I could not believe how many so-called grief-stricken mourners had not even bothered to enter the Funereal Chapel. Most were chatting amiably with one another and some were even smoking! One Music Hall artistes I recognized was actually sitting on a stone sarcophagus with a large cigar in his mouth, whilst holding forth in a conversation with another actress.

The Requiem mass completed, it was now time to take Bella's box, coffin or whatever to the Mausoleum, that Loge had purchased and made available with his *'unflinching generosity,* as he kept reminding us, and there, at the vault, inter her corpse, or what remained of it.

Loge, armed with a conveyance map from the *Particulars of Sale* document, as to the precise of the location of the Mausoleum structure, led the cortège as we marched through the fog-laden aëther that had settled over the cemetery. Loge made it abundantly clear to all who could hear him that it was as a result of his natural *'unflinching generosity'* just who was responsible for the purchase of this Mausoleum, to which we were headed to inter Bella's remains.

"Nearly there now, just past the next Mausoleum according to my location conveyance map which I was given upon purchase of the tomb," Lodge kept repeating this assurance, as we tramped around the fog-bound cemetery evidently lost!

"Indeed," he said, "looking at the conveyance document and the artist's impression of the limestone-built Mausoleum, with its rather fetching carved alabaster statue of a grief-stricken angel standing guard over the bronze door entrance to the vault, is a very tasteful and elegant feature. I might have one carved as well, and have it stand guard at my Mausoleum at Brookwood, when I too, *pass-over* on that fateful day and be interred there."

We tramped down one wet graveled avenue and up another, past imposing monuments, Temples of the Dead and Mausoleums and all to no avail. We only stopped to enable other mourners to catch their breath. Such was the speed of the forced funeral march towards the Mausoleum, where ever that Mortuary Temple was located.

Eventually, our cortège was on the move again, marching past colonnades containing an ornately designed, if solemn, columbarium. We marched down yet another avenue filled with Temples to the Dead and shrines, this time it led us to the Egyptian Avenue of the Dead in which there were constructed several ornate and elaborate Mausoleums, but none was the one we were searching for.

Accordingly, our funeral procession, marched out of the Egyptian Avenue of the Dead, down the avenue of the Lebanese Cedar with a profound hope our erstwhile Mausoleum was there ready to receive Bella's corpse.

It was not and we spent the next forty or so minutes wandering around in the fog with absolutely no idea where we were or what we were supposed to be doing dragging a corpse about the cemetery.

Farther down one particular avenue our attention was arrested by the sight, just visible in the fog, of a Mausoleum of distinct sinister aspect. It was built in style of an ancient Egyptian kiosk, with four solid walls slanting inwards at the top and a colonnade of four columns addressing the avenue, in which we were marching.

Behind those columns, of which the inner two were broad and tapered to a capital in the style of splayed leaves of a papyrus plant, but in contrast the two adjacent outer columns were square and undecorated. The external walls and columns of the tomb supported a monstrously overhanging curved Egyptian architrave, in the form of a *hollow and roll* that supported the stone slab roof.

On the front façade to this vault, forming a portico, immediately behind the columns, was a door architrave in the shape of a metal Masonic winged image above there cessed doorframe cut into the wall of the tomb into which two large burnished copper doors had been positioned. However, apparent even to us, were signs that the copper doors had been forced, because they were both hanging off their hinges.

Immediately opposite that Mausoleum, was another

structure that in comparison, appeared modest. It was again in the ancient Egyptian style and built upon two high steps forming the plinth. Four walls slanting inward made up the structure that was capped with a low six foot high pyramid. Each of the walls were built of blue granite slabs upon which were intricate raised patterns repeating the raised door frame outline and symbols that would make sense to the initiated, but alas to none of us in our cortège.

The door opening into the vault was wide at the base and narrowed toward the top as though reflecting the overall pyramid concept behind the design of this blue Mausoleum. I noticed that the door opening had been filled in with ferro-concrete and sealed with just visible adamantine chains for added strength, to prevent any person gaining access into this chamber housing the sarcophagus.

Other Mausoleums were of indeterminable architecture with no discernible style. They merely showed that the builder had simply placed large masonry blocks one upon each other in order to create a massive monolithic edifice of stone, no doubt so constructed in order to repel the inquisitive, allowing the interred to repose in undisturbed peace. Or perhaps to contain within the sealed stone structure something that must not be allowed to roam Highgate Cemetery.

The more somber of the sealed Mausoleums were those large foreboding edifices reflecting an ancient Egyptian style of architecture. In so doing their designs, based on those large ancient structures, deployed huge megalithic blocks of limestone to create gigantic monumental mortuary temples, Mausoleums, to house several sarcophagus containing recently interred corpses.

Most of these elaborate Mausoleums had only a single

entrance to the inner tomb, which was either bricked up for eternity or, was guarded by huge bronze doors. This megalithic monumental style of Mausoleum construction was the most prevalent at the Highgate Cemetery, containing within its precinct, guarded by high walls, a vast city of the dead. Its long avenues were formed not of buildings wherein the living dwelt but of stone mortuary temples, burial vaults and Mausoleums housing the dead.

Such were the impressive and fantastic temple structures in this massive necropolis that one almost expected to witness a ghostly procession of the gods into Valhalla, escorted by their winged Valkürian warriors. We however, did walk down several more avenues of Mausoleums, including one Mausoleum that was in the process of being constructed. We could see its massive internal stone walls partially built, but now showing clearly the outline of the crypt that would eventually receive the sarcophagus and adjacent mortuary chapels connected by small openings in the walls.

The complex designs of these burial vaults for the dead were readily apparent with its various rooms and doors connecting one vault to another chamber. A singular fact emerged as we walked through this land of the dead. Quite a number of the larger more extravagant of the Mausoleums had the appearance of having been at some stage set on fire! The walls of each temple and burial vault had been scorched and blackened by intense flame. Some structures had partially collapsed as a result of the blaze and in so doing had exposed the interiors of various tombs revealing their sarcophagus.

On other Mausoleums a stone bust of a head, an urn or other decorative masonry features had cracked or disintegrated into ruin due to the intense heat of a fire.

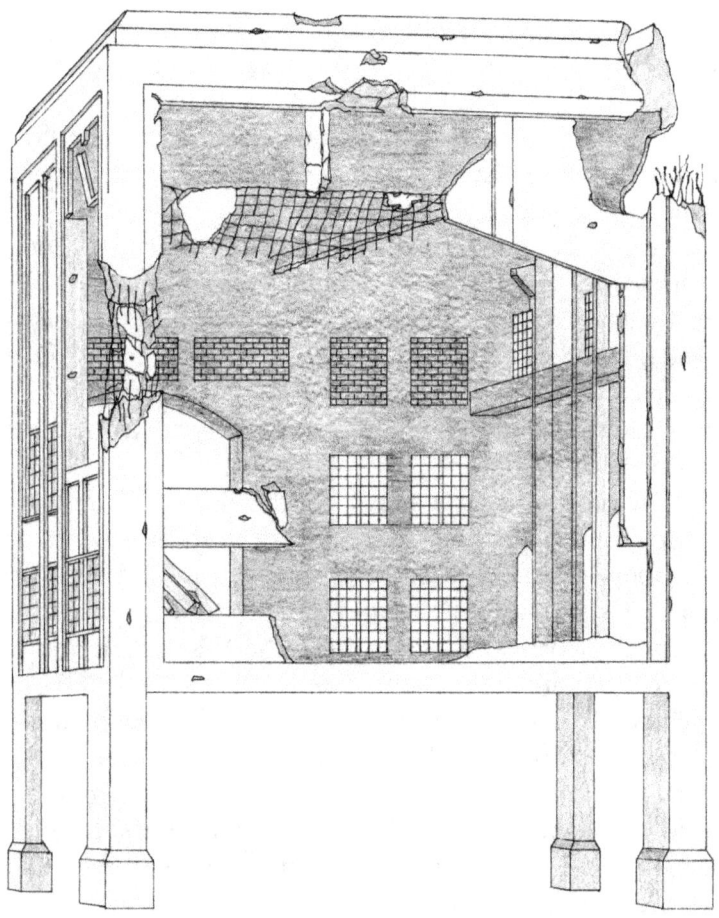

Destroyed Mausoleum Highgate Cemetery

Some of the stone ornamentation on several tombs had been struck with heavy objects. On other mortuary temples the columbarium had been compromised and a few of the columns had been toppled, leaving the masonry dangerously unsupported, as though it were floating in the fog-laden aether.

Why had these monuments to the dead been so

attacked, I asked myself? Was it because the persons, in whose memory they had been erected, had behaved badly during their lives to other people? Other Mausoleums showed that they had been built in a great haste with little regard for the foundations upon which the edifice had been constructed.

Some were in the final throes of chronic subsidence, as indicated by the abnormal acute angles their structures now leaned at and grotesquely out of true. Their fate was now being determined by nature, rather than concerned relatives, who had abandoned their duty to this tomb unable or unwilling to maintain it as a Mortuary Temple to the diseased.

As we continued our search for the elusive Mausoleum Lodge tried to keep those who comprised the dwindling members of the cortège still interested in reaching our goal. That is to inter Bella; and leave at double-quick time for nearest bar, and get on with the Wake of Remembrance, the highlight of the day.

"The Mausoleum has been constructed using the finest limestone blocks with ornamental dressing of black *Elusian* marble and no expense has been spared in so doing. The weeping angel all very tasteful I assure you!" Loge would utter from time to time. However, at that moment suddenly the cortège veered right into another graveled avenue and continued past several ornate and lavish Mortuary Temples.

"Nearly there now, just past that Mausoleum over there, according to my location conveyance map of the tomb," Lodge kept repeating that as we tramped around Highgate Cemetery.

Our cortège continued to march aimlessly around the Necropolis, some members of which were actually smoking cigarettes and shouting at each other. Others indulged in fits of uncontrolled laughter enough indeed, I thought, to wake the dead, by whom we were surrounded, and outnumbered of course.

Not far to go now," said Lodge, "I think it is that building over there. Yes I feel certain that is the Mausoleum, with the detached alabaster statue of an angel looking forlorn and desolate at the bronze door to the structure. We did approach the Mausoleum in the vain hope it was the correct Temple of the Dead. However, we had doubts even before we got there, since there the forlorn looking angel supposedly on guard was nowhere to be seen. The alabaster statue of the angel had either been stolen or removed to some other corpse's dwelling!

However, before Jack and I could marshal our thoughts to deal with this outrage, the cortège was on the move again, marching at a maniac's pace as our feet crunched the wet gravel of yet another fog-bound avenue of the dead."

Eventually, we finished up back at the Funereal Chapel where we had started out from. We had been tramping around the fog-bound cemetery for just over two hours dragging poor Bella in her pressed wood coffin with handles and hinges of string in search of a phantom Mausoleum that Loge had paid ready money for.

It was Lloyd who registered the cortège's collective feeling of frustration and disappointment.

"Why do we not just leave the coffin in this Funereal Chapel rather than dragging it about a north London bone yard in a futile search for a non existent Mausoleum," suggested Lloyd, nearly breaking into song as she said so.

"No!" insisted Lodge, "no, Bella must be treated with dignity, and I for..."

"What by being dragged around Highgate Cemetery," interrupted Lloyd, "with absolutely no prospect of rest for the wicked? There is neither Mausoleum, nor even a hole in the ground into which we could repose what there is left of Bella!" advised Lloyd.

"I tell you, the Mausoleum is around here, probably that structure over there," insisted Lodge, "we are in fact nearly there now, just past that Mausoleum over there according to my location map in the *Particulars of Sale*, conveyance document!"

"Come on dearie, the bloke over whom you had some *sway* has done for you!" said Lloyd, much to the general low laughter which mourners repressed by putting black-edged handkerchiefs to their mouths.

I with Jack and the others abandoned Loge to his vigil in the Funereal Chapel. Alas, it was gradually becoming evident, that we were not going to locate a vacant Mausoleum, of any description, real or apparent, with or without weeping alabaster angel standing guard, at least not in this cemetery.

Accordingly, we left the Funereal Chapel and joined the other grief-stricken mourners on their way out through the fog-bound cemetery to the main entrance gates.

We did eventually reach the imposing stone gated entrance and came across Aloysius sitting on his Barouche carriage bench with his four black-plumed horses waiting patiently.

"Are you able to take us back to the St. Pancras Hotel Aloysius?" asked Jack.

Aloysius turned his head down towards Jack and looked at him. He then looked about him.

"I shall wait here for my master," replied Aloysius, "it is quite probable that he might need my assistance, for he is not a particularly strong when it comes to physical exertion."

It was Dan Leno who now came walking out of the fog towards us.

Theo Houston and Jack Mitchell out of New York?" he inquired.

"That is correct," replied Jack.

"A few of us are heading back into the West End where we have arranged a little Wake of Remembrance, a farewell party for Bella, back stage at the Vaudeville Theater. We have a couple of spare seats in our char à banc, if you should care to join us."

We took them up on their thoughtful offer.

1. Loge had ingested rat poison to create the grey tint to his feature
2. Funereal Rite
3. Benediction
4. Symphony No 2 in C Minor

Chapter 31

The Saga Goes On

Naturally enough, both Jack and I had been devastated on being informed about the fact that Bella had *Passed Over*, but even more distressed on learning how this tragedy had occurred at the hands of her husband, Doctor Crippen. Her funeral had been somewhat of a travesty, both during the indecent haste that the Requiem mass was conducted in, and our futile search for a non existent limestone Mausoleum in which to inter Bella's corpse, or what there was left of it.

Jack and I were now guests of a few Music Hall artistes, as we accompanied them from Highgate Cemetery back into London. It did not take much for the inevitable to erupt unanimously. Sure enough by the time we were approaching Camden Town the singing had started and our char à banc, swayed to the lyrics being expressed loudly. People stared at us as we appeared from out of the fog and into their purview. They would stop walking on the pavement and instead look at us clearly supposing that we were hopeless cases, destined for the institute for the criminally insane, located just down the road at the St. Pancras Hospital.

Our songs became extended and more vociferous and louder. Ironically as we in fact past the lunatic asylum, some of the inmates began to join in our verses and sing along with us! Such was our manic behavior in that char à banc, as we rattled by the lunatic asylum, I was convinced the coachman would drive us up to the main gateway, and there deliver us to the wardens for our own protection.

"Anybody for the nut house?" yelled George Robey, which gained maniacal laughter from the grief-stricken mourners in prolonged unceasing mourning en-route to a Wake of Remembrance.

The carriage driver, alas did not, but rather continued along Crowndale Road and into the Pancras Road heading in the direction of the St. Pancras Hotel. Jack was too busy singing the *'Girl from Idaho'* to notice our familiar location. At length we drove down the Pancras Road which took us past the eastern aspect of our hotel and then turned right into the Euston Road. The fact that we were now clattering along a major busy thorough-fare in no way impeded the ardor nor enthusiasm for which our itinerant minstrels displayed in singing in remarkable unison, verses from various Music Hall songs.

Indeed, this impromptu recital represented nothing more that a wild mobile departure from what they are all dab hands at. Notwithstanding the rapid succession of songs, or in spite of them, our coach driver drove his char à banc off the Euston Road and headed south into a myriad of back streets and squares, none of which were familiar to Jack or me.

However, at one stage in our peregrination, we appeared to be progressing along the side of a hotel which I recognized as being that of the Hotel Russell. Loge had pointed this structure out to Jack and myself previously since it evidently had some significance for him, which was but lost on us. We then turned left and continued on into the Southampton Row.

I was beginning to recognize my way around London. And remembered that it was hereabouts, only a few days a go, that we met with a serious carriageway incident involving Lodge's Barouche carriage, an omnibus, a dray wagon and a Hackney carriage which exploded into smithereens upon impact with a tramcar!

Since our Barouche carriage was wrecked in the incident, that fact necessitated us having to exchange our mode of transport and instead ride the tramcar to Waterloo. I recall the tramcar terminated at one of the most peculiar building I have ever seen, in particular, a building called the Necropolis Rail Road Building. We finished up there in order to reach our destination; that of the Canterbury Music Hall nearby and to where we were then headed at the time.

Lodge, had at the time described the function of this building with inordinate enthusiasm. It was a building given over to receiving corpses which were destined en-route to Brookwood, a gigantic Necropolis about thirty miles outside of London. It was to this building, effective a mortuary, where the deceased would be delivered and then on to the Necropolis Rail Road, which would transport that coffin by train to Brookwood Necropolis.

Jack and I first saw the building, albeit vaguely in the fog, its mannerism made an immediate impression upon us both. It was constructed to a height of four storeys with a deep red terra-cotta cladding to the façade of the building, which had been transmuted into a dull purple colour by the effects of the fog.

On first sight, the building did not look extraordinary, but upon closer examination, its appearance revealed certain aspects and peculiarities in its design and construction. Notably, the huge arched portal taking up all the ground floor façade and indeed

Necropolis Rail Road Building

reaching up to the *piano-nobile* located on the first floor of the building.

I also recall that Lodge was very keen that we should avail ourselves of this unscheduled opportunity to look around the building. This included visiting the opulent *Chapelle Ardent,* for those unfortunate mourners who were unable to accompany the corpse on its final journey to Brookwood. Quite why he thought that we ought to do this, even now eludes me as to the rationale of his idea. The building, though handsome, presented nothing more than a functioning mortuary; or as Jack described it in his blunt way as being basically, a corpse depository!

Eventually our liveried coachman reached the Aldwych and upon doing so wheeled our char à banc into the Strand along to the Vaudeville Music Hall located in that road. The façade of the Music Hall, was unprepossessing, but displayed several classical design features, including a symbolic pedimented attic front and an open loggia addressing the Strand, similar to the arcade one could expect to see at the Oxford Music Hall. These architectural mechanisms, of course, were all intended to impress patrons entering this establishment, despite its name.

Our char à banc came to an abrupt halt and almost immediately the singing stopped. Unanimously, the grief-stricken mourners assumed a dignified seriousness and reverent silence. Upon reaching the Stage Door entrance of the Vaudeville Music Hall in Southampton Street, each veiled mourner, with veils drawn down and their head bowed, stepped down from the char à banc and walked solemnly with a slow measured step across the pavement and into the Vaudeville Music Hall.

Once inside the theater, Jack and I were, in double quick time, escorted by Leno along several corridors, the walls of which were painted white and punctuated with

Vaudeville Music Hall

sepia tinted silver nitrate Daguerreotypes of the very Music Hall artistes, some of   whom now were running to the bar at the back stage Wake of Remembrance.

When Jack and I eventually walked on to the back stage, the Wake was well underway with empty bottles already littering the floor. Some Music Hall artistes were already displaying signs of being emotionally overcome, and not with unrelenting grief, I hasten to add. It was my sincere hope that the safety curtain would not be raised only to reveal to a stunned audience this back stage scene of licentious and unbecoming behavior by their favorite Music Hall performers. None the less, undeterred we joined in the Wake and within seconds had availed ourselves of a bottle of whisky and two deep glasses from which to drink.

Looking around the wreckage we noticed Marie Lloyd in deep conversation with the impresario, Sir Augustus Harris, the manager of the Drury Lane Theater located conveniently nearby in the Covent Garden.

A few minutes later Marie Lloyd, drew herself away from Harris and came up to Jack and offered her hand to him.

"Remember me Jack; we met at the New Bedford Music Hall the other evening?"

"Of course I do my precious Greek Goddess in human form," Jack crooned, whilst taking and kissing her hand.

"Cor you're a one! I told you there and then, London born and bred I am, 'oxton [1] in fact, nothing Greek about me. And speaking of Goddesses; where that Lodge got to, still searching for his elusive Mausoleum? There is one born everyday. I have heard of people being taken in over a horse race or buying a house or even a Public House that did belong to the person offering it for sale. But a Mausoleum, for cash, in Highgate, in the fog!" guffawed Marie Lloyd. "A Mausoleum, and a limestone one at that?"

I observed you were talking with Augustus Harris the renowned impresario. Might he be offering you a position somewhere?" asked Jack.

"Him," replied Lloyd, "the venerable *'Father of Modern Pantomime'* he would like to engage me for the lead rôle in the pantomime version of Robinson Crusoe, but the censors will not hear of it. And, besides, I consider that I am above all that now. What do you think Jack? After all, our *'Augustus Druriolanus'* can always resort to that Emma Eames, Jean de Reszke, Emma Calvé or if worst comes to worst, Nellie Melba; for she is *always* available! Mind you they will have to contend with the likes of Dan Leno, Harry Nicholls or even Herbert Campbell who usually play that Drury Lane Theater every Christmas."

"Marie, might not you re-join the *Three Graces* and assume your rightful place at the top?" smoothed Jack, still holding Lloyd's hand.

"Jack," she replied, "I should not want to sing for Lodge again for all the tea in Cheng. And as for the remaining *Graces*, they do not need my help to fall off their perches. I've got no airs and graces; I sings proper, as like I sing from the heart!"

At that moment, Eva Carrington, overcome with either emotion or alcohol, fell into a table with bottles of drink upon it; knocking a few to the floor which smashed and in so doing destroyed at least thirty minutes worth of drink. Another artiste who went to help Eva to her feet also slipped on the wet floorboards and promptly joined her in a heap of black crêpe and veils.

At the same time a very audible argument could be heard between Ellen Terry and the even more loquacious Kate Meyrick about the altruistic rôle of Music Hall artistes.

"I am an *actor* capable of rendering Shakespeare, not some *performing artiste*!" Ellen Terry was heard to screech out before collapsing to the floor in a stupor.

"You could not render a wall with plaster," came the considered repost from Meyrick, who in turn fell against a nearby convenient wall.

Whilst Jack was occupied resuscitating the dying art of inanity, I approached another intact drinks table, erected into makeshift bar attended by a stagehand acting as a bar-tender. Having got a re-fill I turned around to survey the scene of chaos and unbecoming behavior where dignity, and her less fortunate sister, respect, had abandoned us to our alcohol-induced fate. However, at that moment I became aware of a person, in the background, attempting to play a monumental work for pianoforte.

I recognized his attempt at playing the melodic paraphrase on the serenely beautiful transcription of *Echoes of Valhalla'* by Edward Plesse. The pianist's interpretation was off key and playing not at *allegro non troppo* but rather at *allegro vivace*. I mentioned this disappointment to the bar-tender who responded in a manner I did not expect.

"Well this is not exactly the Bechstein Hall [2] but the back stage of the Vaudeville Music Hall and during a Wake of Remembrance, in fact!" he advised.

"Well," I replied, "I realize this all too well, I am merely saying that the pianist, today at any rate, is not at his best. That music he is playing is called *'Echoes of Valhalla'* [3] by an excellent fellow, name of Plesse. And the way that pianist is attempting to play it, is more capable of inducing ear-ache than instilling a profound feeling of sonority and appreciation of sublime progression of harmony, as intended by Plesse!"

"Can you do any better?" asked the bar-tender of the makeshift bar.

"As it happens, yes I could. But, since I am relaxing and therefore not on public call, you might like to avail yourself of the new improved Electro-chromium-plated Aëolian Pianola out of Fifth Avenue, New York," I responded.

"Really!" said the bar-tender, whilst polishing his wine glasses in an agitated manner, "I prefer the American Angelus player-piano as it happens."

"I have enjoyed immensely those contraptions' ability to extemporize faultlessly, such harmony and sonority of chord, which I sincerely believe the days of the pianist, such as the one over there, are numbered. Certainly no establishment's appointments, including this back stage, can be complete in the absence of a New Improved Electro-chromium-plated Aëolian Pianola. Think about it sir! Having an Aëolian Pianola and the facility for having music played for you at any time and perfectly, so that you could never tire or become bored listening to your favorite pianoforte works!" I replied.

"Is that so? You will be telling me next that the new domestic upright piano, like that one being played over there, will replace the grand piano?" said the bar-tender, in tones I detected as being those of facetiousness.

"Sir," I said, "it is a surety. You may count on it sir, count on it!"

"And in turn the domestic upright piano to be replaced by the Aëolian Pianola?" retorted the bar-tender.

"Be advised of it sir, for it is a certainty, the Aëolian Pianola will sweep all before it into oblivion, as it assumes its rightful place in the Pantheon of improved machines, as the only purveyor of mechanically contrived music!" I said.

"Very interesting," said the bar tender, "very interesting."

"I remember one particular Aëolian Pianola," I said, inspecting my refilled glass of whisky, "I had the pleasure of listening to, actually in an establishment not far from here. The Aëolian Pianola seemed then to have had a mind of its own and indulged infrequent bouts of almost empyrean tenderness and flamboyancy. Especially whilst tackling the particularly difficult section of a piece of music called '*Benediction de Dieu dans la solitude*' by the Abbé Franz Liszt..."

"A mind of its own, it is a mechanical contraption, not a person?" said the bar-tender interrupting me.

"The Aëolian Pianola, can be anything to anyone," I continued, "as it progressed its way though the multiplicity of arpeggios and scales. Both ascending and descending in harmony to the dominant melody, as the machine assumed a manic interpretation, as if to demonstrate just how talented it was. Astoundingly, I remember people stopped talking, and diverted their attention to this *impromptu* virtuoso recital by an Aëolian Pianola.

"It was truly an accomplished display by the machine, which culminated in its vibrating with mechanical activity, as if working itself into an exquisite delirious frenzy as it approached the closing section of the piano transcription. It did so with the mechanical interpretation of the wildly chromatic display of brilliance of the '*Invocation*' bringing the music to an acclaimed and triumphant finalé.

"I must confess. I really did expect those people who had been witnessing this Aëolian Pianola's solo performance début to burst out in to sustained applause; I was delighted when I saw that they did so, and in fact erupted into a mælström of sustained applause!" I said.

The bar-tender's response to my reminiscences of my enjoying listening to an Aëolian Pianola, was rather unexpected. I became aware of the fact that he was looking very obviously behind me, and not at my face. I turned around out of interest, only to find myself looking at the irate pianist who had over-heard my conversation about his playing and my recommending the Aëolian Pianola as his possible replacement.

"Can you do any better at the upright?" the pianist demanded, with a cigar hanging out of his mouth.

I looked down at the pianist. A stage hand I thought, judging by the fact he was wearing a pair of heavy thorn proof rustic colored Harris Tweed trousers, which were held up by wide braces. In addition, he wore a collarless faint striped shirt.

"Are you then perhaps by way of being a radical?" he continued, his voice full of aspersion.

And with that Parthian shot, aimed at me, I made my mumbled excuses in reply. I then abandoned the make-shift bar to the irate pianist and the bar-tender, both of whom were looking at me, as though I were a registered idiot on reprieve whilst making derogatory remarks about my person and, behavior.

It then dawned upon me that I had in fact just been involved in a ridiculous conversation, with the bar-tender about pianofortes, mechanical or otherwise. I concluded that I had indeed made of fool of myself talking absolute nonsense and displaying all the concentrated naïveté of an idiot. This realization was reënforced by the evident comparison with other grief-stricken mourners, also intent on anything remotely physically possible here at the Wake of Remembrance for Bella in the back stage of the Vaudeville Music Hall.

I had no sooner concluded this when I found myself talking with a group of Music Hall artistes, who included Nelly Power and Little Tich. George Robey, then joined us and held out his hand to me.

"Please to meet you Theodor, is it?" he inquired.

"Delighted to make your acquaintance George," I responded.

"Just call me 'Prime Minister'," he replied laughing.

"Oh, I should prefer to call you 'First Lord of the Treasury', so much more informal," I said.

That witticism fell straight to the floor; as did with a crash, Jules Léotard, the well-known daring man on the flying trapeze, who apparently lost his balance and slipped.

"We saw you in conversation with Vesta about her playing that domestic upright piano. Poor soul she cannot play a note, but always tries to regale us at every opportunity when ever there is a domestic upright available to her. Mind you, she does get better though, especially when she has got few drinks down her neck!" remarked Little Tich.

"I saw no Vesta Tilley and I certainly do not recall speaking with her," I said, questioningly, looking down at Little Tich, who indeed was.

"The pianist, with the cigar hanging from her mouth, who came up to you, at that bar when you were talking with the bar-tender about mechanically contrived music emanating out of an Aëolian pianola," said Little Tich, "that was our Vesta."

"But that pianist was a fellow, a stage hand I thought, wearing, I distinctly remembered, a pair of heavy thorn proof Harris Tweed trousers held up with braces and wearing a collarless faint striped shirt and…" I offered.

At that moment those assembled around me burst in to uncontrollable fits of laughter.

"That is our Vesta, our Vesta Tilley alright, playing the piano," said Robey, "she could not wait to get out of her grief-stricken and deep mourning look of black bellowing velvet dress edge in black silk. Together with wearing an oversized large black hat complete with attached mysterious veil pulled down over her face.

"At least when she is in public, it is all very much lady like. But in private, a man's suit any day for our Vesta; she would infinitely prefer to get into a men's clothes where she feels infinitely more comfortable, than swan around in a ball gown!" advised Robey.

"But did I not see her sitting in that char à banc, we drove down in earlier from Highgate Cemetery? At the time, I distinctly recall, she was decked out in wreathes of black and wearing a bellowing black velvet dress edge in black silk matching an oversized black hat," I asked.

"You certainly did, and she wore the same when she stepped off the char à banc and crossed the pavement, in public, to enter this Vaudeville Music Hall. But, once out of the public gaze, then it is back to the usual attire of men's' clothes," informed Robey.

It was just trying to figure out the implications of what Robey had imparted to me when I felt somebody pulling at my coat sleeve complete with black armband. I turned around only to come face to face with Little Bo Peep! She introduced herself whilst waving and shouting at other grieving artistes attending the Wake.

We spoke at length about her impressive *act* which I congratulated her on.

"Oh that is very kind of you sir," she said, whilst dropping a shallow curtsey, "but I seem to remember you as that kind gentleman who gave me your paisley patterned handkerchief, when I was limbering up my crying in the dressing rooms in the Hungerford Music Hall a while ago!"

"I do indeed remember. At the time, Jack and I were being escorted by Lodge to the manager's office in the depths of the Hungerford Music Hall up against the

Charing Cross Rail Road Bridge. I thought that you were genuinely distressed and upset," I responded.

"Oh you remembered then?" said Bo Peep.

"I do indeed," I replied, "and the half burned mannequins lashed to the corridor walls. And, also the Monologist who appeared quite beside himself with forlorn anxiety and repressed terror and I can still see him in my memory. There, in those lower levels of the Hungerford Music Hall, we saw him dressed in a loud yellow Prince of Wales check patterned suit and wearing a purple fez. At the time he appeared to be very disconsolate, and with his hands, was wringing continuously in a forlorn manner a long piece of blazing red silk cloth. He did this whilst having a very intense and animated conversation with his reflection in a large gilt-framed mirror."

"Oh you mean Jeremy. He is fine when he is performing on the stage, because he knows full well that he can hit the bottle afterwards; but not before he has done his *turn* on the boards!" informed Bo Peep.

"We had only just arrived from New York," I continued, "and our exploring the depths of that Hungerford Music Hall was quite revealing. Though not as much as our following Lodge into the superstructure of the Charing Cross Rail Road Bridge. My heart nearly failed on no less than two occasions!"

"You were following Lodge; do you not mean Theseus?" inquired Bo Peep.

"Theseus?" I asked.

"Yes, we call him Theseus, on account of his scheming ability to formulate convoluted and complicated stratagems equal to the mythological Theseus negotiating his way out of the Minotaur infested Labyrinth of tunnels!"

"Interesting," I responded, "because where Log…Theseus then took us, was almost the equivalent of the Labyrinth, in that we found ourselves beneath the Charing Cross Rail Road Bridge stumbling around the girders and arches. I remember at length, we came to an iron door the surface of which was covered in a rusting patina. It was to this door that Lodge applied his shoulder, forcing it open inch by inch. We all three of us eventually succeeded in squeezing through the aperture before Lodge slammed the iron door closed behind us.

"We found ourselves in a chamber, the air in which was cold and not from the Music Hall building. It was fresh air, though with a smell and dankness to it. It turned out we were in an upper section of one of the foundation arches that supported immediately above us the Charing Cross Railroad Station and the beginning of the rail road bridge over the Thames Lodge had informed us in an nonchalantly manner.

"Quite why Lodge had brought us to the foundations

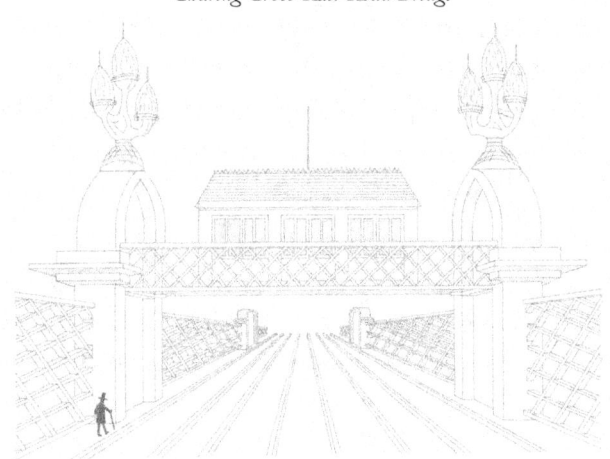

Charing Cross Rail Road Bridge

upon which this Hungerford Music Hall is built and buttresses a rail road bridge was lost on me, but I do remember being filled with trepidation at the prospect of being within one of the arches supporting the mighty weight of the Charing Cross Rail Road Station and its rail road bridge filled me instantly with a foreboding.

"I did not obviously expect the whole masonry structure to come crashing down upon us, crushing the very life out of our souls. But, the possibility of such an event, caused a very real presentiment of fear to become evident to any intelligent imagination!" I offered.

"That sounds like Lodge, making a big deal about visiting the manager of the Hungerford Music Hall, Marmeduke Gatti in his subterranean domain. Marmeduke shuns the sunlight. Strong sunlight makes him turn peculiar," announced Bo-Peep.

"Well your tearful act is impressive and you are to be commended," I said.

"Oh no, no, it was all part of the act. But do let me introduce you to a friend of mine," said Bo Peep, laying aside her shepherdess' crook and outsized glass of vodka, and reaching into her voluminous bag. In an instant she produced a face, a familiar face, with a fixed manic expression upon it.

It was Judd, our erstwhile ventriloquist's dummy we had abandoned in the Criterion Theater after his exhibitionism and over confident behavior at our expense. Together with his outrageous and overt sympathies with the Nihilists and hecklers, who, at the time, were demanding his immediate emancipation from bondage that Jack and I were apparently guilty of subjecting him to!

"The last time I saw little Judd here was when we were playing the Criterion Theater the other evening and his head departed from his shoulders and went rolling around the stage floor much to the disgust of the hecklers and Nihilists embedded in the audience who were demanding his release from servitude, If you can believe that!" I said to Bo Peep.

"I most certainly did. That is why I went down to the dressing rooms, where I found him bound up and discarded and rescued him. I call him Marmeduke. Is that not correct my precious?" asked Bo Peep of the ventriloquist's dummy.

"It is an axiom of life, I have always maintained," replied Marmeduke, to my utter astonishment, "that I shall not be consign to oblivion, for I too have my rôle to play on the world's stage. I may well be fashioned from the finest woods, but I have feelings and expect, no demand, dignity!"

"We called him Judd…" I said.

"Not anymore. He is now Marmeduke, a name much more befitting his expansive character and sensitive personality," informed Bo Peep.

"Marmeduke or what ever, is a wooded doll, a ventriloquist's dummy, or an ex prop," I replied.

"No, I am not!" insisted Marmeduke.

"That is right," confirmed Bo Peep, "aside of which he has a lovely genuine smile and is altogether quite cute, is that not the case Marmeduke?"

Marmeduke on this occasion deigned not to reply, but stared manically into oblivion.

"You like his smile, what you mean, that manic grin expression he is wearing?" I asked.

"I do not think Marmeduke is very impressed with you Theo," informed Bo Peep, "and anyway, better take Marmeduke home now, as I think he looks quite exhausted and more than a little piquéred."

And with an inordinate show of farewell, Little Bo Peep made her apologies and departed waving and shouting wildly at everybody. Even Marmeduke was disposed, despite his exhaustion, to wave as well to the assembled grief-stricken mourners, all of whom were in various stages of deep morning at this impromptu Wake of Remembrance in the back stage of the Vaudeville Music Hall.

At this juncture the Marie Lloyd and Jack came marching over to say something to Robey. Then in an instant, the Wake of Remembrance stopped dead as Lodge appeared at the side of the back stage area. He looked about the place surveying the wreckage generated by the Wake and the bodies lying on the floor. He still looked like the chief unceasing grief-stricken mourner in perpetual deep mourning sporting his black silk armband. Which, I noticed had been sewn into his coat sleeve. Indicating permanence of remembrance for Bella, which I think was sincere.

He did not move, but continued to look about the back of stage and the mourners still standing. The top hat he wore, complete with black ribbons trailing at the back, and black crêpe material wrapped around it, conferred upon him a distinguished look. Despite Loge's effort to look the part of the grief stricken soul in everlasting deep mourning, he did in fact still retain touches of gray to his worn face.

He then noticed where we were standing and came over towards us with a dignified measured walk. He swerved and manœuvred, like a seasoned waiter, through various groups of people, and side-stepped those inert bodies on the floor. Presently came up to Jack and me and shook our hands. He astutely ignored Lloyd who feigned interest in a nearby gilded cherub mounted on a faked stone pedestal.

Jack pulled himself away from Lloyd and shook Loge's hand for quite sometime. He even patted him on his shoulder, which on this occasion Lodge refrained from looking over.

This was Jack's way of trying to show empathy for Loge, who had during the time of our acquaintance with him, shown nothing but kindness and unswerving confidence in our abilities. He had without any reservation introduced us to numerous persons and therefore, opportunities to assist us perform successfully in London.

We both felt that in his time of sadness and reflection at the loss of Bella, of whom, Jack and I knew, he was fond, that we should like to indicate our appreciation and sympathies for him.

We spoke at length about the future and in particular his loss of one of his *Three Graces*.

"But as I said previously Loge, surely you must be able to pick up contralto or soprano or whatever to replace Bella?" inquired Jack.

"As I said then Jack," replied Lodge, "contraltos are as cheap as life itself; it is a soprano that I really need to replace Bella."

It was while we were listening to Lodge attempting to explain some details regarding the phantom Mausoleum, that all of a sudden his facial features assume a look of dread. Concerned, I went to support his arm, for I feared the worse. I thought that he was about to endure his supreme moment, and collapse down to the back of stage floor, alongside half the members of the assembled Music Hall profession, who at this very moment were lying upon it. He seemed to go into a trance as I shook his arm, on which was sown the black silk armband.

The gray tinted patches on his face, that we had noticed earlier when we met Loge in the foyer of the St. Pancras Hotel before embarking on the final journey to Highgate

Cemetery, were still in evidence. I looked at Jack. He returned my concern by shrugging his shoulders.

Lodge, so it seemed was looking into the middle distance as though staring at oblivion. Instinctively, I turned my heads for no reason other than to see what could possibly have caught Loge's unswerving attention and induce such a profound catatonic [3] re-action in him.

"It was at this precise moment, and I shall forever remember it as so.

The vision was standing next to the makeshift bar, the same bar at which I had previously made a fool of myself. I could not believe my eyes. Nor indeed could Lodge. I understood immediately now why Lodge had gone into a mental cataleptic state. It was *the* woman, the Woman in Red! And from a fluted glass, was pouring champagne down her throat in an abandoned manner.

Jack had resumed his talk with Lloyd and Loge was joined by Little Tich and Jules Léotard. The well-known daring man on the flying trapeze, who by now had picked himself up from the floor but still appeared unsteady on his feet and who could barely hold on to his wine glass, let alone a trapeze frame

Both Little Tich and Jules Léotard had inveigled Loge to describe further the singular episode of the phantom Mausoleum. To which Loge accented. And, Lodge did so with unadulterated enthusiasm and relish, now coming to realize that this catastrophe in being cheated out of his Mausoleum, was fast becoming a way to gain undeviating attention. Even more so than had he actually interred Bella in the tomb structure.

I decided to approach the Woman in Red since she was standing by herself.

"Good afternoon Ma'am," I said, daringly, "may I introduce myse…"

"I know precisely who you are," she interrupted, "you are friends with that sybarite Lodge."

She then turned her back on me, drained her glass of champagne and banged it down on the makeshift bar. The bar-tender, on his own initiative, re-filled the fluted glass with champagne.

"And you are a wronged woman!" I responded, "I was at the Crush Bar in the New Bedford Music Hall the other evening when you had your intimate conversation with Lod..."

"You mean when we had that almighty argument for the delectation of those crowded in that bar," she said, interrupting me yet again, "well I meant every word I uttered, as God is my witness."

"Well I do not know much before my arrival in England from New York, only recently. Up until a few days ago I did not even know who Michael Lodge was, let alone his history or indeed his dealings with other Music Hall artistes," I said.

"You would do well to disassociate yourself from him; for he can only be the ruin of you eventually, as he has tried unsuccessfully to ruin me," she replied.

"I could hardly abandon him now. He is after all in a state of shock and distress over Bella's death, and manner of it. Being the chief grief-stricken mourner in eternal deep mourning he needs friends at this time of painful sadness and reflection," I responded.

The Woman in Red looked at me and then pointed with her empty champagne glass in the direction of where Lodge was standing.

"I remain contemptuous in my belief of that fact," she said.

I turned my head around slowly. Had there been a trap door in the back of stage floor, then I would have willingly have fallen through it and risked the resultant injuries to my bones.

For there in full sight of God, man and *Gus* the theater cat was Lodge. As the chief grief-stricken mourner in continuous and profound mourning, he was dressed appropriately, in a black frock-coat complete with arm-band and trousers made of herringbone patterned broadcloth. His black patent leather boot had upon them a deep shine showing that they had been particularly well varnished. His white shirt, the collar of which was fastened with a stone of pure black jet to match his top hat with black crêpe wrapped around it, complimented his deep mourning attire.

Amongst this funereal garb and profound loss and sadness was a face, albeit a grayish looking face. Upon his facial features was a smile, a beaming smile the width of his face, which showed the world an array of perfect white teeth through which a deep and sustained laughter could be heard.

"Well the saga goes on," said the Woman in Red.

I could not reply.

"And you were saying," said the Woman in Red, "about your lending him emotional support in this, his hour of grief? The only support he really needs now, is physical support, before he falls over on to the floor laughing."

"Bar-tender, another whisky and make it large, my good man" were the only words I could think of saying. I felt like a fool, an utter fool for the second time this afternoon, and at the same makeshift bar too.

"So you are from America, New York in fact?" she asked, much to my surprise as I was looking into my glass at the time and not expecting her to talk to me, having just made another, more definite faux pas.

"I am, all the way from the Gramercy Park district in fact. The name is Houston, Theodor Houston and I am very delighted to make your acquaintance Ma'am," I said, almost gushingly.

"Queenie, call me Queenie," she said, speaking in the polished key of C sharp, as a duchess might do so.

We sat down on a couple of nearby chairs, or stage props, covered in a stained moiré striped silk fabric. Queenie then re-arranged her attire and got out her red leather cigar case. From this case, that Queenie held in one hand, and using the fingers on that hand, and with great dexterity, pulled out a Trichinopoly cigar, which she lit by striking a match on the sole of her boot.

We then got to talking. During which, I remarked upon her performance at the New Bedford Music Hall in Camden Town. In particular, how she controlled the audience, in addition to making them release their emotions in a way I had never witnessed before, in my entire professional stage career. I was very impressed, and told her so.

She, for her part, seemed genuinely moved by my remembering the performance and recognizing her abilities.

"Do tell me Theodor, are you one of Lodge so-called protégés?" she asked.

"Theo, Queenie, please call me Theo. And no, I am not a protégé of any one, least of all Lodge. No he is a someone we met, or rather, more accurately, he looked us up, when we were performing at the Chicago World's Columbian Exposition at the Majestic Theater. We agreed to accompany him to England and here try our luck at rejuvenating our *act* which, in all honesty, unlike yours, had gotten a little rusty. So here is for safety and here we are!" I replied

"I have never been in Chicago, or America for that fact; but should love to try my hand out there, especially doing Vaudeville," intimated Queenie.

"I suspect that you may be disappointed Queenie. Vaudeville, as I have at last come to realize by experiencing London is not the same as Music Halls here in the Metropolis. When I said earlier, that I thought your performance stunning, especially in how you controlled your audience, in addition to urging them to release their emotions, I really meant it. In my stage career going back too many years, I have never witnessed anything quite like it," I reposted.

"When you say Music Hall is not the same as Vaudeville, what exactly do you mean Theo?" inquired Queenie.

"What do I mean? Much to my cost I assure you. Let me please explain. When Jack and I met with Lodge in a bar…" I said.

"That figures," said Queenie.

"…in a bar in Chicago he effectively offered us a rôle in Music Hall in London on the basis he was looking for new *talent* to amaze his audience and for their delectation. I remain even today slightly confused in what Lodge felt then at the time, we could offer his audience. Still we packed our bags and here we are. But, it did not take to long to realize one particular pertinent fact that hit us, as it were, like a freight train.

"George Leybourne, the manager at the Imperial Music Hall suggested it, just before we went on stage, but in such a nonchalant manner that his warning was lost on us. I remember now verbatim exactly what he said to us, because later, after we had abandoned the stage, his warning, his ominous warning, was all too apparent to us.

"'Gentlemen,' Leybourne had said, 'please allow me to offer you some advice. Not that you need it, but none the less, it may prove to be useful to you. Firstly, Music Hall in England is not the same as Vaudeville is in America. Secondly, what you term as Vaudeville in America is not the same as Variety Theater in England. And thirdly, what in England might be considered Burlesque would be termed Vaudeville in America. But then gentlemen I feel certain that you know this. Good luck!'

"We did not understand at all those crucial differences amongst the four definitions; and very much to our cost. His offer of good luck, was on that occasion, entirely wasted and subsequently our début on his stage turned into a fiasco, a débâcle even, of a kind I have never experienced before in my stage life. It was probable that the audience in the Imperial Music Hall on the fateful night thought us imbecile. But that negative experience got me to thinking.

"I realized eventually, especially after seeing you Queenie perform at the New Bedford Music Hall in Camden, that yours was a highly polished *act* responding to and controlling an audience. An audience, I might add, in the main, made up of intelligent, affluent or knowledgeable people in the middle of the largest Metropolis in the world governing the largest empire created on earth.

"Did we honestly suppose that our previous *turns* or *acts*, which may have been acceptable in lesser or smaller theaters, in New England or the Mid West, were really going to go down well with a sophisticated audience, the kind of which we experience at the New Bedford Music Hall or Imperial Music Hall? No!

"It would be easy to think that Music Hall, certainly in London, is a non stop series of anecdotal recitation, song or *turns*. It is not. It is much more complex and an audience, with its wide range of expectation, is going to demand fulfillment on a level that only a seasoned practitioner can provide. You are one those accomplished persons Queenie, but your skill would be wasted on the audience back home who are not as well attuned to a national concept of esoteric humor, as the English are.

"Put it this way Queenie. Members of a large family living together will come know each other intimately, because of familiarity. They will read easily moods, concern, euphoria or other emotions affecting the family. A stranger to that family will be at a loss from the very beginning. Because he will not, immediately, be able to understand that unwritten esoteric code of communication between members of that particular family which is born of experience.

"The same principle may apply to artistes or performers out of their depth elsewhere. And sometimes the transition can fail as with Marie Lloyd when she toured New York. I saw her. And while, yes she made an impact, it was at great expense to her reputation, which caused problems with her later. Though Queenie, I do wish you every bit of luck, should you decide to tread the boards in America, though secretly, I do not think that you operate on luck, but rather gauge your audience intelligently!

"In this respect, I was only discussing with my stage partner Jack…" I said.

"You mean that fellow over there attempting to do an impromptu matinée performance of the Can-Can without any coördinated precision; aided and abetted by Dot Hetherington, Marie Lloyd and Gertie Millar?" interrupted Queenie, pointing with her Trichinopoly cigar at the intrepid dancers. "It can only end in disaster at best or an undignified débâcle at worst, but certainly not alas, to critical acclaim."

I also noticed that before Queenie put the Trichinopoly cigar back to her lips, she flicked the not inconsiderable excess ash straight onto the back stage floor!

Queenie had no sooner done that, than Jack, Marie and Gertie all fell back, as predicted, into side curtain which broke from its upper rail and collapse down engulfing them in an avalanche of black curtain material and a cloud of choking dust, to the sound of spasmodic, if faint sporadic applause.

The more I looked at Queenie from close up some stirred in the back of my mind. It was as though I knew her. I naturally put this down to having seen her twice; once in the New Bedford Music Hall and the other time, of course, was at the Oxford Music Hall, in Oxford Street. But even so, her mannerism and gestures were familiar to me.

"Is it your intention to stay in London, or will you return to the United States?" she asked, bringing me out of my reverie.

"Yes!" I said decisively, "it is very much my intention to stay here in London."

"Why is that so?" inquired Queenie, handing me her empty fluted glass, that I took from her hand and glided over to the makeshift bar, with the obvious instruction to the patient bar-tender?

"Because I have come to appreciate," I replied from the bar, "and indeed become very fond of the established Music Halls in London and the dedicated artistes who perform tirelessly in them. You yourself, of course Queenie, being, as it were, of a nobler cast and indubitably, *pares inter pares*!" 4

"Oh Sir, you are so, so kind!" responded Queenie, in a mock *Southern Belle* accent of the type prevalent in our southern states back home in America. I handed a replenished glass of champagne to her and resumed my seat.

I would dearly have liked to have responded to her humor, except at that very moment, Loge, decidedly drunk, came staggering over to where Queenie and I were sitting. I say came over, it would be more accurate to describe his progress as being erratic and circuitous than direct. At length he did gain our position and stood in front of us swaying gently from side to side. He looked decidedly dishevelled, and even his crêpe encased top hat, was slightly battered and perched to one side of his head, at a jaunty angle, as it were.

"So how are we Queenie, come to say your farewells to our Bella then," spluttered out Loge.

"Our Bella, what, have you taken possession of her corpse already? I got the impression that she was married to some quack doctor out of Michigan, according to a telegram in *The Daily Telegraph*. Mind you, I can appreciate what you are trying to intimate. Bella probably did have a better friend in you Lodge, than in her erstwhile husband. Who by way of showing his friendship; done her in!" said Queenie, in all seriousness.

"*Passed-over*, Bella has *passed-over,*" said Lodge producing a black edge handkerchief with which he then proceeded to blow his nose, but only after looking over both shoulders.

"If you wish, but it is not the fact of her *passing-over*, what ever the preposterous terms means, but rather the manner of her *passing-over*, that is to say Lodge, quite simply, her being done in. More importantly, what have you done with her corpse? Were you able to find your elusive Mausoleum which, according to my reliable sources in rumor, idleness or gossip, you purchased for cash earlier today?

"Or did you inveigle your impudent man-servant

Aloysius to assist you in carting Bella's body back to your Bleak House and laying her corpse out on the kitchen table, and doing a morbid Rossetti? [5] Or, shall we read about such goings on in your Bleak House in the Bergen Avenue in the next edition of Rickard von Kraff-Ebing's instructive little booklet, such was your undying friendship?" inquired the Woman in Red, Queenie.

"How dare you! How dare you imply anything of the kind; that is unworthy of you? Bella and I… we were just good friends and nothing more. Our professional relationship was purely platonic," insisted Lodge.

"Now you mention that," replied Queenie, "I can well believe it!"

Lodge opened his mouth to reply but instead looked over his shoulder. Not in response to his monomania affliction, but rather to make sense of the commotion behind him. It centered on Cinderella, who had made an appearance and was remonstrating with one of the fairies from the *Corp de Ballet*, the whole troupe of which, had also turned up to pay their last respects to Bella. Whilst availing themselves at the bar, which I noticed, that they had been drinking at for quite some time.

It may have been at Cinderella's instigation; we could not determine immediately on account of the sudden mêlée which resulted in feathers and bits of taffeta erupting from the commotion. But in the next instance, the innocent gilded cherub that seemed to be in the midst of it, was unceremoniously toppled from its faked stone pedestal, down to the floor. But, in a way, it would never be able to regain that expression again, of sylvan look upon its face, at least not this side of eternity.

Which may not be such a bad outcome; for I had noticed that cherub's face when entering the back stage, and have never encountered such a look of concentrated malevolence in its chubby facial features, of which the stuff of nightmares are made.

The fact of the cherub, having been downed, seemed to have brought order, or a least an uneasy peace, which descended on the *Corp de Ballet* from which Rachel D'Arcy and her Ukulele, materialized unscathed, closely followed by Cinderella, who also emerged and staggered in our direction towards us. She then stopped for a moment, thought, and then veered decisively towards the makeshift bar and yelled at the bar-tender.

"A large glass of vodka my good man and be quick about it!" she advised.

The patient bar-tender, without any discernable change of facial expression, duly obliged.

This Cinderella, is of course, Little Bo Peep, who because of her secret guises, is able to play two totally separate rôles in the same Music Hall on the same night. Every body thinks they are two different artistes! She is clever in more ways than one, and thus gets over the *Exclusivity Clause* which prevents other performers from doing what she does all the time.

Her earlier entrance, as Bo Peep, was designed deliberately for all to see she was here in attendance. Her leaving the wake later, as Bo Peep, was equally noisy and obvious for all to realize. After a suitable interval, Cinderella materializes and is in the middle of a commotion, again for all to see her. The idea is of course people will remember seeing Little Bo Peep and Cinderella during the course of the Wake!

Cinderella completed her staggered walk and joined us, or rather engaged with Loge. At the same time Cinderella's three ugly sisters, in the persons of danseuses Mademoiselle Ariel, Mademoiselle Gillert and Mademoiselle Ada also turned up and loomed large over the demur seated Lodge.

"What have you done with Bella, you know the corpse?" was Cinderella's polite opening inquiry, "because the last we saw of you was marching around a grave yard dragging poor Bella in her card-board coffin behind you trying to find a new home for her. Well did you, no, no, I mean did you find a spare tomb for her?

"Come to that, what is going to happen to those *Three Graces* of yours now that there are only two left? Who will be the next one to go tragically, Dot Hetherington or will it be Kate Lawrence? One thing is for sure Loge, be grateful you have now only got *Two Graces* to fight with; I have got three ugly sisters to contend with on a daily basis," said Cinderella, as though she had a speech impediment.

At which point she collapsed into a nearby gilded cathedral chair, the padded seat of which was covered in a stained moiré silk.

"Do you not think that you have had…"

"Loge, I have not even started yet; and I will thank you to attend to your own business, not mine?" said Cinderella, who then immediately swallowed a deep draught of neat vodka from her large glass and then breathed out noisily.

"How are you Queenie, still singing beautifully for your supper?" asked Cinderella, "and has Loge here come to beg forgiveness of you for treating you shamelessly, what with breach of promise and such. You should take Phyllis Broughton's stance in this matter and sue him for every chocolate penny he possesses, eh Lodge?

"I will bet that you have a few chest loads of those pennies secreted about Bleak House in the Bergen Avenue, guarded over by the manic, if loquacious, Aloysius who, I might add, Lodge rescued from dire straights in the East End," informed Cinderella.

"I do not deal in chocolate or any other kind of penny I deal with fiduciary notes or banker's draft," replied Lodge visibly irritated by Cinderella's vicious, if unprovoked attack upon him. "And, for the record, I found Aloysius wandering around the East End starving and ragged. And as you know my *unflinching generosity,* can never know any bounds – for that in itself, remains an impossibility."

"All very laudable Loge, but what were you doing out in the East End, wandering around for what, picking up strafes and such like? That is what we want to know?" inquired Cinderella, who then again drank deeply from her drink and breathing out in her usual dainty way, as befitting a prim Cinderella.

Others, I noticed, joined our group, curious as to what was happening, since both Loge and Cinderella were raising their voices with each reply to each other.

"Despite your dubious missionary work in the East End, Loge, and saving the demented Aloysius from himself or indeed a fate worst than death, but now only to find himself finished up in Bleak House. I will wager that he now wishes to God that he could swap places with either the imprisoned Count of Monte Cristo or the geezer in the Iron Mask; whichever would be preferable than the living death extant in that peculiar house of yours.

"Your so-called faithful man-servant Aloysius, was over heard talking with other flunkies only today whilst they were all waiting at the main entrance into the Highgate Cemetery during Bella's funeral. What he had to say about your house in the Bergen Avenue was quite instructive. He had described the place quite openly to his fellow flunkies as being; 'once as a veritable Bleak House, twice as that living death and no less than three times as working there being almost as if one were being fated by death!"' said Cinderella.

"Hearsay, utter and vicious hearsay, I can tell," replied Lodge.

At this remark, the assembled grief-stricken mourners attending the Wake of Remembrance for Bella, fell into uncontrollable fits of laughter, much to Lodge's chagrin.

Cinderella continued, unabashed.

"Even your so-called faithful retainer scoffs at you behind your back, can you blame him? You treat all before you as though they were but numbers to maintain Box Office receipts, your only real love in this world. As indeed you have treated our Queenie here, shamelessly. And, from whom even now, you have neither grovelled for an apology nor forgiveness from her bountiful and generous personality!" informed Cinderella.

Queenie said nothing but looked at Lodge, smiled and merely put her fluted glass of champagne to her nose in order to smell its bouquet. It was Marie Lloyd, in the arms of Jack, who continued the attack on behalf of Cinderella, who by now was showing signs of fatigue.

"Well, Lodge, what about your treatment of Queenie here, who done you no harm?" inquired Lloyd, giggling, very much as Bella used to do so.

Lloyd's giggling became infectious as others joined in the laughing. It is because she stood up to you over the strike. That is why you give Queenie a hard time, is that not the case?

"All of us here, in the back stage of the Vaudeville Music Hall, also desire precisely what Queenie wants. We want a stop to exploitation, the removal of the notorious *Exclusion Clause*, better pay and an end to doing unpaid matinée performances, and not only...," said Lloyd, interrupted by ecstatic clapping which then erupted into an uncontrollable mælström of applause.

To my great surprise, Edna May walked into this applause, thinking, no doubt, that it was for her! I had noticed a poster, as we approached the stage door entrance that she was reprising her rôle here at this Vaudeville Music Hall, as Violet Grey in the *Belle of New York*, which I saw in the original run years ago in New York City. She was very good then, and I remembered, when we playing the Bridge Street Music Hall in her home town of Syracuse, upstate New York, that she was a warm-hearted humorous girl.

This momentary diversion caused by Edna May's arrival did not in any way prevent Lodge from raising his hand and bringing it down slowly in an effort to quell the sustained applause. It did not work and he was compelled to stand there for quite some time as the clapping continued unbridled. I got the distinct impression that some were clapping just to prevent Lodge from speaking; or at least his checking them. At length the ovation died away as the assembled mourners resumed their drinks and arguments whilst dispersing and leaving Loge without an audience to explain his motives.

"May I introduce you to Edna May, a fellow American performer?" I asked Queenie.

"I should be delighted to meet your friend Theo," Queenie responded.

We left Lodge with a manic look in his eyes staring into the middle distance as the chief grief-stricken mourner at Bella's Wake of Remembrance.

1. Hoxton
2. Now the Wigmore Hall, London
3. In the pianoforte transcription
4. First amongst equals.
5. The painter Rossetti had his dead wife laid out on the kitchen table for seven days in case she revived

Chapter 32

The Mistress of Guise

It was in a pensive mood that Jack and I took our break-fast. I was still considering the implications arising from the Wake of Remembrance for Bella Elmore, who, sadly was done away with by her doting husband, Dr. Crippen. During that Wake, that had gone on until well into the night, I did meet the Woman in Red, Queenie. Also Jack and I simply did not realized how such prodigious amounts of alcohol could be consumed in just the one session without the need to organize another Wake of Remembrance.

"Better get a move on Theo; for we have been summoned by Loge to meet with him at his attorney's office in the Wellington Road in a place called St. John's Wood. He has kindly provided directions to enable us to get there, using the urban rail road," said Jack.

"Why, what are we supposed to be doing with him?" I inquired, not really in the mood to go gallivanting around a fog-bound Metropolis, as the white opaque windows panes of the Grand Dining Room indicated to me.

"I do not know Theo, other that the fact he has requested our presence at twelve o'clock noon," advised Jack.

"That is fine Jack," I replied, "but I am to take tea with

Queenie, the Woman in Red this afternoon at four o'clock in a place called Claridges in Brook Street. Just where is that street in relation to this Wellington Road, is it far?" I asked.

"Not far Theo, a carriage drive away. But tea with the Woman in Red eh?" said Jack, rising from the break-fast table, "I will see you in the foyer, say in twenty minutes?" replied Jack, consulting his steel case pocket watch.

Accordingly, a few minutes later, we left the comfortable confines of the St. Pancras Hotel for the infinitely discomfort of the acrid fog still swirling around the phäntasma-goric façade of the hotel and the urban rail road station. We were not long in the fog, as we soon gained the platforms of King's Cross Metropolitan Station.

Having entered the station precincts, Jack went to purchase two train tickets whilst I entertained myself reading a preposterous advertisement poster plastered to one of the walls of the ticket office, regarding electro-magnetic medicine.

We had only just reached the platform when a train painted with green livery came roaring into the station. It blasted down the side of the platform edge pushing the dense fog before it as it progressed along passed us. Jack and I climbed aboard and sat down on the wooden cross benches.

"This train is of the Metropolitan District Rail Road, so we will have to change at Baker Street Station for a train of the Metropolitan Rail Road. Moments later with a lurch our train steamed out of the station and into a tunnel.

"Just what do you suppose Lodge wants to do with us in his attorney's office, sue us?" I ventured.

"He cannot be too pleased with how things turned out yesterday at Bella's funeral or Wake of Remembrance. A

CURE OF DISEASE WITHOUT DRUGS OR MEDICINE

With the patented Airtight Dry Cell Pocket Battery, which furnishes 4000 Electro-Magnetic Vibrations Per Minute.

ARE you afflicted with either Partial or Total Deafness? Catarrh, or Catarrhal Deafness, Rheumatism, Neuralgia, Lumbago, Gout, Nervous Debility, Any other Disease, from any cause or of any Length of Standing ?

DR HUBER'S ELECTRO-MAGNETIC DRY CELL POCKET MEDICAL BATTERY SUPPLIED WITH CONDUCTING CABLES, ARMATURES TO FIT ANY PART OF THE BODY OR LIMBS AND ADJUSTABLE EAR & NASAL ELECTRODES

The Battery and different Appliances can be used by all the members of an entire family for various ailments.

Trial of Batteries and Appliances and Electrodes FREE at our office at

'THE DR. HUBER'S DRY CELL POCKET MEDICAL BATTERY CO.'
35 Tottenham Court Road (3rd. door above Windmill Street entrance) London, W.

lot of people, it seemed to me, were queuing up just to impart their feelings on to him. At least in this respect, he appears more sinned against than he is sinner," Jack said, pensively,

Our train came to an abrupt halt in the Portland Road Metropolitan Station. A minute or so later it continued in to the Baker Street Metropolitan Station.

"We change here Theo for the Metropolitan Rail Road, the old St John's Wood Rail Road that will take us to Marlborough Road Metropolitan Station," said Jack, consulting the cable-gram from Lodge giving instructions on how to get to his attorney's office.

We alighted from the train and made our way along the westbound platform with other passengers at an agonisingly slow pace and up into the Main Hall. It was then with apprehension that we walked up to railway servant attired in his black uniform with red piping and asked him for directions to the platform from which we might avail ourselves of train that will take us to Marlborough Road Metropolitan Station.

He looked at us in a condescending manner. Accordingly, we braced ourselves to receive his inevitable and predictable facetiousness for which these rail road servants are renowned.

"Platform four and leaving in five minutes," he advised, before turning and fielding a further polite inquiry from another passenger.

We did make our way down to platform four, as advised, and whilst waiting there for our train, I indulged in my habit of reading the gaudy advertisements posted to the walls of the platform and searching for the most outrageous.

I did not have to search for long and soon found one insisting on the inherent virtues of an improved and

Baker Street Metropolitan Station Main Hall

Extra-Refined Pear's Amber Soap – Matchless for the Complexion. Another promoted the rather implausible health benefits of Bovril Meat Extract. Wedged in between them, was a poster proclaiming the advisability of taking Scott's Emulsion of Pure Cod Liver Oil.

Further down the platform wall were other advertisements, one of which introduced a dark beverage called the *Coca~Cola*, perhaps unknown to the English, but very well known in the United States, or at least on the eastern seaboard. However, the poster assured me; it was as 'Refreshing as it is Delicious!' and I could quite believe in this claim, as the beverage was laced with a generous amount of cocaine. Adjacent was a bill informatively advising the public that Allsopp's Pale Ale was now available in bottles. About that information I did make a mental note.

An exaggerated claim that Sanitas Disinfectant Fluid Destroys Disease seemed rather overoptimistic to me but in comparison did lend credence, at least, to the claim emanating from an advertisement that Paterson's Camp Coffee 'Is The Best as it is Incomparable!'

Other people on the platform then surged forward as a train in purple livery was backed into the station along the platform upon which we were standing. We had no sooner boarded the train, than it began to glide along the platform edge and into the fog-laden aëther above the permanent way of the Metropolitan Rail Road.

A few minutes later we steamed into St. John's Wood Road Metropolitan Station. Again, we waited here for quite some time before continuing up to Marlborough Road Metropolitan Station. Having gained that station's platform, we alighted and made our way up through the station and into the Marlborough Road. The fog here appeared thicker than at St. Pancras. So it was with grim determination that we marched off down the road, in accordance with our instructions, in the direction of Wellington Buildings, where Loge's attorney has his office.

Our walk was in silence and not very long. Eventually, we reached the address. It was a substantial and imposing building comprised of various businesses and practices. We approached the threshold of the building, which was set inside a vestibule, and dominated by a highly polished cruciform-panelled, double-leaf mahogany front door. Upon these doors was an array of gleaming brass plates with the names of various legal practices inscribed upon them. We had arrived at the right building, if nothing else, I thought.

Jack pulled at the adjacent bell wire and a faint tinkle announced our presence. Presently, the hall light shone through the semi-circular glass window above the door, which suddenly opened and a uniformed Concièrge, in the tunic of a commissionaire, materialized in the door frame.

Upon advising him of the nature of our visit, he

Wellington Buildings, St. John's Wood

beckoned both us into the hallway. After a few moments, he then instructed a page-boy to escort Jack and me to Lodge's lawyers. The page-boy duly obliged and led the way up a broad green-carpeted staircase to the *piano-nobile* into an office. There the receptionist escorted us down a red carpeted corridor and into the office of the senior partner of the legal practice. Upon being ushered in Lodge got out of his comfortable leather armchair to greet us. The senior partner too also rose from behind a large ornately carved mahogany desk with inlaid red leather to its writing surface.

"Ah, Mr. Houston and Mr. Mitchell, please do take a chair," said the partner, as he waived us into two Chippendale chairs facing his desk. We duly obliged and made ourselves comfortable on the moiré silk covered padded seats.

We duly sat down opposite his desk. On each of the two corners of the desk nearest to us, was a bronze lamp radiating a soft light through an opaque and patterned glass lampshade. In between these lamps was an elaborate and pretentiously decorated red marble inkwell and combined quill stand.

Jack talked to the senior partner about various things.

I therefore took the opportunity to look about his office in an idle, nonchalant manner. His office was well appointed with expensive items of furniture ranged around a large airy room with a high ceiling, from which was suspended an intricate brass and crystal chandelier.

On the walls, covered in Regency striped paper, were large gilt-framed paintings of sylvan scenes, including a Claude Lorrain that I recognised. Set into one wall, were three elongated ceiling high French windows leading out onto a balcony fenced with iron railings. Pulled back and secured with gold coloured twisted cord were curtains of brocade. Against the opposite wall was constructed an extensive library filled with legal tomes and reference books.

The floor of his office was uncarpeted and bare, made up of elm floorboards, which created a soft warm appearance. In the corner of the room was a Chatwood's Burglar and Fire Resistant safe, no doubt bulging with confidentiality and secrets about Lodge, which would make interesting reading, I thought. The room resembled more the office of a *dilettante* than a hard-headed attorney, I concluded.

However, during my visual peregrinations I became aware that Jack was trying to elicit information out of the attorney, whilst very skilfully evading his inquiries of us. One thing that I did notice was a document on the senior partner's desk. It was a legal document tied up with pink ribbon, in fact a conveyance attached to deeds. Nothing unusual in that given we were in a lawyer's office. What was unusual was the fact the conveyance referred to '…a Mausoleum, constructed of limestone, located at Brook-wood, in the County of Surrey, near London.' What was Lodge up to, I conjectured, was this to be Bella's final resting place?

It was Lodge who formally opened up the meeting.

"We were just discussing the fate that befell Bella and how we are still shocked by it. However, such a loss drives one to perhaps think more clearly and to put things into perspective. In this respect I have decided to make you an offer of engagement with me on a permanent basis, if that is agreeable to you both," said Lodge, much to our surprise.

"I shall be happy to do exactly that. Do you have any specific notion as to what you require in addition to the standard clauses?" inquired, the attorney of Lodge, whilst rising from his buttoned down red leather chair and pulling at a nearby bell rope.

"Yes I do have a specific request to amend the contract. I wish to remove the *Exclusivity Clause*, in this contract, as I shall be doing so in all my contracts with various artistes. This clause is wrong and does prohibit the free movement of talent by persons who ought to be encouraged to perform widely and without penalty for so doing, for the delectation of the Music Hall going public," informed Loge.

The senior partner looked askance at Lodge. But it was Jack, however, who got up from his chair and walked over to Lodge. He held out his hand which Loge shook.

"Good man Loge, good man," said Jack.

I too rose from my comfortable Chippendale chair and shook Lodge's hand warmly.

"What is the deal?" asked Jack, reverting back to his forthright manner.

"I have jotted down some ideas of how I should like the contract to be drafted in conjunction with anything you two might wish to incorporate into the document," said Lodge, in a very conciliatory way.

We chatted for a little time about general conditions

and what we all hoped to gain. It was obvious that Lodge had undergone a change of heart. Perhaps, Bella's death had, in fact moved him in more ways than one, and it could be, as he intimated, that such a loss makes one think more clearly and to put things into perspective.

For myself, I could hardly contain myself in being the first to inform Queenie of the fact that it is Loge's intention to remove the repressive and unpopular *Exclusion Clause*, as a standard condition in all previous contacts issued by him.

Just then a knock upon the door was heard and a secretary walked into the office.

"May I offer you refreshment gentlemen?" she asked.

"Rather", Jack enthused, in a mock English way, "tea, Jackson's of Piccadilly, the Jubilee blend."

"Would that be a concoction or diffusion?" responded the secretary, taking up Jack's facetious challenge!

"The former," I answered, for myself and Jack.

"Really?" the secretary replied, and then she looked at Lodge and the partner, "the usual stiff brandies for you two?"

"Yes thank you, that will be all," said the senior partner.

Our drinks duly arrived, as did the draft contracts on heavy grade parchment for us to sign.

After we had considered the contracts and signed them, the senior partner had champagne brought in and together we all four of us toasted our respective and inextricably linked futures.

Thus it was that Jack and I left Lodge with his attorney as we made our way back to Marlborough Road Metropolitan Station, with more than a skip in our step.

"Have you noticed Jack," I said, "it is always the short meetings, lasting but the time it takes to have a drink, that the best deals are struck?"

"Absolutely!" responded Jack.

As we approached the station, I realized that indeed the station building was quite impressive, and not without beauty. Of course when we arrived here earlier we left the precincts of the station building and headed off down the road, away from the station. Accordingly, we had no reason to look behind us.

It was only when we were approaching the building that we both realized its inherent architectural merit.

"I sure as hell did not expect that," said Jack, echoing my thoughts exactly.

"What this Marlborough Road Metropolitan Station?" I asked, somewhat perplexed at Jack's remark.

"No, Theo," replied Jack, "I was referring more to our meeting with Lodge and his attorney. Some how I was mentally expecting a major confrontation with Lodge, or at least his lawyer."

"Well as usual, Loge is full of surprises. I never expected to be signing contracts with him today or indeed on any day in the near future," I responded.

We walked silently into the station building and stepped down to the platform. We did not have long to wait before an engine came bursting into the station

Marlborough Road Metropolitan Station

hauling several coaches painted in the Metropolitan Rail Road's livery color of purple. We boarded and continued our conversation in the confines of an empty carriage. A few moments later we were moving and gaining speed to the extent we moments later blasted our way through the St. John's Wood Road Metropolitan Station without stopping.

A few minutes later we steamed into Baker Street Metropolitan Station. Presently, having gained the platform, I got off the train, but Jack elected to stay on it in order to make his way back east to our hotel. However, before parting, we agreed to meet up at the Oxford Music Hall at seven o'clock this evening where we shall take a red plush private box and be royally entertained for our delectation!

Within a few minutes of waiting I managed to hail a passing Hansom carriage and trundled off, as per my instruction to the carriage driver, to Claridge's for my rendezvous with Queenie, the Woman in Red.

My Hansom carriage clattered over the Marylebone Road and down into Baker Street. Our progress was slow in comparison to the rail road journeys I had just made with Jack. However, whilst we made our way down the street, I had ample opportunity to examine from the seat of my Hansom carriage a particular building that Lodge had pointed out to Jack and me a few days ago when we were also travelling down Baker Street.

His remarks were aimed more at Jack, than me but I do recall Lodge saying that some famous detective, possibly a Pinkerton man, resided in that house at number 221 Baker Street on the junction of Dorset Street. Apparently, there have been several stories written about this detective including one, I recall was called the Hound of the D'Urbervilles. Aside of which, the Georgian

House in Baker Street

house, whilst architecturally elegant, did not look like the residence of a famous detective; more the home of a physician.

"Can you step on it?" I said to the carriage coachman, fearing at this rate of progress, that I would be late for my meeting with Queenie, which I determined was certainly not going to be case.

"Can you not see there is fog ahead of us?" retorted the Hansom carriage driver.

"I can see that and I can also see that I am going to be late, which is not going to happen, so do not give me excuses, just move it," I instructed.

My driver did increase his pace somewhat, but that did not prevent me from sitting on the edge on my buttoned down red leather upholstered seat.

Finally we came to Oxford Street over which we cantered into a roadway called North Audley Street. To my surprise we came across a thoroughfare called Lees Place, opposite which was located the Embassy of the United States. This imposing winged red brick majestic looking building, with corner stone dressing and the façade of which, reflected a restrained Federal design [1] complete with a masonry eagle perched on top of a pediment above the main door entrance.

We then turned sharply into a large square, the name of which I did not see, but a minute or so later we clattered thankfully into Brook Street and pulled up outside the Claridge's Hotel, with two minutes to spare.

"See what you can do when you try," I said to the coachman whilst handing him his fare and a large tip.

Having just arrived just in time for tea with Queenie, I stepped down from the Hansom carriage to the roadway I then looked up at the imposing red brick façade of Claridge's Hotel. Impressive I thought as I made my way inside and immediately saw Queenie, in the foyer dressed as the Woman in Red and looking every much a goddess. We greeted each other and I escorted her into the salon in order to take tea with her.

It was whilst drinking our Jackson's of Piccadilly, Coronation blend tea that I appraised Queenie of Lodge's decision to remove the *Exclusion Clause* in all contracts extant with Lodge and other artistes. She appeared genuinely pleased, as indeed, so was I for her.

"I am glad that Loge has seen sense and, in my opinion," Queenie said, "he has made a very good decision. He shall not regret it, nor will he continued now to earn the scorn of his detractors, of which they are legion. And, I think, Loge is absolutely correct when he said to you that such a event as losing Bella could make one more think clearly, prioritize what is important and to put things into perspective.

"Though Theo, I suspect that you and Jack were more than instrumental in persuading Loge, as he likes to be called by his close acquaintances. I think he listens to you both, especially you Theo," remarked Queenie.

We spent a very enjoyable afternoon in the salon drinking tea and smoking cigars whilst talking about what Queenie intends doing now that the *Exclusion Clause* was no more. In addition, we also discussed what Jack and I will be doing on the London stage as protégés of Loge.

Queenie fell in eagerly with my suggestion of meeting Jack at the Oxford Music Hall, and it was with that intention in mind that we abandoned the salon in Claridge's Hotel and stepped into fog-laden twilight and then into a waiting Phäeton carriage with highly varnished side panels.

Our liveried coachman took us through the silent fog-bound streets of Mayfair and eventually emerged into

Regent's Street, next to Vigo House of peculiar repute. Queenie, not surprisingly was fully acquainted with the antics rife in the dome on the roof of this infamous house. Having turned left into the Regent's Street, our Phäeton carriage continued up and then turned right into Soho along Great Marlborough Street, and indeed past the new Palladium Theater, built recently to the designs by the prolific architect, Frank Matcham. Queenie pointed out this and other salient facts to me.

"This Palladium Theater was opened on St. Stephen's Day to great commendation offering a *'Grand Variety'* of accomplished *acts* by a wide range of artistes, such as Nellie Wallace or even Martin Harvey, an acclaimed actor in the classical tradition," informed Queenie. "Before they constructed the Palladium Theater, the notorious Corinthian Bazaar, together with the equally infamous Hengler's *Grand Cirque* occupied the site."

Eventually we came across Poland Street and made a left hand turn into it and up to the Oxford Street. There we alighted and walked into the Oxford Music Hall.

Other carriages of all types were depositing people who in their furs, silks and top hats were making their way into the foyer, and so were the costermongers very much in evidence, Queenie noticed, and pointed out to me. I began to look around for Jack, but did not in fact have to undertake that task. Within moments of arriving in the foyer, a voice addressed us.

"Queenie, Queenie, up here!" we instinctively looked about and then looked up to the ceiling. There in an opening into the *piano-nobile,* and leaning over a brass railing was Marie Lloyd waving frantically at Queenie.

"Up here Queenie, come up here!" insisted Lloyd.

Both Queenie and I ascended the curved red carpeted grand staircase up to where Lloyd was standing with Jack.

Jack I noticed was clutching a wad of theater tickets. Queenie and Lloyd rushed at one another as though long lost friends having just found each other. I shook Jack's hand.

"Got a crimson plush private box and champagne laid on to celebrate!" advised Jack.

"Celebrate what, our being signed up with Loge as his protégés," I inquired, "or the removal of the *Exclusivity Clause*?"

"Neither, but rather you and the Woman in Red, Queenie," answered Jack, with a smile on his face whilst motioning me to follow Queenie and Lloyd into the Crush Bar.

As usual, there were more impromptu *acts* and *turns* going on in the Crush Bar, than what we might expect on the stage in the nearby auditorium. And, so it was with great reluctance that we abandoned our prime position at the Crush Bar for our red plush private box. Having gotten here, I looked around the auditorium from our privilege position in our red plush private box.

The costermongers and their women, in the stalls, as usual, were forthright and bold in their varied opinions on anything or anyone. And, offered quite freely, advice or insult to other members of the audience who were looking for their seats. And, with whom an argument with total strangers, seemed to them, to be perfectly reasonable. Whilst indulging in the, *behavior*, some of the women would wave and fan themselves with their shabby feathers in an exaggerated, and perforce, suggestive manner.

Within a minute of our taking our red velvet covered comfortable seats and refilling our glasses of champagne, the dark purple safety curtain ascended revealing a forest scene just before twilight.

In an instance, the *Cremorne Belles* had tip-toed on their arches on to the stage, whereupon they performed a slow formation dance with neither musical accompaniment nor song. They danced, in fact, as though they were but fleeting shadows of the closing day. After ten minutes of this complex choreography, they gave way to another *act* which involved an Aëolian pianola.

It was our old friend Flora Miller, dressed in a flowing white satin gown who positioned herself in the soft limelight so as to engender a look of angelic innocence about her person. That contrived innocence, evaporated almost the moment the danseuse began to sing for her supper, to the accompaniment of the Aëolian pianola.

She sang verses of such a blatant nature, about being in the garden shed looking out amongst the cabbages and leeks, which made me, feel weak at the knees listening to them. She continued singing to the accompaniment of the sublime tinkling of arpeggios emanating from the Aëolian Pianola that struggled to keep up with her frenzied attack on musical harmony and verse.

I felt vulnerable in having to endure this *act*, involving as it did the Aëolian Pianola, which she stroked tenderly during her recital of verses, some of which were so lewd to a degree, that I did not know were extant on the London stage, even though Jack and I had in fact witnessed her performance in the recent past at the Hungerford Music Hall at Charing Cross.

It followed that her singing these verses again, caused acute embarrassment. To say the least, that I could see from our private box, especially to the audience in the Dress Circle, but not to the occupiers of the seats that made up the stalls, most of who chanted their equally vulgar responses. Queenie and Lloyd seemed thoroughly entertained by Miller's lyrical renditions.

What she had to sing about the *'Lost Chord'*, still a childhood favorite of mine, upset me, making me feel vulnerable – quite! Her rendition, in *D flat*, I noted, not for the first time had caused me to reëxamine my profound understanding of Victorian sensibilities and emotional response to religious music. Consistent with her singing and dancing was her cavorting at the Aëolian pianola, which she still continued to stoked tenderly in a highly provocative totally unabashed and suggestive manner. Rather as Rachel D'Arcy does with her Ukulele. She sang a verse of a song which I recognized and invited the audience to join in the chorus.

"Altogether now," she exhorted the audience, while she sang verses laced with vulgar and lascivious innuendo, quite clearly audible over the audiences' singing the normal accepted verse! Marie Lloyd could hardly contain herself and sang loudly and clearly and with gusto in duly obliging Flora.

"She is an absolute gem of the first water," Lloyd kept repeating this accolade throughout Flora performance. At one stage Flora, in approaching the finalé to her questionable rendition, actually managed to get most of the costermongers in the cheap stall seats, to stagger up on to their feet to chant out their coarse responses and at the end of which attracted thunderous applause and great verbal acclaim.

Other *acts* and *turns* were performed on the stage before us and for our delectation, which involved the audience in an informal way.

It was against a background of disruption, such as this, that the artistes on stage had to contend with. And, accordingly, which made them resort to being even more outrageous and impudent in order to gain the attention of a distracted audience, especially the mass ranks of the costermongers occupying the stalls.

At one point, two girls on the stage were inquiring of each other through verse, very suggestive notions. One of which was, '*Who is your lady friend?*' and '*Where is your pet baboon I saw you walking out with last night?*' Much to the occasional delight of an audience who appeared as equally happy to be able to make their own entertainment, rather than watch the antics on, or indeed off, the stage. The actors on stage fared no better, most of who spent their engagement returning a continuous volley of abuse with equal impromptu wit.

Despite this essential requirement to *ad lib,* the *acts* were varied as they were invariably sultry and all I noted, where I could understand, were riddled with lascivious innuendo. There seemed to be a general chaos surrounding the order of appearance of the *acts* according to the playbill and at one point, there was some confusion between the artistes, as to who should be on the stage doing their turn.

This, I noticed, whilst drinking my champagne, that this was a recurring problem in Music Halls. In fact a quite audible argument developed between the competing groups of artistes much to the delight of the disconcerting audience, who revelled in this impromptu entertainment of the real variety. Certainly, if the language deployed by the arguing contestant artistes, was anything to gauge by.

Eventually, the management of the Music Hall appeared, and cleared the stage, a task they were obviously used to performing on a regular basis. In so doing they cleared the way for another odd character, a Monologist in fact. He stepped smartly in to the limelight wearing a ridiculously tall stove-back top hat, voluminous striped trousers and a face and a countenance of such repellent ugliness as to defy description. His condition, however did not in any way impede the confidence with which he applied his skills, as an artiste in reciting a series of verses back to front and backwards as well as talking interminable nonsense!

The audience, in the cheap seats, erupted into ecstatic applause, for what sounded to me, at least, to be a rather nonsensical dialogue. That the words were impressed with innuendo, could never be in doubt, and were intelligible only to the few, certainly not contained in the Dress Circle, though perhaps in our red plush private box quite possibly.

The stage was now set again in a subdued lighting whilst another girl limped onto the stage. I recognized the face next to hers. It was our erstwhile ventriloquist's dummy, Judd, or Marmeduke, as he has now been re-christened. He was in the arm of Little Bo Peep, who immediately commenced a dialogue with him.

"This is my new friend Marmeduke," announced Little Bo Peep to the hushed audience, "say hello Marmeduke, say hello to the nice people out there. Go on."

Marmeduke declined to do so. Nothing new there, I thought. But instead, Marmeduke wore an even more manic expression, involving bearing his teeth, and moving his head from side to side in an arc for the whole audience to see.

"Marmeduke, say hello to the audience," insisted Bo Peep.

"I do not want to and I hate you. Put me down this instance," replied Marmeduke, "put me down, now."

"I most certainly will not," said Bo Peep, "you are a naughty boy Marmeduke for disobeying me."

"And you are a horrid ugly girl and cannot even look after docile lambs without losing some to an even more stupid fox than you," said Marmeduke, "and not only that, this silly girl has kidnapped me. There I was, sleeping in my card-board box after a particularly exhausting *act* on the stage at the Criterion Theater, when this fat ugly girl, you see before you here, stole me and refuses to let me go home!"

"That is not true," said Bo Peep, "I rescued you from oblivion and certain obscurity or possibly being sold as matchwood!"

"Rather that I be useful as a matchstick, than have to look at your ugly face, "said Marmeduke, "put me down, now I demand my freedom!"

At this point Little Bo Peep burst into tears. And, using my paisley patterned handkerchief, attempted to stem her tears from rolling down her plump pink cheeks.

Then it happened. We and the entire auditorium, gasped in horror, as we witnessed Marmeduke slap Little Bo Peep across her face! This had the effect of sending Po Peep down to the stage floor. Before long both Bo Peep and Marmeduke were rolling around on the floor, much to the excitement of the audience who in unison rose from their seats. They did so in order to get a better view of the mêlée, which was now erupting in full view of members of the audience. Need less to say the audience went wild with excitement, as two stage hands came on to the stage, in an attempt to wrestle Marmeduke from Little Bo Peep, who was now beside herself with tears and screaming.

Within moments, Bo Peep had picked her self up from the deck and leaning on her shepherdess crook, burst into song about having polio and being condemned to limp for the rest of her short life, that is, if the consumption did not get her first. She then let her song trail away, as though she had not the breath to power the words out of mouth and limped off the stage to avalanche of sustained and loud applause.

There is a new *act* involving Judd or Marmeduke which Jack and I never thought about. Obviously, Marmeduke has gotten himself a new *act* and the audience seems to like it! Not with standing that fact, our Little Bo Peep was quite an accomplished ventriloquist too, by any standard.

After a suitable pause the two infamous danseuses came on in the persons of Jessie Bateman and Lina Cavalieri who spent an inordinate time strutting around the stage almost sizing each other up as though they were about to engage in a physical assault upon each other's person.

This of course, was very much the case in those original Pleasure Gardens, such as those of Cremorne, Vauxhall, Ranelagh or indeed Marylebone, as the precursor to the Music Halls, where boxing matches between female contestants was very much an accepted, indeed expected normality. In addition, given the entertainment, in the main, consisted of to bull-baiting, cock fighting, overt gambling and general *unbecoming behavior* as licentious and debauchery both of which were practised on a large scale, in those Pleasure Gardens.

I think we were probably about to witness a resurgence of the later, but at length nothing happened. It may have just been an interesting thought provoking interlude, as both danseuses retired from the stage gracefully and their dignity very much intact.

That was a signal for a mass evacuation of the auditorium to several strategically located Crush Bars, one of which we repaired to during the interval. On returning to our box, drinking our champagne, the safety curtain again ascended into the stage attic revealing a scene depicting a gingerbread cottage set in the same forest clearing. However, on this occasion, it was not twilight but rather night complete with a full moon suspended precariously on the stage backdrop above the cottage.

The distinct but feint sound of a pianoforte, off stage, could be heard playing pieces of music I recognized as being from   Robert Schumann's *Neun Waldszenen für Klavierstüke.* [2]

After listening for some minutes of this delightful music, the back drop scenery wobbled as the cottage door opened, creating an opening from which a shaft of yellow light poured out illuminating the floorboards of the stage. It was through this cottage door that Cinderella emerged looking battered and disheveled.

She still wore her top hat and white silk ball gown onto which sequins had been sown. Together with her out sized pit boots, clearly several sizes too big for her, but into which iron studs had been nailed into the soles. It was in these ungainly boots that Cinderella clumped around the stage.

When the ovation had died down, Cinderella came up the edge of the stage, up against the footlights and leaned forward into the distance. She put her hand up against her eye brows and peering into the audience, announced that she had, at long last, been released from the drudgery of being a frustrated '*Angel in the Home.*' [3]

She then burst into a song about how she rally would rather sing for her supper; than clean her sisters' dirty pots and pans and rinse their beer bottles. And how she related her dream of going to the ball, wearing dainty glass slippers and not these hob-nailed boots, her ugly sisters forced her to wear. Despite the fact Cinderella was, wearing those large hob-nailed boots, did in no way, impede her ability to skip and almost float over the stage; and even attempt a *Pas de Deux,* which she executed flawlessly and with grace.   She completed her *act* by inviting the audience, who did not need to be asked twice and who accepted readily, to join with her in singing, *'You shall go to the Ball!'*

The women in the audience took her up on her invitation, often singing louder than Cinderella herself. It was as though this song was an open invitation for all and sundry to try their hand at singing. Still strutting around the stage like a *Southern Belle* complete with a bellowing white ball gown, Cinderella addressed the audience. In particular the women in the cheap seats and exhorted them, with her sweet accent and winning ways, to, *'assist me'* in my song, *'I Do Declare!'* as her finalé.

It was quite some time before the ovation had died down after Cinderella's elegant abandonment of the stage, through the open cottage door, which slammed shut after her, still full of the joys of freedom from her ugly sisters.

The auditorium was then plunged into a sudden darkness as the town gas mantles were turned down. A silence descended upon an expectant audience. Gradually in the gloom a single very weak shaft of yellow limelight was focused on a solitary figure standing immediately in front of the back drop of red velvet curtain and facing the audience with his head bowed down, as though in anxious thought.

From where we were sitting in our box I could just make out in the subdued light, that the fellow on the stage was wearing a loud *Prince of Wales* yellow and brown check patterned suit and an outsized red Derby hat, pulled down low over his eyes. This however, did not conceal his blond hair, tuffs of which were visible protruding out below his red Derby hat. On his small feet he wore a pair of scuffed boots, which were neither of the same style or indeed color! His hands were peculiar, in that they appeared rigid and tinted to a gray hue.

Gradually he lifted his face upward to the Dress Circle immediately in front of him. He then turned his face from right to left in an arc across the auditorium and finished by looking up in our direction and at our box in which Queenie, Marie Lloyd, Jack and I were all sitting.

The features upon his face were now becoming clearer, especially his nose which looked like it had been stuck on as an after thought to the general facial assembly. His face was peculiar too, in that it had an unnatural color to it; almost pure white with a visible painted area of rouge to the cheeks. His eyebrows were bushy and partially concealed his deep sunken black eyes.

But, these obvious features paled into insignificance, when compared with the glaring manic expression he made with his open lips revealing two rows of closed teeth.

He then walked slowly in a measured step to the front of the stage. In so doing the footlights from the floorboard level below illuminated his face, and in so doing created shadows coming up from his chin. These shadows had the effect of turning his manic expression into one of an exaggerated grotesque image. The audience remained silent throughout and even a few costermongers were moved to remain respectfully quiet whilst they witnessed this new *act* being performed in front of their very eyes.

He stood at the very precipice of the stage, swaying as though in a breeze. His arms merely hung loosely at his side whilst his head assumed a circular motion with the occasional flash of teeth reënforcing that unnerving manic expression. Then as if he were being lowered, by unseen supports, he knelt down on one knee, as though in genuflection and began with a low murmur to annunciate his inner thoughts.

These low sounds soon developed into a plainchant

about how, as a baby in the forests, he was taken from his home beneath a leaf, resting on the forest floor, and put into bondage. How he was only fed just enough to ensure he did not fade away. He paused at this point and again with his manic expression caused by bearing his teeth, turned his head in a wide sweep for all in the auditorium to see.

He then got up, and walking about the stage in a loose-limbed manner, as though he were a puppet being controlled by hidden wires, proceeded to sing about his fervent hope of release from being manipulated and controlled by others. To this lyrical sentiment the costermongers and, indeed some in the Dress Circle, finally failed to control themselves. And, indeed, erupted into unbridled applause with some even inducing a mild form of delirium into their re-action to this fellow on the stage.

The applause was tremendous and in response the performer to off his red Derby hat and bowed to the audience. The instant re-action in our private box was not limited to just me; it also involved Jack too. We both looked at each other, then down at the stage upon which was the bowing performer was still responding to the audience's' approval of his *act*.

Then the awful realization dawned upon Jack and me; the fellow on the stage below us, was nothing more than a re-incarnation of our erstwhile, if discarded, ventriloquist's dummy, Judd! It was none other than Judd, come to life but by whom? The prospect of Judd having an independent life on the stage, filled both Jack and I with a nameless foreboding, as I felt aghast at the idea. Jack and I sat there champagne in hand stupefied at what we had just witnessed. It was Queenie who said it.

"Cinderella, Bo Peep call her what you will. She is

always re-inventing herself into different guises. I have known her, I think, for at least nine years, and I do not know her name or what she really looks like. Each time we meet, which is usually in dress and back stage, just before either of us goes on to do our respective *turns*, I see her only in her stage attire and never in her off-stage dress. She is truly an enigma. And, it is possible that we know her in other guises!" informed Queenie to a stunned Jack and me.

Marie Lloyd was too busy screaming at, well *Judd*, for an encore, to which demand, *Judd* willingly obliged. At the conclusion to a series of encores the audience, sensing that the entertainment really now had come to an end, at least in the auditorium, stampeded for the nearest Crush Bars. We sat in our private box drinking the remainder of our champagne and looked about the now empty auditorium.

Not a word was spoken amongst us. Even the loquacious Lloyd kept her silence. I think we all new what was going through our minds and hearts, as we sat there in the empty auditorium, in which we all four of us plied our craft in making people smile at worst, or at best laugh at us. For myself, I knew that I had reached a turning point in my stage life and knew now exactly what I shall be doing in future.

It was with these thoughts that we left our private box and headed out into Oxford Street still in the grip of the pervasive perennial fog. We all chatted for several minutes while waiting for our respective carriages to take us to our destinations. We all agreed to meet again soon.

Eventually Jack and I made our way back to the St. Pancras Hotel. Before going in however, I beckoned Jack to stop and suggested that we smoke a Trichinopoly cigar together. Only recently when we first arrived in London, we had both of us stood outside here in front of the St. Pancras Hotel contemplating our futures.

We were now compelled to do the same again. Our experiences of London and the Music Halls that we visited had raised some points which needed our consideration, and decision.

Jack took this to be a sign from me that I wanted to talk with him on something important. We had often done this in New York, and indeed elsewhere, where we just stayed put for a few minutes and enjoyed a cigar whilst considering our immediate future.

We smoked in silence, whilst the smoke from our cigars defused imperceptibly with the swirling fog about us. In front of the powerful image of the St. Pancras Hotel, the phäntasmagoric façade of which was still able to present itself to us, despite the swirling fog.

We were at a point in our lives, where decisions, important decisions, were going to have to be made, and with far reaching consequences. I was happy to do so.

"Jack," I started in, "we have learned a lot whilst in London. In answer to an inquiry from Queenie yesterday at Bella's Wake of Remembrance, I replied that it is my intention to stay on in London. Irrespective of the fact we have signed contracts with Loge, my decision would have been the same. What are your thoughts on this matter?"

"Do I really need to tell you Theo?" answered Jack.

"No, Jack Mitchell, you do not have to," I responded, "and I know that!"

"Theo," said Jack, "this is where it is at, here in London, and it is here that we shall find what it is we are looking for; not just on the stage, but also off it."

A solitary Brougham carriage waited beneath the near by Porte Cochère. We both considered it as we finished

St Pancras Hotel

our Trichinopoly cigars and instinctively broke out into uncontrollable laughter at our decision.

On gaining the foyer, a bell-boy from the Concièrge approached us and handed Jack a cable-gram. It was from Lodge, Jack informed me, having ripped open the buff-colored envelope which had contained the message. On reading the contents, Jack said nothing but simply handed over the cable-gram to me. I read it with trepidation.

++SORRY COULD NOT BE WITH YOU THIS ++
EVENING ++++ IMPORTANT +++ AUDITIONING
++ 3RD GRACE TO REPLACE BELLA STOP.++
WILL CALL BY BREAK-FAST ++ STOP.++
LOGE.

The following morning whilst Jack and I were taking break-fast, in the Grand Dining Room, we neither of us could contain our curiosity and burned for the appointed time when Lodge would turn up. He did not disappoint and approached our table on the dot of nine o'clock.

Accompanying him was a face that looked familiar but difficult to place. Then it hit me like a freight train. She was Elizabeth Firth, a singer out of New Jersey. From memory a good singer, but I did not realize or think that she was a soprano. Jack, from Jersey City new her quite well, as was evident when he rose to shake her out-stretched hand.

Still that vocal requirement clearly did not deter Lodge from elevating Elizabeth, as soprano, up to the Pantheon of the Great! Well at least up to one of the *Three Graces,* that is probably the equivalent in aspiration or achieve-ment, in Lodge's estimation.

"Elizabeth is, alas able, with the ease of the gods to command the undeviating attention of an audience," said Lodge, beaming with smiles.

"Oh sir you are so kind," responded Elizabeth, in a distinctive New Jersey accent and returning an even broader smile to Loge, who blushed somewhat, at this overt demonstration.

"Elizabeth has been trained in the operatic scale and will make a splendid replacement for Bella," insisted Lodge.

I am throwing a little party by way of celebration tonight at my house in the Bergen Avenue. We need to talk about starting you off at the Imperial Theater in the Royal Aquarium & Winter Garden. See you at seven o' clock gentlemen," said Lodge, as he walked out arm in arm with his new soprano from New Jersey.

Jack and I looked at each other regarding Loge's new soprano. We also realized in an instant something else, something much more profound. And it was what we had been searching for. As I continued to looked at Jack, much went through our minds without a word being uttered or a facial expression being made by either of us

We both new in our hearts, that the decision to stay in London, under the aegis of Loge, was the correct one to have made, and we had done so.

We both instantaneously burst out into uncontrollable laughter which attracted the attention of our fellow diners in the break-fast room at the St. Pancras Hotel, that we will now have to vacate and find a permanent home some place else.

But I also realized precisely, by our bursting out laughing at the break-fast table, precisely what it was that Jack and I had not discovered in the Majestic Theater in Chicago, when we were compelled to confront our fears. It was neither the hecklers nor indeed the Nihilists; it was us! Except that we totally misunderstood what was happening. Including the ability to recognize challenges presented right in front of our very eyes! I knew now why this was so.

The whole concept of Music Hall; ranging from the Supper Rooms, to Vaudeville, to Burlesque to saloon bars in Public Houses to the infamous Pleasure Gardens to Music Halls, and now perhaps to the Variety Theater, demonstrates that the saga goes on. It moves with each innovation and demand. And, in this respect, practition-ers such as Bo Peep - Cinderella show how it can be done.

Cinderella is not frightened of the future; because she will make that future her own. And for knowing her, she has shown Jack and me, I am convinced, the way forward. And, for imparting that precious knowledge to us, she is certainly more than welcome to keep that Judd!

1. Equivalent of late Georgian architecture
2. Forest Scenes: Nine Piano Pieces
3. Women who worked at home were assigned this title

Index